Dear Reader,

When Pocket Books decided to bring *Stormswept* back into print, I was thrilled at the chance to revise and refresh another novel I'd penned long ago under the name Deborah Martin. My early works set the stage for my career to come: first, the historical detail, passionate action, and darker tone of the Deborah Martin novels. And later on, the sensual entanglements, witty repartee, and lighthearted spirit of my recent Regency series, the Sinful Suitors and the Hellions of Halstead Hall. Both styles are infused with the sexy romantic liaisons my readers have come to expect in my books.

In *Stormswept,* Lady Juliana St. Albans is reunited with dark and daring Rhys Vaughan, the husband she thought had abandoned her after their wedding night years ago. Battling mistrust, yet longing for the love they once shared, they must unravel a maze of mystery and menace to find love again. In this tale of desire and deception, I heightened the drama, enriched the story line, tightened the dialogue, and stoked the heart-pounding sexual tension between these entangled characters. I hope you enjoy this story, whether it's a past favorite or a new adventure for you to relish!

Sincerely,

Sabrina Jeffries

HOW THE SCOUNDREL SEDUCES

"Scorching . . . From cover to cover, it sizzles."

—*Reader to Reader*

"Marvelous storytelling . . . Memorable."

—*RT Book Reviews* (4½ stars, Top Pick, K.I.S.S. Award)

WHEN THE ROGUE RETURNS

"Blends the pace of a thriller with the romance of the Regency era."

—*Woman's Day*

"Enthralling . . . rich in passion and danger."

—*Booklist* (starred review)

WHAT THE DUKE DESIRES

"A totally engaging, adventurous love story with an oh-so-wonderful ending."

—*RT Book Reviews*

"Full of all the intriguing characters, brisk plotting, and witty dialogue that Jeffries's readers have come to expect."

—*Publishers Weekly* (starred review)

The *New York Times* bestselling "must-read series" (*Romance Reviews Today*)

The Hellions of Halstead Hall

A LADY NEVER SURRENDERS

"Jeffries pulls out all the stops . . . Not to be missed."

—*RT Book Reviews* (4½ stars, Top Pick)

"Sizzling, emotionally satisfying . . . Another must-read."

—*Library Journal* (starred review)

"*A Lady Never Surrenders* wraps up the series nothing short of brilliantly." —*Booklist*

TO WED A WILD LORD

"Wonderfully witty, deliciously seductive, graced with humor and charm." —*Library Journal* (starred review)

"A beguiling blend of captivating characters, clever plotting, and sizzling sensuality." —*Booklist*

HOW TO WOO A RELUCTANT LADY

"Delightful . . . Charmingly original." —*Publishers Weekly* (starred review)

"Steamy passion, dangerous intrigue, and just the right amount of tart wit." —*Booklist*

A HELLION IN HER BED

"Jeffries's sense of humor and delightfully delicious sensuality spice things up!" —*RT Book Reviews* (4½ stars)

THE TRUTH ABOUT LORD STONEVILLE

"Jeffries combines her hallmark humor, poignancy, and sensuality to perfection." —*RT Book Reviews* (4½ stars, Top Pick)

"Delectably witty dialogue . . . and scorching sexual chemistry." —*Booklist*

SABRINA JEFFRIES

WRITING AS
DEBORAH MARTIN

Stormswept

Pocket Books

New York   London   Toronto   Sydney   New Delhi

Pocket Books
An Imprint of Simon & Schuster, Inc.
1230 Avenue of the Americas
New York, NY 10020

This book is a work of fiction. Any references to historical events, real people, or real places are used fictitiously. Other names, characters, places, and events are products of the author's imagination, and any resemblance to actual events or places or persons, living or dead, is entirely coincidental.

First Pocket Books paperback edition July 2016

POCKET and colophon are registered trademarks of Simon & Schuster, Inc.

For information about special discounts for bulk purchases, please contact Simon & Schuster Special Sales at 1-866-506-1949 or business@simonandschuster.com.

The Simon & Schuster Speakers Bureau can bring authors to your live event. For more information or to book an event, contact the Simon & Schuster Speakers Bureau at 1-866-248-3049 or visit our website at www.simonspeakers.com.

Interior design by Leydiana Rodríguez

Manufactured in the United States of America

10 9 8 7 6 5 4 3 2 1

ISBN 978-1-4516-6554-3
ISBN 978-1-5011-3099-1 (ebook)

To librarians everywhere, including my husband.
Without you, I couldn't have done my research for this
back in the early '90s. Thank heaven for interlibrary loan!

PROLOGUE

*J*uliana St. Albans knew hardly anyone at her betrothal dinner. Her family had invited only the cream of Carmarthen society, so most other guests were English nobility connected with her betrothed. A twenty-course feast awaited them, champagne already flowed freely, and a costly orchestra was playing.

She would have preferred less ostentation, but whatever Darcy St. Albans, the Earl of Northcliffe, wanted, he got. And her brother wanted to impress everyone with his newfound wealth, particularly her husband-to-be—Stephen Wyndham, Marquess of Devon.

Believing the marquess to be as ambitious as himself, Darcy had already invested in a mining project with Stephen. But her kind and considerate betrothed was nothing like her bullying brother. Stephen was more like Rhys.

As the image of a tall, lean man with eyes blue as the Celtic sea leapt into her mind, she frowned. Why couldn't she evict Rhys Vaughan from her thoughts?

I'm not betraying him by doing this. I'm not!

He was dead, for pity's sake! She had a right to be happy, to have children at last. At twenty-seven, she wasn't getting any younger. And since her one glorious night with Rhys six years ago hadn't given her a child . . .

A blush stained her cheeks. "Oh bother." Lifting her skirts, she headed for the stairs. She refused to spend one more *moment* thinking about a man who hadn't even tried to write her in the years before his death.

As she descended the wide staircase, the guests—and her betrothed—turned to watch. The attention made her squirm, especially when Stephen's hot gaze raked down to linger on the swells of her breasts. Why did that make her uncomfortable?

When she reached his side, he offered her his arm. "The beauty has arrived at last."

She took it with a smile. She was being silly. Of course her betrothed found her desirable. And she couldn't have children unless he did. "Good evening, my lord. You're looking handsome this evening."

Before he could reply, the others crowded around them offering congratulations. One elderly woman leaned in. "I suppose you'll be moving out of Llynwydd, Lady Juliana."

Stephen spoke for her. "Since Llynwydd belongs to her, of course we'll repair there from time to time. But we shall live at Wyndham Castle in Devonshire."

"That will certainly be a more pleasant place to reside," the woman said. "And no doubt easier to manage, since you won't have to deal with stupid and incompetent Welsh servants."

Juliana bristled. "I beg your pardon, but I do not hire stupid or incompetent servants. My Welsh staff is exemplary."

Squeezing her hand, Stephen hastened to add, "Juliana's been fortunate in her choice of servants, but I'm sure she'll find mine more agreeable. They're all thoroughly English."

As the woman sniffed and moved off to relate Juliana's comments to her friends, Juliana bit back the impulse to correct Stephen. Thoroughly English indeed! If the surly staff at Wyndham Castle were indicative of the English nation as a whole, then England was in sad straits.

"Is my sister waxing poetic about the Welsh again?" her other brother, Overton, came up to ask.

Stephen flashed her an indulgent smile. "You know Juliana. She defends everyone."

Unlike Darcy, Overton would probably rather be hunting with his rapscallion friends than hobnobbing with his peers. "I was wondering if you know that fellow by the window. He's been glaring at you two ever since Juliana came downstairs. He looks familiar, but I can't place him."

When Juliana turned to look, Overton added, "Damn. He must have walked off while we were talking. I'll point him out later. Don't like the looks of him. Not a congenial sort, I'll wager." Overton glanced at Stephen. "Hope he's not one of your friends."

"Oh, I doubt it." Stephen scanned the room. "He's probably some acquaintance of Darcy's."

While the two men continued talking, Juliana's mind wandered. She wished she'd seen the man Darcy had spoken of. All this attention from strangers was unnerving. As mistress of Llynwydd, the estate her father had given her, she'd led a solitary life. But Stephen had already warned her that they'd be doing a great deal of entertaining at Wyndham Castle.

She hated entertaining. She much preferred the challenge of running her estate, even though her parents and their English friends had thought it scandalous that a woman should live away from home and manage property alone.

Fortunately, the Welsh tenants and staff didn't care who ran Llynwydd as long as it was done efficiently, especially since it made a good profit, which had eventually silenced her family's objections. A pity she had to leave it all behind.

A servant stepped into the drawing room and announced that dinner was served, but Juliana scarcely noticed, wondering if she'd made a mistake in agreeing to marry Stephen. It wasn't as if she loved him. She felt a great deal of affection and respect for him, but was that enough? Darcy's marriage amply illustrated that matches not based on love could be disastrous.

Glancing at her sister-in-law, Elizabeth, Juliana tensed. The woman wore her usual carved-ice expression, which never cracked, even in the presence of her husband. Darcy's reasons for marrying the young heiress had been thoroughly mercenary. But were Juliana's reasons for marrying Stephen any different?

Yes, they were. There was nothing wrong with marrying for companionship. Even Llynwydd was lonely at night, in the dead of winter. She was tired of being alone. She wanted a husband and children.

Besides, she liked Stephen. They'd do nicely together.

Before she knew it, the meal had passed, and Darcy rose to begin the evening's toasts. "Welcome, my friends, to this celebration," he said in stentorian tones. "A year ago, this fine gentleman, the Marquess of Devon, came to court my sister, Juliana. And as luck would have it, they found favor in each other's eyes."

A shadow passed over his face. "Although my father died before he'd had the chance to meet his lordship, I know he would have approved of the marquess. Lord Devon is one of the most respectable, intelligent, and engaging men I've ever known."

Darcy stood a little straighter, looking almost military in demeanor. "So tonight, my friends, I'm pleased to announce, on behalf of my mother and my late father, the betrothal of my sister to this honorable man."

He held up his glass, his face flushing with pleasure. "A toast! To Lady Juliana and her husband-to-be, Stephen Wyndham, the Marquess of Devon! May their joy be unbounded!"

The guests raised their glasses, preparing to cheer—but another voice rang out from the other end of the hall. "I dispute that toast!"

Darcy looked incredulous, as the other guests hesitated with their arms suspended in the air as if by invisible wires. Juliana's heart dropped into her stomach.

She searched for the man who'd spoken and found him at the other end of the ballroom. Towering over the other guests, he stood in the shadows, where she couldn't make out his features. Was this the fellow Overton had spoken of?

He was dressed more soberly than her guests, and his entire bearing bespoke arrogance. The gasps of those around him had little effect, for he carried himself forward with the invincibility of a battleship.

He snatched a glass from a guest's hand as he passed. "I would propose another toast entirely."

Something in his voice tweaked her buried memories. It couldn't be. His accent wasn't right. And as he came closer, she could see he wore the expensive attire of a lord, not the modest garb of a radical. What's more, he was too big, too self-assured, and entirely too imposing to be . . .

But try as she could to deny it, her fear became a certainty as he strolled up the aisle to the head table. She stared at the broad shoulders, at the black curls cropped at the chin framing an arresting and painfully familiar face. She rose, not realizing that she did, disbelieving the evidence of her own eyes.

Darcy seemed to regain his wits. "What preposterous rudeness is this? I don't know you, sir, and I'm certain you weren't invited. Leave at once, before I have my footmen throw you out!" He signaled to a servant, who hastened toward the stranger.

With a sinister clang, the encroacher withdrew his sword and the summoned footman fell back.

Sure of his audience, the man came to within six feet of her. "If anyone should have been invited, 'tis I. But then, I'm sure you treacherous blackguards thought yourselves well rid of me." He scanned the head table with a scathing glance. "Otherwise, you wouldn't be engaging in this farce."

With her heart in her stomach, Juliana stared at the man's face. 'Twas impossible!

Stephen jumped to his feet. "Treacherous blackguards! I'll call you out for that, sir!"

"Ah, but you have it all wrong, Lord Devon. *I* should call *you* out. Ask Juliana."

Stephen shot her a questioning look, but Juliana took no notice as the man fixed his gaze on her, searing her. Her throat tightened and her knees shook. Only one man had those blue eyes. And for a moment, her heart leapt and she wanted to bound over the table into his arms.

Then she saw the coldness in his eyes, the anger in his face, and the urge fled.

"You should have told him, Juliana." His voice held an edge of fury. "'Tis an important thing to leave out of any discussion about betrothal."

"It c-can't be tr-true," she whispered, stumbling over the words.

His eyes narrowed. "What? That I've returned? That I've come to reclaim my lands . . . my inheritance . . . and you? Oh yes, love. It is true."

The entire company was thrown into confusion, except for her brothers, who looked as if they'd commit murder any moment. It was like seeing a corpse rise from the grave.

"Rhys, please." She clasped her chair as her knees began to buckle.

With an expression as cold as the frostiest winter, Rhys lifted his glass in a toast. "To Juliana, my darling wife. I've come to take you home."

And for the first time in her life, Juliana fainted.

PART I

Carmarthen, Wales
July 1777
Six years earlier

If you marry a green youth,
you will cut the sprouting corn;
and you may find that the harvest
is too stormy to be borne.

—ANONYMOUS, "STANZAS FOR THE HARP"

1

As sweet is your pose
As a riverbank rose
Or a posy where lily or lavender blows.
— HUW MORUS, "PRAISE OF A GIRL"

Juliana St. Albans gestured at the tall young man who stood stiff and sober before the crowded room. "Is that Rhys Vaughan?" He seemed different from the other Sons of Wales sitting in the basement of Gentlemen's Bookshop in Carmarthen. "That can't be him. He looks too quiet."

Her Welsh lady's maid, Lettice Johnes, snorted. "For what? Did you expect a hard-drinking, hard-boasting gambler like his late father, the squire?"

Juliana swept her gaze around the room. "I expected none of this." In her naiveté, she'd thought to find serious young men discussing politics in earnest voices . . . not this rabble of hotheads.

"I don't suppose you want to go home now?"

Lettice sounded so hopeful that Juliana had to smile. "Not after I went to all the trouble of dressing like a poor Welsh servant to follow you here."

"I should never have told Morgan I would attend," Lettice grumbled. "And I shouldn't have let you stay once you showed up. He won't be happy about that."

"It's not your fault. If your sweetheart wasn't always so heedless of his surroundings when he courts you, I wouldn't have overheard him mention the meeting." And Rhys Vaughan's part in it.

"Pray God none of the Sons of Wales recognize you. They'll think you a spy, and Lord only knows how they'll react."

"No one will guess who I really am." Juliana wore her simplest gown, a mob cap to cover her telltale red hair, and a Welsh shawl. It was the perfect disguise.

"If your father finds out you were here consorting with 'those dirty Welsh,' he'll give you a thrashing. You'd best leave before you get into trouble."

A pox on Lettice for always trying to tell her how to behave! At twenty-one, Juliana wasn't a child anymore. Why, most women were already married, bearing children, and running households. Surely she was old enough to attend a late-night meeting of Welsh radicals.

"Will you stop haranguing me if I promise not to get caught?" Juliana snapped.

"This meeting won't be the 'romantic' Welsh poetry and history you fancy. It'll be rough men waving their arms and shouting about politics."

"They're not shouting now."

"They will be, once Rhys Vaughan starts to speak his piece."

Juliana glanced to where the squire's son stood beside

a burly shopkeeper, waiting for the meeting to begin. The men in the audience were scowling and making sarcastic comments as the squire's son strove to ignore them.

"Why are they so hostile to him?" Juliana asked.

"The young Mr. Vaughan has been away a long time at university and on the Grand Tour. Since his father loved to talk of how the English would save Wales, this lot is suspicious of the son."

"But children don't always take after their parents."

"Aye. Heaven knows you're nothing like yours." Lettice flashed her a speculative glance. "You came just to see Mr. Vaughan, didn't you?"

Her maid was far too perceptive. "Of course. I wanted to hear his lecture. He's speaking about the Welsh language, isn't he?"

"Aye, but that's not why you're curious. After what your father did to the Vaughans, you want to see what the son is like. So what do you think of the man whose inheritance your father stole?"

Juliana stiffened. "Papa didn't steal Llynwydd. Squire Vaughan was a profligate man who lost his estate through his own recklessness. He shouldn't have played cards at such high stakes if he hadn't been prepared to lose."

"Perhaps. And perhaps your father shouldn't have agreed to such high stakes. A man's estate is his life." Lettice leaned closer. "Some claim the squire was drunk when he made that bet. And some claim your father cheated, in his eagerness to get a fine estate to use as your dowry."

Juliana winced. "I don't care what the gossips say. Papa won that estate fairly."

"Then why deed it to you? Fathers don't generally give their daughters ownership of their dowry properties, especially when the family's finances are strained. He wants to protect Llynwydd from whoever might challenge his claim."

"That's not true." Papa had only been trying to secure Llynwydd for her so Darcy couldn't appropriate it for himself after Papa died. "But I'm sorry the squire's son has no more inheritance now."

"Aye, and no father, either."

Guilt assailed Juliana. The squire had killed himself after losing his estate. And all because of what Papa had done to protect her.

She'd come here hoping to find Mr. Vaughan to be as much a profligate as his father, someone she could despise. Instead, she found a sober fellow too serious for his age.

And far too handsome. He had an unblemished brow, a determined mouth, and the strong jaw of a man of character. He didn't look much older than she, yet unlike other young men, he didn't fidget or shift from foot to foot like an impatient heron. His regal reserve and arrogant stance obviously came from good breeding. Like Darcy, he exuded confidence. His neat clothing wasn't extravagant, but it was certainly finer than that of the others.

Yet he shockingly wore no wig. Like a common Welsh laborer, he kept his lustrous black hair tied back in a queue. And his eyes were all passion and fire . . . blue and wild and fierce, like the crashing waters of the Welsh sea.

He must have sensed her watching him, for he turned his gaze to her. She caught her breath, afraid he might see through her flimsy disguise. But when he gave her the barest half-smile and his gaze moved on, her breath whooshed out of her.

He wasn't at all like other men of rank she knew, who were cold and lackluster even when they smiled at her. Like King Arthur, Mr. Vaughan thrummed with power. Arthur had been Welsh, too, a scholar and not a warrior. She could almost envision Mr. Vaughan admonishing his knights to uphold the ideals of the realm.

Oh bother! As usual, she was making everything romantic. Rhys Vaughan wasn't an Arthur, and certainly not a king.

"There he is, the devil," Lettice muttered.

Juliana looked over to see Morgan Pennant coming down the row toward them. The handsome printer in his thirties always smelled of ink and paper. Men generally trailed after Lettice like lapdogs, but only Mr. Pennant had captured the maid's affections. Unfortunately, his involvement with the Sons of Wales had forced her to keep her courtship secret. But she hadn't been able to keep it from Juliana's curious eyes.

As Mr. Pennant sat down beside Lettice, he laid a proprietary hand on hers, then leaned forward to see who her companion was. When he caught sight of Juliana his smile faded, and he shot Lettice a quizzical glance. "What's she doing here? 'Tisn't a place for an English girl."

"She followed me after she heard you invite me. You did say Mr. Vaughan would be talking about reviving the Welsh language." Lettice shrugged. "Once she was here, I couldn't send her home alone, could I?"

"I don't like it," Mr. Pennant grumbled.

Lettice patted his hand. "You needn't fear that she'll speak of it to anyone."

"I know." Mr. Pennant glanced over at Juliana, who was trying to look as innocent as possible. "I'm more concerned for her safety. You mustn't let Vaughan know who she is."

"Certainly not," Lettice said.

The crowd's gabbling increased as the shopkeeper stepped forward to the podium, and said in Welsh, "Today we are privileged to have with us Mr. Rhys Vaughan, son of our own Squire Vaughan."

"Aye," called someone from the crowd, "the *great* Squire Vaughan." The sarcastic tone drew laughter from the crowd.

The shopkeeper went on, reciting Mr. Vaughan's affiliation with the Gwyneddigion Society, a well-known London group supporting Welsh causes, but the crowd grew only more hostile.

Juliana couldn't keep her eyes off Mr. Vaughan's hardening features. The poor man! When he scanned the crowd, a dark scowl beetling his forehead, she waited until his eyes met hers again, then flashed him an encouraging smile. His eyes widened, then became unnervingly direct.

As she continued to smile at him, some of the sternness left his face. He kept his gaze trained on her even as he took his place behind the podium. There, he laid out his notes and drew a deep breath. "Good day. I'm very pleased to be here."

As low, angry mutters punctuated the tense silence, his expression grew grim. He surveyed the room, pausing at her, and once more, she gave him a reassuring smile.

"I am a man without a country. As are all of you." Rich and resonant as thunder in the mountains, his voice raised goose bumps on her skin. "And why is that?" He paused. "Not because England holds us captive to strange laws. And not even because the cloak of the English church sits poorly on our shoulders. Nay, we're without a country because our language has been stolen."

A fervent energy lit his face as he warmed to his subject, and he shook a sheaf of legal papers. "When you go to sell your cattle, what language is your bill of sale written in?"

While he waited for an answer, she held her breath. Then a man called out, "English."

Mr. Vaughan smiled coldly. "Aye. And when you choose a book of verse from the lending library, what language is it written in, more often than not?"

"English!" cried a few men in unison. They'd begun to sense his sincerity. Looks of concentration replaced their scowls.

His voice hardened. "And when you stand before the Court of Quarter Sessions to defend yourself for breaking their laws, what language do they use to condemn you?"

"English!" several shouted.

He nodded, waiting for the noise to subside. "English. Neither our mother tongue nor the tongue of our forefathers, but a bastard language thrust upon us against our will." He scanned the room. "You may wonder why I talk of language at a political meeting. You may think it doesn't matter what the squires and judges speak, as long as good, honest Welsh is still used in the streets."

He dropped his voice. "But how many Welsh in Carmarthen no longer speak their native tongue?" Leaning forward, he said in confidential tones, "I myself was sent to England, first to Eton and then to Oxford, because my father believed the English were our saviors and would give us a say in their government as long as we followed *their* rules and spoke *their* language."

He slammed his fist down on the podium. "By thunder, he was wrong! And he died because he believed in the English!"

The ring of pain in his voice made Juliana wince. But she wouldn't shrink from the words of this fierce-eyed Welshman. He spoke the truth, even if it was painful to hear.

"My father died," Mr. Vaughan went on in a voice soft as a whisper, "because he'd lost his country . . . and his language." Every man in the room hung on his words, emotion glistening in their eyes. "And when he wrote his dying words, do you know what language he wrote them in?"

"English," came the murmur from the crowd, following the ebb and flow of his voice as if they were one with him.

"Aye. English." He gripped the edges of the podium. "How long before the Welsh tongue is a quaint memory, like the fading memory of Welsh conquests? How long before we are nothing more than an English county, with an English heart and an English soul?"

Many in the crowd nodded.

His voice rose to a clarion ring. "I say that a man without his own voice is a slave! I say that when the English take away the red dragon's fiery tongue, they take away his power!" He paused, his expression dark and earnest. "Will you let that happen, my countrymen?"

"Nay!" the crowd cried as one.

"Will you let them trample our identity into the dust?"

"Nay!" They shook their fists.

He smiled, his audience in the palm of his hand. When his next words came, they were quiet and more powerful than any ranting. "Then we must follow the example of our companions in America."

Several gasps pierced the air. Many in Wales sympathized with the colonists, but plenty also opposed their rebellion. Juliana had heard her father argue many times that the American revolt would only end in a loss of men and wealth for everyone. Talking about it in glowing terms was seditious.

Mr. Vaughan held up a pamphlet. "Some of you have heard of our countryman Richard Price, who writes on the American war. In his *Observations on the Nature of Civil Liberty*, he says the natural rights of men should prevail over English law." He paused. "I agree with him. It's time to found a Wales governed by all the people—not just a few squires."

That was met by stunned silence.

"The American Declaration of Independence states, 'We hold these truths to be self-evident, that all men are created equal.' Yet here in England, Welshmen are far less than equal to their English lords."

"Aye!" cried voices from the crowd.

"We, too, want equality!" he shouted.

"Equality!" they shouted in return.

Lettice rose. "And at what price? My grandfather fought the English, and he died for it. Thanks to him, my family lost everything. Is that what you and your friends want? Do you wish your wives and sisters and children to starve for the cause of equality, while you and your brave friends fight a futile battle?"

When everyone gaped at her, Juliana waited for Mr. Vaughan to mock Lettice's womanly concerns as Papa and Darcy would have done. But Mr. Vaughan settled his disquieting gaze on Lettice and smiled. "I believe, Miss Johnes, that though it may cost some lives, this isn't a futile battle. I believe we can succeed."

Lettice wasn't appeased. "Every man thinks that, but many fail. Then we women are left holding the country together without our men!"

Before Mr. Vaughan could answer, a voice piped up in back. "If ye need a man, Lettice, I'll be glad to satisfy ye. Come by the shop anytime!"

"You wouldn't know what to do with me if you had me!" Lettice retorted.

"Never know until you try!" called another raucous male voice. Mr. Pennant cast the man a vicious glance and half rose in his seat.

Mr. Vaughan pounded the podium. "Enough!"

The crowd quieted.

"Miss Johnes asked a legitimate question. All I can say is, this cause will eventually bring better things for all of Wales, women and children included. And isn't that worth the cost?" He held up the pamphlet. "Mr. Price thinks that it is. But don't take my word for it. You must read his essay yourself."

How smoothly Mr. Vaughan had led the conversation

out of dangerous waters. A pity he hadn't further addressed Lettice's statements. Why *weren't* women's wishes considered whenever men went to fight for their causes?

Mr. Vaughan drew several pamphlets from a box and waved them before the crowd. "Hitherto, Price's essay has only been available in English, but I've translated it into Welsh. Here are printed copies, along with a work by Price's friend Thomas Paine. I've brought pamphlets for all."

The crowd nodded their approval. Political writings were rarely made available in Welsh, and certainly not writings on such controversial topics.

Mr. Vaughan was already handing out pamphlets. "Take as many as you like," he urged. "Read them. Think about them. Then think about your country. It's time the Welsh understand why the colonists are fighting English oppression. And why we should do so as well."

People grabbed at them, pushing and shoving to get copies. "There's more in the front," Mr. Vaughan declared.

The disorderly crowd completely disintegrated as some people rushed forward to stuff their pockets with the pamphlets, while others gathered to whisper, cautious of approaching the seditious materials. Mr. Pennant neared the front as well.

"I wonder how Mr. Vaughan managed this," Lettice whispered to Juliana. "No local printer with any sense would have risked printing it."

"Perhaps the owner of this bookshop has a connection to one in London? It couldn't be Mr. Pennant. He's going up to get one for himself."

"Hmm." Lettice scowled. "That could also mean he's trying to hide his involvement. And he'd certainly qualify. He's local and he has no sense. He's also well-acquainted with Mr. Vaughan, but I swear I'll have his head if he did something so dangerous." Lettice set her shoulders. "I'm going to ask him. You stay here, all right? I'll be back in a moment, and then we'll leave."

Juliana nodded as Lettice slid into the aisle without waiting for an answer. Shrinking into her corner, Juliana watched people surge from their seats.

Unfortunately, Mr. Vaughan was moving through the crowd toward her, shaking a hand here and speaking a word there. His frequent glances at her warned her of his intention to waylay her. She searched for Lettice, but the maid was arguing with Mr. Pennant at the far end of the room.

Dear heaven. Juliana had best avoid Mr. Vaughan. But as she reached the end of the aisle, he did, too, and blocked her exit.

Clearing his throat, he thrust a pamphlet at her. "Would you like one?"

She swallowed, waiting for him to notice the quality of her clothing and denounce her. But when he merely pressed the pamphlet upon her, she took it.

As she did, his fingers brushed hers. The brief contact made her feel suddenly warm in the damp cold of the basement. Stuffing the pamphlet under her arm, she dropped her gaze. "Th-thank you," she said in Welsh, praying that her accent would pass muster.

He flashed her a smile. "Would you tell Miss Johnes I'm sorry for the other men's insulting remarks?"

"Yes."

She tried to slide past him, but he caught her arm. "I hope *you* didn't take offense."

"Of course not. But I must go home."

He released her, only to follow her down the aisle. "Why so soon? Miss Johnes is staying. Can't you?"

By that time, she'd reached the door. She passed into a dimly lit hall and headed for the stairs, shaking her head.

Once more he caught her arm. "Here now, I think you've been lying to me."

Her heart hammering in her chest, she lifted her face to his. He didn't appear angry, but she couldn't be sure in the faint light. "What do you mean?"

"I think you did take offense at what the men said, else you wouldn't run off so soon."

Relief flooded her and she forced a smile. "I promise their words gave me no offense. Now please excuse me—"

She headed up the stairs, but he hurried to block her way once more, halting a step above her. "Then perhaps 'tis my speeches driving you off."

"Oh, no! You were wonderful!" Then she groaned. That wasn't the way to escape him.

A blazing grin transformed his serious features. "Thank you." Taking her hand, he rubbed his thumb over the knuckles, making her short of breath. He stared down at her hand, seemingly at a loss for words. But when she tried to pull free, he said, "You know, 'twas you who helped me speak so well. Everyone else seemed determined to dislike me, but every time you smiled, I felt welcomed. You had such sympathy in your expression that it emboldened me."

She blushed. Papa always chastised her for being too familiar with people, but she couldn't help it. Occasionally someone just captured her interest.

"If you don't mind my asking," he went on, "what is your name?"

"M-my name?"

Her distress seemed to amuse him. "Yes, your name."

Dear heaven. She looked beyond him for Lettice, but the hallway in which they stood was empty. Everyone else was still inside.

"Is it so difficult a question to answer?"

She stared down at the tapered fingers that held fast to hers, like ropes mooring the ships at the docks of the Towy. How was she to set herself adrift of him? "I must go, sir."

A mock frown creased his forehead. "'Let her who was asked and refused him, beware!'"

Her caution was momentarily forgotten. "Why, that's Huw Morus's 'Praise of a Girl'!"

"You know of Morus?"

"Of course!" Enthusiasm spilled into her voice. "He's one of my favorite poets, and that's my favorite poem by him. I have every line memorized. Let me think . . . what is the rest?"

When she bit her lip in concentration, his voice dropped into an enticing rhythm, "'Give a kiss and good grace / And pardon to trace, / And purity too, in your faultless face.'"

"Oh . . . yes." Too late, she remembered the words . . . and their inappropriateness. The color rose in her cheeks.

His thumb traced circles on the back of her hand. "I think he wrote the words just for you."

She tried for a light tone. "Hardly. Morus died before I was born."

He laughed. "For a servant, you're quite a scholar."

Bother, she'd forgotten her role! And if she stood here like a goose much longer, letting him say such adorable things, she'd give everything away. "That shows how little you know about servants."

"I know you have beautiful eyes, like rare emeralds winking in the sun. Poets write paeans to eyes like yours."

Why must he be as silvery-tongued as all those poets? "You shouldn't say such things to me."

Now his fingers stroked her palm, sending strange shivers up her arms. "Why not? Have you a husband?"

"Nay, but—"

"A sweetheart?"

She shook her head. Then seizing on the only thing she could think of, she said, "I'm not worthy of your attentions. Please, I must go."

But her words seemed only to hearten him. "Nonsense." He descended to her step, putting him so close she could feel his warm breath on her forehead. "I don't care if you're a servant. Since I have no estate, it scarcely matters. So perhaps I'm unworthy of *you*. At least you do honest labor, while I am still finding my place in the world."

His self-doubt tugged at her heart. "But you *have* found your place in the world, don't you see? You show people the truth. That's important."

Satisfaction glimmered in his eyes. "Do you find it important, my nameless friend?"

His nearness was crumbling her resolve. "Yes."

"You are my friend, aren't you?"

"Yes."

He drew her toward him. "Good, I can use a friend these days." His eyes searched hers. "'Give a heart that's alight / With kindly delight, / Gentleness, faithfulness, and we'll do right.'"

Before she could even register the next verse of Morus's poem, Mr. Vaughan was lowering his head. Then he pressed his mouth to hers.

At first she was too shocked by the intimacy to move. No one had ever touched her like this. No one had ever been *permitted* to touch her like this. It was the utmost affront to her dignity. And the utmost excitement of her life.

Instinctively, she closed her eyes, wondering if Arthur had kissed Guinevere in this manner. But as Mr. Vaughan moved his lips over hers in a tantalizing rhythm, even those thoughts disintegrated.

When she made a sound deep in her throat, he caught her about the waist, forcing her to clutch his shoulders to keep from falling. The movement brought her flush against him, her skirt crushed between them, and she felt sure he could hear her heart pound madly in her chest.

He kept kissing her, scattering thrills through her body like a ploughman sowing seeds. His mouth was soft and coaxing at first, a mere breath against hers. But as he prolonged the kiss, he shaped her mouth to his with more insistence until she went utterly limp.

"My lady!" came a sharp voice in English. "Juliana! Stop that at once!"

Hearing Lettice's voice was like hearing the voice of God descend from the heavens. With a gasp, Juliana jerked back from Mr. Vaughan and turned a guilty face to Lettice, who had pushed through the crowd into the hall, followed by Mr. Pennant.

Mr. Vaughan ignored them to smile at her. "At last I know your name."

Then Lettice was beside her. "Come," she said, pulling Juliana away from Mr. Vaughan. "We must go home."

"No, stay!" Mr. Vaughan called out.

As Lettice dragged her up the steps, Juliana looked back at him regretfully. "I'm sorry, Mr. Vaughan. I told you I had to go."

Lettice paused at the top to shove Juliana behind her and glare down at him. "You're a fine man, and I wish you luck, but Juliana is not for you!"

Mr. Vaughan's eyes blazed as he took a step up. "Why not?"

"It's better to let the women leave," Mr. Pennant said as Lettice thrust Juliana out the door and into the street.

"I knew something dreadful would happen if I let you stay." Lettice broke into a quick stride, still clasping Juliana's arm. "You must not have told him who you were, or he wouldn't have been putting his hands on you like that."

"I tried to get away from him, truly I did. But he was so . . . so . . ." Wonderful. "He quoted Huw Morus to me. He quoted 'Praise of a Girl.'"

"Aye, I'll bet he did. He's smooth as a fine brandy, that one. But brandy also has a bite, and so does he. That squire's son isn't what you need."

Juliana tipped up her chin. "It was merely a kiss." The only kiss she'd ever had, and it had stripped her youth from her in one clean swipe.

"Juliana!" came a shout from behind them. Mr. Vaughan had broken free of Mr. Pennant.

Instinctively Juliana turned, but Lettice yanked her forward. "Don't look back. You'll only encourage him."

Juliana choked off her protest. Lettice was right. Rhys Vaughan might speak like an angel and kiss like someone out of a Welsh myth, but the minute he found out who she was, he'd spurn her. Better to get the pain over with now, before she let herself hope too much.

So when he called her name the second time, she kept walking and didn't look back.

2

Such my woes, sorrow's harvest,
She, day-bright, won't let me rest.
Spellbinder, lovely goddess,
Speaks to my ears magic, no less.
— DAFYDD AP GWILYM, "HIS AFFLICTION"

Rhys stared hungrily after the woman named Juliana. "Tell me who she is."

"Forget about the girl, all right?" Morgan snapped.

"Why?"

"As Lettice said, she's not for you."

Coming from Morgan, that stung, and his friend was wrong anyway. Rhys could still feel her lips softening under his, could see her brilliant eyes grow dreamy at his words.

But why would Miss Johnes and Morgan say such a thing? Wait—hadn't Miss Johnes called Juliana "my lady"? Surely not.

Though that would explain why she was "not for him." Servants didn't speak cultured archaic Welsh, or know poetry or have such soft skin. She should have smelled of lye, not lavender. "She's isn't a servant, is she?"

Morgan sighed. "Nay."

"I'll make a nuisance of myself trying to find out who she is, if you don't tell me."

"Trust me, you don't want to know."

"Why not?"

"For one thing, she's English."

Rhys's jaw dropped. "But she spoke beautiful Welsh."

"She's fluent in it. From what Lettice says, she's a bit of a bluestocking, and likes to read Welsh tales and such."

The blood rushed to Rhys's head as he tried to remember if she'd had an accent. God, as if he could tell. English was his own native language. Father had always made them speak it at home. He'd learned Welsh from the servants.

Then something else Morgan said made his throat grow dry. "A bluestocking? How did a bluestocking come to be a friend of Miss Johnes?"

With a sigh, Morgan turned back toward his shop. "She's Lettice's mistress."

"Mistress!" A slow dread burned through him. "And her name?"

Morgan glanced at him with pity. "Lady Juliana St. Albans. Her father is the Earl of Northcliffe."

Feeling sick, Rhys stared at Morgan. Northcliffe had killed Father as surely as if he'd pushed him into the river himself.

Then he remembered how sweetly Juliana had encouraged him during the lecture. "I don't believe you!"

"She followed Lettice here this eve, and Lettice didn't send her home."

God help them all. As he realized why the woman must

have sneaked into their meeting, Rhys tensed. "That little, conniving—"

"Here now, don't talk that way about the lady. I understand why you're upset, but—"

"Lady?" Rhys whirled on him. "What was the 'lady' doing at a gathering like this?"

"Just curious, I suppose. Lady Juliana does like Welsh things."

"By thunder, why didn't you warn me who she was?" He felt like breaking something, like tearing into someone, anyone. Why did she have to be Northcliffe's spawn?

"So you could badger her for her father's crimes? Lettice would've cut out my tongue if I'd caused trouble for her mistress."

"Her mistress could cause trouble for us! She could name our members to her father, and we'd all find ourselves hounded by the burgesses. You know how fond the press gangs are of carrying off radicals to serve in His Majesty's Navy."

"She wouldn't turn us over," Morgan protested, a bit nervously.

"She might do it for her father."

"I don't think so. Besides, she's only a girl."

"Nay." Rhys thought of her soft body pressed to his. "Lady Juliana is not 'only a girl.' "

"Perhaps not, but you're accusing her of being a spy." Morgan laid a hand on his shoulder. "You're thinking with your cock. She's a pretty thing you can't touch, so you're taking that out on her."

Rhys recoiled from the truth in Morgan's words. "Don't

talk to me as if I'm some green lad. I know all about her family's damnable tricks. Leave me be, and I'll take care of this."

Morgan's eyes narrowed. "What do you mean?"

"That's none of your concern." Rhys stalked off, wanting to be away from Morgan and his too-sound logic.

"Don't do anything foolish, lad!" Morgan called after him.

Rhys kept heading for the river. "Damn, damn, damn. Not only English, but the earl's own daughter."

He could still hear her saying she wasn't worthy of him. What stupid answer had he given? Ah yes, that he might not be worthy of her since she did honest labor. Hah! Her "honest labor" was sneaking about at night, spying on her father's enemies, seducing them with her smiles.

He pounded his fist into his palm and tried to blot out her image, the intent expression she'd worn as he'd talked, the satiny texture of her cheek, her yielding lips—

Damn her for doing this to him! How could a woman look so innocent and be so deceitful?

And she'd certainly looked innocent. Not so much beautiful as arresting. The wide eyes and full mouth had seemed to signal a generosity of spirit, as well as an unconscious sensuality. She hadn't flirted, hadn't smiled coyly, and she'd kissed with an untutored wonder.

His eyes narrowed. Obviously, he was more easily fooled by appearances than he'd thought.

By now he'd reached the bridge. He strode along it, then stopped at the railing to stare into the swirling waters where his father had leapt to his death.

"May God have mercy on his soul."

Anguish hit Rhys anew. If only he'd been here a month ago, instead of racing back from Paris, summoned by an urgent letter from his father that read, "I lost Llynwydd, son."

Why hadn't he followed his instincts the first time Father suggested sending him away? He should have refused to leave. But Father had insisted that he acquire an "education befitting a gentleman."

That was all well and good for a boy who didn't have to shore up the family estate at every turn, who hadn't spent his holidays poring over Llynwydd's books. Left to his own devices, Father had never been able to settle his mind to work, and he'd always relied too heavily on a land agent who overlooked his outrageous expenditures.

So while Rhys had played the dutiful son in Paris, making stupid notes on French architecture and history and art by day, and meeting with philosophes at night, the damned Earl of Northcliffe had deceived his father into gambling away Rhys's inheritance. While Rhys had been traveling back across the Channel, numb with shock from his father's letter after it finally reached him, his father had been throwing himself into the Towy. Rhys had arrived just in time to watch them pull the body from the river.

"Well, Father," he said, looking down into the unforgiving waters, "I'm a squire now. What good is my proper education to either of us?"

The whistling wind was his only answer.

He stared out into the unfeeling night. "But I'm going to make it right. You'll see."

He'd already been to a solicitor about the possibility of regaining Llynwydd. The man claimed Rhys had a chance of winning a dispute over the property, since his father had not been "in his right mind" when he'd signed it over to the earl, and since there were rumors that the earl had cheated. The solicitor and his agents had been gathering facts for the case, having already notified the earl that Rhys was disputing the transfer of ownership.

But apparently Lord Northcliffe had his own methods for stopping Rhys—like sending his daughter to the Sons of Wales meeting, where she could take note of every radical in the place. Such knowledge would be useful to a man known for intimidation.

Well, Rhys would put a stop to that. He'd go to Northcliffe Hall and set the damned earl straight before this spying business went any further. And if Lady Juliana was there, he'd set her straight, too.

The next morning, Juliana sat in the breakfast room, swirling her spoon in her hot chocolate. How *wonderful* Mr. Vaughan had been, so learned, so . . . fiery.

Lettice had spouted nonsense about how a man would say anything to get a woman in his clutches, but Mr. Vaughan wasn't like that. He was passionate, like her, and couldn't contain his feelings about things that mattered.

She was still staring dreamily into space when the sound of loud voices in the foyer jerked her from her reverie. Wondering who would call so early, she rose and went out into the hall.

"I don't care what time it is," said a familiar voice. "I want to see his lordship immediately!"

She froze beside the staircase. Though her view of the foyer was blocked, she recognized those ringing tones from last night.

The door to Papa's study opened from the other side of the staircase and, oblivious to her lurking in the shadows, he stormed into the hall. She crept forward, her heart in her throat as she peered around the edge to see her father come face-to-face with Mr. Vaughan.

Two footmen were attempting to reason with Mr. Vaughan, but he was standing firm. He looked exactly as she'd remembered him—all lean muscle animated with a vibrant energy that put the spark in his eyes and the glow on his face. Why on earth was he here?

Father glowered at him. "What is the meaning of this, sir? You cannot force your way into a man's house without—"

"I am the son of the man you ruined," Mr. Vaughan said. "William Vaughan was my father."

Father gestured to the footmen, who returned to their posts. Then he turned his hard-eyed gaze on Mr. Vaughan. "I heard you'd returned to town."

"I'm sure you did. If none of your other spies told you, then I suppose you heard it from your daughter."

Juliana's knees buckled. So he'd found out who she was. But why tell Papa that he knew her? Didn't he know what trouble he'd get her into?

"What do you mean, my daughter?" Papa demanded.

"Don't pretend you didn't send her to spy on me and my friends last night."

"Last night?"

Mr. Vaughan thought her a *spy?* What happened to all his sweet words? And his gentle kiss?

"I should have expected this of you," Mr. Vaughan went on. "You couldn't allow the wheels of justice to take their slow turn. No, you had to skulk behind your daughter's skirts, sending her out to do your dirty work."

How dared he! She'd obviously been quite wrong about his nobility of mind. He was beastly, simply beastly! If she were a man, she'd walk right out and thrash him!

But she could only watch helplessly as her father drew himself up, a vein bulging in his forehead. "You, sir, are insane if you think my daughter would involve herself with your band of ruffians!"

You tell him! Perhaps Papa would refuse to believe Mr. Vaughan's words. Perhaps he'd dismiss them as trouble-making nonsense.

Mr. Vaughan dashed those hopes. "Your daughter's name is Juliana, is it not?" Then he proceeded to describe her with an accuracy as astonishing as it was damning.

Juliana buried her face in her hands as her father sputtered, then shouted, "Juliana! Juliana, girl, you come down here at once!"

How could she face Papa's temper, especially in front of that betraying wretch? Yet she must defend herself. Not that Papa would listen to her.

She could cheerfully throttle Mr. Vaughan. The wicked creature obviously didn't care that he was ruining her life.

"Don't take it out on the poor girl," Mr. Vaughan said,

and for a moment, Juliana thought him repentant. "'Tisn't her fault that she isn't as practiced at deceit as her father."

The urge to throttle him surged again.

"Juliana!" Her father's tone brooked no argument as he started for the stairs. He'd keep at it until the entire household had come to watch.

With a sigh, she emerged from behind the staircase. "Here I am, Papa."

Taking her by the arm, he dragged her in front of Mr. Vaughan. "Tell me truthfully, girl: Do you know this man?"

She considered lying, but that might force Mr. Vaughan to elaborate on her adventure. "Aye, Papa."

Her father's hand tightened painfully on her. "Is he telling the truth? Were you at this gathering of his friends last night?"

She cast a glance at Mr. Vaughan, whose face was stony and remote as he stared at her without a whit of concern. Any guilt she'd felt for misleading him last night rapidly dissipated.

"Were you?" Papa repeated, shaking her.

Lifting her chin in defiance of them both, she said, "Aye."

Her father shoved her away. "Go wait for me in the study. I'll be there presently to administer your punishment."

A tremor of fear skittered along her spine. "Please, Papa, let me explain—"

"Go to my study!" He shook his thick finger in that direction. "Now, or I'll cane you thrice as hard!"

With a shudder, she backed away. She'd seen Papa angry before, but not like this. Still, she mustn't let him reduce her to a quivering puddle, or it would go worse for her. With all the dignity she could muster, she stalked off to the study.

Rhys watched her go, uneasiness settling in his gut. What in the devil was this? An elaborate show for his benefit? Surely the earl wouldn't cane his daughter for this, would he? She'd done only what he'd put her up to.

But she'd been caught. Perhaps her punishment was for that. A surge of unwarranted pity made Rhys tighten his fists. "You shouldn't punish Juliana for merely carrying out your orders."

The earl remained silent until the study door opened and closed. Then he fixed Rhys with a cold gaze. "I assure you, sir, I wouldn't send my daughter within ten miles of you and your scoundrel friends. If I needed spies, I'd use one of my sons or a servant. I'd not send an innocent girl into a nest of vipers, even to crush the likes of you!"

The logic behind the man's words struck Rhys hard. If the earl spoke the truth—and somewhere in the fog of Rhys's anger it seemed plausible—then Juliana was about to receive a caning.

And it was all his fault.

At that thought, he snapped, "If she didn't go at your request, then why in God's name was she there?"

Northcliffe's eyes narrowed. "I have no idea. The girl has strange notions about the Welsh, to be sure, but I'd never thought to see her sneaking about at night."

A chill shook Rhys. Morgan had said she liked to dabble in Welsh things, and he hadn't seemed concerned about her presence at the meeting. Had Rhys jumped to conclusions?

"Your 'wheels of justice' don't worry me," Northcliffe went on. "I acquired Llynwydd fairly, and I'll hold what is mine, no matter what some upstart Welshman thinks to do about it!"

"You didn't 'acquire' that estate. You stole it. And I intend to prove it."

They glared at each other a long moment, hatred boiling up between them.

"We shall see, my boy." Northcliffe summoned his footmen, then motioned to Rhys. "Escort Mr. Vaughan to the gate. I never want to see his scurrilous face in this house again."

Rhys smiled grimly. "I can see myself out. And don't worry, Northcliffe. I shan't set foot here again until you resign your claim to Llynwydd. Which you will do one day, if I have anything to say about it."

Ignoring the earl's derisive snort, he left, with the footmen trailing after him. But as soon as Rhys passed through the wrought-iron gates and heard them clank shut behind him, he paused to stare back through the bars, his anger replaced by a more unsettling emotion. Guilt.

Juliana was in there awaiting a caning. If she truly had attended the meeting for her own reasons, then she was suffering due to *him*.

Belatedly, he remembered her flawless command of Welsh and her quoting of Welsh poetry. Today she'd worn an expensive blue satin gown, but the undersides of her cuffs had been as dingy as his from having well-inked paper rub against them. She was clearly a scholar. And scholars were rarely spies.

"Damn it all!" He moved along the stone wall, searching for a way to get back in.

It wasn't as if he could do anything. He couldn't leap into the earl's study and whisk Juliana away. But he also couldn't let her be caned.

Perhaps he could create a distraction to get her father away from her. Or find her afterward and soothe her hurts. Beg her forgiveness.

When he came to an oak branch that extended several feet over the wall, he decided he could probably reach it. Then he could climb up the wall and jump over—

A rustling on the other side gave him pause. The sound seemed to move up the oak. Puzzled, he stared up into the tree. When he caught a glimpse of blue satin, relief surged through him. He should have known Lady Juliana wouldn't stay to be beaten. Running away seemed to be her specialty, thank God.

More satin spilled over the top of the wall as she crept backward along the branch. He saw a flash of shapely calf before her silk hose caught on the bark. She grabbed at it, but her hair, a rich coppery red that had been hidden from his sight last night, masked her face and blinded her.

He moved under the branch just as she lost her balance and fell right into his arms. Clearly startled, she shoved her hair from her face, but when she saw who'd caught her, she scrambled out of his arms.

"What are you doing here?" she demanded.

"Catching you."

"Why? So you could make sure I got my caning? Are you planning to march me back in to Papa?"

He winced. If he hadn't already been convinced she was innocent, her wounded tone and attempt at escape would have done it. "Nay. I thought I'd rescue you, instead."

She brushed leaves and twigs from her gown. "I am doing fine rescuing myself, thank you very much."

"What are you planning to do—hide?"

"Not that it's any of your concern, but yes. Until Mama can talk Papa out of my punishment. Or at least get it reduced."

"That works?"

"Sometimes." Her stiff look sent guilt spiraling through him. "I had to do something."

"Thanks to me and my blundering." He tugged an acorn from her hair.

But when he couldn't resist letting his fingers linger over the silken strands, she swatted his hand away. "How dare you! First, you get me in trouble, and then you act as if it never happened!"

Her words lacerated his already beaten conscience. "What I did this morning was unconscionable, and I am sorry. I can say nothing in my defense."

"Quite true."

The throaty timbre of her voice made him ache to touch her again, but he knew better than to try. "You must understand—your father and his candidate for Member of Parliament are persecutors of radicals. When I found out you were his daughter—"

"You decided I was his *spy*. I understand quite well, you . . . you *diawl*!"

Her use of the Welsh word for "devil" took him off

guard. As she flounced off toward the woods, he hastened after her.

"You ignored my obvious sympathy for your cause and for you," she said, "and instead imagined horrid things of me. I know Papa committed a great wrong against your family. But I had naught to do with it!" She stomped through the grass, heedless of how it ruined her skirts. "But because I am a St. Albans, you decided I was in it up to my neck." She halted to fix him with a piercing stare. "Correct?"

"Something like that," he muttered, irritated that she had so succinctly described his mad thoughts over the last night.

"So you came to Papa with your suspicions, instead of to me." Her voice caught. "Even though last night you praised my eyes and quoted Huw Morus to me. You told me . . . Oh, it doesn't matter what you told me. All of it was lies anyway."

"Not so!"

"Aye." She eyed him as if he were a snail. "Lettice explained it to me. A man will say anything to pull down a woman's defenses, so he can get at her person." Her sweet mouth trembled, and he felt like a bastard all over again. "You said all those lovely things to get me to kiss you, yet it meant nothing."

"That's not true. I meant every word."

When he reached for her, she backed away. "If you lay a hand on me, I'll call the footmen."

"And let them carry you back to your father?" As she blanched, he caught her hand. "Please, Juliana, you must believe me. This morning was a temporary madness. Last night when I met you, I realized I'd met my ideal woman. Then I discovered you were out of my reach. It infuriated me to have you snatched from my hands before I'd had a chance to know you. That's why I struck out today."

"Against me."

"Nay, against everything that took you from me. Unfortunately, that included you."

She cocked her head. "You're speaking in riddles and trying to confuse me." She tried to snatch her hand from his.

He wouldn't let go. "I know this sounds insane, but from the moment I saw you smile at me, I wanted to know everything about you."

She pressed her lips together. "Your pretty words won't work this time. I know your game now."

Damn it all, why did he want so badly to convince her he wasn't an ogre? He ought to be running as fast and far away as he could. Lettice was right—she wasn't for him.

Yet something in him rebelled at the idea. He clasped her hand against his heart. "What can I do to change your mind, *anwylyd?*"

"Don't call me that. I'm not your 'darling.'"

But he could see her wavering. "Tell me how to make up for my poor behavior. I can't take your caning for you, but I could tell your father I was mistaken, that I saw some other woman at the meeting."

She snorted. "Too late for that."

Clasping her about the waist, he drew her close. "Doesn't it mean something to you that I came back to rescue you?

Don't my apologies mean anything? That's why I was under that tree: I was going to pull myself up on that branch and go after you."

He bent close, and she sucked in her breath. He wanted to taste her again, to crush her mouth under his, to revel in its warmth. Her lavender scent filled his nostrils, driving him more insane. He pressed a kiss into her hair.

"Please, you mustn't—" she whispered.

"Touch you? Kiss you? I truly can't help myself when I'm with you."

Glancing back at the estate walls, she stiffened. "Oh no—Papa has sent my brothers looking for me."

Two burly young men were indeed coming round the corner of the wall. He recognized Viscount Blackwood, the earl's heir. Swiftly Rhys pulled her into the forest, praying that the men hadn't seen them.

But when he tried to drag her deeper, she halted. "Please, I must go back. They won't rest until they find me, and if they find you with me, 'twill be very bad for me."

"I want to protect you. You shouldn't suffer for my error—"

"It doesn't matter. I can endure the caning, now that I know—" She broke off, coloring.

"Yes?" Lifting her hand to his lips, he pressed a kiss into her palm. "Now that you know what?"

She ducked her head shyly. "That you no longer believe those awful things you said. That you didn't lie last night."

"I don't. And I didn't." He stroked her hair. "Do you forgive me?"

"Yes."

That sent his blood thundering through his veins. He didn't deserve her kindness or trust. He shouldn't desire her, or let her desire him. Yet he did, and he would.

He held her close. "Stay awhile." He managed a smile. "Give your mother time to plead on your behalf."

She cupped his cheek, looking as if she might do as he asked. But just then one of her brothers called out, "Darcy, I see something over there . . . in the woods!"

She pushed him away hard. "Go!" When he hesitated, her voice turned pleading. "If you care for me at all, run and don't come back. Because if they find me with you, I'll be caned within an inch of my life."

Only that gave him the strength to flee into the woods. But he halted a short distance away and hid to watch as her brothers caught up with her.

"Juliana, you little fool, you're in big trouble now," said the viscount. "Father will have your hide for running off!"

"You could tell him you couldn't find me," Juliana said hopefully.

Her brother shook his head. "This isn't like when you were a girl and I hid you from Father. If you don't come now, 'twill be worse for you later. So it's better to get it over with."

Despite the man's sympathetic tone, Rhys had to fight the urge to jump out and snatch her from her brothers. But thrashing her brothers would only get her in more trouble.

By thunder, this was a damned mess! He shouldn't have come at all. And he certainly shouldn't have held her again, allowing her to steal once more into his heart.

Look at me, lurking behind trees, longing after an English-woman, and one beyond my station at that. She ought to hate me. I ought to hate her.

Yet he didn't. And given the chance, he would see her again. That was what worried him most.

3

Where there's love it's all in vain
to draw the bolt or fix the chain;
and locks of steel, where there's desire,
and doors of oak won't hold that fire.
　　　　—ANONYMOUS, "STANZAS FOR THE HARP"

*N*ight was falling as Darcy smoked a cigar before dinner on the terrace of Northcliffe Hall. When he saw Lettice leave the house, glance about her, and head for the woods, he frowned. She must be meeting someone. It had to be a man, or she wouldn't be so secretive about it. But who might it be?

Lettice was *his*, damn it. As soon as he and Lady Elizabeth married, he meant to make the Welshwoman his mistress. Though Elizabeth's dowry would bolster the family fortunes and her breeding would make her an excellent hostess for social affairs, she was too cold to warm a man's bed.

Unlike the lovely Lettice.

Stubbing out his cigar, he followed her at a discreet distance until she halted in a clearing, and a tall Welshman in modest dress emerged from the shadows.

God rot it, he knew that fellow. Morgan Pennant, the printer. He had a shop on Lammas Street.

Darcy scowled as Pennant drew Lettice into his arms and kissed her. Was Pennant the reason that she'd stopped encouraging Darcy's kisses of late? With jealousy boiling up inside him, he edged closer to watch from behind a tree.

After letting that bloody Welshman kiss her for far too long, Lettice jerked back. "I swear, Morgan, you try my patience. I told you last night, find someone else and leave me alone."

"Yes, I can see how much you want to be left alone," Pennant said dryly, pulling her against him. "You certainly came at my summons."

"Only to make sure you never 'summon' me again." She glanced around nervously, and Darcy flattened himself against the tree trunk.

"You don't mean that." Pennant tried to kiss her again, but she turned her head.

"I don't want to lose my position. I won't ever be forced to scrabble for a living like my parents, and that's what I'll get if I keep on with you." She pushed Pennant away. "I know you printed those seditious pamphlets for Mr. Vaughan. One day you'll be found out, and I don't want to be linked with you when you are!"

Darcy's eyes narrowed. Was she speaking of the same Mr. Vaughan who was his father's enemy? The one who'd landed Juliana in trouble this morning? And what was all this about sedition?

Pennant laughed. "I told you last night, they were done in London. Nothing to do with me."

Lettice turned her back to him. "I'm no fool. I know you'd do anything for your fellow Sons of Wales."

Darcy clenched his fists. That deuced group of radicals? Father and the burgesses had been attempting to stamp them out for some time. Lettice was right to be concerned. Being mixed up with that lot would definitely get her turned off if Father found out about it.

Not one whit put off by her words, Pennant came up behind her to clasp her about the waist. "I won't let your silly suspicions change what lies between us."

"It's already changed it. I shouldn't even have gone last night. 'Twas very foolish. And after your idiot friend came today to make accusations against my poor Lady Juliana, I ought to wash my hands of you entirely."

"That wasn't my doing, and you know it."

"Still . . ." When Pennant began nibbling her ear, she leaned her head back against his chest with a sigh. "Can't you just forget about the radicals?"

Pennant turned Lettice to face him. "Nay, sweetheart, I cannot. And you don't truly want me to. If I were a puling coward who paid lip service to English laws, then grumbled about it in the taverns, you wouldn't love me."

"I *don't* love you, you fool!"

Dragging her against him, Pennant kissed her with a passion that made Darcy rage. The scoundrel! 'Twasn't right that he should have Lettice!

When Pennant stopped kissing her, he chuckled. "Say again that you don't love me, and I'll show you again that you're lying."

She clung to his shoulders in near desperation. "You devil,

how could I care for a man who doesn't have the good sense to see the danger he puts himself—and his friends—in?"

"You've nothing to worry about. If I'm found out, you and I will start anew in London, or perhaps even America. You can be sure I'll never leave you to the tender mercies of your master." He stroked her cheek. "But no one will find out unless you tell them."

"I swear I'll never tell!" She threw her arms about his neck. "Oh, you will be careful, won't you?"

"Only if you promise to keep meeting me." His voice grew serious. "I couldn't bear it if you truly broke with me."

"I must be ten kinds of a fool . . ." She paused. "But God help me, I do love you."

His answer was to kiss her again so passionately, Darcy had to dig his fingernails into his palms to keep from leaping out and tearing into the too-handsome printer.

But if he jumped in now, Lettice would side with her lover and Darcy would never have her. There were better ways to get what he wanted.

First he'd see what he could find out about Pennant's and Vaughan's activities.

Then he'd make sure Pennant was no longer around to tempt Lettice.

The scent of roast duckling, mingled with the sugary smell of cinnamon apples, wafted up to Juliana where she lay on her bed. Her mouth watering, she thrust her head under her pillow.

Mama had prevailed upon Papa not to cane her, so he'd

chosen confining her to her room for the next two weeks and sending her to bed without supper tonight, when her favorite meal was being served.

She would rather have been caned, just to have it done and over with.

Then again, perhaps not. Papa had been furious. He might truly have hurt her, especially after she'd refused to tell him what meeting she'd attended and who'd taken her there. She'd never seen him so enraged.

Had last night's adventure been worth it?

Aye. One kiss from Rhys Vaughan had been worth all of it.

Like as not, she'd never see the smooth-tongued Welshman again. She wished she could get a note to him, to explain . . .

She punched the pillow. What was there to explain? That she wished she were a Welsh girl who could kiss whomever she wanted? It was true. At the moment, she'd rather be a scullery maid than a lady.

The door swung open, making her jerk her head around. Her mother slipped into the room and came to sit on the bed beside her. "I wanted to make sure you were all right. You do understand why your father punished you, don't you?"

Juliana swallowed her resentful words.

"He merely wants what's best for you, dear. If you're to make a good marriage, you must learn to control these wild urges of yours. You cannot simply go off on your own. There are men who would—" Her mother broke off, lips tightening.

"Would what?"

Mama dropped her voice as if speaking of a deadly secret. "Assault your person."

Juliana's eyes widened. Lettice hadn't told her that. "You mean they would hit me?" Juliana didn't count Papa's canings as hitting; that was merely punishment for transgressions.

"Not exactly." Mama looked pained. "Men can assault a woman in other ways. They can touch a woman . . ." Her mother trailed off, obviously embarrassed.

"You mean, like kissing them?" Juliana added helpfully.

Her mother glanced up, startled. "What do you know of kissing?"

Juliana dropped her gaze. "I-I've watched Lettice."

Her mother's sigh of relief sounded loud in the room. "That maid of yours is entirely too forward with men for an unmarried woman. But then, she's Welsh."

What did that have to do with it? "Do only Welshwomen let men kiss them like that?"

"An unmarried Englishwoman would never allow a man to kiss her, unless he were her betrothed, of course. Even then, it would be a buss on the cheek, no more. Only married people may kiss on the mouth . . . and . . . well, touch each other."

Mama's voice grew brittle. "But men have trouble curbing their intense . . . ah . . . feelings. So women must be the strong ones and hold them at bay."

Mr. Vaughan's kiss had made her feel all tingly and pleasant inside. She'd wanted to stand there kissing him forever. "Don't women have intense feelings?"

"Certainly not! Not proper Englishwomen and well-bred ladies. The Welsh are different, because they have impure blood. But English ladies are a higher breed—strong feelings aren't in our constitution. There *are* a few unmarried women willing to be any man's paramour, but certainly no one who travels in our circles."

Juliana knew the word "paramour" had something to do with living in the same house with a man who wasn't related to you either by blood or by marriage. But the word sounded so foreign that she'd dismissed it as a Continental peculiarity. "These few unmarried women . . . they're English?"

Her mother sat up straight on the bed. "In name only, I should think. Their behavior demonstrates that they're not—" She broke off. "I shouldn't have mentioned it. In any case, you mustn't think about women with such impure blood. *You* aren't of that kind, not with your breeding."

"So you're saying that if a woman, even an Englishwoman, lets a man kiss her and likes it, she has impure blood."

"Of course." Her mother's eyes narrowed. "You're awfully curious about this, Juliana."

She managed a smile. "Well, my window is over the garden, so I see the servant girls with their sweethearts go by. I never could understand why they kiss so much."

Her mother gave a tight-lipped smile. "And now you do."

Impure blood? That explained *everything*—why she felt so different from her family, why they always told her to control her emotions when she only wanted to let them out. That must be why she loved Welsh things and had "strong feelings" when Mr. Vaughan kissed her.

"I'd best return downstairs, before I am missed and your father loses his temper."

Juliana scowled. Mama's meek acceptance of Papa's commands had always angered her. Perhaps *that* was her impure blood, too, making her want to fight instead of bow her head and take her medicine as Mama said a lady should.

After Mama slipped out the door, Juliana got up and wandered to the window. Feeling hemmed in, she opened it and rested her arms on the sill.

Now when her family talked about the Welsh as if they were odd creatures, she would know why she didn't agree. Why she found Welsh stories about heroic conquests much more exciting than the English lady's manuals Mama made her read. She had impure blood.

She didn't mind hearing that she was flawed. Ladies with impure blood seemed to have all the fun.

Suddenly, she heard a rustling in the oak that grew near her window. A form appeared on the branch a couple of feet above, and she opened her mouth to scream. Then the figure said, "It's me, Rhys."

"Mr. Vaughan? Good Lord! What are you doing?"

Now she could see his face. "Coming in to talk to you."

Then before she could react, he dropped to hang from the branch. "Move away from the window, my lady."

It was either do as he said or watch him fall. With her heart in her throat, she got out of the way as he began swinging back and forth until he veered close enough to hook his feet over the sill.

"You fool!" she hissed and hurried forward to help him climb inside. "If you'd fallen, you might have been killed!"

He dusted off his breeches, then turned a gleaming gaze on her. "Are you so worried for me, then?" Grinning, he strode across the room to latch her door.

Dear heaven, she'd welcomed a man into her bedchamber and let him lock them in together. This wouldn't do at all. "You shouldn't be here."

"I know. I told myself I should stay clear of you and your family. But I had to find out if you survived your caning." Taking off his coat, he tossed it across a chair. "When I glanced through the windows downstairs and didn't see you with your family in the drawing room, I started circling the house, searching for a way in. That's when I spotted you, looking like an angel in white."

The compliment softened her. A little. "Well, you must go. Someone might find you here, and I'll be in even more trouble than I already am."

He winced. "Was the caning too very awful?"

She shook her head. "As I'd hoped, Papa changed his mind about it after Mama talked to him. But I'm not allowed to leave my room for two weeks." Her stomach growled. "And I was sent up without dinner."

His eyes darkened. "I'm sorry for getting you into trouble."

She shrugged. "It's done now. No use crying over it."

"But at least I can help enliven your confinement."

"Oh, no, you can't *stay*," she cried as he drew a parcel from his coat pocket. "Mama might—"

"I brought you a gift. As a sort of apology."

That stunned her into silence.

He thrust the parcel at her. "I should have brought you bread, I suppose, but no gift can really make up for the trouble I got you in."

"No . . . I mean . . ." She took it from him with a tremulous smile. "I can't believe you brought me a present."

When she unknotted the string around the parcel, the burlap wrapping fell away to reveal a book. She caught her breath at the title—*Gorchestion Beirdd Cymru*. Which meant, in English, *The Masterpieces of the Welsh Poets*.

"There's no Huw Morus," Mr. Vaughan said, "but it has poems by Taliesin and Dafydd ap Gwilym—"

"It's delightful!" She lifted her gaze to him. "'Tis the most wonderful present anyone has ever given me."

He let out his breath. "You like it."

"How could I not?" She caressed the leather-bound volume. "I have lots of Welsh history books, but only pieces of Welsh poetry transcribed for me by our servants from their own small collections. I've never had a whole book of poems to myself."

He smiled. "That's because there are few in existence. The Morrises in London did that one."

Opening the book, she thumbed through the pages, careful not to crease the spine. "How did you get a copy in such a short time?"

"'Tis my own."

Her pulse quickened. She flipped to the front and saw his name written in ink on the flyleaf.

"I have a small library of Welsh books I carry about with me," he added. "That's one of them."

She held the book out regretfully. "You mustn't give me your only copy—"

"I want to. I knew you would appreciate it." He covered her hands with his.

Her breath grew unsteady. "How can I ever thank you, Mr. Vaughan?"

He smiled. "You could start by calling me Rhys."

When his eyes locked with hers, dark and searching, she said, "I'll cherish your gift always, Rhys."

He stared at her as if caught up in a magic spell. And it must have been a spell that kept her from drawing her hands from his or looking away. Then he took the book from her to lay it on a nearby table and drew her close. She could hear the quickening of his breath, see the pulse beat in his throat.

"You honor me by cherishing my gift," he whispered.

She didn't speak a word, afraid to shatter the spell. He was going to kiss her. And she wanted him to. So, so much.

His kiss began as the merest mingling of breaths, their lips just touching, but as she slipped her arms about his waist, he groaned and covered her mouth with his.

Hunger had already made her light-headed, and the softness of his mouth and his musky scent engulfed her in a dizzy, unfamiliar pleasure.

"Juliana," he whispered against her mouth. "Sweet, sweet Juliana."

Her eyes slid shut. "Rhys."

He altered the tenor of their kiss, pressing harder and skimming his tongue along the seam of her lips. "Open to me, *cariad.*"

Dear heaven, he'd called her his "love."

She opened her mouth to answer and felt his tongue plunge inside. Shock held her motionless until he began to explore her mouth, sparking a wanton heat inside her. Over and over, he thrust his tongue between her lips. The bold strokes made her yearn to feel him pressed more closely to her, but when she tightened her arms about his waist, he moaned.

She jerked back. Had she hurt him? But he stared at her wild-eyed before dragging her back for a kiss so intense, it scarcely let her breathe. Then he scattered kisses over her cheeks, her jaw, her neck.

Each touch of his lips bedeviled her with fierce urges until need spread through her body like hot honey. Freeing his hair of its ribbon tie, she raked her fingers through his unruly curls.

Suddenly she heard footsteps in the hall. She twisted away, and he swore under his breath. The light footsteps paused outside her door, then continued past.

After they heard a door open and close, he asked, "Who was it?"

"Mama, probably going to her room." She stared up at him. "Lettice will come soon to help me undress for bed. You mustn't be here when she does."

A faint smile quirked up his lips. "I wouldn't mind watching."

She reddened. "You shouldn't talk that way."

"You're right. Why waste time talking?"

He reached for her once more, but she slipped from his grasp. "I'm serious, Rhys. You must leave. If you're not concerned about Lettice finding you here, then think of this: Papa will soon follow Mama to bed, and if he discovers you here—"

"He might make good on that caning."

"He's really not as bad as he seems."

With a hard glare, he snatched up his coat. "Don't speak to me of your father's good points. I'm well aware of the man he truly is—the sort who would steal a man's estate from his family." The firelight flickered over the unyielding lines of his face. "But I suppose you don't believe that he did."

"I don't know whether Papa came by your estate fairly, but I do know he shouldn't have taken it. I only wish I could do something."

His expression softened. "I don't expect you to. As you said, you're not to blame for it."

His generous dismissal of her guilt only increased it. If Papa hadn't wanted a fine dowry for her, Rhys might even now be sitting comfortably in his own drawing room. What would he say if she told him that Llynwydd was hers? He'd probably accuse her of lying again, and she couldn't bear that. Besides, it wasn't as if she could change the fact.

"I'd better go." He donned his coat. "I've done what I came to do." His gaze flicked to her lips. "And more than I should have."

"Won't you come again?" Oh no, she shouldn't have blurted that out.

He sucked in a ragged breath. "You mean, here? To your room?"

"Only if you want to."

"I want to." He tipped up her chin to flash her a look of blazing desire. "I'll return as often as you wish—every night, if it pleases you."

"Just make sure to come after everyone is asleep and Lettice has left, so we won't be found out."

With eyes glittering, he traced a line along her jaw. "I don't think you realize what you're suggesting."

She turned her face to kiss his palm. "Perhaps not. But I don't care."

He swallowed hard. "By thunder, I must be insane to let you put me through this *uffern dân*."

"I wouldn't want you to suffer the 'fires of hell' for me, but I believe I like your form of insanity."

With a choked cry, he dragged her to him for another long, plundering kiss, and his hands roamed her body, taking new liberties. Then he released her to head for the window, where he climbed up onto the sill. "Are you sure about this?"

She ought to take back her words. But wouldn't it be lovely to see him again, to have more time to talk of poetry and the Sons of Wales and . . . oh, just everything? He'd explain to her what it meant to have impure blood. And he wouldn't laugh at her enthusiasm for Welsh things, either.

"I'm sure."

"Then I'll be here tomorrow." Without warning, he jumped for the branch.

Her heart leapt into her throat, but he caught the branch easily, then shimmied down the trunk.

Once on the ground, he gazed up at her. "Tomorrow," he mouthed.

She nodded, lingering at the window until he was gone. Pray heaven that tomorrow came soon.

4

Much love will you see,
And my heart and its key,
My dear, if you say you will come with me;
But if you draw back
'Tis a perilous lack—
My life is so wounded, there's no return track.

—HUW MORUS, "PRAISE OF A GIRL"

A week later, Rhys passed through the gardens of Northcliffe on silent feet. Every night began the same, with him determined to keep his hands off Juliana as they talked of Huw Morus and Dafydd ap Gwilym, of the Gwyneddigion Society and the war in the colonies. She had an uncommon thirst for knowledge. It was as if the sheer outrageousness of his presence in her bedchamber freed her to ask any question that popped into her head.

If they'd only talked, it would have been fine. But they'd done more. Every night ended the same, with her in his arms as he kissed and caressed her. Two nights ago, he'd finally unbuttoned her nightdress, which had been tormenting him as much by what it concealed as what it revealed. Then he'd slid his hand inside to cup the soft, heavy warmth of her breast.

Just remembering it made him harden. After her initial shock, she'd allowed him to stroke and then pluck at her nipples, teasing them to firm little points. She'd even let him suck them with all the greed that had built in him since the first time he'd seen her. Her skin was smooth and firm, like ripe fruit luscious to taste. He'd wanted to go on tasting her forever.

Then last night . . . damn it all, he'd pressed his advantage too far. They'd been arguing about some Goronwy Owen poem when he'd pulled her onto his lap to kiss her. That had led to hot, sweet caresses, and before long, he'd inched his hand under her nightdress to stroke the triangle of curls between her legs, to finger her flesh, already wet for him, and stroke it until she moaned.

It had been a week of such delights.

And a week of sheer hell.

He swore under his breath as the familiar heaviness in his loins grew almost painful. Tonight he would put an end to this limbo one way or the other. He couldn't go on endlessly craving her body. He wanted to wake up with her at his side after going to sleep in her arms. He wanted to rescue her from her bastard father.

Right now, however, he couldn't even rescue her from himself. That was why he'd arrived early. Knowing that Lettice might show up any minute would keep him from going too far. If Juliana rejected his proposal, he wouldn't stay and torment himself further. And if she accepted, he could wait a few days to enjoy her delights.

He climbed up the tree outside Juliana's bedchamber. From the branch, he watched her through the glass. She was at her dressing table, combing her hair, and he sucked in his breath. The mass shimmered like a cascading flame with each stroke.

He shifted uncomfortably. Perhaps it was only lust that drew him to her. Perhaps he was being a fool to care for her.

Thrusting that disturbing thought from his mind, he pulled out some pebbles. It took only a few to catch her attention.

She hurried to throw open the window. "You're early."

"I'm coming in."

As soon as he'd cleared the window, she said, "Lettice will be here in a little while. We won't have much time."

"I know. That's why I'll come right to the point. I brought you a gift." He drew out an oblong object wrapped in cloth and handed it to her.

When she unwrapped it, her eyes widened. "Why, 'tis a spoon."

"A *llwy garu.*"

A pink flush touched her cheeks. "A love spoon. The gift Welshmen give their sweethearts."

"Aye. I carved this one myself for you. Morgan showed me how. It took me most of the week to complete it."

She ran her finger reverently over the handle's intricate Celtic crosses, ending in two entwined hearts next to the spoon's bowl. "It's lovely. I've seen one before, but this is the first anyone has ever given to me."

"And the last, I hope."

"What do you mean?"

He took a deep breath, then plunged in. "You know I leave for London the day after tomorrow. I want you to go with me."

Cradling the love spoon in her hands, she sat down on the bed. "Are you asking me to be your paramour?"

"*Uffern dân*, I'm doing this badly." He took a seat next to her and seized her hand. "I thought you understood: A love spoon is more of a gift from a suitor to the woman he wishes to marry."

A shuddering breath escaped her. "Marry?"

"Aye." He kissed her hand. "I'm asking you to run away with me, to go to London as my wife."

She was silent a long time. He forced himself to wait for her answer, not to press her while she was still absorbing his words. Yet not until she pried her hand from his did he realize he'd been squeezing it so hard.

Rising from the bed, she went to her dressing table and stared down at the book he'd given her. "Why do you wish to marry me, Rhys?"

That wasn't the answer he'd expected. He stood up, a sudden pain tightening his chest. "What do you mean?"

"Do you hope marrying me will force Papa into acknowledging your claim on Llynwydd?"

Was that how she thought of him, as some bastard out to get his estate back at any cost? "Your Papa and his paltry claim on Llynwydd have nothing to do with this. And if you can think so after this past week, then I see I made a mistake coming here."

Anger choked him as he pivoted toward the window,

but she hastened to block his path. "Please don't go. I merely need to understand. We've shared things that I've never shared with anyone, but you haven't once said . . ." She thrust out her chin. "Men marry for many reasons. I have a right to know yours."

What a fool he was. He thought he'd shown his feelings for her, but women liked words—and he'd never said them. "I could say I want to marry you because I want to make love to you, and that would be true."

She colored prettily, though she didn't turn away.

"And I could say I want to marry you because you and I both love poetry and Wales. That would be true, too." Taking her face in his hands, he stared into her eyes. "But the main reason I want to marry you, Juliana St. Albans, is because I love you. With all my heart."

Astonishment spread over her face to end in the most brilliant smile he'd ever seen. "I love you, too, Rhys Vaughan."

Her words shattered the tight knot inside his chest. "You'll run away to marry me?"

Her face clouded over. "Can't we simply ask Papa for permission to wed?"

He gave a bitter laugh. "Certainly. I'm sure he'd be honored to have his enemy, a penniless dog of a Welshman, for a son-in-law.'"

She sighed. "I suppose you have a point."

"By thunder, I *am* a dog for asking this of you. I have some money, but until now my main hope for the future was in regaining my estate. Now I'm not so sure how wise that is. My fighting your father would put you in an untenable position."

"Perhaps not." She gave a secret smile. "You see, I—"

"Nay." He pressed a finger to her lips. "I don't want to talk about that. I won't have you thinking I'm marrying you to get your aid in regaining Llynwydd. I'm marrying you because I love you and you love me. Once we're married, we'll sort the rest out. Even without the estate, I have prospects. I can teach. Or I can continue to work for Morgan if I have to."

She smiled. "So it *was* him who printed those pamphlets."

He gripped her arms. "Who told you that?"

"Lettice thought perhaps . . . well, she said—"

"She shouldn't be saying anything, damn it all! Morgan would be in great danger if anyone knew."

"I shan't tell a soul, I swear. Besides, if you're to work for him to support us, that would be cutting off my nose to spite my face, wouldn't it?"

Glancing at her aristocratic features, he winced. "I'm a bastard to be denying you the wealth you deserve. Your father no doubt plans to marry you to a duke with vast estates."

"I don't want that." She trailed her finger over his cheek. "I only want you."

With a moan, he kissed her. Soon he'd be able to kiss her whenever he wanted, to linger in her arms. The thought sent his blood racing anew.

It took all his will to break the kiss. "Listen, *cariad*, I've much to tell you, and we have little time. Tomorrow night I'll come as soon as Lettice is gone. We'll go out the window." When she blinked, he added, "Don't worry, I'll bring a ladder. I found one behind the stables." He took a deep breath. "We'll go straight to the bishop's house. I've already bought the license."

"The bishop will wed us?"

Rhys grinned. "He's my godfather, and none too fond of your father. After we're married, we'll take the night coach to London." He paused. "No one here suspects that we've been meeting, do they?"

She shook her head.

"So it'll take them a while to discover where you've gone. Even if they guess that you've eloped, they'll head for Gretna Green, which would send them north. By the time they figure it out, we'll be in London and too well-established for your family to do anything but accept the marriage."

"But I can't go without saying *anything* or they'll worry. Can't I leave a note?"

"Absolutely not." When her face clouded, he softened his tone. "Sorry, my darling, but that's too risky."

She dropped her gaze. "You're right, of course."

He tipped up her chin. "Promise me you'll do as I ask."

"I promise."

Suddenly he heard a tapping at the door. They froze.

"It's me," came Lettice's voice.

Rhys drew back. "I'd better go."

Lettice tried the door. Swearing under his breath, Rhys strode for the window. "I'll be here tomorrow night. If you change your mind, leave the window closed, and I'll know not to bother you."

"I won't change my mind. You can be sure of that."

Lettice rattled the door and called out, "Juliana? Are you in there?"

"Go," Juliana urged. "Before she makes a fuss."

"I love you. Remember that."

She pressed a kiss to his cheek. "I love you, too. Now go!"

Juliana watched as he stood on the sill and jumped for the branch. He caught the branch and climbed down with a leonine grace, then blew her a kiss.

Lettice hissed, "I don't know what you're up to in there, but I'm going to fetch your mother!"

Racing to unlock the door, Juliana opened it just in time to catch Lettice striding down the hall. "Lettice!" she called to the maid.

Lettice returned warily. She entered and swept the room with a searching glance. When she caught sight of the open window, she went to look out of it.

Juliana held her breath. But Rhys had apparently made his escape. Frowning, Lettice shut the window. "You shouldn't let in the unhealthy night air. You'll make yourself sick."

Juliana's gaze landed on the love spoon she'd laid beside the book on her dressing table. As Lettice strode for the wardrobe, Juliana snatched up the book and the love spoon and hid them under the chair cushion.

"I-I was looking at the stars. 'Tis a beautiful night."

"Aye, so beautiful you were woolgathering and didn't hear me knock?"

"I dozed off. And you know how soundly I sleep."

Lettice stared at her hard. Then shaking her head, she

turned to open the wardrobe and, without further comment, helped Juliana undress.

Somehow Juliana managed to keep from blurting out her news. But once Lettice was gone, she sank onto her bed with a dreamy sigh.

She and Rhys were to be married! And the foolish man thought he was damning her to an impoverished future—ha! He'd be delighted to find that in marrying her, he'd regained his estate.

Or would he be suspicious instead? Any mention of Papa infuriated him, and he sometimes seemed uncertain of her. How might he react when he found out that Papa had taken Llynwydd for her? Would he worry that people would claim he'd married her for the estate? Might he even refuse to go through with it, because of how it would look?

Perhaps she shouldn't tell him anything until they were wed and on their way to London. Then it would be too late. Besides, he'd asked her not to speak of Llynwydd, so she'd only be doing as he asked, right?

And once they were joined forever . . .

Juliana threw out her arms and began to dance about the room, remembering how Rhys had touched her most private places and made her burn last night and filled her with wild exhilaration. Tomorrow night he would do that again to her, only this time, he wouldn't feel compelled to stop. She would *finally* know the full enjoyment of having impure blood.

Tomorrow night, Rhys would initiate her into all the pleasures of love. She could hardly wait.

5

Like honey musk is
Your unconcealed kiss,
The kernel of your lips I cannot dismiss.

—HUW MORUS, "PRAISE OF A GIRL"

Juliana and Rhys left the church on his horse long after midnight. Rhys's chest pressed hard against her back, and she shuddered with anticipation. She was glad to be married, but the secrecy bothered her.

So did his silence. Did he doubt the wisdom of the marriage, now that they were bound forever?

The longer they traveled the rutted road, the more she worried. The moon cast an eerie light through the mist, and the wind whispered dire predictions. Then an owl flew across their path hooting, and she jolted up straight with a cry.

"Don't worry, my love, 'tis nothing." Rhys tightened his grip about her waist. "You're not having any regrets, are you?"

Had she been so obvious? "Of course not."

He nuzzled her hair. "I wouldn't blame you if you did. I

asked a great deal of you—to leave your family and abide with me 'in sickness and in health, for richer or poorer.' I might be poor for some time, depriving you of luxuries you're accustomed to."

The dear man was as anxious as she. "I don't care about that. You're all that matters to me."

"You shan't regret marrying me. I swear I'll make you happy."

She settled herself against his hard body. "And I swear the same."

As the horse clopped along, Rhys said nothing else, instead speaking with soft kisses and caresses, his fingers stroking the underside of her breast as he nibbled on her ear. By the time they reached the White Oak Inn on the outskirts of Carmarthen, she'd forgotten every misgiving.

Until Rhys's low curse jarred her. "The coach isn't here. We were to board it immediately, to prevent anyone from finding us. I was told it generally arrives before two a.m. It must be nearly that now." As a groom ran to take his horse, Rhys dismounted, then helped Juliana do so. "Where's the London coach?"

"Ain't arrived yet, sir. They sent a boy on ahead to say they'd be late by an hour or two."

Rhys grimaced. He arranged with the groom to have his horse cared for while they were away, and for the bags to be put on the coach when it arrived. Then he told Juliana, "We can't stand out here waiting, and we can't sit around inside where anyone can see us. An hour may turn into five. We'd best take a room."

Five! If she and Rhys didn't leave soon, her family

would come across the note she'd penned for them when they awakened. Though it said nothing of where they'd gone, still . . .

Rhys took her arm. "Something wrong?"

She didn't dare say she'd disobeyed his instructions. "Everything's fine."

He led her inside and found the innkeeper, a hawkish-looking man whose dark eyes flitted about the room as if searching for malcontents. He looked a bit familiar to Juliana, but she couldn't think why.

Rhys said, "My wife and I need a room for a few hours to await the London coach."

The innkeeper eyed Rhys suspiciously. "Begging y'r pardon, sir, but can ye prove y're married to this woman?"

"Of course." He showed the man the marriage license, careful to keep her last name covered up. "We're headed to London so I can introduce my wife to my family."

"I see, Mr. Vaughan. Well then, I believe I've one room available. If you'll come with me . . ."

They followed him to the stairs, but Rhys paused there. "I've forgotten something in our bags." Flashing her a mysterious smile, he turned to the innkeeper. "Take my wife up. I'll be there shortly."

As she and the innkeeper climbed the stairs, Juliana felt the man watching her, but her discomfort with that was quickly eclipsed when he ushered her into their room and she saw the bed.

The innkeeper walked around, showing her where the chamber pot was and extolling the virtues of the room, but she paid attention to none of it. All she could think of was lying with Rhys in that bed. The mere thought of it warmed her all over. And made her nervous, too.

Just then, Rhys entered, a book tucked under his arm. He paid for the room and asked the innkeeper to notify him when the coach arrived. Within moments, they were alone. She didn't know where to look, what to say to break the awkward silence.

Then he held out the book to her. "This is my wedding gift to you." He flushed. "I suppose it's vain of me, but . . . you see . . . these are poems I wrote myself."

"Truly?" Intrigued, she turned the pages, skimming the Welsh verse copied out in a bold, male handwriting.

"The last few were written for you."

She flipped to the back and read aloud, "'Mine is a dank and cheerless song / Hung with heavy tears as long / As Juliana sits above / And is not mine to love.'"

"Not quite Huw Morus," he said. "But it captures how I felt when I feared you might reject me."

She clasped the book to her chest. "How could I, when you bring me such wonderful gifts?"

"So it's my gifts you married me for, eh? What a greedy little thing you are."

As he snatched her to him, she giggled. "I am greedy, you know. For your presence, for your smiles, for—"

"For this?" He brushed a kiss over her lips.

She sighed. "Oh yes."

"So you like my wedding present," he said huskily as he reached up to bury his hands in her unbound hair, crushing the strands between his fingers.

"Aye. 'Tis wonderful." Remembering the rolled-up parchment in her bag, she said, "And I have a gift for you, too. I will fetch it."

"Later." He buried his face in her neck, then began to kiss a path along her throat to her ear, making her shiver with excitement. "We've all the time in the world for that."

True. Later she'd show him the deed to Llynwydd. Later she'd reveal that she, too, could give presents. But now . . .

He sucked her earlobe, and she moaned. Who'd have thought one's ears could be so sensitive?

Then he drew back to shrug off his coat and toss it on a chair, fumbling for the ties of her stomacher. "Are you very tired? Do you wish to sleep?"

Why was he eyeing her like that? And what did he mean, sleep? Surely he didn't think they could remain here for hours. "We really don't have enough time for that," she said, thinking of the note in her room.

"Not for sleeping," he said in a low rumble. "But for other things."

"Like what?"

Without a word, he removed her stomacher. "Has your mother or Lettice ever explained what a man and his wife do in the bedroom after they're married?"

She blushed. "Like kissing and . . . and touching? Mama said it was only permitted between married people."

"Yes, and we're married now." His intense stare frightened her a little. "Did she tell you what kind of touching takes place?"

"Not exactly." Thinking of when he'd caressed her between the legs, she turned a bright red. "I imagine it would be like . . . what we did before."

"It will. But we shall do much more," he rasped.

Oh no, *now*? What if they missed the coach? What if they were discovered? "We don't have time to do 'much more,'" she said, unable to hide the panic in her voice.

He searched her face. "Is that what's bothering you—our lack of time? Or are you simply scared of what we're going to do?"

She hesitated. He looked as if he might eat her alive, and she was reminded that they hadn't known each other long. "I don't know."

"Tell me this, then. Do you like it when I kiss you?"

"Yes, I do," she couldn't help admitting, afraid to meet his gaze. "I know it shows I'm not well-bred, but I can't help it and—"

"Wait, wait." He lifted her chin. "What do you mean?"

"Mama explained that men have strong feelings that well-bred women lack. She said only women of impure blood like Lettice feel that way, so since I . . . well . . . get excited when you touch and kiss me, I figured I must have impure blood."

He looked stunned.

She swallowed hard. "You don't mind that I have impure blood, do you? Mama says all the Welsh and Scottish and Irish have it, and even a few Englishwomen, although well-bred women like me aren't supposed to."

Something flickered in his eyes. "Your mother was wrong. Plenty of Englishwomen, even well-bred ones, have the feelings you speak of, although they pretend otherwise."

"Why would they pretend?"

"Because people like your mother hold them to such an

impossible standard that they don't dare admit the truth." He pressed a kiss to her forehead. "Believe me, you have the purest blood of any woman around, and your enjoyment of what we shall do in this room together in no way reflects upon that."

Should she believe him? The way he made her feel had to be scandalous. Still, if he didn't mind her having scandalous feelings, why should she? "You said we'd do more than kiss and touch. What did you mean?"

She felt his dark smile to the tips of her toes. He grasped one end of the neckerchief tucked into her bodice and drew the piece of silk toward him so it whispered over her skin like butterfly kisses. Then he skimmed his knuckles over the swells of her partially exposed breasts, making her breath catch in her throat.

His voice sounded almost strangled when he answered, "I think 'tis something better understood in the doing. All I ask is that you trust me."

That had an ominous ring. "Why?"

"Because I intend to give you pleasure." Then he began to undress her, showering her with hot, fervent kisses that made her blood race.

Only when her corset fell away, leaving her in just her shift, did she pull back. Her high-necked nightdress hadn't been nearly so revealing, and she felt almost naked. Still, with the fiery look he gave her, she scarcely noticed the chilly air.

But when he began undressing, too, it gave her a start. After the night he'd caressed her beneath her nightdress while remaining fully clothed, she'd assumed lovemaking was one-sided—he did things to her and she let him.

Apparently not, for he now wore only his breeches. And when she lifted her hand to stroke his bare chest and he growled, "Yes, touch me. God, please touch me," she needed no more invitation to explore the dusting of black curls, the well-defined muscles, the skin taut and smooth over hard sinew, like silk over steel.

Unlike her brothers, who were built like battle-axes, he was lean and sleek as a rapier and nearly as frightening, for she could feel the strength he held in check. The longer she stroked his skin, the more quickly his chest rose and fell, as if he couldn't quite catch his breath.

Oddly enough, neither could she. Especially when he moved her hand to the buttons of his breeches, his eyes darkening to a rich cobalt. She jerked back in shock.

"I don't suppose you're ready for that," he said in a rough rumble. "Never mind. I can do it."

He undid his breeches and removed them, although mercifully he left his drawers on. This time when he took her in his arms, she felt something she hadn't noticed before, a hard bulge between his thighs that pressed into her skin.

"Juliana," he said hoarsely, "I want to touch you all over, as a husband touches his wife. Will you let me?"

All over. It sounded wonderful. And scary, too. "Yes."

He wasted no time in slipping his hand inside her shift to cup her breast. With a happy sigh, she pressed herself into his palm. He'd done this before, and she'd liked it. A lot.

He thumbed her nipples until they tingled, then filled both hands with her breasts. When she clutched his waist, he ravished her mouth, delving deep with his wicked tongue. She scarcely noticed when he dragged her shift down her until it whispered to the floor about her ankles.

"Oh, Rhys," she whispered, twining her arms about his neck.

"There's more, my love. So much more." He gave her a scorching look as his hand slid sensuously down her belly to the secret, aching place between her legs. Unlike that night in her room, he was bold about what he wanted. Not content with merely cupping her and rubbing the cleft, he stroked further, until she felt his finger plunge inside her.

What in heaven's name? She tried to pull away, but he wouldn't let her, capturing her mouth with a possessive kiss. This time his tongue stabbed restless and deep as his finger probed inside her. Soon her faint urge to protest faded. What he was doing was so delicious, she wanted more. His fingers created a strange ache and then soothed it, all at once. Blindly, she grabbed his shoulders, wanting him to . . . to . . .

She didn't know what. When she arched into his hand, rubbing against his palm, he whispered, "You like that, don't you? You're so warm, so wet . . ."

He bent to seize her breast in his mouth and she clamped his head to her in a kind of half-mad joy that made no sense. It was like the quick pierce of fear and anticipation whenever she raced her horse. His mouth drew on her breast, hot and ravening, making her body hum with excitement, especially in that place between her legs where his fingers still plundered her.

Then he drew back to shuck off his drawers before

walking her backward to the bed, his mouth scorching kisses over every inch of skin he could find. He tumbled her down and lay half over her, one knee parting her legs. She wanted his fingers inside her again, but didn't know how to ask for such an embarrassing thing. When his knee brushed between her thighs, she arched upward in an unconscious bid for more.

With a sound half-laugh, half-groan, he caught her face in his hands. "Listen to me, my dear, wanton wife. I'm going to put myself inside you. 'Twill hurt a bit at first, but I'll make it as easy for you as I can."

You've already put your fingers inside me and it didn't hurt, she wanted to say, but he silenced that with kisses, long, hungry ones that intensified the sweet ache in her lower belly.

Then his legs were between hers, spreading her thighs apart, opening her to his questing fingers. Suddenly those were replaced by something else, something long and hard and wholly unfamiliar, sliding up inside her.

She tore her mouth from his. "Rhys, what—"

"Trust me," he choked out. "I promise I'll be gentle."

As that mysterious part of him pushed deeper, stretching her inside, she wiggled beneath him. "Oh, but you're not! It feels . . . too tight. There's something wrong!"

"Nay, 'tis always this way the first time for a woman." He kissed her neck, then slid his tongue along her jaw.

"How do you know? You're a *man*," she snapped.

"Trust me, my love. If you'll relax a little, it will go better."

He worked his hand down between their bodies, then

caressed the hidden nub that seemed to be the source of all her enjoyment. She gasped and arched upward, planting him further inside her.

But that wasn't enough for him, for he inched forward. "Hold on, love, and 'twill be all right in the end." Then he thrust deep, making her cry out as something tore inside her.

"Rhys," she whimpered helplessly. "Please . . ."

His mouth cut off her protest, all warmth and sweetness. Then he moved again, drawing out, then in, then out in a motion that at first gave her discomfort.

"Never forget that I love you," Rhys whispered against her lips. "It gets better, I promise. But you must relax."

She tried to do as he bade, and to her surprise felt the intrusive pressure lessen. And as he slid into her with slow, long strokes, his movements even began to warm her.

"Ah, *cariad*," he murmured, "you feel so good, so tight." He lowered his mouth to feed on hers, making her forget the invasion in her nether regions.

The more he caressed her mouth while driving that hard part of him into her, the less discomfort she seemed to feel. Her breath started to quicken and her heart to pound in anticipation of she knew not what.

Soon conscious thought forsook her. Her body seemed taken over by a wonderful bundle of urges that made her cry out without meaning to, arch up without her mind giving the command, and strain toward a greater closeness with him.

Apparently he felt it, too, for he abandoned any attempt to be gentle. His arms bracketed her body, the muscles straining as he fell into a driving motion that put him deeper inside with every thrust. To her shock, she reveled in the lusty way he plunged into her, keeping her breathless. He was consuming her . . . no, he was annihilating her and in the annihilation was such . . . untold freedom. To give one's body up like this . . .

"Juliana . . . my love . . . *fy annwyl mhriod* . . ." he said, but she was so beyond thought she scarcely heard him calling her his "darling wife."

He drove himself into her until they merged like two streams joining a torrent rushing to the sea. The current swept them both up, pushing them faster and faster toward the edge of a cliff by the dark, wild ocean, their limbs tangled together.

She strained against him, feeling the roar of pleasure in her ears. She didn't know when she began chanting his name, writhing mindlessly beneath him, with him.

"Juliana!" he cried hoarsely. "My God, Juliana!"

"Yes . . . oh yes . . ."

Suddenly he gave a mighty thrust, and it was as if they both hurtled over the waterfall and into the thunder of vast, crashing waves. With a choked cry, he poured his seed into her and she reveled in the feel of it, clutching him to her until she was swamped by an enjoyment she'd never dreamed of.

For a moment, she feared she'd drown in it, die like this in his arms. Her body shook, and only when she realized that Rhys's body did the same did she lose her fear.

Some time passed before the wildness subsided. Rhys buried his head in her neck with a sigh, his whiskers tickling her skin. He stayed silent so long, she almost feared he might be dead. She felt near to death herself—and yet utterly satisfied.

Nothing she'd ever experienced compared to this. If this heaven was allowed only to impure women, then she pitied all those Englishwomen with pure blood.

After a while, his weight began to crush her. "Rhys, I can't . . . breathe."

With a groan, he shifted off her, lying on his side and propping his head up with one hand. He bent to kiss her shoulder. "Sorry, my love. You make a pleasant bed."

Now that he no longer lay atop her, she felt an odd stickiness between her thighs. She looked down to see blood smearing her skin.

She sat up in alarm. "Good Lord, I'm bleeding!" Although she felt only a vague soreness between her legs, he must have wrought terrible damage inside her.

"It's all right." He laughed, pulling her back into his arms. "A virgin usually bleeds the first time a man takes her."

She eyed him uncertainly. "Are you sure?"

"Quite sure, dear wife of mine." He kissed her on the lips. "But the second time is much less messy . . ." Trailing off with a meaningful smile, he slid his hand over her breast.

She could feel his arousal growing against her thigh, but his certainty about the blood worried her. "How do you know so much about what happens when a man . . . when he . . ."

"Makes love to a virgin?" He smiled. "Well, other men

warn a man of these things. 'Tis a pity women aren't as forthcoming about such matters to each other."

"True," she said absently, but her mind now wandered to Rhys's apparent experience with women. He'd undressed her so easily. He'd seemed to know exactly how a woman's clothes were fastened, and how they came undone. "Am I the only woman you've ever done these things with?"

His smile faded. "You're the only virgin."

Jealousy surged through her, startling in its intensity. She tried to sound nonchalant. "So you've made love to another woman."

"No one that mattered, I assure you."

"Who, then?"

He groaned. "None of them are even worth talking about."

"*None* of them? More than one?" She thought of him touching other women's bodies, kissing them and sliding his fingers deep inside them. Mama had told her people only did these things with the ones they married. Was that a lie, too?

He slipped from the bed and went to the washbasin. After wetting a towel, he washed her blood off himself, then returned to the bed and sat down to cleanse her.

"You're not going to tell me, are you?" she asked.

A muscle worked in his jaw. "Do you really want to hear a recitation of the women I've bedded?" When she just stared at him, he said, "All right then, there was Mrs. Abernathy, the young wife of one of my tutors, who invited me to tea when her husband wasn't home, and the dairymaid at Llynwydd—"

"Enough." She realized she *didn't* want to know any of it.

"Listen, my darling wife." He leaned over her. "There were only a few. They were experienced women who wanted to have a tumble with a young, randy buck of tolerable looks. It meant as little to them as to me." He kissed her, his eyes solemn. "And not a one of them was good enough to touch your boots, do you hear? Not a one."

The look in his eyes warmed her, but she was still confused. "Some of these women were . . . married?"

He sighed. "Some of them."

"But Rhys, I thought married women weren't supposed to . . . well, do these things with men who weren't their husbands."

A cynical smile played over his lips. "You thought right. But as you've seen, lovemaking is quite pleasurable. People sometimes do it for its own sake, not because of any deep feelings for the person they join with. If their husbands—or wives—won't oblige them, or don't give them pleasure, they may not choose to abide by society's rules."

She sucked in a breath. "Did I give you pleasure?"

"Oh yes. A great deal of pleasure."

"So then you will abide by society's rules." She didn't think she could bear it if he made love to other women after making love to her.

He looked stricken. "Of course. What I did before . . . 'tis what most young men do in their salad days." He stroked her hair. "But people who love each other don't need anyone else. And I love you very much. It shall take me till the end of our lives and beyond to express how much."

How could she stay peeved with him when he said such

sweet things and looked at her with such adoration? She could forgive him those other women as long as he was hers, now.

When he saw her smile, he let out a long breath. "All right?"

"All right." Then she added, "And I shall abide by society's rules, too. I promise."

He quirked one eyebrow up. "You'd better. Some men beat their wives for such behavior, you know."

"Oh?" Her eyes went round. "You would never beat me for anything, would you?"

Lowering himself to cover her, he murmured in a husky voice, "Never. I plan to cherish you all my life." He nudged her knees apart as he bent his head to suck her breast, starting an ache deep inside her. "Beginning now, *cariad*."

Then he demonstrated exactly how he intended to cherish her.

6

A tryste with Morfudd true I made,
'Twas not the first, in greenwood glade,
In hope to make her flee with me;
But useless all, as you will see.

—ANONYMOUS, "THE MIST"

Darcy and his brother rode like fiends toward the White Oak. Juliana had run away with that damned radical Vaughan. He would never have believed the boy who'd been sent to alert them, if he and Overton hadn't found Juliana's room empty and a note left there for the family that read:

Dear Papa and Mama,
    Don't be alarmed. Rhys Vaughan and I have decided to marry, and since we knew you wouldn't allow it, we've run off together. Please try to be happy for us. Rhys and I are very much in love, and hope you will come to accept this marriage in time.

With great affection,
Juliana

Just thinking of it made his blood boil. "When I get my hands on that scoundrel, I'll kill him!"

"The boy said they were already married, so they must have left the house hours ago," Overton replied. "They may be gone by now."

"Could Vaughan have gotten a special license?"

"The Welsh bishop might have given him one. He's none too fond of Father."

So how was he to deal with Vaughan? Killing the bastard wouldn't be wise. Too many people knew of the battle between the squire and Father, so if Vaughan were found dead, the family would be under suspicion, and that would hurt Darcy's political plans.

But having a deuced radical for a brother-in-law wouldn't help his plans, either. Besides, Darcy hated that Vaughan was using this deceitful way to get his hands on Llynwydd. Juliana would soon discover that Vaughan hadn't married her for love, though he'd somehow seduced her into believing otherwise.

And if she'd been so blind as to run off with the man, she wouldn't listen to reason. So how was he to get her out of this once he wrenched her from Rhys? What if the marriage had been consummated? He had to manage this so Juliana wasn't ruined, by having either her reputation sullied or her heart broken.

When they reached the inn, the owner ran out to greet them. "My lord, I hope I wasn't mistaken about recognizing your sister, but I felt sure—"

"You weren't mistaken." Darcy glanced up at the darkened windows. "How long have they been here?"

"More than an hour, I'm afraid." The innkeeper dropped his gaze to the ground. "And I believe they've been . . . ah . . . using that time to . . . well . . ."

"I understand." Darcy clenched his fists. The bastard. So much for putting a stop to the consummation. "Where are they?"

"Their room is at the top of the stairs, but Vaughan came down a few moments ago to ask about the coach and get food. My servant is making a cold supper for them while Vaughan waits in the kitchen."

Darcy dismounted. That gave him an idea for another way to deal with this problem. He paused to think through everything, to consider every avenue.

Then he turned to the innkeeper. "Here's what I want you to do, my good man. Find some excuse for luring that scoundrel out here without telling my sister. My brother and I will deal with him." He handed the innkeeper an ungodly amount of money and watched the man's eyes widen. "That is yours, as long as you keep silent about whatever you see this night—and that includes not saying a word to my sister. Agreed?"

"Yes, my lord."

As the innkeeper headed back inside, Overton growled, "We should go in and slit the bastard's throat, the more public the better. Let them see what happens to the man who defiles our sister!"

"Aye, and let them hang us afterward. Father's influence couldn't get us out of that, I assure you." Darcy's mouth tightened. "Don't worry, I've got plans for our Mr. Vaughan. When I'm through with him, we'll never have to worry about him again."

～❦✑✑～

Rhys walked down the hallway of the White Oak. The innkeeper had told him the coach had arrived and the coachman wanted to speak to him. Rhys hadn't heard much noise coming from the inn yard, but then, he was having trouble concentrating on anything tonight.

That came from bedding his lovely wife, no doubt.

He smiled. Juliana was his in every way now. No more torturous nights lusting after her while he lay alone in his bed. No more torturous days wanting to speak to her and knowing he couldn't.

Their life ahead might be difficult, but he could do anything with her at his side. His lack of an estate made no difference, and tonight he thought he could even tolerate her family. Ah, the poets were right to say that love would make a man mad. It surely had made him so.

But madness was pleasant indeed when shared with Juliana.

Rhys walked out into the inn yard, then stood there blankly. There was no coach here.

Suddenly something hit his head, and everything went black.

When he came to, Rhys found himself lying on a cold earth floor in what seemed to be a cellar. Voices argued from beyond an open door, but he had a devil of a headache and couldn't take in the words. He sucked in a deep breath and got a mouthful of rank-smelling air, and when he tried to stretch his cramped limbs, he discovered his arms and legs were bound.

"*Uffern-dân!*" How long had he been lying here?

The arguing voices didn't seem to hear him, but a voice beside him said, "Rhys? Devil take them, they got you, too?"

"Morgan? What in thunder is going on?"

"'Tis a press gang. While they were dragging me in just now, I heard them say they're taking us aboard ship to serve in His Majesty's Navy. The damned wretches."

Rhys's blood ran cold. It couldn't be. Only a while ago, he'd been making love to his new wife at the White Oak. But he had no idea how long he'd been lying in this stinking, dank hole. "Where are we?"

"I don't know; they put a sack over my head when they took me. But I suppose it's some tavern near the docks. They got me when I came home after meeting Lettice."

Rhys's heart pounded. "It can't be a press gang. They don't take people like us—craftsmen, squires' sons. They take sailors."

"And radicals."

"Aye, but what good could we be to them? I don't know a sail from a bedsheet, and I'll tell them, I will!"

"Don't waste your breath," Morgan muttered.

But Rhys had already pushed himself into a sitting position. "You there, outside! I want to talk to you!"

Silence. Suddenly, the doorway was filled by a bulky man carrying a lantern. When he held it up Rhys saw his face, and shock went through him. It was Darcy St. Albans—Viscount Blackwood, heir to the Northcliffe title and Juliana's brother.

Had the viscount found out about him and Juliana? But how? And what in thunder had he done with Juliana?

Rhys glared at the viscount. "What's this all about?"

The man fixed him with eyes as cold as the icy sea. "You thought you'd finally pulled it off—gotten Llynwydd in your clutches. Well, thank God you didn't succeed."

What? Was the man referring to Rhys's attempts to have the acquisition of Llynwydd investigated by the authorities? "I have no idea what you mean."

Blackwood's face tightened. "Don't pretend you didn't know that Juliana owns Llynwydd. After my father won it from yours, he made it her dowry—even went so far as to deed it over to her."

"You're lying. She'd have told me."

Confusion crossed Blackwood's face before he masked it. "If she didn't, I'm sure your solicitors did before you approached her."

"I knew nothing of it." Rhys cast the man a glance of withering scorn. "I married your sister because I love her."

Blackwood's expression hardened. "I doubt that. But it hardly matters. You won't have Llynwydd after this night, to be sure."

Rhys tasted fear. If Llynwydd was indeed Juliana's, there was only one way the bastard could take it. "You plan to kill me."

"Nay." Blackwood set the lantern on a shelf. "'Tis what I ought to do, but Juliana begged me not to. My sister has a soft heart—even if she did want you out of her life, once she found out what being married to you would mean. And as usual, she called on me to clean up the mess."

Rhys gritted his teeth. "What in God's name are you talking about?"

"Juliana and her penchant for getting into trouble, then leaving it to her family to extricate her. Only this time, she's gone too far."

Rhys fought to ignore the man's words. Juliana did tend to run away when she found herself in a sticky situation.

"*Sais yw ef Syn*," Morgan murmured.

He is a Saxon, beware.

Morgan was right. "She wouldn't betray me," Rhys growled.

"Then why are you here?" Blackwood drew a snuff box out of his pocket. "By the time you two reached the White Oak, she realized she'd made a big mistake—that marrying you meant giving up any chance at a husband of title and great wealth. Even with Llynwydd back in your hands, you'd have to struggle to put it to rights."

Blackwood inhaled a pinch of snuff. "For some peculiar reason, she'd been blinded by your Welsh charm. Perhaps she'd even enjoyed your advances. But faced with the reality, she saw how foolish she'd been to marry a penniless Welshman who was only interested in her for her property. Juliana acts on impulse at times, but she generally comes to her senses afterward."

Memories swam through his head. Juliana's skittishness after the wedding. How she'd been alone with the innkeeper while Rhys had gone back to get her gift. How she'd even wanted to leave him to fetch her gift for him.

Worst of all, he remembered the night of his proposal, when she'd asked if he was marrying her to get Llynwydd. Had she mentioned then that it was hers? Surely he'd remember that.

Then other images crowded in—their encounters in her room, the sweet way she'd accepted his proposal, her joy in their joining. No, he'd stake his life on her willingness to wed and bed him.

"Juliana wanted our marriage. She'd never back out of it like a coward, and she'd certainly never send you to kidnap me!"

"Believe what you want," the viscount said with a shrug, "but ask yourself how my brother and I knew where to find you." He paused to let that sink in. "She had the innkeeper summon me as soon as you reached the White Oak. She probably thought to have us rescue her before you could—" He clenched his fists. "We were too late for that. But not too late to deal with her mistake."

"Don't listen to him," Morgan said. "You know Lady Juliana would never be so fickle."

"Morgan's right," Rhys said. "And she'll give you no rest when she finds out what you've done!"

The viscount snorted. "Once you're aboard that ship you're as good as dead, for you'll not escape His Majesty's Navy. You're lucky I didn't just kill you, but in deference to her feelings I gave her the choice of impressment, and she agreed to that since it would allow her to be free of you in the least scandal-provoking way possible."

Rhys gaped at the bastard. There was no way in thunder Juliana would have had him impressed. Obviously her brother had thought this whole thing up himself. "Even the British Navy doesn't allow men to be impressed solely at the whim of an English lord."

"Ah, but they do impress radicals to teach them a lesson. And after Juliana told me about what you and your friend there have been up to, printing sedition and passing it out in the streets, that gave me the perfect solution."

Rhys heard Morgan curse, and clamped down on the doubts Blackwood's words were rousing. It would have been easy for the bastard to find out that Rhys had distributed the pamphlets. But there were other printers in Carmarthen and many in Wales. In fact, Blackwood had no reason to believe Rhys hadn't had the pamphlets printed in London. So how could he have found out that Morgan had printed the pamphlets? Unless Juliana had told him.

"I don't know what you're talking about," Rhys said.

The viscount scrutinized his fingernails with a bored look. "Juliana told me about the meeting that you spoke at, and recounted all you said about the Welsh language. And she told me about the pamphlets you two printed up."

Could someone else have betrayed them? If so, who?

"I was happy to oblige her," Blackwood went on. "With you gone, no one need know about your havey-cavey wedding. We can arrange a proper marriage for her. And Llynwydd will be a plum for a more worthy gentleman."

"The bishop who performed our ceremony will have something to say about that!" Rhys spat.

Blackwood's eyes narrowed. "Will he risk tangling with my father? I doubt it. He may be Welsh, but he still answers to the Church of England, and they might frown on a man giving a license to a known radical and a young Englishwoman. I don't think your bishop is quite that brave. If he is, we'll insist on an annulment. 'Tisn't what we'd want, of course, but—"

Rhys let out a roar that made Blackwood jump back a step. "This marriage has been consummated!"

"Ah, but if Juliana claims you were impotent and you're not there to refute her, then everything is done. Over. Complete. She's free to marry another, with a fine property to attract him."

Rhys gritted his teeth, wishing he could wipe the smug smile from the viscount's face, wishing the man's words weren't so convincing. He made himself remember Juliana's face as she'd sworn to love, honor, and obey him for a lifetime. She'd meant her words. He could swear she did.

But someone had summoned her brothers to the inn tonight. It wasn't likely that they'd figured it out on their own, for they hadn't even known he was seeing Juliana, and she'd promised not to leave a note telling them about the elopement. He'd certainly told no one where they were going, not even the bishop. And she *had* been alone with the innkeeper while Rhys had gone back to the horses . . .

He beat back his doubts. Whom would he believe—a black-hearted Englishman like the viscount? Or his sweet Juliana?

His sweet Juliana . . . who'd always run off at the first sign of trouble . . . at the meeting . . . after her father's threat to cane her . . . He'd heard Darcy tell her that day in the forest that he wouldn't hide her anymore. And she'd relied on her mother to get her out of her caning.

Yes, his sweet Juliana did have a penchant for acting impulsively, then doing whatever it took to avoid the consequences. If she'd thought that he'd somehow learned

Llynwydd belonged to her, would she have balked at the marriage?

Worse yet, she had known that Morgan had printed the pamphlets. And she was, after all, a pampered young English noblewoman.

He cursed himself. He knew Juliana. Pampered she might have been, English she certainly was, but she wouldn't run from their marriage. Would she?

He fixed Blackwood with a threatening gaze. "I won't listen to your lies about my *wife*. She will be my wife until the day I return, and I *will* return. You can be sure of that, you son of a bitch!"

"If you do, it'll be your death." The viscount gestured to Rhys's neck. "I'll make sure they hang you and Pennant as deserters!"

"If you won't release me, at least release Morgan," Rhys gritted out. "No matter what you think, he had nothing to do with those pamphlets. I had them printed in London. And if Juliana says otherwise, she's lying."

A dark smile creased Blackwood's face. "Is Lettice lying, too, then?"

"You whoreson Englishman!" Morgan exploded. "If you think to malign my woman as well—"

Blackwood's harsh laugh cast a chill on the already cold room. "You two are such fools. Women are cowards at heart. All I had to do after I brought Vaughan here was confront Lettice with what Juliana had told me. She confirmed it as soon as she realized what hot water she was in." He gave Morgan a hard stare. "Once I knew for certain you'd been involved, of course I had to take you, too. We can't have you radicals stirring up the Welsh—not with an election nigh. Lettice understood that."

"Nay, she would never betray me," Morgan choked out. "She couldn't—"

"Of course she could." Blackwood shoved the snuff box into his pocket with vicious energy. "When it came to choosing between her post and a Welsh radical, she certainly didn't throw herself into poverty."

"I don't believe it," Morgan whispered. But his anguished tone said he might.

The viscount drew himself up. "Well, that's that. I've tarried here long enough. Now that you know why you're being impressed, I hope you'll not trouble the men with questions. They've been well-paid to ignore them."

Rhys felt as if a boxer had been pummeling him, each blow primed to hit his most vulnerable spots.

The viscount turned for the door. "I'll leave you two gentlemen to your thoughts. After all, once you're aboard ship you won't have much time for thinking, will you? And remember what I said. Return to Wales and you're dead men. I'll see to it myself."

With that, he was gone, leaving them in total darkness once more.

"You know he's lying," Rhys said.

"Did Lettice tell Juliana who printed those pamphlets?"

"Yes."

"So she did know." Morgan cursed under his breath. "I told Lettice not to tell her. She swore she'd not say a word to anyone."

An acrid taste filled Rhys's mouth. "You know women. They can't keep secrets."

Morgan's breathing grew heavy. "Yes, but to tell Blackwood? If he didn't find out from either of them, then from whom?"

"A spy in our midst, perhaps? One of our compatriots?"

"Our compatriots didn't know who printed them. You even told them it was a London printer."

"Perhaps someone overheard us discussing it." Rhys stared blankly into the darkness, praying that was the answer.

But even if Blackwood had found out about the pamphlets through spies, that didn't explain how he'd known where to find Rhys tonight.

Rhys could explain how Blackwood knew about the Sons of Wales, and even why Juliana hadn't told him about Llynwydd. Perhaps she hadn't known it belonged to her. Perhaps Blackwood was simply lying about that.

But Rhys couldn't explain how Blackwood had known where to find him. That was the one piece of damning evidence that ate at him. And he couldn't forget how nervous she'd been when they reached the inn.

"At the moment, it hardly matters whether the women betrayed us," Morgan said. "I don't think we're likely to get out of this. I have no weapon." His tone hardened. "I was out courting."

Rhys thought of all he'd heard about the navy, which was forced to resort to impressment because conditions were so bad on a British man-of-war that men died and deserted at alarming rates. Rhys had heard of the wretched food that bred disease, of the floggings ordered by tyrannical captains. Some prisoners, when given the choice of the navy or death, chose death. Juliana couldn't have wished such a nightmare on him.

"What do we do now?" Morgan asked.

Rhys clenched his fists, the stone floor scraping his knuckles. "We survive. And one day we return. Because no matter what that son of a bitch Blackwood says, we *will* avenge this."

7

I gaze across the distant hills,
Thy coming to espy;
Beloved, haste, the day grows late,
The sun sinks down the sky.

        —WILLIAM WILLIAMS PANTYCELYN,
        "I GAZE ACROSS THE DISTANT HILLS"

*N*ervous and tense, Overton rode beside his brother back to the inn. When they'd found Juliana sleeping upstairs hours ago, they'd decided to leave her there while they dealt with her husband. But now the sun had risen well above the horizon, because Darcy had insisted on waiting at the tavern until the ship pulled out of port.

It worried Overton. The whole scheme did. "I hope you know what you're doing. The press gang didn't like taking a squire, even after you gave them all that money and said Vaughan was a radical."

"I don't care. The blackguard carried off our sister for his own devious purposes. Don't you understand? They consummated the marriage! That deuced bastard would have been our brother-in-law if we hadn't acted. And once

Juliana realized he desired her only for her property, she'd have been miserable. Is that what you wanted?"

No. But this whole business didn't seem right, especially with Vaughan being an Oxford man and a gentleman. "Perhaps he truly cares for her."

Darcy snorted. "The daughter of the man who stole his estate? I doubt it." They rode into the inn yard. "Besides, Juliana deserves better. Trust me, if we'd let it go on, a week from now she'd have been regretting the marriage and asking us for help."

Overton remained silent as they dismounted. This just all made him bloody uneasy.

As they approached the inn, Overton caught Darcy's arm. "I heard those cruel lies you told Vaughan. The poor chap will suffer in the navy anyway, so why kick him when he's down?"

"Because if he believes Juliana loves him, he'll return to take advantage of her. Vaughan must be forced to realize he'll gain nothing by coming back."

Overton shivered. "What if he still attempts it?"

"After the navy gets through with him, he won't want to come near Wales." He patted Overton's shoulder. "Don't worry, brother. He'll struggle through the navy, slink off into some corner of the world with his tail between his legs, and thank his good fortune that he needn't deal with us ever again."

Overton chafed at his brother's condescending tone. Rhys Vaughan hadn't seemed that sort of man to him. "Well then, what if Morgan Pennant comes back? He looked rough."

"A printer?" Darcy chuckled. "You certainly are spooked by shadows."

"I just don't understand why you said all that rot to him about his sweetheart and got him riled up. You told me you only wanted to rid the town of radicals." He crossed his arms. "Now I wonder if you did this to get him out of the way, so you could have Lettice."

Darcy glared at him. "I hope you don't voice that theory to anyone but me, dear brother. Remember, when Father dies, I'll hold the purse strings. And I never forget a slight. Do you understand me?"

Overton blanched. Darcy had never threatened him, but then, he'd never needed to. Overton had always deferred to his brother's superior intellect. In return, Darcy had always made certain Overton received sufficient funds for hunting and gaming.

"Well?" Darcy prodded. "Say you'll support me, no matter what."

If Darcy wanted this so badly that he'd make threats to get it, Overton dared not cross him. "I'll support you."

"Come on, then."

Moments later, they found the innkeeper and determined that Juliana hadn't left her room. "I think she might have fallen asleep. 'Tis awful quiet up there."

"Good." Darcy gave the man more money and reminded him once again of the story he was to tell anyone who asked. "And be sure all those in your employ say the same."

The three of them climbed the stairs. Darcy paused outside the door. "Remember, this is our first visit to the inn. We know nothing about Vaughan's disappearance."

When Overton nodded, Darcy gestured to the inn-keeper to unlock the door. Then he threw the door open.

Juliana was asleep. But as soon as Darcy boomed out "Where is he?" she jolted awake.

Overton averted his face as she immediately sat up, exposing her nakedness. And though she scrambled to cover herself with the sheet, rage surged through him to see her obviously deflowered.

"Where is he?" Darcy, too, wore a tortured look as he strode inside and scanned the room. "Where's that scoundrel Vaughan?"

Darcy was so convincing that Overton had to remind himself it was merely an act. Clutching the sheet to her chest, Juliana watched Darcy prowl the room with an expression of growing horror.

Darcy fixed her with a fierce gaze. "Where's Rhys Vaughan, Juliana?"

She looked pitifully bewildered. "I-I don't know. I fell asleep and then . . . What are you doing here? How did you know where to find us . . . I mean, me?"

"Mother found your note this morning, and we've been searching inns ever since. When we got here, the innkeeper said there was indeed a young couple staying here." Darcy cast her sheet-wrapped body a look of contempt, and poor Juliana cringed. "I see we came too late to rescue you from that fortune hunter, but not too late to make him face the consequences. So tell us where he is!"

"What time is it?" Juliana asked.

"Milord," said the innkeeper, in keeping with Darcy's instructions, "the maid told me Mr. Vaughan came downstairs a few hours ago and went out. She didn't stay around to see him come in, and I assumed he was up here—"

"Where did he go, Juliana?" Darcy demanded. "Tell us!"

Tears welled in her eyes. "I don't know!"

Guilt stabbed Overton.

Darcy snatched up her clothes and threw them at her. "Then you're coming home with us."

"No. I want to wait here for my husband."

"So you really did marry that fool Welshman."

Juliana tilted her head back regally. "Yes. And there's naught you can do about it."

Darcy's tone was deceptively casual. "Prove you're married. Show me your marriage certificate."

Overton held his breath. If they could get their hands on the certificate they could make the marriage disappear entirely, provided the bishop cooperated.

Juliana, however, dashed those hopes. "I can't. I'm not sure where it is. Rhys might have it with him."

Overton and Darcy exchanged glances. Neither of them had thought to search for papers on Vaughan's person. And the ship had already sailed. If Vaughan ever returned with that certificate . . .

"The marriage certificate is gone," Darcy said coldly. "And so is your husband. It appears, madam, that Vaughan has abandoned you."

"No! He wouldn't have. Why marry me, then leave?"

"So he could bed you and take your lands. But he's nowhere in sight, so you might as well come home with us."

She turned an imploring gaze on Overton. "I must wait for him."

Overton bit his tongue to keep from telling her everything. But even if he wanted to go against Darcy, doing so now would be futile. Telling poor Juliana that her husband had just begun a lengthy stint in the navy wouldn't exactly comfort her.

"Listen, love," he heard himself saying. "There's no point in waiting here by yourself. Mother is sick with worry. Come back to the house, and I'm sure this good innkeeper will send your—" he nearly choked over the word "—husband on to Northcliffe if . . . *when* he returns. I'll bring you back here later, if you want."

When Juliana cast him a grateful smile, he swallowed his guilt. In truth, she was lovely, and it would be a bloody shame to waste her on a chap like Vaughan, who might indeed have married her for her property.

He and Darcy were doing what was best for her. She deserved a better husband. And with that thought, he silenced his conscience.

It had been hours since Juliana had left the inn, where there'd been no sign of Rhys. Their bags—and the deed to Llynwydd—had still been there, intact. Something awful had happened to him; she just knew it. But what?

And now Papa wanted to see her. Worried sick, she descended to the ground floor. As she reached her father's study, Lettice emerged from the shadows, her normally vibrant eyes dull and red.

"What is it?" Juliana asked.

"Have they not told you? Everyone's been out looking for your husband and heard that the press gangs were about in the wee hours this morning. Someone reported seeing them take two men aboard a rowboat." Lettice's voice wavered. "My Morgan . . . and your Rhys."

Juliana's stomach roiled. "No. No. Not Rhys, not my husband—"

"It's true, my lady." She swiped away fresh tears. "I asked around myself. No one's sure which ship they were meant for. Several set sail from Carmarthen Bay this morning, and the boat likely headed for one of them. The other Sons of Wales think the burgesses learned who was responsible for those pamphlets and told the press gangs to take them."

"It has to be a mistake! Who would have known where to find Rhys?"

"Anyone might have sent word to the press gangs."

She thought of Rhys aboard an English man-of-war and shuddered. He wasn't a seaman. How would he survive?

Suddenly the door to her father's study opened and her mother stepped into the hall. She flashed Lettice a reproachful look before turning to Juliana. "Come in, they're waiting for you."

As soon as Juliana entered, her heart sank to see Papa and Darcy scowling at her. Even Overton looked worried.

But nothing touched her. Not Papa's shouting, not Darcy's frowns, not Overton's obvious discomfort. Juliana could only think of what Lettice had told her. Rhys and Morgan taken by the press gangs. The thought swamped her in an acid tide of terror. If only she'd gone downstairs with Rhys. If only—

Suddenly she realized Papa was asking her a question. "Are you listening to me, girl?" Rage made his eyes bulge.

"Yes, Papa." How calm her voice sounded. And how odd that her fear of him had vanished. It was as if the marriage ceremony had transformed her. She was no longer Lady Juliana St. Albans, but Rhys's wife, Lady Juliana Vaughan. She had a husband now; she didn't need her family's approval.

Her father's ramrod posture didn't alter. "We'll have the marriage annulled. You'll tell the bishop that it wasn't consummated, and—"

"But it was consummated."

Her father looked at her as if a doll had suddenly opened its porcelain mouth to speak to him. But she was his doll no more. She was married, and wouldn't stand for him treating her like a little girl.

They were trying to make this marriage go away, and she wouldn't let them.

"That doesn't matter," Darcy bit out. "You'll tell the bishop whatever Papa says."

"I certainly won't. I won't let you erase my marriage."

"I'll lock you in your room forever, girl!" her father roared. "I'll keep you from eating and—"

"You can't bully me anymore. None of you can. Only my husband can tell me what to do. If you bring me to the bishop, I'll tell him the truth—so don't even think it."

"Come now, Juliana," Overton cajoled, "this is the best way. We've heard that the man's been impressed."

A tight fist closed on her heart. "So it's true?"

"A piece of good fortune for us," Darcy said. "Now you

don't have to live out a miserable existence legally bound to a man who didn't want you."

Though Darcy's words lacerated her, she thrust out her chin. "He did want me. He still does."

"Even if that's true, he'll be at sea for years," Papa said.

"Perhaps he can escape."

"He'd be a fool to try. The punishment for desertion is hanging. Or if you're lucky, whipping through the fleet."

"Aye," Darcy said. "The master-at-arms takes the unlucky deserter in a boat from ship to ship, and at each stop the deserter receives lashes from that ship's boatswain. I heard tell of a man who was dead by the time they reached the last ship. They flogged him anyway. When they buried him, the flesh was completely flayed from his back."

Bile rose in her throat. "My poor Rhys!"

"And even if he doesn't escape, he'll be lucky to survive," Darcy went on relentlessly. "They treat sailors abominably on those warships—flogging them for any infraction, feeding them maggoty biscuits—"

"That's enough, Darcy!" Overton bit out.

But Juliana was already numb. How would her dear, sweet husband bear it all?

"In any case," Darcy said, "he'll not be back for a long time. So this whole thing can be fixed if you'll just—"

"Nay!" Juliana choked out. "I love him. He'll return someday, and when he does I'll be waiting. I know he'll find me as soon as he can."

"No doubt," Darcy snapped. "So he can get his greedy hands on Llynwydd. 'Tis why he married you, isn't it?"

"He didn't know Llynwydd belonged to me. He married me for love."

"None of this matters!" Papa roared. "There's been a scandal, and we must keep it quiet. You'll get this marriage annulled, girl, or I'll force you into it."

"Now, Horace," her mother said, "stop shouting at the girl. It does no good to be like that."

Juliana's courage wavered. Could Papa force an annulment? He couldn't make her agree to one, but if he pressured the bishop, could he bring it to pass without her? She couldn't let that happen.

She considered her choices. There was only one—a colossal lie. "If you try to annul my marriage, I'll make sure every man, woman, and child in this town sees my marriage certificate and knows the truth of what happened."

Darcy scowled. "You said you didn't know where the certificate is. You said you thought Vaughan had taken it."

She forced herself to sound calm. "I lied. And I have it now in a safe place where none of you will find it. So either you let me have my way in this, or I shame the family by revealing what I've done."

Papa paled and, for a moment, actually looked vulnerable. "You wouldn't do that to me, would you, love?"

Something twisted inside her heart. He never called her "love" unless he wanted something from her. "I don't want a scandal any more than you do, Papa. I wouldn't want to bring shame on the family, or on Rhys. But I am his wife."

Darcy came from behind the desk, his expression calculating. "What if Vaughan doesn't return? What if we never hear from him again? What if, God forbid, he dies at sea? You'd likely never know it. You'd live your whole life in some half state between widow and wife, never having a family or a husband."

She fought to ignore that harsh truth.

Darcy shot their father a glance. "I have a proposal that might settle this to everyone's satisfaction. If Juliana doesn't wish an annulment, she doesn't have to get one. We can ask the bishop to keep silent about the marriage, under the circumstances. I'm sure he'll agree. As for anyone else who knows about it—like the innkeeper—I've already ensured that they'll keep quiet."

She eyed her brother warily.

"Why don't you also keep quiet for now, Juliana?" he went on. "Take time to consider what you wish to do. There's no hurry. You may decide you're unwilling to sacrifice your future for the memory of one Welshman."

She surveyed the expectant faces of her family. In truth, she wasn't up to facing people right now, to telling them about her marriage when she had only sorrow in her heart.

Still . . . "What if I find myself with child?"

"Oh, mercy," her mother squeaked, and her father looked ill.

Although Darcy's expression grew more stony, he held her gaze. "Then we'll announce the marriage, of course. Still, it's unlikely. You only spent one night together, didn't you?"

Turning crimson, she nodded.

"So what do you think?" Darcy prodded. "Why don't we give it a little time and keep it quiet until you make up your mind?"

As Juliana stared at him, a great weariness stole over her. It had been a long day and night. Darcy's words held too much logic for her to ignore. Yet wouldn't she be betraying Rhys if she did as Darcy asked?

She sighed. Yes. But she had few other choices. And Darcy's proposal did have merit. It would give her time to explore possibilities, to determine if she could buy out Rhys's service or something. As soon as Rhys wrote to say which ship he was on, she could take care of it.

But if she stayed here with the family, they'd try to change her mind and get an annulment. She thought of all the plans she'd made with Rhys. Then her brow cleared. "All right, I'll consider it." The group breathed a collective sigh until she added, "But only under one condition."

"Condition?" her father growled.

"That I live at Llynwydd in the meantime."

"Llynwydd?" her mother protested. "Alone?"

"Yes." Juliana cast them a defiant glance. "It belongs to me, after all."

"I should never have given it to you," her father grumbled. "Perhaps if I hadn't, none of this would have happened."

"But you did, and I won't give it back. It belongs to me and Rhys. And until he returns, I want to live there and make certain it's cared for properly."

"Of all the stupid ideas—" her father began.

"If you don't allow it, Papa, I'll trumpet my marriage to the rooftops. I'll tell everyone I know, and devil take the scandal."

She stared at her father with a resolute expression. He

scowled, but the fight seemed to have gone out of him. For the first time in her life, she realized he was looking terribly old. And worn down.

She softened her voice. "Please, Papa?"

Anger flickered in his eyes, but he quelled it. "Very well, girl, as you wish." He stiffened. "But I tell you this: If I ever get my hands on that scoundrel Welshman, I'll wring his bloody neck, I will."

She was too relieved by his acquiescence to protest.

Her heart wrenched in her chest. She had a home of her own now, even if she had no husband to share it with. Rhys was gone, and it might be years before he returned.

Nonetheless, having Llynwydd to care for was something. All she could do was hope that fortune would smile on her, and bring Rhys back to her soon.

PART II

Carmarthen, Wales
June 1783

Hard blow, why care where's my home,
You broke faith, and it grieves me.
—LLYWELYN GOCH AP MEURIG HEN,
"LAMENT FOR LLEUCU LLWYD"

8

O, when you eye all Christendom's
Loveliest cheek—this girl will bring
Annihilation upon me . . .
—DAFYDD AP GWILYM, "THE SEAGULL"

The harsh smell of vinegar roused Juliana, but it took the sound of arguing voices to drag her fully from her faint. She caught snatches of words—"liar," "crazy Welshman," and "my wife."

She forced her eyes open to find her mother holding a ghastly bottle to her nose. Brushing it away, she attempted to sit up, but Overton said, "Don't rush it, love."

He looked so pitying that she turned to him and not her mother, who was near hysterics. "Is Rhys truly here?"

With a nod, Overton moved to let her see across the room. Stephen stood silent and angry at the window, the very picture of the haughty lord, and beside him stood Darcy, his face red. The object of both men's fury was the man she still could hardly recognize. Rhys Vaughan.

Ignoring Overton, she sat up. They were no longer in the

ballroom, surrounded by guests. Her family had whisked her into the drawing room, for which she was grateful, although they'd done it only to minimize the scandal.

But none of that concerned her as much as Rhys's miraculous appearance.

The three men on the other end of the room hadn't yet realized that she'd awakened. They were busy bandying forth phrases about "rights" and "betrayal" and "honor," which gave her a chance to study the husband she hadn't seen in six years.

Such a long time. Had Rhys really been so tall? Or so handsome? To be sure, his finely tailored clothing made him look more imposing and sophisticated than before, but there was something else, too. Years ago he'd emanated an enticing blend of flame and raw energy, but she could tell by how he parried her brother's verbal thrusts that the flame and energy had been banked into a furnace that burned even hotter. His obvious control frightened her as his unstudied fervor never had.

And he seemed determined to pick up their lives as if nothing had happened. Her temper flared. Six years without a single letter; no message of any kind to tell her he'd survived the navy. The investigator Darcy had helped her hire had turned up nothing until a year ago, when he'd found a mention of Rhys's death in a ship's log.

Yet Rhys had obviously not died. In fact, while she'd struggled to bring Llynwydd into its glory, waiting for him, fearing for him, and finally mourning him, he'd been off somewhere prospering, judging from his fine clothing. And he was obviously here to stay.

I've come to reclaim my lands . . . my inheritance . . . and you. I've come to take you home.

He meant to continue as if the years of silence were nothing. He wanted to take ownership of the estate she'd nurtured, to benefit from the work she'd performed, when he'd apparently not cared enough even to let her know he was alive.

If he thought she'd simply acquiesce to his plans, he could rot in hell. Six years was a long time to be silent, blast him.

Six years is an eternity, Rhys thought as his attention was caught by a movement on the other end of the room. He turned to see Juliana rise from the settee, her face set stubbornly.

"I'd like to participate in this discussion," she said in a surprisingly steely voice.

Lord Devon and her brother, the new Earl of Northcliffe, pivoted toward her, breaking off their argument. With everyone's attention on her, she marched forward.

Despite his attempt to quell it, the vise about Rhys's chest that had been tightening ever since he'd first seen Juliana this evening became painful. Dressed in a golden satin gown that showed her assets to their best advantage, she'd come down the stairs to that English lord with her face alight, and he'd wanted to roar his protest. That had been a surprise.

He'd expected to feel elation as he'd stood before them and made his announcement, watching Juliana's face spread o'er with alarm. But he hadn't expected the hard clutch of memory about his chest.

No matter what he told himself about her character, he couldn't forget that she was his wife, that those soft, red lips had once parted beneath his kisses.

At twenty-one she'd been pretty, her green eyes bright with the promise of youth and her full figure a lusty young man's dream. But now . . .

Now she was beautiful. She was damned exquisite, with a lush form and a lovely face. In the years he'd spent wishing he could make her feel a tenth of his tortures, he'd forgotten about the pleasures of her, the way her hair flashed copper in the candlelight, the quick turn of her hand when she spoke.

Tonight he'd had ample time to watch and remember.

Cursing himself for falling once more under her spell, he rubbed the scars on his wrist to remind him of his purpose. "I see my wife has finally chosen to join us."

"You keep referring to her as your 'wife,'" Northcliffe cut in. "You have no proof of any wedding."

Under other circumstances, Rhys would have been amused by Northcliffe's petty attempt to put a good face on things in front of Lord Devon. But he was not amused now. "I suppose a marriage certificate won't suffice?"

Everyone gave a collective gasp. Except Juliana.

Northcliffe turned on her. "A marriage certificate? Does he have a marriage certificate?"

She nodded stiffly.

Rhys drew it from his pocket and waved it at her. "This should serve to jog your memory about our marriage—the one you conveniently forgot."

"If I'd wanted to forget our marriage," she said, her voice full of dignity, "I'd have had it annulled."

"Not having the marriage certificate might have made that difficult." Rhys slid the certificate back in his pocket. "And I'm sure my godfather, the bishop, wouldn't have agreed to such a scheme. So you just waited until he and his wife died. Then there were no more witnesses and no need for an annulment. No need for a public scandal."

"But there will be an annulment now," Northcliffe put in.

"Now that you're acknowledging the marriage?" Rhys quipped, with a knowing glance in Lord Devon's direction. The man had gone pale.

"Yes," Northcliffe bit out.

"No. There will be no annulment," Rhys said savagely.

"Why not?" Juliana asked.

Rhys leveled a withering glance on her. To her credit, although she colored, she didn't flinch from his gaze.

"Have you forgotten," he said in a silky voice, "that our marriage was consummated? Or will you pretend it wasn't?"

"Consummated?" Lord Devon broke in bitterly. "Is that true, Juliana?"

Rhys watched with pleasure as her mouth trembled and her confidence faltered. His puny taunts scarcely repaid her for the loss of his illusions, but they did give him a certain hollow satisfaction.

"You don't have to answer," Northcliffe warned.

"But if you don't," Rhys told her, "I'll be forced to give

your betrothed a detailed account of our joyous wedding night . . . how you cried out my name as I—"

"That's enough, Rhys." Juliana's face was deathly pale, emphasizing the fragility of her slender throat. Her lovely, silken throat. He cursed inwardly. Why did he notice such things now, knowing what she was?

She turned to her betrothed. "I'm so sorry, Stephen. I never thought this would happen. I thought—"

"Is he telling the truth?" Lord Devon demanded.

"Yes, he is."

"Oh dear, now you've gone and done it!" exclaimed her mother as she collapsed onto the settee.

Lord Devon looked shattered, the very picture of a cuckolded husband.

Poor sot, Rhys thought. A cuckold and not even married yet. Still, a few weeks more and the marquess would have been full owner of Llynwydd. Rhys's tone hardened as he faced his wife. "Now that we all agree, there will be no more talk of an annulment."

"If you'll both claim that the consummation didn't take place, we can still have the marriage annulled." Northcliffe shot an imploring glance at Lord Devon. "Then Juliana could marry his lordship, as planned."

Lord Devon stiffened. "But I could not marry her." He turned to Juliana with pity in his eyes. "I'm sorry, my dear, but I have family obligations to consider. And my reputation. You understand, don't you?"

Juliana nodded, but Rhys could tell she didn't understand at all. A welter of emotions assailed him: anger at Lord Devon for his callousness, anger at her for caring about the damned marquess, and anger at himself for noticing her reactions at all. This was what he'd wanted—to separate her from her wealthy nobleman, to make her face the consequences of her unthinking actions years ago. He should be delighted that she was hurt!

But when Lord Devon took her hand and she stared up at him with regret, Rhys felt his insides twist.

"If you'd only told me the truth in the first place," Lord Devon said, "if you hadn't lied to me—"

"Lying to you was a necessary part of getting you to marry her, you fool." Rhys couldn't keep silent in the face of their obvious feelings for each other.

"Stay out of this, Rhys," Juliana said. "'Tis none of your concern."

"I hadn't realized the betrothed takes precedence over the husband," Rhys snapped.

She flinched, but otherwise ignored him to take Lord Devon's hands in hers. "I'm sorry I didn't tell you, Stephen. I believed him dead, or I'd never have allowed you to propose."

Rhys gritted his teeth. What rot! She'd wanted Rhys out of her life precisely so she could gain a better husband. The little liar.

"And I do understand why you feel you must withdraw your offer." She gazed up into the marquess's face with the look that had once entranced Rhys.

It entranced the marquess still, for he said fervently, "Let me know if there's an annulment, and I'll speak to my solicitor. Perhaps . . ." He trailed off with a sigh. "I hope you'll understand if I go now. I can't bear—" He shot Rhys a hard look. "You must work things out with your husband."

Releasing her hands, he left the room.

Juliana's mother, who'd been watching in horrified disbelief, shrieked, "The scandal! The dishonor! Oh, mercy on my life, what shall become of us?"

"Call Elizabeth in here," Northcliffe urged his brother.

St. Albans went to summon Northcliffe's wife, who was attempting to get rid of the guests in as subtle a manner as possible. She hurried in to cast her husband a quizzical look.

"Have the guests all gone?" Northcliffe asked her.

"Only the local ones. I couldn't very well throw out our houseguests. You'll have to take care of that."

Northcliffe shot Rhys an angry glance. "I will. Later. For now, take Mother upstairs and stay with her. She can't handle discussions of this nature."

With a nod, Lady Northcliffe helped the dowager countess from the room.

Then Northcliffe whirled on Rhys. "You must agree to an annulment. You can't do this to Juliana."

Rhys raised an eyebrow. "After what she's done to me, I'm letting her off easy."

Juliana whirled to face him. "And what have I done to you that's so dreadful that you purposely reappear on the eve of my engagement to torment me? To snatch my betrothed from me?"

The surprise in her voice came as a shock. "How dare you act as if you don't know? How dare you pretend you didn't collude with your brothers to have me impressed?"

She stared at him, aghast.

That only stoked his anger. "I wouldn't have blamed you for having second thoughts about our marriage. 'Twas an ill-fated union from the beginning." His throat tightened. "But then to behave like a coward, instead of telling me . . . to summon your brothers behind my back and bid them to rid you of me—I can't forgive that. You may have thought you were doing me a favor by saving me from death and letting me be impressed instead, but I nearly died from it anyway."

Her face had grown bloodless, but he went on relentlessly. "Unfortunately for you, I didn't. My ship was captured by the Americans after I'd served three miserable years, and they gave me the choice of imprisonment or fighting for freedom with them. I chose to fight. And they rewarded me well. Very well."

"Which means you were either a privateer or a spy," Northcliffe interjected, "for 'tis the only way a man gains wealth during a war."

Rhys's dark chuckle seemed to disconcert his enemy. "If you think to use any of that against me, think again. Being taken captive by the Americans doesn't constitute desertion, so you can't have me hanged. What's more, the war with the colonies is over, and I took part in negotiating the peace. As a consequence, I've made some powerful friends—like the Dukes of Grafton and Rockingham. They've assured me that my debt to the nation has been paid."

He reveled in Northcliffe's shock. The current leaders in Parliament, Grafton and Rockingham, firmly supported the colonists. Of course, they wouldn't have countenanced Rhys's privateering, but Northcliffe needn't know that. And in truth, they'd listened to Benjamin Franklin when he'd presented Rhys as a model representative of both British and American concerns.

He smiled. The irony of that statement still amused him.

"I don't understand," Juliana broke in. "Why on earth would you think I'd summoned my brothers to the inn? Or had you impressed?" Her eyes widened. "Did your years in the navy make you mad?"

How dared she act innocent? "No, the madness was in trusting you. God, I was so enamored of you that it took several floggings for me to accept what you'd done."

He caught her arm, and she flinched from his touch. Good. Let her fear him. She seemed to understand that better than love. "But after I sent letter after letter and all remained unanswered, I had to accept it was true."

"*What* letters?" she demanded.

He ignored her. "I considered never coming back—making a life in America and abandoning any dream of Wales. But once the Duke of Grafton made it possible for me to return without repercussions, I realized I had to, if only to make you face the marriage you ran from by having me impressed."

"I did not have you impressed. You've lost your mind!"

"Then why are you preparing to marry another, as if our wedding never existed? And not just any man, but a wealthy English marquess—exactly the kind of man your brother said you would find." His voice turned menacing.

"So don't pretend you had no part in it. The innkeeper at the White Oak confirms what your brother told me six years ago—that you had him send me aboard that ship because you wanted to end our marriage!"

His voice had risen to a shout, but he didn't care. He'd waited an eternity to confront her with her act, to watch her tremble as she realized he'd returned to exact vengeance.

And she did tremble, but not with fear. With anger. "My brother!" Wrenching her arm free, she turned to her brothers. "Which of you told him these lies? *Which?*"

"Darcy," St. Albans responded, stepping away as if to give his sister fighting room.

And she looked as if she were spoiling for a fight as she turned on the earl. "Why would you lie to him like that, Darcy?" Her voice seemed to catch, and a look of betrayal spread over her face. "Why?"

Northcliffe shot a quelling glance at his brother. "Now, Juliana, you know you wanted him gone. And when I brought him to the ship, I told him the truth: that you had cold feet about the marriage. I'd have killed him if you hadn't suggested the impressment, so you have nothing to be ashamed of."

"You had him impressed?" she hissed. "And then you acted as if . . . Oh God, how could you have *done* that to me? To both of us?"

"Come, love," he said in a gentle voice. "This pretense is foolish. I know you didn't want me to tell him the truth back then, but I was so angry about his marrying you for your dowry that I said more than I should have."

"You told him that I'd sent my own husband off to a terrible fate. How could you speak such lies!"

"There's no point in pretending to innocence now, Juliana," Northcliffe said soothingly. "He knows everything, so we'd best deal with the bastard and see if we can negotiate some arrangement mutually acceptable to us all."

She looked stunned into silence. Then her eyes narrowed. "What about the letters he speaks of? They came *here* for me, didn't they? And you never sent them. And that man who told me Rhys was dead . . . It was all your doing, wasn't it?"

Northcliffe shrugged. "If that's the way you want it." He turned to Rhys and said blandly, "I lied. It was all my doing."

She trembled, and Rhys tensed against the sympathy that spiraled in his gut. She was merely angry that her brother had told her secrets.

With a wild look in her eyes, she marched over to grasp her brother's coat. "Tell Rhys the truth." She shook him. "How can you lie about me like this?"

Northcliffe pushed her away, no doubt disgusted at his sister's pretense of innocence.

It ate at Rhys, too, no matter how much he told himself it was an act. "Stop accusing him, Juliana. Yes, Northcliffe handed me over to the press gang, but you were the only one who could have summoned him to the inn that night. No one else knew we were there. And you and Lettice were the only ones who knew that Morgan and I printed those seditious pamphlets, which gave Northcliffe the excuse to have me impressed. Are you going to explain that away, too, in this foolish attempt to save yourself from me?"

She rounded on him, her eyes confused. "I don't know how they found us. Perhaps from the note—"

"What note?" he said, pouncing on her slip.

Guilt suffused her face. "I left a note that said we'd eloped. But that's all it said, I swear. I didn't tell them where we'd gone."

"As I recall, we'd agreed not to leave any note."

"I know, but I couldn't let them worry."

"So you're saying that your 'note' is how they knew to come to the inn only an hour after we got there?"

"An hour? What are you talking about? They came the next morning and told me—" Suddenly she whirled on her brothers. "You must have come while I was asleep. Is that when you caught him, and told him these terrible lies?"

"Stop it!" Rhys hissed. "Do you think I'll believe this invented tale? You might as well give up all hope of that, for the innkeeper says you sent him to get your brothers while you were alone with him, before you and I even made love."

"Then he lies!" Desperation was in her voice now.

"The innkeeper lies. Your own brother lies. Even your betrothed has abandoned you, now that he's seen your true character. So why is everyone lying about you, if you're so innocent?"

"I don't know." Her voice dropped to a pained whisper. "But no matter what they say, I loved you then. I wanted to be your wife. I would never have summoned my brothers."

He fought the despair that her use of the word "love" in the past tense dredged up. Even knowing her to be a fickle, foolish woman, she could affect him, and that was dangerous. "Someone brought them there at four in the morning, long before anyone would have found your note. And what about the pamphlets? No one knew who printed them but you and Lettice."

Anger flared in her face. "You and your friend Morgan pranced about town with a devil-may-care lack of concern for what happened, and you blame me for that? I'm sure it wasn't the secret you make it out to be. Why, at the meeting—"

"Which you boldly sneaked into, then fled from when you realized you'd acted impulsively. Just as you married me, then fled the marriage after you changed your mind." He smiled, knowing he had her trapped.

She recoiled. "Is that who you think I am? Some irresponsible fool who'd marry you, then change her mind on a whim?"

"Not only on a whim, but because you thought I'd married you for your property. The night I proposed, you accused me of wanting to marry you to get Llynwydd. I denied it, but you persisted in your fears, didn't you? And once we were married, you let those fears persuade you that you'd made a big mistake."

"And that's when I'm supposed to have summoned my brothers and told them to pack you off to the navy?" She shook her head in disbelief. "Nothing I say will convince you that I couldn't have done such a thing, will it? You've tried and sentenced me, and I'm to have no word in my defense."

"I'm relying on the evidence, wife—and the evidence says you betrayed me. Perhaps you did it not knowing what impressment would mean for me, but you did it all the same."

She whirled on St. Albans. "And you, Overton? Shall you let Rhys believe Darcy's lies, and say nothing in my defense?"

St. Albans glanced at his brother, then said unsteadily, "I know you for what you are, Juliana."

"A foolish nitwit who'd send her husband off to certain torment to avoid her marriage? Is that what you know me for?"

Lord Northcliffe barged forward. "That's enough, Juliana. You were young, and no one blames you for behaving as you did." He turned to Rhys. "Except your husband. And in light of your dislike of your wife's behavior, sir, I would think you'd welcome an annulment."

"No annulment," Rhys repeated.

Lord Northcliffe paled. "But surely, now that you know all of it—"

Juliana glared at her brothers. "You see what your plotting has wrought? Now I'm married to a man who believes horrendous things of me yet refuses to release me." She faced Rhys. "You want to ruin us all? Fine. Divorce me."

"Divorce?" her brother exploded. "Certainly not!"

"This is none of your concern, Darcy. You've already meddled quite enough, thank you."

Rhys stared at her. A divorce would make it impossible for her to marry again. How strange that she'd risk it. But perhaps she thought her obvious attractions would

ensure that matters turned out her way. And they probably would.

"No divorce," he said evenly. "You had your chance to be
rid of me legally, and you didn't take it." His eyes narrowed
to slits. "You know, if you'd asked for an annulment that
night, I would have given it to you. I loved you that much."
His tone hardened. "But you didn't ask. You took a more
treacherous road, and now you're mine, Juliana. And you'll
be mine for as long as I want you."

"You mean for as long as you wish to torment me." Her
chin came up and her eyes glowed with bitterness. "That's
what this is all about, isn't it? You want to keep me in
your power so you can punish me for a slew of imaginary
crimes, not first of which is being English."

He stiffened. "Being English is certainly a deficit in your
character, but I could have tolerated it if you hadn't frivolously thrown me into the lion's den."

"I never did that, but of course you don't believe me.
You always were a suspicious man, Rhys Vaughan. I should
have known you'd never trust me. It was all a sham—the
soft words and kindnesses. Inside, you waited for me to
make some mistake so you could show me to be the unworthy Englishwoman you already believed I was."

She said it with such conviction that he had to grit his
teeth against the emotions she roused. "Stop twisting the
past! I didn't make you unworthy—you proved yourself
so. You took a man's life and played with it, never caring
what destruction you wrought!" He jerked back his cuff to
show the scars on his wrists. "This is only one illustration
of what your actions brought."

At the sight of the thick scars, she gasped. Then, to his surprise, she touched them and lifted a tortured gaze to him. "'Tis a terrible thing you've endured." She clasped his hand. "But I swear it was not of my making. I could never have—" She broke off with a sob.

It was the first time she'd touched him since his return, and it seared him deeper than any flogging. He snatched his hand from her, damning her for her pity. By thunder, she still had the power to move him. After all this time, she could make him believe her innocent when everyone said otherwise.

"We've wasted enough time discussing this," Rhys managed. "You're my wife now, and nothing will change that." He turned to address her brothers. "There will be no annulment, no divorce." His eyes narrowed. "Nor, I hope, will you attempt to continue plotting against me. For if you try to destroy me, this time I'll bring all of you down."

"You're going to do that anyway, aren't you?" Northcliffe gritted out.

Rhys surveyed the new earl, who'd grown leaner in his absence, as if the privileges of power and money had been gained at a cost to his physical self. The young man looked older than his years, especially with the powdered peruke on his head. Rhys had heard of Northcliffe's successes— how he'd taken the reins after his father's death and climbed upward until he associated with some of the greatest men in London.

Northcliffe might sputter and complain about Rhys's plans, but he wouldn't thwart him. Not, at least, until he'd considered the consequences. "I shall not take my revenge that way," Rhys said, relishing the power he held over his enemy. "Not if you give me what I want—my wife and my estate. Much as I prospered during my years in America, 'tis Wales I love, and 'tis in Wales I'll stay."

Grabbing Juliana by the arm, he pulled her to stand beside him. "I merely wish to make sure that my wife lies in the bed she's made, as I had to lie in the bed she made for me."

Sheer terror flared in Northcliffe's eyes. "And what does that mean, exactly?"

"From this night on, Juliana is my wife in every way. We'll spend tonight at my town house, but tomorrow we head for Llynwydd. You are not to interfere, unless you wish to relinquish your tidy position in England's political hierarchy. If you cross me, I'll do whatever it takes to ruin you."

Northcliffe stiffened. "You want us to stand by and watch while you torment our sister?"

Rhys shrugged. "I won't beat her, if that's what you think." He leveled a threatening gaze on the two men. "But I will deal with my wife as I see fit, and I won't tolerate your interference."

Casting his brother a long, meaningful glance, Northcliffe hesitated. Then he sighed. "All right."

Juliana glared at Rhys. "And what if I refuse? What if I tell you to go to hell?"

She certainly had changed since he'd first met her. Years ago, she wouldn't have even uttered the word "hell." But she'd soon learn that strong words had no effect on him.

"I don't think you fully appreciate the precariousness of your position. It's not too late to put a good face on this, to tell the world that it was all a misunderstanding. We eloped and then you thought me dead, so you hid the elopement from the world. Eventually society will forgive you for that, especially if we live publicly as husband and wife."

She stared at him stony-faced.

"But if you resist me," he continued, "I'll reveal what really happened. I'll show off that lovely marriage certificate and bemoan the fact that you went to terrible extremes to get out of our marriage."

"No one will believe you."

"They'll believe me over a woman who nearly committed bigamy. And you'll never be able to hold your head up in society again."

"If you hate me that much, why do you want me as your wife?"

He lifted a hand to trail his fingers over her cheek. She flinched from him, and unexpectedly he felt dismay. Dismay? Hadn't it been his goal to have her at his mercy all along?

Angry at himself for being so affected by her reactions, he drew back. "There are reasons I might give, of course. I need you to maintain my hold on Llynwydd. And I want an heir." He waited until that last remark registered. "But the truth is, I simply refuse to give you the pleasure of being free of me."

To his surprise, she met his gaze boldly. "That works both ways, dear husband. I may not be free, but neither are you. And if you persist in tormenting me because of Darcy's foolish lies, I swear I'll make your life hell."

He stared into her flashing eyes, wondering if she'd always been this stubborn. Or this achingly beautiful.

"Then it's hell we'll be headed for, Juliana. Because this time you won't escape our marriage."

9

Too great desire is evil,
Every step unlucky still!

—DAFYDD AP GWILYM,
"TROUBLE AT A TAVERN"

When the doors closed behind Juliana and Rhys Vaughan, Darcy slammed his fist against a wall. "That deuced bastard!"

"Aye," Overton said. "And you just gave him carte blanche with our sister. Have you gone mad? Don't you see what you've done?"

Crossing to the sideboard, Darcy poured himself two fingers of whisky. "What the hell did you want me to do?" He downed the whisky in one gulp.

"Tell the truth! I should have told it myself, but—"

"But you knew what I'd do to you if you did." Darcy threw the glass at the wall, feeling only the faintest satisfaction at the sound of breaking glass.

Overton looked pasty as he dropped into a nearby chair. "I can't believe you did that to her. There's no telling what Vaughan will do, now that he believes she betrayed him."

"Don't you think I realize that?"

"Then why did you lie?"

Darcy stared blindly ahead. "At first I hoped he'd agree to an annulment if I held to my story and painted a foul picture of Juliana."

"And when he refused to get one? Why didn't you tell him the truth then, so they could at least have an amiable marriage?"

"He won't hurt her." Darcy knew he was trying to convince himself of something he didn't quite believe, but he kept on. "He still cares for her, or he wouldn't want her so badly."

"You're a bloody fool if you believe that. He just promised her a marriage in hell. You'd stand by and let her live it, when a word from you would end it?"

"Which am I to choose—a marriage in hell for Juliana? Or complete destruction for the family? He said he'd do nothing to us, as long as we let him have Juliana and Llynwydd. But if we tell him the truth, those assurances are gone. He'll destroy us. Grafton and Rockingham are his friends, for God's sake! Do you know what would happen if they ever turned against me? I'd lose everything I've accomplished!"

Overton frowned. "It would be worth it to have Juliana happy."

"I'm in a marriage from hell myself. And he said he wouldn't beat her." Staring at the door Vaughan and Juliana had left through, he remembered how the bastard had spoken of being flogged. Deuce take it, what would a man who'd suffered so do to the woman he thought had caused it?

And to the men who really did cause it?

"After a few weeks with her, sweet as she is, he'll come around." But his assurances sounded hollow even to him.

"No matter how you excuse it, you've still made her the scapegoat for your crimes. Poor innocent Juliana, who never spoke badly of anyone in her life."

Every word sliced through Darcy. He sank into a chair and buried his face in his hands. "How was I to know he'd return? How was I to know he'd make something of himself?"

"It was a stupid business—all of it. She loved him, and we hurt her. But we can fix it now."

Darcy lifted his head. "What about Mother and Elizabeth? What about everything we've gained? Juliana wouldn't want us to risk everything for her. Vaughan's the vindictive sort. Surely you can see that."

Overton jumped to his feet. "Aye, and he'll be vindictive toward Juliana if we don't tell him the truth!"

"I don't know if he'd believe it. He's already spoken to the innkeeper. He's sure to find anything we say suspect."

"Did you tell the innkeeper to lie, too?"

Darcy rose. "Vaughan's last letter here made me worry, so I instructed the man what to say if Vaughan ever sought the truth. Honestly, I thought Vaughan would write him, and after receiving confirmation of Juliana's behavior, would decide against returning."

"What of that man who brought proof of Vaughan's death? Did you pay him to lie, as well?" When Darcy remained silent, Overton exploded. "You bastard!" A look of disgust filled his face. "What a treacherous web you wove! You lied to Juliana, you lied to her husband—"

"I thought I was doing the right thing for all of us."

Raking his brother with a contemptuous gaze, Overton said, "'Twasn't the only reason for your plotting, I daresay. You did it for Lettice—admit it."

"Shh!" Darcy hissed, glancing toward the door. "Elizabeth will hear you."

"Elizabeth knows about your mistress, you dolt. *Everyone* knows. You're not the least bit discreet. I daresay Lettice doesn't know you were behind the impressment of her sweetheart, does she?"

Darcy's stomach twisted into knots. A pity that sometimes his brother could be astute indeed.

How to answer him? To win Overton to his side, he'd have to play on his sympathies, and that meant telling the truth. "No, Lettice doesn't know I was behind it. And I don't want her to know . . . ever."

"Well, she's sure to find out now. Vaughan will tell her out of sheer spite."

Darcy grimaced. "Aye. And Pennant might have returned with Vaughan." And if so? Were the tales he'd told Pennant strong enough to keep the man from Lettice? "Now you know why I tried to prevent their return. I love Lettice. She's the only thing that keeps me sane. I can't survive her leaving me—or taking away my only son."

The thought of that nearly killed him. He choked back the doubts about Edgar's paternity he'd nurtured through the years. It didn't matter that the birth had taken place eight months after Pennant's impressment. Edgar was *his* son—his! "A pox on Vaughan! Why did he have to return?"

"I don't know, but now that he's back, what will you do about Lettice and Edgar?"

"I'll hope she never learns the truth. And if she does, I'll pray that years of taking care of her will compensate for my sins. Perhaps when she sees how far I went to secure her love, she'll not hold them against me."

"For a man of intelligence," Overton remarked dryly, "you're surprisingly stupid when it comes to women."

He hated that Overton was probably right. "Do one thing for me: Don't tell anyone the truth until I see how Vaughan acts. There's a chance he won't bother speaking to Lettice, since he assumes that she, like Juliana, betrayed her lover. But if Vaughan learns the truth, his first strike will be to drive Lettice from me."

"Juliana is sure to tell her. And Lettice isn't the sort of woman you can easily fool. Then there's the boy—"

Darcy clenched his fists. "Just give me some time to think of a way out of this mess. Time to tell Lettice myself." He fought to swallow his pride. "Please, Overton. Bear with me awhile longer."

With a sigh, Overton nodded. "But not much time. If you haven't come up with anything in a few weeks—"

"I'll tell Vaughan everything. I swear."

As Rhys led Juliana out into the dark night, she roused from her numb state to look around at the lanterns lighting the walks for her engagement party. If not for Rhys, she'd be dancing in Stephen's arms. He'd be treating her with his usual kindness and consideration, and later he'd kiss her while she closed her eyes and . . .

Thought of Rhys.

A curse welled up in her throat. She'd been so stupid! To have wasted all those years pining for him, comparing every man she'd met to him. He was a distrustful arse, pure and simple.

As Rhys led her toward the entrance, she stole a glance at the man she'd once worshipped. He was as handsome as he'd ever been, if not more so. And he still had that orator's voice.

But in every other way, he'd changed. Angry lines were etched into his forehead, and his jaw seemed permanently clenched in a rage she barely understood. As she stared at his cold profile, despair washed over her.

Had their time together meant nothing to him? The Rhys she'd fallen in love with hadn't been quick to believe lies about her.

No, that wasn't true. She remembered the first time he'd come to Northcliffe Hall, when he'd accused her of spying. The Rhys she'd fallen in love with had been just as quick to believe the worst of her.

But at least back then he'd recognized his tendency to jump to conclusions. And he hadn't been able to act on his assumptions in such a sweeping manner. Now he had a frightening power over her. A power that her wretched brothers had sanctioned, blast them!

She gritted her teeth. When she got her hands on Darcy again, she'd strangle him! She should have done so the minute he started lying to Rhys. But she'd been too stunned to believe it. What madness had possessed him?

And Overton, too! Tears started in her eyes, and she swiped them away, hoping Rhys hadn't noticed. Her brothers were traitors and didn't deserve her tears. I'faith, they deserved to be hanged!

She must have made some choked sound, which attracted Rhys's attention at last. "Don't worry," he said, "I shan't make you walk all the way to my town house. My carriage is just outside the walls. I didn't want to rouse questions earlier by having it bring me to the doorstep, so I came in the way I used to."

The reminder of how he used to slip onto the grounds, how he used to love her, roused her temper. "Oh yes, you were very good at sneaking into places."

"As I recall, I was invited."

She remembered how quick she'd been to welcome him into her bedchamber. He'd probably thought her the worst of wantons.

Was this to be her punishment? A constant litany of her faults? If so, she had a surprise for him. She couldn't do anything about his misreading of the past and her character, but she could refuse him the satisfaction of rousing her anger every time he sought to wound her.

Tense and silent, they reached the gates, which the gatekeeper opened as he saw her approach. No doubt the news had traveled through the household like wildfire. It was all she could do to face down the curious gatekeeper.

The carriage that awaited them was surprisingly fashionable. A liveried coachman sat on the perch, and the horses were a pair of matched bays. Apparently, Rhys hadn't lied about his improved circumstances.

That only deepened her despair. While he'd been amassing a fortune, nursing his unfounded distrust of her, she'd been mourning him. And all he could see was betrayal.

Still hurt by that, she refused his help when he reached to hand her up, even though it meant clambering into the carriage in a most unladylike manner.

As she settled herself on the plush seat, he took the one opposite her. "If you think to annoy me with your petty shows of resistance, Juliana, you might as well give up. Nothing you invent can compare with the many 'annoyances' the captain of the HMS *Nightmark* invented for impressed landsmen."

She merely stared out the window as the carriage rumbled away from Northcliffe.

"And ignoring me won't work, either," he drawled.

Her gaze shot to him, and she winced at his gloating smile, which showed he thought he'd had the last laugh.

But her temper must have shown in her face, for his smile cooled. "Tell me, *cariad*, did you ever look at your betrothed that way?"

He spoke the Welsh endearment with an absolute contempt meant to wound. With as much cool nonchalance as she could muster, she said, "Unlike you, Stephen never deserved my anger. He was always sweet to me. I never even had to raise my voice to him, for he, at least, was a gentleman."

"A rich, powerful gentleman. A pity he never saw your true self until today. He might have saved himself some grief. But with all that money and position hanging in the balance, you had to hide your true self."

She searched for some retort that would stop him dead. "Just as you did when you courted me, speaking lies and giving me gifts. With your estate hanging in the balance, you had to hide your true self."

When his smile faded completely, she felt a moment's satisfaction.

He leaned forward to glower at her. "You know I was unaware that Llynwydd belonged to you. That had nothing to do with why I married you, no matter what you thought."

"That's not what Darcy said. And of course, he always speaks the truth." *Hah! Wriggle out of that one!*

"And you believed every word he said."

She leveled a solemn gaze on him. "No. Because I knew in my heart what you were. 'Tis why I waited so long for you."

"So long?" He gave a harsh laugh. "Yes, you waited at least until a marquess came sniffing after you." His eyes shimmered in the dim light. "How long did you wait before you let him court you, before you went hunting for a husband?"

She hid her hurt. He had a right to ask it, she supposed. "Surely you heard what Darcy said. Stephen came to court me only a year ago. I didn't encourage his overtures until Darcy's investigator told me you were dead."

"Which was a lie."

"Yes, but I believed it—or I wouldn't have let Stephen court me at all."

"And the little matter of your previous marriage didn't come up. I wonder, how did you plan to deal with your Stephen on your wedding night?"

She couldn't prevent the guilty flush that spread over her face. "I was hoping he wouldn't notice."

"Or perhaps that wasn't even an issue." His voice grew more cutting. "Perhaps he'd already sampled your delights and knew he was getting damaged goods. I daresay any man who'd had you wouldn't have cared about your lack of innocence. Not once he'd discovered what a wanton you are in bed."

She shot up in her seat. "How dare you! Stephen would never have—"

"Did you tell him about that convenient tree outside your window, so he could enter your bedroom at night and take you at his whim?" He leaned forward, breathing heavily. "Did you cry out every time he thrust deep into you, as you did with me? Did you—"

"Stop it!" Sobs welled up in her throat. "Stop saying such awful things! You're the only man who's ever touched me that way, and you know it!"

He fell back against his seat, panting hard, like a savage beast that had just run its poor prey to ground.

She fixed him with an accusing gaze. "I meant it when I promised to be faithful to you."

"Obviously your definition of faithfulness differs vastly from mine."

"What did you expect? That I'd languish away forever, believing you dead? You never sent any word. If I'd known you still lived, no power on earth would have kept me from awaiting your return. But I didn't know, don't you see?"

"So you say," he bit out.

She forced herself to be strong, to fight him with his own weapons. "And you? Were you faithful to me, as you promised on your wedding night?"

He stared at her. "Are you asking if I bedded other women?"

She nodded, unable to speak the words. She shouldn't have brought it up. She'd already spent her years at Llynwydd remembering their wedding night, knowing that he'd bedded one of the dairymaids. Many a time she'd tortured herself, wondering which of the buxom women was the one who'd known him intimately.

He hesitated, as if uncertain whether to tell her. Then his jaw tightened. "What do you think? In America there were plenty of willing wenches who wanted to bed a war hero and didn't mind being loose with their reputations. Do you think I threw them out of my bedchamber?"

Each word was designed to cut deeply. And he certainly drew blood.

Still, she fixed him with a steady gaze as the coach shuddered to a halt outside a town house. "I think you're a two-faced devil with one set of standards for himself, and another for his wife."

For a long moment, he simply glared at her. Then he thrust the coach door open and pointed to the town house door. "Get inside! Now!"

With all the dignity she could muster, she stepped down from the coach and walked primly up the entrance steps, scarcely noticing the expensive Palladian home with its marble columns and sashed windows. All she could think of was how to get out of this mad marriage with Rhys. She couldn't continue in it when he sought to destroy her at every turn.

She heard him behind her and hastened her steps to avoid his touch. She needn't have worried. He kept a marked distance from her as the doors opened before them, manned by servants who'd been watching from the windows.

A portly man stepped forward and bowed to Rhys. "All the rooms are in readiness as you instructed, sir."

"The master bedroom is finished?"

"Yes, sir. We had a time getting it ready in only a week, but it's done."

"Good," Rhys said, staring absently about him.

Juliana followed his gaze. Everything looked newly furbished. Too late, she remembered gossip among the tradesmen about the eccentric American who'd bought the old Webberley town house. Dear heaven, if she'd only realized . . .

Then the implications of that sank in. Instead of coming to speak rationally to her the minute he'd arrived in town, Rhys had sneaked into her engagement party like a thief, then aired his grievances before all of society.

"Will that be all, sir?" the servant asked.

Rhys nodded. "We leave for Llynwydd in the morning. In future, I'll notify you in plenty of time whenever we plan to be in residence." He cast her an enigmatic glance. "For tonight, you and the other servants are dismissed. We don't wish to be disturbed."

Her gaze flew to his. There was an ominous meaning behind his words. "I shall require a maid to help me undress—"

"We do not wish to be disturbed," he repeated.

The servant wisely disappeared through a door off the downstairs hall.

"Come, my dear wife," Rhys said, "let me show you the master bedchamber."

"I'd rather just go to my own," she said as they ascended the stairs. "I'm sure I can find it myself."

"Oh, no." He clasped her arm, making it clear he wouldn't tolerate resistance. "I fully intend to accompany you to your room. And to bed. I wouldn't miss that for the world."

Good Lord. They'd reached the top of the stairs already, and the master bedroom proved to be the first door on the hallway. Frantically, she sought some delaying tactic, but before she could find one, he'd opened the door and urged her inside.

Mouth dry, she entered and glanced around. The room shouted masculinity. The dark woods, the rich blue velvet curtains and bed drapings made her feel like a trespasser. A pair of man's boots, newly polished, sat at the foot of the bed. His. This was his. All of it was his.

She faced him warily. He'd come in behind her, and now made a point of locking the door and putting the key in his pocket.

When he stared at her as a hungry man stares at a succulent hen, then sat down to remove his shoes, she sucked in a harsh breath. I'faith, he planned to bed her. Now. Tonight.

Was this to be her punishment? Did he truly think she'd let him take her, as if years hadn't passed between them? If so, he was in for a surprise.

He stood and strode to a table against a window where a crystal decanter of bloodred liquid sat. With slow, deliberate movements, he poured two glasses. "Wine?"

She shook her head. If his plan was to seduce her, she would soon disabuse him of that notion. She was no longer the untried, foolish girl he'd enticed with poems and gifts. She knew her own mind now, and he was *not* simply going to pick up where they'd left off. Not after all the lies he'd believed about her.

As he sipped from his glass, his gaze raked her with the insolence of a horse trader picking a prize mare. "I can't believe I'd forgotten how truly beautiful you are."

When she said nothing to that, he set the wine aside and rounded the bed toward her. Curious to see what he would do, she stayed still as he approached. He stopped mere inches away, reaching up to draw a jeweled pin from her hair.

A cursed trembling began in her body as he removed the pins until her hair tumbled down about her shoulders. He was so close she could touch him, could brush her fingers over the clean-shaven chin and the thin blade of a nose if she wanted. His wine-scented breath feathered over her face, summoning up long-buried memories—of the way his mouth once covered hers, teasing, possessing.

She fought the memories. This wasn't the Rhys who'd taken her with care on their wedding night. This was the Rhys who believed her a schemer and a liar. And as long as he did, she wouldn't let him seduce her.

He lifted her hair, letting it fall over his hands, then rubbing the strands between his fingers. His eyes glittered as he stared at it in the candlelight. "I'd also forgotten how soft your hair is." As she held her breath, her emotions rioting, he stroked the mass over her shoulder.

Suddenly he stiffened and jerked his hand back, pivoting away. He crossed the room, his expression grim as he picked up his wine again, not looking at her.

"Take off your clothes." He gulped some wine, then set the glass down hard on the table.

"Not until you leave."

He faced her, eyes wild. "Perhaps I didn't make myself clear earlier. You're my wife now, and I'm never leaving again." He trailed his gaze over her body. "When I said I intended to take you and my estate back, I meant in every way. And if you're wise, you'll try to appease my anger instead of playing the innocent."

The words drove deep. "I'm not playing at being innocent."

"One day you'll admit the truth. But in the meantime, I expect you to obey my commands as you promised to do when you spoke your vows so frivolously. So take off your clothes. Now!"

That was his plan? To take her by force?

She thrust her chin out at him. "Make me."

He started. "I will, you know. I'll tear the clothes off you myself. And I'd hate to ruin such a lovely and expensive gown."

Yet he made no move toward her. And when she didn't take off her clothes, he growled, "Fine. I'll go first." He removed his neckcloth, then his cutaway and waistcoat. "Your turn."

"I won't. You can't force me to."

He stepped toward her, fists clenched. "Take your damned clothes off! I wish to see what I paid in blood for!"

The frustration in his face gave her pause. Perhaps she should attempt a different tactic. If this wasn't just about punishing her by humiliating her, if he still actually desired her, then somewhere inside him was the Rhys she'd married—the one who'd actually been in love with her.

There was only one way to be sure.

So she unfastened her stomacher, then her bodice, skirt, hoop, and petticoats. And as she bared her arms and shrugged out of her armor, she was rewarded by his gaze darkening and his face growing taut with undisguised hunger.

He *did* still desire her. That was something, at least.

"The stockings," he said hoarsely. "Take off your stockings."

Heart pounding, she stepped out of her slippers, then lifted her shift only high enough to untie the garters and draw down her white silk hose. She felt his gaze following the slide of them down her legs. In spite of everything, it sent a thrill through her.

"Now the corset." His voice sounded more unsteady.

"I can't undo it by myself."

Her words seemed to jerk him from some dark prison. With a curt nod, he came to stand behind her. She sucked in a quick breath when she felt his fingers unknotting her laces, brushing her skin as he drew the corset apart. It reminded her of what they'd been like together in that inn room on their wedding night.

Could they ever be that way again?

When the corset dropped to the floor, he stepped in front of her, his eyes devouring her. "Now the shift."

"Your turn," she said coolly.

He tensed, then gave her a tight nod. "Very well. Perhaps you *should* see what your betrayal wrought." Jaw clenched, he tore off his shirt. "Have you ever witnessed a man being whipped? Have you any idea what happens to a man after several floggings with a cat-o'-nine-tails?"

When he pivoted to show her his back, she gasped. She'd expected scars, but the reality was far worse. There were no scars on the upper back at all. It was simply an expanse of mottled skin that looked like healed pulp. There were scars lower down in the small of his back, however, where the cat apparently hadn't reached as well, leaving a dense mesh of white lines on the skin.

She'd heard of the horrors men suffered in the navy, but she'd never dreamed anyone could be so cruel to another human being. His beautiful back, so proud and finely shaped, was covered with healed welts. What pain had he endured to have a back like that? And what other pains had he not yet told her of?

He left nothing to her imagination. "They clean the cat after every stroke, to make sure it doesn't become so clotted with blood and flesh that it's ineffective. And when they're done, they wash the back with brine so it will heal. Men generally pass out from the shock of salt water against torn flesh—if they haven't passed out already. But the skin does heal. Until the next flogging, of course."

Bile rose in her throat. How many such floggings had he suffered? And how had he endured them at all? No wonder he was so furious at her, if this is what he'd thought she'd done to him.

He whirled to face her. "The law supposedly allows no more than six strokes, but a tyrannical captain may order up to three hundred with impunity. And I had a tyrannical captain . . . a cruel man who hated the Welsh, especially known radicals." He stared past her at the wall. "He had me flogged for the least infraction, and for some I didn't commit."

Pity welled up in her. "Oh, Rhys, I'm so sorry you suffered."

His gaze snapped to hers. "I didn't tell you so you could pity me. I told you so you'd understand a fraction of what you did to me when you decided marriage didn't suit you after all."

"I didn't—"

"Enough!" he thundered. "I don't want protestations of innocence from you, nor pity, either. I want only one thing from you tonight. So take off your damned shift!"

The violence of his words shook her, but she refused to let him cow her. Somewhere inside was the man she'd once loved. She knew it. And perhaps seeing her in the flesh would remind him of how they'd been together, and stop his attempts to torment her.

As her shift slipped to the floor, he dragged in his breath and scoured her with his gaze, pausing at her breasts, her belly, the juncture of her thighs. She swallowed hard. If he could endure countless floggings, she could endure this. So when his eyes moved slowly back up her body, burning like blue flames as he assessed her every attraction, she made herself stand proud.

By the time he brought his gaze back to her face, his expression had altered, softened. "Do you know how many times I survived a flogging simply by remembering you? The curve of your hips . . . the full weight of your breasts . . . the silkiness of your skin . . ." He walked up to her, then lifted his hand to run a finger down her throat, over the swell of one breast and then over her belly.

It was such a sensual gesture, almost sweet, that for a moment she forgot how much he'd changed. For a moment, she half-believed that the old Rhys stood before her, coming to her as she'd dreamed of him doing every night for the past six years. She waited, breath held, for him to kiss her.

Instead he shook his head, as if coming to his senses. He yanked his hand back. "Lie down," he commanded, unbuttoning his breeches. "On the bed."

She stared at him, shocked by the change in him. Was this really what he planned—to take her like an animal, to reduce their former lovemaking to a bestial act in payment for the many bestial acts committed against him?

No. She wouldn't let him.

"Lie down, I said!"

"Not when you're like this. I won't let you punish me by doing something you will regret later."

"I won't regret it," he bit out, as if trying to convince himself. "I swear I won't."

Faced with his stubbornness, she kissed him. To remind him of what had been, of who they'd been together.

He froze, and for a moment, she wondered if she'd made a mistake. But then his mouth opened over hers, and he was kissing her roughly, deeply, with soul-devouring thrusts of his tongue that made her weak in the knees in spite of everything.

Then his hands were caressing her breasts, and his mouth was ravaging her, and she was truly lost. This couldn't be the same man who'd coldly told her a few minutes ago to undress, who'd threatened to take her with violence. This man was a lover.

Or a seducer. With a shudder, she fought the flood of warmth that centered in her loins. It was all a trick. She must stop this.

But she couldn't. She simply couldn't.

She fought to concentrate on how he'd believed her brothers' lies, but she could only remember what he'd been to her. And when he bent to close his mouth over her nipple, hot and sweet, drawing and tugging on it, she went soft all over.

"Please . . ." she whispered, hating him for making her capitulate so easily.

His hand slipped down between their bodies, cupping her, fondling her intimate places. Wherever he rubbed, she burned, and when he continued the magic, she opened her eyes, amazed that he could still rouse her body so thoroughly after all the years of silence.

He had closed his eyes and was now sucking her breast as if he'd craved it for an eternity. Suddenly his finger slid inside her, delving deep. She couldn't help it. She moaned and closed her arms about his waist.

At the touch of her hands on his back, he stiffened and his eyes shot open. He glared at her, his breath unsteady, his face a mask of anger.

She watched him in total confusion. What had she done?

"Damn it all, Juliana!" Cursing foully in Welsh, he shoved away from her. He buttoned up his breeches with furious movements, though his arousal was still visible beneath them.

She stared at him. "Why are you angry? This was what you wanted, wasn't it?" Her voice grew bitter. "To seduce me, have me fall into your bed willingly again?"

"It took very little to get that from you, didn't it?" he snapped. "It took very little to have you moaning and writhing with pleasure!"

At first embarrassment made her blush, but as she realized that he seemed angry that she'd responded, she grew cold inside. "If you didn't want me to have pleasure, then what did you intend? To make me fear you?"

He scowled at her, not saying a word.

"That's it, isn't it?" The truth created a hollow ache in her stomach. "You meant to make me suffer as you suffered, to punish me."

"'Tis what you deserve!"

"It isn't. And somewhere in that bitter heart of yours, you know it. You don't truly want to hurt me. 'Tis why you gave me pleasure, why you touched me with gentleness."

"That's a lie!" He stalked toward her as if to renew his

assault. But when she lifted her face to him in challenge, her eyes unafraid, he whirled on his heel and headed for the door.

"Damn you!" he hissed. Then he unlocked the door and stormed out.

She held her breath, waiting for him to return and make a liar of her by attacking her in earnest. But when he merely locked the door from the outside and strode away cursing, she collapsed onto the bed, finally allowing her tears to flow.

She didn't care what he claimed. For a few minutes, he'd forgotten all the lies he believed about her. For a brief time, he'd been the Rhys she'd loved.

And that glimpse heartened her. Somehow, she'd won the first battle.

But how many more battles like this could she endure?

10

O how I long to travel back,
And tread again that ancient track!
That I might once more reach that plain
Where first I left my glorious train

—HENRY VAUGHAN, "THE RETREAT"

*L*ettice opened the door to her son's room, careful not to wake him. It was a nighttime ritual, checking on Edgar before she went to bed.

Tonight the full moon cast its kindly light over his sweet face, kissing his soft cheeks with moonbeams. His childish features were so painfully familiar to her. She'd tried not to notice over the past few years how much more he looked like Morgan with every passing day, but it was impossible not to.

Darcy, however, saw none of it. It sometimes amazed her that he never questioned why his "son" didn't resemble him.

She closed the door, her throat tightening. If Darcy ever did realize how she'd tricked him . . . what would he do? What would *she* do?

Glancing around the modestly furnished bedroom she shared with Darcy whenever he visited, she sighed. In truth, Darcy treated her like a queen. He came to her often and brought her endearing gifts. She had her own cottage away from prying eyes, and plenty of time to care for it.

Of course, the townspeople looked down on her for being the mistress of a married English nobleman whom they despised. Still, she tried not to let it bother her. At least she had a home for her and her son.

Besides, Darcy treated Edgar well, since his wife had given him no children. Although he couldn't acknowledge Edgar as his son except to her, he gave Edgar a generous allowance and promised to educate him as a gentleman. And Edgar thought the world of "Uncle Darcy."

So why wasn't she content? Why was it that, whenever she looked into Edgar's sparkling black eyes, she thought of the one man who'd made her melt with just a touch? Darcy couldn't do that. Their lovemaking was pleasant and adequate . . . but with Morgan it had been a glorious feast, a celebration of joy.

A knock at the door downstairs disturbed her thoughts. Darcy? He'd said the engagement party would go late and that he wouldn't see her for a day or so, but perhaps he'd changed his mind.

She hurried down and opened the door without a second thought. "I didn't expect—"

Her words caught in her throat. Standing before her was a ghost—a flesh-and-blood ghost she'd never hoped to see again.

The years melted away. "Morgan! Is it really you?"

His only answer was a hard stare.

She wanted to throw herself into his arms and cry for joy, but the chill in his expression halted her. What was wrong? Why did he look at her so sternly?

Then she remembered. She was another man's mistress now. And he couldn't have found her without learning that.

Her heart sank. He'd changed a great deal. His clothing was richer than before, and he wore it with the arrogance of a man of position. A jagged scar creased one of his cheeks, and his hair was quite long.

But his black eyes were what truly showed the years, for they were no longer merry. They were solemn and unsmiling. And they remained fixed on her with an unnerving intensity.

"May I come in?" he rasped.

"Yes, of course." She stood aside to let him pass. She shut the door and slumped against it, needing something to hold her up. The shock to her heart was so great, she didn't know if she could absorb it. Morgan was here, alive and standing before her. But he was obviously not happy to be here.

Somehow she contained her tumultuous emotions, so that the words that sprang to her lips showed none of her feelings. "Would you like some tea?"

He turned from surveying her cottage to fix her with that same icy gaze. "You see your 'true love' after six years and all you can do is offer him tea?"

The sarcasm he put into the words "true love" wounded her. He'd been gone for years without a single letter, and now he expected everything to be exactly as it had been before? She swallowed her hurt, smoothing her expression into one of nonchalance. "To be honest, after all this time hearing nothing from my 'true love,' I'd assumed I didn't have one anymore."

Her coldness seemed to rouse him from his aloofness. He came toward her, fists clenched. "I sent a letter to Northcliffe Hall. It was returned with the words 'No longer at this address' written across it. I didn't know where else to look."

"Obviously you found me tonight."

His eyes glittered. "Yes. I went to Northcliffe Hall, and they told me of your whereabouts. And of the nice cottage that your lover, the new Lord Northcliffe, bought for you."

As his contempt washed over her, righteous anger surged. How dared he accuse her! Thanks to his dangerous politics, he'd left her pregnant with no way of supporting herself, no possible future. Yet he'd expected her to wait for him? Forever?

Dragging in a bracing breath, she met his gaze. "It took you a very long time to come searching for me. I know you must have served in the navy for a while." She trailed her gaze over his rich attire. "But obviously you went on to greater success. I suppose making a fortune in some far-off country kept you too busy to return." She straightened her shoulders and walked toward the fireplace.

But he caught her arm. "What kept me busy was finding a way to return without being hanged for desertion!"

All the stored-up resentment of six years exploded in her. "If you hadn't gotten yourself involved with those damned

Sons of Wales, you wouldn't have had to worry about it! If you hadn't printed those wretched pamphlets—"

"And if you hadn't told Northcliffe about them!"

"What the devil do you mean?"

He thrust her away, disgust contorting his face. "I didn't believe him when he said you'd betrayed me." His sweeping gesture encompassed the cottage. "But I talked to the servants and discovered how long you've been here. Ever since I left, you've lived here as his mistress." He shook his head. "You were obviously willing to go to any extent to stay out of poverty, weren't you?"

She gaped at him. "What did Darcy tell you? Did you see him tonight?"

"No. If I had, he'd be dead for what he did to me." He drew in a ragged breath. "For what he and you did together."

Her heart's pace slowed to a crawl. "A pox upon't, what did he do? What is it you think *I* did?"

His eyes narrowed. "You know he had me impressed."

She staggered back, her legs suddenly too weak to hold her up. Somehow she found a chair and dropped into it. She shook her head mindlessly. "Darcy? Are you sure?"

Morgan clenched his fists. "Quite sure. I'll never forget how he gloated about how you'd confirmed that I was the one who'd printed those pamphlets. How you'd done it to keep from losing your damned position."

She jerked up straight in her seat. "I never told him that! I wouldn't have! How could you even believe it?"

"It's hard not to when you're sitting here as his mistress, obviously snug as a cockle in the cottage he paid for!" His voice rose to a shout. "How stupid do you think I am? You expect me to believe you had no part in it?"

"Yes, I do!" Jumping from her chair, she prepared to give him a thorough set-down, but a childish voice coming from the stairs stopped her. She turned to find Edgar standing on the bottom step, rubbing his eyes.

"Mother, why are you shouting?" He eyed Morgan with curiosity. But when Morgan gave him a hard stare, he fidgeted. "Good evening," he said bravely, then destroyed the effect of his manly speech by sticking his thumb in his mouth.

Edgar only sucked his thumb when he was frightened. She said quietly, "Go back to bed, Edgar. Everything's all right, and we'll try to be more quiet."

"Wait." Morgan looked Edgar over. When her son stared at him with a trace of fear, Morgan softened his expression and went down on one knee. "Good evening to you, my boy."

With mixed emotions, she watched Morgan examine Edgar's features. She wasn't sure she wanted Morgan to know he had a son—not after what he'd accused her of. Even if he was telling the truth and Darcy had spoken such lies about her, how could Morgan have believed them?

"Your name is Edgar?" Morgan asked.

"Yes, my lord." Edgar's eyes were round as saucers as he stared at the big stranger.

A faint smile touched Morgan's lips. "You needn't call me 'my lord.'"

Taking his thumb out of his mouth, Edgar cocked his head to one side. "But I call Uncle Darcy 'my lord.'"

Morgan's smile faded. "That's because . . . 'Uncle' Darcy is a lord. I'm not."

"What should I call you then?"

"'Sir' would do nicely, I suppose."

"Yes, sir."

"I've seen your mother, and now I've met you, but where is your father?"

Lettice cursed under her breath. Must he torment poor Edgar like this? She stepped forward to intercede, but Morgan gave her a hard glance that froze her.

Edgar shifted from foot to foot and stared down at the steps. "I haven't a father, sir." He screwed up his face into a frown. "Other children do, I know. Is it odd that I have no father? I mean, Mother says Uncle Darcy is as good as a father."

Morgan visibly tensed. "And do you like Uncle Darcy?"

Edgar's face brightened. "Oh yes, very much. He brings me lovely presents. And he likes to play quoits. Do you like to play quoits?"

"Of course."

Lettice could stand it no more. "Edgar, it's time for you to go back to bed. It's very late."

Morgan stayed the child with one hand. "Only one more question, and then you must do as your mother says." His voice shook. "How old are you?"

Lettice closed her eyes and sighed.

"I'm five. My birthday was this past May Day. We always have a jolly time. I'll be six years old next May Day, and a very big boy."

Morgan remained silent an endless moment. She could almost see him figuring the dates.

After scrutinizing Morgan carefully, Edgar blurted out, "Would you like to come to my birthday party?"

Morgan stood up and patted Edgar on the head, but the pat turned into a caress before he drew back his hand. "I should love to."

Lettice bit her lip to keep from crying. "Go to bed, Edgar," she choked out, and this time the boy obeyed.

As soon as they heard the upstairs door shut, Morgan whirled on her, eyes alight. "Does Northcliffe know that Edgar is my son?"

She turned away, trying to hide the emotions she knew must be blazing in her face. "Who said that Edgar is your son?"

"Don't lie to me. I can look in his face and tell he's my child."

Her only answer was a barely stifled sob.

Coming up behind her, he made her face him. "Does Northcliffe know?"

"No! Why in God's name do you think I'm here? Why do you think I've been with him all this time?"

He stared at her, uncomprehending.

"When the press gang took you," she whispered, "I had just realized I was pregnant. And on that same day, the old earl dismissed me without a reference for 'consorting with radicals' and not properly watching out for Lady Juliana." Her voice rose. "I was with child, and without a position or family, and you were nowhere to be found!"

She planted her hands on her hips. "So when Darcy asked me to be his mistress, what do you think I said? 'No, my lord, I'd rather take my chances that some fool would hire a pregnant woman'?'No, my lord, I prefer to wait endlessly for my lover while my child and I starve'?"

Rage made her voice shake. "What would you have had me do, Morgan? What grand plan had you made for me, in case you were punished for your illegal activities?"

He stared at her, clearly stunned. "The old earl dismissed you? But Darcy said you betrayed me in order to keep your position!"

"I didn't betray you. I never would have. But my position was precarious, and my association with you was all it took to have me lose it!"

The color drained from his face. "Good Christ, I never dreamed . . . You didn't tell me you were pregnant . . . I didn't know . . ."

"I had only just found out myself. But even if you'd known, would you have stopped what you were doing?"

Pacing the room, he muttered, "I don't know . . . perhaps . . ."

"And another thing," she bit out. "Why in God's name would I have betrayed you to Darcy, when I was carrying your child? I'd have been a fool to endanger my child's father!"

Morgan flinched, then turned to stare at her, the truth dawning on him. "So Northcliffe lied. You had nothing to do with the impressment."

"I told you, I knew nothing of it!"

Remorse shone in Morgan's eyes. "Devil take it, I'm sorry. I'm so sorry, love. I . . . I didn't believe him at first. I truly didn't." He paused. "But you don't know what hell Rhys and I went through. Our captain flogged his men at the slightest provocation. Rhys suffered through many floggings. Fortunately, I had only a flogging or two once the captain discovered I was a good cook. That was my salvation."

She stared at him wide-eyed. He'd suffered. She could see it in his eyes. "I've heard life on a man-of-war is horrible."

"Aye," he clipped out. "And after a while you start to hate anyone and anything that put you there."

Her anger had dimmed, but the hurt burned even brighter. "Even your 'true love'?"

He closed his eyes against the accusation in her voice. "Especially your true love, if you think she betrayed you. Please forgive me for doubting you. I see how wrong I was." Then his eyes shot open, and his jaw tightened. "But Northcliffe is also responsible for keeping us apart. He told me that you'd betrayed me."

She thought of the Darcy she knew, the one who could be infinitely kind. "I don't understand it. He has always treated me well."

"Don't you see?" Morgan stepped forward. "He'd probably been making plans to steal you from me for a long time. That's why he got rid of me."

She couldn't deny the logic of his words. Darcy had never hidden his desire for her. And he'd been right there, ready to make her his mistress after the earl had dismissed her. What she'd construed as an act of kindness had been plotted out from the beginning.

"He was obviously in love with you," Morgan said tersely, "so much in love he'd have done anything to get you."

A tear fell onto her cheek. "He has always said he loves me to desperation. It frightens me sometimes, how much."

Morgan clasped her shoulders. "The question is, are you in love with him?"

She averted her face. "That hardly matters. He's been so kind—"

"Taking away your sweetheart, the father of your son? Is that 'kind'?"

She lifted her tearstained face to his. "I have trouble thinking of him that way. You say he did this terrible thing, but I've never seen that side of him."

He obviously didn't like that answer. "If you won't tell me what you feel for him, can you tell me what you feel for me, after all these years?"

The question shouldn't have taken her by surprise, but it did. And even more surprising was her inability to form a coherent answer. "I honestly don't know."

His hands tightened on her. "I think you do. I think you're merely afraid to answer. Darcy has made a comfortable place for you here, and your misguided sense of loyalty makes you think you owe him for that. But I'm not talking about loyalty or kindness. I'm talking about love."

She wanted to hide her raw emotions, but he caught her chin and made her look at him.

"When you opened that door tonight," he persisted, "in that first second when you saw me, there was joy in your face. Was it born of love? That's all I need to know."

She closed her eyes, hoping to avoid the question until she could ponder her answer. Did she dare tell him the truth? And if she did, what would that mean . . . for her . . . for Edgar . . . for Darcy?

He gave her no time to think. Before she could free herself, she felt his lips on hers, gentle, soft, and every bit as sweet as she remembered.

He still smelled of bay rum, and his mouth still covered hers with blatant possessiveness. She started to draw back, but he clutched her head, holding her immobile as he moved his lips over hers, coaxing them apart until she opened to him, letting him plunge his tongue into her mouth.

His kiss was utterly sensual and as exciting as a kiss ought to be. It seemed to go on forever. When he finally pulled back, her breath came hard and fast, and she was even more confused. How could he still make her blood sing, even after all the time she'd spent with Darcy?

He stared at her, triumph in his eyes. "You do still love me. No matter what you say, I know it. I feel it in my bones."

She hid her face in his shirt, feeling both shame and joy at his words.

"Come with me tonight, Lettice," he whispered against her hair. "Let me make you my wife. Let me care for you . . . and our son."

It took every ounce of her will to resist the plea in his voice, the tempting comfort of his arms. But she couldn't simply wrench Edgar away from his home without giving it careful thought. Nor could she pay Darcy back with such treachery after he'd cared for her. She owed him a chance to explain.

"I need some time, Morgan. I need to speak to Darcy—"

"And listen to more of his lies?"

"At least he took care of me."

"If he hadn't had me impressed," Morgan gritted out, "I would have been the one taking care of you."

"I know." What a coil this was. How could she untangle it without hurting someone? "Still, I owe him a great deal."

Morgan's scowl was etched with pain. "And what of me? Am I to lose you again, because he was here when I couldn't be?"

"Nay!" When his scowl was replaced by a hopeful look, she added, "Come again tomorrow. By then, I'll have spoken to Darcy. And I'll have made my decision."

He looked as if he'd argue, then clamped his mouth shut and strode for the door. But he paused there to stare her down. "Listen well, Lettice. I'm not going to disappear this time. So no matter what decision you make about Northcliffe, I shan't give you up easily. Nor my son. I want you both, and I'll fight for you. Because I know you want me, too. And until that changes, I'll brave any obstacle Northcliffe throws at me to have you."

He went out into the night, leaving her breathless and excited. Pray God he meant what he said. Because despite her indebtedness to Darcy, despite her son's feelings, she wanted Morgan, too.

More than anything she'd ever wanted before.

From where he sat in the library, Rhys heard the clock strike two, but he ignored it and poured himself another glass of brandy. His head ached, his eyes throbbed, yet he welcomed the liquor as it seared his throat.

He should go to bed. Tomorrow he and Juliana would travel to Llynwydd, and he'd need a clear head for that. And for his next bout with his wife.

Groaning, he stared into the flames. His wife. A curse on the witch and her delectable body! What spell had she put on him?

He'd only meant to frighten her, to make her know she could never again ignore him. Instead she'd turned his lesson into a seduction, tempting him to make love to her, to give her pleasure and seek his own pleasure with her.

By thunder, what had happened to him? Had he forgotten so easily all he'd suffered, thanks to her?

An image leapt into his mind, of Juliana standing tall and proud in her nakedness, even as he'd ordered her to lie on the bed. Her soft moan of pleasure echoed in his mind. Despite her anger, he'd aroused her, and remembering it made his loins grow heavy once more.

How could he desire her so fiercely after all she'd done? For the past year, he'd dreamed of this night, of how he would humiliate her and make her beg. Instead he'd been the one humiliated. He'd been the one to flee. Once he'd touched her, he'd been eternally lost.

Her wanton nature made him lose all control when he was with her. He'd forgotten she wasn't like other women. Even now, he could hear her telling him on their wedding night that she had impure blood because she found pleasure in his caresses.

The memory brought a smile to his lips before he caught himself. Damn it all, that had been part of the trouble tonight! All those sweet memories of the first time, when she'd willingly given him her body.

He gulped some brandy to purge his thoughts. By now, he should have lost his pleasant memories. Yet he could still remember their wedding night, and how it had felt to be inside that enveloping warmth—

The door opened. He turned, thinking perversely that he'd conjured her up, but Morgan walked in.

"So there you are." Rhys returned his gaze to the leaping flames. "I wondered where you'd gone off to."

"I went to see Lettice."

Rhys glanced at him. "And how was your faithless lover?"

Morgan's jaw tightened as he took the other chair near the fireplace. "I found her not to be faithless, after all."

With a snort, Rhys pushed the brandy decanter in front of Morgan. "So being another man's mistress isn't a sign of faithlessness?"

Morgan poured himself a glass of brandy. "Yes, she's Northcliffe's mistress. She's also the mother of a child born eight months after we left. His name is Edgar."

It suddenly occurred to Rhys that he'd never asked Juliana about children. But surely she'd have told him if their one union had produced a child. Still, he must question her on it tomorrow.

He spoke more unsteadily. "I suppose Lettice claims this Edgar is yours."

"I *know* Edgar is mine."

Rhys pulled the brandy decanter back. "Perhaps you shouldn't have any more of this. You're clearly foxed."

"If you'd seen him, you'd know he was, too. He's the very image of me, and he's the right age. Besides, she told me he was mine."

"She could have lied."

"Why do so?" Morgan scowled. "She has let Northcliffe think the child is his all these years, which is why the bastard provides for her. In telling me the opposite she's risking everything, since I could reveal the truth to him and ruin things for her. Why would she give me reason to do so?"

"You're going soft on me—ready to forgive her because she's given you a son. Have you forgotten what happened to us? Will you let her insinuate herself into your good graces, now that she has tired of Northcliffe?"

Morgan jerked his gaze from Rhys. "You're a cynical son of a bitch, you know that?"

"Aye, 'tis what kept me alive. And you, as I recall."

"'Tis also what's made you so blind with vengeance that you can't see the truth." Morgan shot to his feet. "Lettice is innocent of involvement in our impressment. And perhaps Juliana is, too. Perhaps Northcliffe concocted the scheme to separate not only me from the woman he coveted, but also his sister from an unworthy Welshman."

Rhys set down his glass. "I see it took little to erase your memory of the night we were impressed. *Someone* betrayed us—at least one of the women did, and probably both. I may be a cynic, but at least I'm not a besotted fool. I didn't fall for Juliana's tearful protestations of innocence."

Morgan began pacing. "I'd believe Lettice over the lies of that twisted sot Northcliffe. And you should believe Juliana over him, as well."

"It's hard not to believe him when he repeats the accusations to her face." Bitterness surged in Rhys anew. "Despite her calling him a liar, he was adamant about Juliana's participation. So even if—and I do mean if—your Lettice is innocent, Juliana is not."

"He still claims she got cold feet, and had us impressed to get out of the marriage?"

"Aye, claims it staunchly." He clenched his fist around the decanter. "So does his brother. And the innkeeper."

"Well, his brother would support anything he says. But the innkeeper—what did she say to *his* accusation?"

Rhys scowled. "Nothing. She 'didn't know' why he would lie. Just as she 'didn't know' who summoned her brothers to the inn in the middle of the night when no one knew where we were." He slid the decanter aside. "And she certainly 'didn't know' I was alive, which is why she was marrying her precious marquess."

"She denied that you'd sent her letters?"

"She claims Northcliffe never gave them to her."

"It's possible, isn't it, if his is a household where he gets the mail first?"

"Aye, it's possible her brother invented everything." Rhys jumped up from his chair. "But it's equally possible she's just trying to get out of things, as she always used to do."

"She was awfully young then."

Rhys stared into the fire. "She never trusted me. The night I proposed, she accused me of wanting to marry her to get Llynwydd."

"You can see how she might have thought that."

"But going behind my back to act on it? I don't blame

her for her vacillations, nor even her fickle character. I blame her for letting me go through hell because she was too cowardly to attempt getting out of the marriage some honorable way."

"That's not all you blame her for, is it? I daresay your anger would be much reduced if you'd returned to find her unmarried."

Rhys shot Morgan a furious glance. "Are you implying that I'm jealous?"

"Aren't you?"

"No. I'm angry that she planned to use my estate to buy that English noble for a husband. If she'd been innocent, she wouldn't have taken up with that damned marquess. She wouldn't have kept our marriage secret!"

"Did you ask her why she did?"

"She claims that some hired man of Northcliffe's found out I was dead. As for why she kept our marriage secret in the first place . . . she didn't say why, but she probably has a tale for that, too. It doesn't matter. Eventually I'll make her admit the truth."

"What if she has a valid explanation for everything? I wouldn't have believed Lettice was innocent, either, until she explained how she'd had to choose between starvation for her and Edgar, or an alliance with Northcliffe. I can't blame her for that."

Rhys stared into the fire. "Juliana's situation is different. I have the word of three people, two of them her damned brothers! Tell me, why in God's name would her own brothers lie about it when they know I would punish her for it?"

"*Do* you intend to punish her? All you said before was that you would take back Llynwydd and your wife. But what will you do with her now that you've got her? What kind of marriage can you have when you trust her so little?"

"What I do with Juliana is my business," he snapped.

"True. But let me give you some unsolicited advice. If, after maligning her character, you discover she's indeed innocent, you may find that after showing her so little faith, she has lost complete faith in you. What will you do then?"

"'That is indeed 'unsolicited advice,'" Rhys growled. "And unwelcome."

Morgan gave him a hard stare. "I only hope you're not making an irreparable mistake." He left the room, closing the door behind him.

Rhys cursed. "I'm not making a mistake."

So why did he wonder if Morgan might be right?

11

> *Despite what good comes from holding land,*
> *World's a treacherous dwelling*
>
> —PERYF AP CEDIFOR, "THE KILLING OF HYWEL"

A persistent clicking resonated through Juliana's dream, then dragged her from a deep sleep. With a groan, she opened her eyes and stared at the wall opposite her.

Where was she? This wasn't Northcliffe, or even Llynwydd.

Then memory flooded her. This was Rhys's town house.

Last night she'd decided the only way to continue was to turn this mad battle of wills into a civil marriage. That was the best she could hope for, with him hating her so. And much as she dreaded living like strangers, that was preferable to fighting him.

She was tired of battles. For years she'd battled her fears, then her grief over what had happened to Rhys. She'd fought her family to keep her place at Llynwydd, and she'd fought the creditors to get the estate on its feet.

When she'd decided to marry Stephen, she'd thought the battles would finally be over.

But thanks to her blasted brothers and their betrayal, she was now in the worst battle of all.

Closing her eyes, she willed back the hurt inside her. She could understand why Darcy lied to Rhys the first time—to keep Rhys away from her. She could even understand why he'd lied to her about Rhys's death, since he'd wanted her to marry Stephen. But why continue after Rhys's return?

None of what had happened the night of Rhys's impressment made sense. Darcy and Overton had clearly come to the inn earlier. But how had they known where to find her? Some faint memory of that night struggled to surface, but she couldn't bring it to mind.

Her brothers' betrayal made no sense, either. Darcy had always been ambitious and strict, but he'd also had moments of kindness. When she was five she'd drawn flowers all over Papa's legal papers with his best ink pen, and while Papa had ranted and sworn, Darcy had hidden her in his closet. He'd always looked after her.

Last night, he hadn't been looking after her. Not at all. She must find out why.

Feeling better now that she had a course of action, she pushed herself into a sitting position—and saw Rhys.

He was just inside the door, his gaze on her. Barefoot and wearing only an open-throated shirt and tight breeches, he looked more like a pirate than a squire, especially when he watched her with a dangerously hooded gaze.

"I came to see if you were up. Your mother sent your clothes this morning. I'll have them brought to you. We'll be leaving soon, and you'll probably want breakfast." His words were crisp as his gaze drifted down.

Too late she realized she was wearing only her shift, which hung low over her bosom.

With a blush, she dragged the sheet up to her chest. "How long have you been standing there? And why didn't you knock?"

"Why would I knock at my own bedchamber?"

"To be polite, perhaps? You do remember courtesy, don't you?"

Her boldness seemed to startle him. Then a dark smile crossed his lips. "I remember lots of things. One of them is how enticing you used to look, all curled up in your bed at Northcliffe. I wanted to see if my memory served me correctly."

His soft words took her off guard. The thought of Rhys watching her sleep made her feel trembly and warm inside. "And did it?"

"No." He stepped forward. "You're much more enticing than I remembered."

His hot gaze alarmed her. She didn't want a repeat of last night. Best to get him off the dangerous subject of his desire for her. "I heard voices in the hallway late last night. Did you have a visitor?"

His expression grew shuttered. "Morgan came to tell me about his visit to Lettice."

"He returned with you? That's wonderful! Lettice must be thrilled." Then she remembered Lettice's circumstances.

"I mean, she must be happy he survived the navy. Though I suppose everything's different between them now."

"Morgan doesn't think so." Rhys snorted. "He means to continue where they left off, if she'll have him. That damned child of hers instantly grabbed his sympathies."

Rhys probably thought Morgan should torment his former love for getting involved with another man.

She shifted her gaze to the curtained window. It reminded her there was a world outside his house, outside his presence. 'Twas the only thing that kept her emotions even.

"I have a question for you," he said into the silence.

"Yes?" She couldn't look at him.

"Did you . . . was there . . ." He paused, seeming to struggle for words. "Did we have a child, too?"

The quiet yearning in his voice shocked her so much that she merely shook her head no.

"You mustn't lie about this," he choked out. "If we had a child, I need to know."

Pain settled sickly in her belly. "I haven't lied to you about anything. And I certainly wouldn't lie about that. Did anyone mention children last night, when you were wresting me away from my family? Don't you think they would have?"

"Actually, I thought you might have sent the babe off to be raised elsewhere." When she swung her gaze to his, anger boiling up in her, he added, "If you did, I won't hold it against you. I just need to know the truth so I can regain my child."

"You don't want truth. You only want more crimes to

lay against me." Her voice dropped to a ragged whisper. "Have you no good memories of our time together? Did the floggings beat them so completely from your mind that you could think I'd send away my own child to be raised by strangers?"

He flinched. "You kept our marriage secret. I didn't expect that. And to keep it a secret, you'd have to hide any child of our union."

She leapt from the bed, not caring that she wore only her shift. "If I'd had a child, I wouldn't have kept our marriage a secret! I'd have shouted it from the rooftops."

"You didn't need a child for that." He balled his hands into fists. "You should have done it anyway, instead of pretending it never happened."

"If I'd wanted to pretend it never happened, I would have had it annulled."

His eyes narrowed. "You didn't have the marriage certificate, and the bishop wouldn't have let you, while he was alive."

She snorted. "Neither of those things would have stopped my father. Papa had the power to force your godfather into making the entire thing disappear." She jabbed a finger at her own chest. "*I* kept him from it. I told them I'd spread the story of my elopement throughout the land if they attempted an annulment."

"You should have done that anyway." His eyes were alight with outrage. "Instead, you hid it like some shameful secret."

"Aye, I did." How different things would be now, if she hadn't. "But Rhys, remember my youth. I'd been wedded and bedded for only a night, then told that my husband was lost to me for years, if not forever." Her voice caught. "And I knew exactly what impressment entailed—that you could easily die at sea."

She turned toward the window, fearing the condemnation she'd find in his expression. "It was hard enough for me to stand up to them and say I wouldn't allow an annulment. You weren't there to give me strength and protect me from my family's anger. So when Darcy suggested . . ."

Oh Lord, she'd forgotten how much Darcy had shaped her behavior. He'd orchestrated it all so well, and in her grief and uncertainty, she'd fallen in with his plans easily. He'd wanted her to hide the marriage so there'd never be a question of her going back to it. And when she'd stubbornly held on to her hopes, Darcy had cut them off by paying an investigator to say Rhys was dead.

Darcy had cold-bloodedly betrayed her, and she hadn't even known it. Tightness built in her chest as she stared blindly at the heavy green brocade in front of her.

"What did your damned brother suggest?" Rhys prodded.

She swallowed back a sob and faced him. "He said there was no point to proclaiming my marriage when you might never return. He pointed out that I might never know if you survived the navy. If you died, who would tell me? Why should I ruin my life, he said, when 'twould be better to wait and see what happened?"

"You mean, to wait and hope that I never returned." Rhys's face wore a look of betrayal so deep, she wondered if anything she said could ever erase it.

Still, she had to say it all. "Perhaps Darcy hoped for that. I never did. But when the investigator Darcy hired for me said you were dead—"

"A pat addition to your story," he muttered. "Except for one thing. There was no evidence of any death for your supposed investigator to find."

"I realize that now. Darcy obviously paid the man to tell me you were dead."

"Can you show me this investigator?"

She scowled. "What do you think? Since my brother's persisting in his lies, he's certainly not going to allow someone he hired to refute them in my defense."

"How convenient for you."

She flinched. "Why won't you believe me?"

"Because you never told your precious betrothed about your marriage, even when you supposedly believed yourself a widow. You did exactly as Darcy predicted—you hid your marriage so you could make a more advantageous one later."

"I didn't hide it for that reason!"

"*Any* reason was a betrayal of what we'd shared."

Guilt overwhelmed her. He was right. In a sense, she had betrayed him by listening to Darcy. "True. But I couldn't bear to face the scandal of an elopement when I had no husband to show for it. And Darcy played on that. He pointed out that I was neither widow nor wife, and that I'd be in that limbo forever unless I kept the marriage secret."

Rhys glanced away, but his jaw began to twitch.

"I was weak, Rhys. Not as weak as you've believed me

to be, but weak nonetheless." She weighed her next words, knowing they would make her even more vulnerable to him. But she had to make him see her side. "In truth, I prayed I'd find myself with child, for then I'd have had part of you with me. Then they'd have been forced to let me announce the marriage."

His gaze swung to her, sympathy sparking in it.

"I wanted your child so badly. When my courses came, I wept for two days."

She paused. The silence drew them in together, into a mourning for what might have been, what never was.

He let out a long-drawn breath. "So there was no child."

She shook her head, clamping down on the tears that waited to engulf her. The sorrow on his face tore at her. "That's when I began keeping the secret. I made them promise to let me await you at Llynwydd, and I moved there under the pretext of caring for my estate. But it was really to avoid their pressure on me to annul the marriage."

He gaped at her. "You awaited me at Llynwydd? For how long?"

She blinked. "I thought you knew. You seemed to know so much else. I've been living at Llynwydd all this time."

"I haven't been there since I reached Wales two weeks ago. I didn't want to go until everything was settled, so I could arrive as owner. I also didn't want anyone recognizing me and warning the family of my arrival. When I asked around, I was told it was closed up."

She nodded. "I closed it up a month ago, when I came to town to plan my engagement party. Until then, I'd been living there."

"As what? Obviously not as my wife."

"Nay, as the owner. 'Tis my property, you know."

His eyes blazed at her. "So you were happy to live in my estate, yet not to acknowledge our marriage."

It sounded so callous when he said it that she got defensive. "I would have been happy to acknowledge our marriage if I'd had any word from you saying you were alive. Or if the investigator hadn't proclaimed you dead."

"The letters." His face paled. "They went to Northcliffe Hall. And you were at Llynwydd."

Her heart began to pound. He understood. He did. "Aye. And Darcy obviously never gave them to me."

He pondered that for a moment. Then his face hardened. "Even if that's true, it doesn't change anything. You set out to keep this marriage a secret from the moment I was impressed, long before you would have expected to hear anything from me, all because you hoped to marry someone else later."

"Can't you understand what it was like for me? You said yesterday that you could forgive me for having second thoughts. So why can't you forgive me for being weak when I believed you were gone forever? I couldn't do anything but wait . . . without word, without hope for the future. So when the investigator told me you were dead, I felt free to let Stephen court me. And to accept his offer."

At the mention of Stephen, he stiffened. "Yes, and while you were preparing to turn over the fruits of my estate to another man, the damned English Navy was draining my lifeblood from me."

"I know. But you escaped, didn't you? And look at you

now. You're obviously successful and wealthy." Bitterness swelled in her. "You spent three years in America. If you'd come back then, instead of waiting—"

"I couldn't. I had no money and no desire to feel the hangman's noose about my neck. And I assure you, those three years in America weren't blissful and carefree." He stared her down. "I repaid the Americans for saving me by risking my life daily. I did it because I wanted to return and needed money to do so, and the most money was paid for the riskiest tasks."

The bleak abyss in his eyes made her ache to comfort him. But how did one comfort a wounded beast who bit anyone who ventured near?

"I won't say what I did," he went on. "You might tell your brothers and get me hanged despite my newly gained influence. But I can tell you this—there are wounds and scars on my body that your countrymen inflicted long after I left the navy."

He yanked back a handful of hair to reveal a long, jagged scar just above his right temple. "This was done by an English saber. I nearly died from it—I was completely unconscious for two weeks. But I survived the same way I survived everything else, by telling myself I had to live to regain what I'd lost: my wife, my home, my birthright. I had to live to repay you for your betrayal."

Stepping close to her, he lowered his voice. "You think to purge me of my anger with all your tales, but 'twas my anger that kept me alive—and I will honor its cry for vengeance."

It took all her strength to gaze into the harsh face that

showed the ravages he spoke of. But she managed it by remembering how that face had once smiled at her, the corners of his eyes crinkling in amusement.

Reaching up, she smoothed her fingers over his scar. "'Twasn't anger that kept you alive. Nor even your thirst for vengeance. 'Twas love. Love for your home. And yes, love for me. 'Tis the love you can't purge, and you hate that."

He froze as she trailed her fingers down his cheek, remembering when he'd welcomed her caresses. He reached to pull her hand away, but covered it instead. For a moment they remained locked that way, his rough hand engulfing her small one.

Then he drew her hand from his face. "You think all your soft words and your touch will save you from me, don't you?" His breath came hard and fast, but he still clasped her hand. "You think it'll make me forget that I found you betrothed to another upon my return, that you hid our marriage from the world, that you toyed with my life without one thought for the consequences."

He lowered his face until it was inches from hers. "It won't, I assure you. No matter what you say, I know you for what you are. And one day you'll beg my forgiveness for what you did to me."

She wasn't as cowed by him as before. She knew now what he would do, and what he wouldn't. "I've told you why I behaved as I did, and you've seen for yourself how callous Darcy has become. If you still choose to think ill of me, I can't change that."

She drew a deep breath. "But regardless of what you

think I did to you, I'm your wife. And thanks to your stubbornness, I'll be your wife forever. So don't you think 'twould be better to find a way to live amiably together? Will gaining your 'vengeance' erase your wounds or ease your pain?"

She waited breathlessly, holding his gaze.

He thrust her from him with a curse. "You expect me to take up where we left off. To act as if you hadn't betrayed me. To forget."

"Nay. But I think you're a practical man. You've seen war, and you know peace is preferable." She sought for words that would bridge the chasm between them, that would spark the good memories inside him.

And words she'd read only a few weeks ago came to her. She said in Welsh, "You know how to 'fashion peace, which is richer than gold.' You know that 'Mercy will never die or grow old.' It's time to fashion peace, don't you think? Time to find mercy in your heart."

He looked stunned silent by her quotation from *The Black Book of Carmarthen*. In his quest for "vengeance," he'd forgotten all the pleasant hours they'd spent discussing poetry and books, all the sweetness between them.

So this was what she must do. Remind him of the sweetness. She must uncover the old Rhys.

His face mirrored his torn emotions. "You're wrong," he murmured in Welsh. "I don't know how to 'fashion peace' anymore. I don't even know what peace is."

She held out her hand to him. "Then let me teach it to you. Let us learn peace together."

For a moment, he wavered with his gaze fixed on her

outstretched hand. Then he turned away. "Get dressed. We leave in an hour." And he was gone.

She stared after him. Despite his commands, she now knew the truth. Inside, he ached for love.

Hope for them sparked within her. She would feed that spark with the tinder of her own precious memories. And perhaps one day soon, the flame would melt the ice in Rhys's heart.

Wiping the sweat from his brow, Rhys shifted in the saddle and looked back as the coach lumbered into view, raising clouds of dust behind it. Juliana was in that coach, riding alone because he'd chosen to accompany the vehicle on horseback.

He twisted the reins about his hand until the leather bit into his gloves. Two hours of hard riding had taken its toll on a head that throbbed from last night's brandy and a stomach that churned as badly as when he'd eaten maggot-ridden hardtack.

Yet he couldn't make himself join her for the last half hour, not even to lie back on soft cushions and close his eyes. Joining her meant enduring her quiet, long-suffering presence, and that he couldn't do.

But this solitude wasn't much better. No matter how hard he rode, he couldn't push her words from his mind.

You know how to fashion peace. This morning he'd expected her to fight, to snap and shout at him. When she did, it was easy to think of her as a light-headed, spoiled flirt who'd ruined his life on a whim. It was easy to remind himself of all she'd cost him.

But when she met him with Welsh poetry, so perfectly spoken that it might have been a bard intoning the words about "peace" and "mercy," all his convictions about her grew shaky.

Then memories crept in. Like that night long ago when she'd sat on his lap and recited the whole of "Praise of a Girl," the Welsh words flowing from her like rich music. Her face had glowed from the pleasures of poetry spoken aloud, and she'd taken delight in the kisses he'd given her after each stanza. There'd been no hesitation in her, no sign of dislike for his penniless state or his Welshness.

Her explanations this morning simmered in Rhys's brain. Her family's pressure on her to have the marriage annulled . . . Darcy's urging her to keep the marriage a secret . . . her reasons for her betrothal . . . All of it rang too much of truth.

He no longer knew what to believe. And every time he thought of her defending that handsome marquess, it made his blood boil.

But when she'd spoken of not having their child . . . The yearning shining in her eyes couldn't have been false. Even now, it sparked a deep desire for something he'd never wanted before.

His child. Their child. Would their children be pale as cream like their mother, or dark like their father? Would their hair capture the sun like Juliana's or reflect the black night like his own?

Thoughts of children led him to thoughts of how children were made. Of how she'd looked in that thin shift that barely veiled the dusky rose of her nipples or the auburn curls below her belly. How her heady lavender scent still made him want to bury his face in her hair . . . in her neck . . . between her legs.

"*Cer i'r diawl!*" She drove him as mad with need as ever. And he was woefully tired of fighting it.

Perhaps he shouldn't. Because she was right about one thing: He didn't want her to lie there like a whore and let him spend himself inside her. He wanted her moaning beneath him, lifting her mouth to his of her own accord to find her pleasure.

Aye, he wanted her willing. He remembered so well how sweet it had been when she was willing. And he wouldn't be giving up anything, to have her willing. It was what they both wanted.

Her words came back to him. *Fashion peace*, eh? Let them fashion peace in the marriage bed. She was right: They had a lifetime together. And as long as he made it clear who would be master in their house, they could have pleasure together.

Of course, he wouldn't let those pleasures negate her duty to make amends. He wouldn't trust her, but he could bed her as often as he wished, and if she drew enjoyment from it, that was even better.

And why should he resist her anyway? He had a right to enjoy his wife's body.

Just then he topped the hill that looked down on Llynwydd, and his breath caught in his throat. Home. He'd finally come *home*.

He was glad that he hadn't come until he could enter the estate as owner, for it made the pleasure more intense.

Llynwydd was his. Every garden, every field, every tenant farm. No one could deny that any longer.

He halted to savor it—the massive wrought-iron gates, the expanse of outbuildings, and the thriving orchards of plum and peach. A lump grew in his throat. The yews his father had planted when Rhys was barely eight were so tall now.

Then there was the squire hall itself—a block of aged brick flanked by the newer wings his grandfather had put in. Sunlight glinted off the white painted railings of the entrance steps, and the oak door looked as solid as ever. At last he could ride up to that very door and walk into the halls of his childhood home with impunity. He had his birthright back, and not even the treacherous St. Albans brothers could wrest it from him.

But Juliana already had.

A knot twisted his gut. After living here all this time, she must have changed things to suit her whims. Some changes were evident from here: a new tile roof on the coach house, expanded stables, and the vine house that showed she'd revived the practice of growing cucumbers and melons at Llynwydd. What else had she altered?

He straightened in the saddle. It didn't matter. Llynwydd was his now. If her changes were good, he'd let them stand. But *he'd* make that decision, not her. She'd soon learn he was master here. When she accepted the role of dutiful wife—and when she came willingly to his bed— he'd accept the peace she offered.

But not until then.

12

I'd go back to my father's country,
Live respected, not lavish nor meagerly,
In sunlit Mon, a land most lovely, with
Cheerful men in it, full of ability.

—GORONWY OWEN, "THE WISH"

When Rhys opened the carriage door for her he was smiling, which made Juliana wary. She wanted to believe he'd considered her words and found them sensible, but given the glint of calculation in his eyes, she doubted that. Yet something had changed in him since this morning.

Behind him, the servants were scurrying out of the entrance door to line up along the railings of the stairway. There weren't as many as usual—when she'd closed the house, she'd had to let some of them go—but their well-scrubbed faces and impeccably clean attire made her proud. At least Rhys couldn't accuse her of hiring a slovenly staff.

No sooner had Juliana alighted from the carriage than her housekeeper, Mrs. Roberts, came rushing up. "Milady, we weren't expecting you or we'd have readied the house. I'm afraid everything is still under covers and all in a muddle." She cast Rhys a quizzical glance. "But it won't take us long to get all in readiness, if you're wanting to stay."

"Thank you," Juliana said. "We will . . . that is . . . Mr. Vaughan and I—"

"What my wife is trying to say is, we'll be in residence at Llynwydd from now on, aside from occasional trips to Carmarthen or London."

Mrs. Roberts's jaw dropped. "In residence?" Then, as the rest of Rhys's words registered, she stammered, "Your wife?" She looked to Juliana for confirmation. "Milady?"

Rhys did the same, his smile widening. Obviously, he planned to enjoy watching her announce her secret marriage to her staff.

Juliana sighed. No telling what Mrs. Roberts, with her vivid imagination and penchant for gossip, was thinking. "This is Squire William Vaughan's only son, Rhys. As you've probably heard from other members of the staff, his family were the previous owners of Llynwydd." She swallowed hard. "Mr. Vaughan is also my husband."

As Mrs. Roberts continued to gape at her, Rhys leaned close to whisper, "Very good, wife. Finally you're learning some compliance."

She scowled at him, but he'd already turned to the astonished Mrs. Roberts. "You are the housekeeper?" he asked in Welsh.

It was the first time Juliana had heard him speak entirely in Welsh since his return, and he clearly had an accent. But the housekeeper seemed surprised to hear him use Welsh at all. "Aye, sir," she said quickly. "I've been with Lady Juliana for six years."

"After Papa acquired the estate," Juliana put in, "he dismissed your father's servants and hired his own. Once I moved here I hired as many back as I could, but most had already found other positions, including your father's housekeeper."

He took a moment to appraise the staff ranged stiffly down the stairs.

Juliana wondered what they were thinking, since they'd all known Stephen. The few servants who'd worked for Squire Vaughan might recognize Rhys, but she doubted it.

Flashing Mrs. Roberts a smile, Rhys drew Juliana out of earshot of the servants. "'Tis best that we get this over with now, so here's what I want you to do. Announce to them, as you did to Mrs. Roberts, that I am your husband and that we've been married for six years. Explain that you thought me lost at sea, which is why you never said anything. They're going to hear rumors anyway—"

"Because you insisted on making this whole thing public."

His eyebrows drew together. "Aye. If I'd confronted you and your brothers privately, I might not have lived to tell anyone else about it." As she opened her mouth to protest that horrible statement, he let out a frustrated breath. "For once, just do as I say, will you? Better to have it over with."

When she still hesitated, he pulled her closer to murmur, "And for God's sake, wipe that expression from your face. You look like a virgin facing the sacrificial knife. Try to appear as if you're actually glad to have your husband back."

"If you're so concerned about how this is done, why don't *you* tell them? Embarrassing public announcements are your forte, not mine."

Amusement glittered briefly in his eyes. "At present, their loyalty is to you. They're liable not to accept me if I thrust myself forward in your place."

"Remind me why should I help you gain their acceptance?"

"You said you wanted peace. Show me that you mean it." His voice hardened. "Because if you refuse to support me in this, you won't have a moment's peace, I assure you."

Glancing at the servants, she realized she had no choice. A battle before the staff was unthinkable. Aside from being mortifying, it would only gain her more enmity from Rhys. Nor would it help matters to have the servants confused by who was in charge. This was between him and her, and she wouldn't give him the satisfaction of seeing her lose her dignity before the staff.

Besides, her people would be loyal to her no matter what Squire Arrogance told her to say, so it wouldn't hurt to acquiesce to his wishes.

With a quick nod, she faced her staff. He settled his hand on the back of her waist, and the slight pressure of his fingers against her spine made her more aware than ever of the reality of their marriage.

If only he were touching her with the tenderness of a husband who cared for his wife. But no, his touch was to control, to aim her in the direction he wanted. And for now, his direction was the only one to take. So she announced her marriage, trying to sound sincere while she fought to ignore the warm hand at her back.

Then he stepped in. "None of you need fear for your positions as long as you're doing your jobs well. But I may change how the household is managed, depending on what I find when I tour the grounds and meet with the housekeeper and agent. At a minimum, there will be more staff. In the meantime, if you have a question about the running of the household, you are to come to me. Is that understood?"

When the servants bobbed their heads, cowed by his commanding stance and firm voice, Juliana suppressed a snort. If he thought peace would be achieved by making her powerless in her own house, he was in for a surprise. She wouldn't let him tear down everything that was good in Llynwydd out of peevishness.

"That's all for now." Rhys pointed to two footmen. "You and you, unload the coach. And Mrs. Roberts, I wish to see you and the agent in the study in an hour. Bring with you the account books and whatever other documents you think might need my perusal. The rest of you are dismissed."

Their faces mirroring their questions, the servants returned to their duties.

"Shall we go in now, wife?" Rhys asked.

His assumption that he'd won made her want to shake him. She kept her temper long enough to enter the house, but as soon as they passed into the drawing room, she pivoted away from him. "There's something you should know before you start changing everything to suit your fancy. Ever since I've been managing this estate, it has gained steadily in profits, which was no small feat. Your father left the place sorely run-down. If it hadn't been for me—"

"I know." He drew off his leather gloves and dropped them on a shrouded table. "Father ran this estate into the ground. He gambled and drank too much. After his death, I'd planned to restore it to its former glory." His tone grew acid. "Of course, my impressment altered that plan for a while."

Folding his hands behind his back, he scanned the room. Although the furniture was covered with white and yellow cloths, he had to be noticing the new Chinese-patterned wallpaper and the fireplace, whose chipped sandstone facade had been replaced with black marble.

"I can see you've done much to restore the place. And for that, I'm in your debt." His gaze snapped back to her. "But 'tis my estate now, and I will see to its care. Which may require some changes."

"Fine." Let the blasted fool think he was running everything. Once his back was turned, her servants would ask her in private what to do. And she'd have no qualms in telling them.

Aye, Squire Arrogance, we'll see how far you get trying to manage this estate without me.

A frown creased his forehead. "You act as if this surprises you. But surely you'd anticipated what would happen upon my return." He cast her a mocking smile. "After all, you told me that you waited for me those first few years. Hadn't you realized I would take charge of my estate upon my return? Or were you so sure I'd never come back that you didn't consider that?"

She caught herself before she reacted in anger. Truth seemed to work better. Tilting up her chin, she softened her voice. "Whenever I thought of it, I imagined you knocking at the door and me opening it. I imagined you taking me in your arms and kissing me until I ached from it, then recounting all your hardships so I could soothe them away." When he looked taken aback by her words, she added, "My dream never passed much beyond that."

His gaze locked with hers, and it took all her strength to meet its intimidating force. He stepped closer until he stood only inches from her, a myriad of emotions flitting over his face—disbelief, confusion . . . desire.

"Your dream never passed beyond kissing?" He stroked her cheek with the backs of his fingers.

The unexpected caress gave a turn to her words that she hadn't entirely intended. Shivers coursed down her spine, then made her tremble. Oh bother, there it was again, that same longing he'd always made her feel. Why hadn't the years crushed it to bits? Why did he alone hold the key to her desire?

An urge toward self-preservation hit her and she backed away, but he caught her around the waist, drawing her to him until he'd fitted her snugly against his lean, hard body. "I have been lax, haven't I?" he whispered, nuzzling her temple. "Already I've been with you several hours today, and I haven't yet kissed you."

Before she could protest that she didn't want him to, he bent his head to brush his lips over hers. After last night she hadn't known what to expect, but it certainly wasn't this.

Confused by the change in him, she stood frozen, and he took advantage of her surprise to toy with her mouth, meeting her lips then sliding away, enticing her with his gentle playing, never quite settling in one place. His hot breath mingled with hers until she lowered her defenses, her body going limp and her eyelids sliding closed.

Then he covered her mouth with his so warmly that her pulse began to race. As her breath caught in her chest, she realized she was sinking fast, falling into the quicksand of seduction he'd always been so good at creating. But when she tried to draw away, he captured her head in his hands, holding her still.

Then the kiss began in earnest. He brought his thumbs down to caress her throat as his mouth fed on hers, coaxing her to soften. In a sensuous invitation to deepen the kiss, he ran the tip of his tongue along the seam of her closed lips.

I can't let him do this.

But it was too much like the dream she'd spoken of. With a sigh, she parted her lips, then heard him groan as he buried his tongue inside her mouth.

She stifled her own groan, but couldn't stifle the memories he conjured up as he drove his tongue into her mouth over and over, marking his possession of her as surely as he'd marked his possession of Llynwydd moments ago. This was not like last night's hard kisses. This was seduction, pure and simple.

And as his hands slid down to clasp her shoulders and

hold her tight against him, the lonely years melted away. Once more they were in her bedchamber at Northcliffe Hall, and he was kissing her for endless hours while touching her with brazen caresses that had made her young, virginal body sing.

Now, however, his caresses were bolder. He covered her breast, kneading it beneath his palm. Despite the layers of clothing that separated her from his intimate touch, she could feel her nipple harden.

This time she couldn't restrain her groan, which brought an answering one from him. He stroked down to cup her bottom and pulled her against him so she could feel his arousal. "Ah, *cariad*," he murmured. "You see what you do to me?"

The endearment shot her arousal to new heights. He *did* care, no matter what he said. He was still hers. Throwing her hands about his neck, she gave herself up to him, to the poetry of his mouth plundering hers in an ancient rhythm more compelling than that of the bards, to the sweet slide of his hands relearning every contour of her body.

Before she knew it, he was drawing aside the robings of her dimity Levite gown and inching down her corset and shift to bare her breast to his fingers. Then his mouth left hers to trail kisses down her throat as he flicked his thumb over her nipple until she whimpered, arching her head back to give him better access.

She was waiting breathlessly for the first touch of his mouth on her breast when a knock at the open door behind her brought her to her senses.

Dear heaven, they'd been kissing here in front of God and everybody! With a violent blush, she pushed away from him and swiftly restored her clothing.

He released her reluctantly. "What is it?" he demanded of the interloper.

She glanced back to see a younger footman, David, blushing almost as furiously as she was. He had a tendency to knock first and look later; this would undoubtedly cure him of that.

"I-I'm sorry, sir," David stammered, "but I wasn't sure where to put the trunks."

"You haven't forgotten where the State Bedroom is, have you?"

"Of course not, sir. But I didn't know if . . . well, I mean, milady has been sleeping there and—"

"Put all the trunks in the State Bedroom. From now on, Lady Juliana will be sleeping there with me."

David's head bobbed again and he fled.

As soon as the doorway was clear, Juliana blurted out, "Did you have to be so . . . to imply . . . Oh heavens, they'll think that—"

"That I plan to share a bed with my wife?" Rhys raised an eyebrow. "I should hope they would realize that."

"But what kind of woman will they think I am, to share a bed with you the night after I'd pledged to marry Stephen?"

When his amusement vanished, she cursed herself for saying such a stupid thing.

He strode over to shut the door. When he faced her, his expression could have frozen fire. "They'll think you're my wife, and not the betrothed of some infernal marquess. They'll think I plan to bed my wife. Because that's precisely what I intend to do. Thoroughly and often. Beginning tonight."

Thoroughly and often. She suppressed the thrill his words gave her. "You may have the State Bedroom, but I won't share a bed with you. There are plenty of other rooms I can sleep in."

He settled an enigmatic gaze on her. "My parents slept in that bed together, and so shall we." Reaching out to skim the tip of his finger over the upper swells of her breasts, he lowered his voice to a silky murmur. "You know you want that. Don't deny you were willing just now. I daresay if I'd laid you down on that settee, you'd have been willing enough."

The crude, self-assured words shattered her hopes for peace between them. He saw her only as a receptacle for his urges, not as a wife.

"Perhaps I would have. But we'll never know, because next time I won't be so foolish." She ignored the hurt that snaked through her insides. She'd deal with that later.

"If you're wise, you'll use that beautiful body of yours to make amends, to soften my heart." He dragged his finger up her throat along the pulse, which cursedly quickened. "I'm very interested in seeing if our last joining was everything I remember."

"Why? I don't understand you. Last night kissing me made you angry, and today—"

"I want you in my bed." He tilted her chin up. "But I want you willing."

Blast him! To him, bedding her meant conquering her. But she wanted it to mean so much more. "You would make love to me, even though you think that I'm fickle? That I betrayed you?"

His mouth went taut. "One thing has nothing to do with the other. Fickle you may be, but you're also lovely and enticing. And you know how to appreciate pleasure. Why shouldn't we appreciate it together?"

Rubbing his thumb along her lower lip, he watched her with a secretive smile.

And despite herself, her breath quickened. Oh yes. She certainly knew how to appreciate pleasure. One touch and, like tinder held to a spark, she erupted into flame. He knew it, too. But that didn't change anything.

"What if I resist you? Will you then resort to force?"

His eyes glittered as blue as the icy waters of the Towy. "I've no need for that. You burn as much as I. And as you said this morning, we have many years ahead of us. Even you can't hold out for an eternity. One day you'll say yes."

"I won't."

"You will." He headed for the door, where he paused to look back at her. "And I'm betting you'll do it soon."

When he went out, she released the breath she'd been holding. Pray heaven he was wrong. Because if he came to her as he had the night of their wedding, and made love to her like *that*, she'd be lost forever.

13

Maybe so sharp is exile,
Not to love were more worth while.
—GORONWY OWEN, "AN INVITATION"

Looking up from the ledger, Rhys rubbed his tired eyes. He should close the windows and call for someone to light a fire in the grate; the room was growing chill and dim as nightfall approached. Soon it would be time for dinner. And after dinner, bed.

He slammed the ledger shut. For two hours he'd studied the management practices of his lovely wife, and he'd learned two disturbing things.

One, despite her youth and inexperience, Juliana had run the estate as efficiently as she'd claimed.

Two, he could think of nothing else but bedding her.

Yet judging from their encounter earlier in the day, he wouldn't be bedding her anytime soon.

He hadn't meant to be so obvious about what he wanted. Women didn't like being told they were desired only for their bodies. He'd planned to be smoother, to seduce her with compliments, even use poetry as he had years ago, when he'd been a starry-eyed fool in love.

But when she'd mentioned her beloved Stephen and reacted in such horror to sharing a bedchamber, he'd had to remind her that she was his wife—*not* Lord Devon's betrothed.

With another curse, he rose to pace the room. Why couldn't he do as he wanted with her? He couldn't bear to force her, and his attempt at seduction had ended with her even more determined to fight him. He knew she wanted him. And God knows he wanted her.

But *why?* As she'd said, why did he want her, when she'd taken six years of his life from him?

Because the damned woman had defied all of his expectations. He'd expected her to be either frightened of him or penitent. He'd expected her to throw herself on his mercy. He'd spent many an hour envisioning the penance he'd require of her before he allowed her a wife's privileges, and each scenario had included bedding her in various enjoyable ways.

In none of his dreams had she firmly declared her innocence. Or refused to share his bed. It drove him mad.

She was an enigma. She'd obviously put all her energy into caring for Llynwydd. He hadn't expected to find her living here, much less improving it. Few women controlled their own properties. Why had she? Merely to garner herself a titled husband?

He surveyed the study. Little had changed from when he'd spent his school holidays trying to put to rights what

Father had neglected. The mahogany desk was sturdy as ever, and the Indian rug still had many serviceable years left. The brass fender and irons were polished to a fine sheen, and the walnut wainscoting was clean of dust and cobwebs.

There was one addition—a stepladder at the end of the bookcase. He scanned the shelves at that spot, noting the novels by Fielding and Richardson, as well as several volumes of poetry by an assortment of poets—Donne, Pope, Dafydd Jones . . .

He spotted a particular gilded spine, and his eyes narrowed. Curious, he removed that book and several others, opening their covers to find his name written on the flyleaves.

They were his, but they hadn't been at Llynwydd. They'd been at Morgan's house when he'd been impressed. Had Juliana brought them here? And why?

Granted, she appreciated fine books as much as he, but the image of her going to Morgan's house to pack his belongings gave him pause. If she'd believed him out of her life forever, why had she bothered with something like that?

No matter what they say, I loved you then. I wanted to be your wife.

Yet she'd hidden her marriage even from Llynwydd's staff. She'd tried to marry again, for God's sake!

Still, everything she'd told him this morning seeped into his mind and he found himself seeking allowances for her behavior, reminding himself of her youth, of how easily her brothers might have manipulated her into doing the wrong thing.

A sobering thought struck him. Perhaps the truth lay somewhere between her version and Northcliffe's. Perhaps she'd balked at the marriage and summoned her brothers, but was pressured by them into letting him be impressed. He could understand why she wouldn't want to admit that.

He replaced the books on the shelf, wishing he knew how to find his way through this morass of lies and half-truths.

The sound of laughter wafted through the open window, and curious, he went over to look out at the pleasure garden below. The object of his torments knelt just beneath his window to clip roses, placing them in a basket held by a child.

Rhys caught his breath until he realized that the boy had to be at least eleven. No child of his. Or hers, either.

Then the child spoke in the lilting Welsh of a commoner. "So you've come back to Llynwydd for good?"

She smiled at him. "Yes. Are you pleased, Evan?"

Her perfect Welsh surprised Rhys again. It didn't fit with his image of a pampered English lady who balked at marrying a penniless Welsh radical.

Evan dug at the dirt with his bare toe. "I suppose. Are you?"

He sounded so hopeful that she leaned over and kissed his cheek. "Of course. I love Llynwydd. And I missed having you help me in the garden."

The lad reddened. "Mama said I shouldn't come and bother you just now, but I thought . . . well, you might need me about. To carry things and kill bugs."

Juliana chuckled. "And I bet you were curious to know why I'd come back."

"We *were* surprised, my lady. You said you weren't returning for a while. Then this afternoon Mrs. Roberts came and told Mama you were here with a husband, but not that man you went off to marry."

Juliana's lips tightened. "Mrs. Roberts is certainly quick, isn't she?"

"Do you think so? I don't. She's too old to be quick."

Rhys stifled a laugh. He'd judge Mrs. Roberts to be in her late thirties, and no doubt proud of her limber legs. But to an eleven-year-old, thirty was ancient.

When Juliana merely smiled, Evan grew fidgety. "So. Did you bring a different husband back or not?"

With a sigh, Juliana rose. "Yes, I did."

"Is he another stuffy Englishman, like that Lord Devon?"

"Hardly." She strolled down the walk toward the garden door as Evan followed her. "Do you remember the man I told you about? The one who went to sea?"

Rhys leaned half out of the window, straining to hear their words.

"Mr. Vaughan?" Evan asked.

"Aye. 'Tis he who is my husband."

Evan replied, but by then they were too far to make out what they said. With a frown, Rhys drew back from the window.

Why had she told the boy about him? Why keep him secret from the staff, yet reveal it to a young lad? And how much had she said?

Suddenly he heard footsteps approaching the study

and realized Juliana and Evan were coming his way. As the door opened he slid into the shadows to continue his eavesdropping.

"I have the paper here somewhere," Juliana was saying. "'Tis a shame it was spoiled by water. Are you sure you won't have an unspoiled piece?" She opened a desk drawer and rummaged about.

"Nay, thanks." With a wistful expression, Evan gave a heavy sigh. "As long as I tell Da I got paper from the rubbish heap, he lets me keep it. Good paper would make him suspicious. He'd ask what I was doing with it, make me tell him, and then take a brush to me for it."

Juliana drew the paper out. "For studying and writing? For trying to better yourself?"

"Da says I'll have to help my brother run the farm one day, and I shouldn't waste my time with foolishness like lessons." He folded the paper reverently and slid it into his grimy pocket.

"You know better, don't you?"

He ducked his head, but nodded.

She put her hand on his thin shoulder. "You ought to be in school. You've got a superior mind that would benefit from it."

The boy shrugged. "He needs me at the farm. He only lets me come here 'cause he thinks I'm helping you with the garden." A worried look crossed his face. "And he told me to be back before dark, so I best go."

"Perhaps if I spoke to him—"

"No!" The lad turned a pleading gaze on her. "'Twill only get me into trouble, my lady."

When Juliana sighed, Evan headed for the door. But he stopped to cast her an adoring look. "Thank you for the paper. 'Tis kind of you to do such things for the likes of me."

"I don't do it for kindness." She smiled. "I do it because you're my friend. And you know if you ever need anything, you can come to me. All right?"

He grinned. "Aye, my lady. I'll do that." Then he was out the door.

Rhys watched as she stared after the boy with longing, and his throat felt suddenly raw. She clearly yearned to have a child of her own.

And seeing her so soft and gentle with the lad when she bore nothing but distaste for her husband made Rhys wish he hadn't made her his enemy from the outset.

Then he stiffened. He'd merely behaved like anyone who'd been betrayed by his wife. He hadn't beaten her or attempted to divorce her. She ought to be glad of that.

But she didn't look glad. She looked . . . lost. With a sigh so heavy it wrenched him, she turned to the desk and ran her hand along the ledger, then studied the papers he'd laid out.

He shifted his feet and must have made some noise in the process, for her gaze jerked up and she spotted him in the shadows.

"Dear heaven!" When he stepped into the dim light, she said, "Blast it, you gave me such a start! I didn't realize you were here."

"I . . ." Damn, how was he to explain his eavesdropping? Instead he changed the subject. "Who's the boy?"

"Evan? He's the son of your tenant farmer Thomas Newcome."

Rhys nodded. "I remember Newcome. A bit of a hothead."

Her lips thinned. "Aye. And he doesn't understand the value of education."

"'Tis common for a farmer to feel that lessons are a waste of time."

"I know, but Evan is exceptionally bright. Before I started tutoring him he didn't read and write at all, and spoke only Welsh. In the four years since then, he has learned to read and write not only Welsh, but English and French as well. And he has begun to learn Greek."

"My God, how old is the boy?"

"Twelve. He has a facility for languages that's nothing short of amazing." She scowled. "And it's wasted, thanks to that father of his."

Rhys rubbed his chin. "Perhaps we should find a way to convince Newcome that his son would benefit from schooling. Surely we can come up with something that won't get the boy into trouble."

"You would do that?"

"Of course. It's to my advantage to have my tenants well educated."

She rewarded him with a brilliant smile that took him back to the first time he'd seen her smiling at him from the audience at the Sons of Wales meeting. It made something tighten in his chest.

"If you could get Evan into school, 'twould mean a great deal to me."

"I can see the boy is important to you. Do you mind if I ask why?"

"He's been my special charge ever since our gardener caught him stealing plums from the orchard. He was brought to me here for a reprimand. Instead, we ended up talking about the books in your library. He was terribly impressed."

She smiled to herself. "So I told him that his 'punishment' was to join me here every day for a month for a lesson in reading. And he's been coming a few days a week ever since. I pay him a small sum to help me in the garden, and then I spend most of the time teaching him. His father is pleased to have his son working for 'her ladyship,' and Evan gets an education, spotty though it is."

Rhys regarded her closely. This Juliana bore no resemblance to the timid, fickle woman he'd despised all these years. "That was very generous of you."

Her face flushed with pleasure, but she wouldn't look at him. "As you said, 'twas to my advantage to have the tenants well educated."

"Was it also to your advantage to run my estate with care and efficiency?"

The change of subject seemed to startle her. Nervously she ran her gloved finger along a bookshelf as if testing it for cleanliness. "What do you mean?"

"I've been over the books. I've talked at length with Mrs. Roberts and your agent, Geoffrey Moss, and they both made it clear you've succeeded in reversing the trend my father began. Why?"

Her smile was bitter. "I had to keep my dower estate in prime condition for my husband-to-be, didn't I?"

"I thought of that. But you could have done it from afar, through Moss." He gestured toward the bookshelves. "You certainly didn't have to gather my belongings from Morgan's house and bring them here. So why did you?"

She flashed him a defiant glance. "You know why. You simply don't want to believe the evidence of your eyes."

As he stood there, uncertain how to respond, she went to the door. "I'll see you at dinner."

Then she was gone, leaving him with an ache in his chest and a hundred new questions.

As jittery as a girl at her coming out, Juliana waited in the dining room for Rhys. She'd been uncertain what to do: Serve him a dinner to remember, the kind an exile would enjoy? Or serve him gruel to repay him for his distrust of her? In the end, her desire for peace and her pride in Llynwydd had won out.

Cook, one of the few members of the old staff, had told her that Rhys liked Welsh rabbit and *cawl*, so Juliana had insisted upon those. The table was set with the finest china and silver. She'd instructed the staff to be on their best behavior, to prove themselves as competent as she'd told Rhys they were.

She'd even dressed with particular care, wearing her periwinkle gown of jacquard striped silk and her best embroidered stomacher. She would show Rhys she could be a proper wife when she wanted.

If he couldn't appreciate it, then that was his loss and he truly was a boorish, unmannerly beast. And next time, she'd serve the gruel.

"I'm not late, am I?" his voice rumbled from the doorway.

Her heart fluttered. Clamping down on her nervousness, she faced him with a smile, determined to set a tone of pleasant cordiality.

That seemed to startle him, but he responded with the devastating smile that had once captured her heart. "That color suits you." He walked toward her. "You look lovely this evening."

To her surprise, he caught her hand and kissed it, then brushed his lips over the inside of her wrist. "Very lovely," he added as he lifted his head.

His gaze seared her with a heat that started a fire in her belly. Oh, why did he always do this to her?

"You look very well yourself," she managed.

"Careful now, such extravagant praise will turn me vain."

The words reminded her of the old teasing Rhys. Who still hadn't released her hand. "Then I'd best watch my compliments," she said lightly. "We can't have you strutting about in fuchsia breeches, like the fops in the Macaroni Club."

He laughed. Lacing her fingers through his, he drew her to her seat at the end of the table, then strode back to his place at the head.

For the first time since last night, he looked entirely relaxed. His perfectly tailored breeches and coat accentuated his muscular thighs and shoulders. Years of hard labor at sea had reshaped his body, adding bulk to his chest, arms, and legs, while thinning his face. Where once he'd been a rapier, he was now a sword. Which probably explained why she found him so much more intimidating.

And so much more handsome. The lines etched in his face removed any hints of youthful indecision, and his unpowdered hair, tied back in a queue, gleamed blue-black in the candlelight. She was glad he eschewed the fashion for powdered wigs and patches.

"The Americans have a song about the Macaronis," he said as he took his seat. "It's called 'Yankee Doodle.' I heard it sung in a tavern once, before a battle."

"How does it go?" she asked, wanting to keep him in this amiable mood.

He sang it for her, and she could envision him in a colonial tavern rousing the troops. Her throat tightened. Poor Rhys, forced to fight for another country's freedom instead of his own.

The servant brought in the *cawl*. Rhys looked down into the bowl, and his smile faded as he stared at the traditional blossoms of marigold floating in it.

Oh dear.

He lifted his head. "Do you know how long it's been since I've had Cook's wonderful *cawl*?"

Relieved, she kept her voice light. "Six years?"

"More. I was abroad for the Grand Tour when Llynwydd . . . changed hands." He ate a spoonful, and a blissful smile crossed his lips. "Double her salary. Give her whatever she wants, but make sure she serves *cawl* at every meal from now until doomsday."

Juliana couldn't keep the delight out of her laugh. She'd have to kiss Cook. Double her salary? It was worth that to see his face light up. And to hear him speak to Juliana as a partner in their marriage.

"So *cawl* wasn't a regular item on the menu in America, I take it?"

He tore off some bread and dipped it in his soup. "Not in America, or the navy." When her face fell, he seemed to regret his mention of the navy, for he added hastily, "But there were other interesting dishes in America."

"Oh?" She ate a spoonful of soup. "Like what?"

"Clam chowder, for one," he said between mouthfuls. "'Tis merely clams in a cream soup, but the Americans add some sort of spice. 'Tis a delicious dish if the right cook does it."

She set down her spoon, eating forgotten as she remembered all those women he'd said had shared his bed. "And who cooked it for you?"

He seemed not to notice her sudden sharp tone. "My landlady. I lived in a boarding house when I wasn't at sea. That's how I saved so much money." He flashed her a grin. "You should have seen this terror of a woman. Gray-haired and pug-faced, she'd have made two of you, and if anyone entered her kitchen, she threw them out with one huge fist. But the woman did know how to cook."

She relaxed. Somehow she couldn't see Rhys sharing a bed with an Amazon like that. "Tell me about your time in America. I've only read about the colonies, and I've always wondered if the truth is as intriguing as the stories."

He shrugged. "All right. What do you want to know?"

The next hour passed in a pleasant haze. From Rhys's description of the colonials, she gathered that they were quite a mix—the English-speaking Dutch of the Hudson Valley, the Scots in North Carolina, the warring tribes of Indians, and the English themselves, who were divided in their loyalties. He'd traveled up and down the coast privateering, and had seen more unusual things in his three years than she'd seen in a lifetime.

Courses came and went—lampreys in galantine, roast goose, boiled leeks with bacon, and preserved apricots—but she scarcely tasted a bite. She hung breathlessly on Rhys's every word about men who painted their bodies and went half-naked into battle, about wooden stockades and dense forests, and something called moose roaming free.

"It sounds so wild," she said as he finished his second serving of Welsh rabbit, the toasted cheese on bread that his countrymen were so fond of. "How do people raise families and have peaceful lives with Indians whooping down about their heads?"

He chuckled. "I'm afraid I've given you as distorted a look of America as the books. You were such a good audience that I was driven to exaggerate. 'Tis only wild in the untamed forests inland. Life in the coastal cities is quite civilized. People go to the theater and to church, and children attend school every day. It's not as different from Wales—or England—as you might expect."

Just then, the servant brought in an elaborate puff pastry that Juliana knew Cook had been working on ever since their arrival. Rhys gestured to it with a laugh. "I must say, I've not seen a pastry as ornate as that in America. Obviously, Cook is still outdoing herself."

As the servant began to cut servings, Rhys settled back in his chair and drank deeply of his wine, looking very lordly as his gaze lingered on her. He was different tonight. Though he wore the arrogant expression of a man sure of what he owned, there was also invitation and promise in his look.

He set his wineglass down. "Cook wasn't the only one who outdid herself. This was truly a feast. If I'd asked for every dish myself, I couldn't have chosen a better meal. You must have been preparing for this ever since we arrived."

"Believe it or not, I've been planning this meal ever since you left Wales. I thought surely that if . . . *when* you returned, you would wish to have the dishes you'd been deprived of while you were . . . abroad." She couldn't bring herself to mention the navy.

"Thank you for caring that much. It isn't what I . . . Actually, I didn't know what to expect."

He was being so truthful, she couldn't help saying, "After last night I did consider serving you gruel, but Cook would have none of it. She wanted to amaze you with her talents."

His eyes grew thoughtful. "And did *you* want to amaze me with your talents, too?"

She toyed with the pastry on her plate. "Perhaps."

"I'm suitably impressed. With the house, the furnishings, the staff . . . You've done well by me, even if it wasn't for me you were doing it."

She started to retort that *everything* had been for him—but had it? Or had she done it to prove her worth in a world where a woman was often only measured by her docility as a wife?

Even before she'd been told he was dead, her pride in Llynwydd had ceased to be linked to him. As her hopes of seeing him again had faded, her thirst to improve Llynwydd had increased. She'd found joy in making it special for both her staff and her tenants. None of that had anything to do with him.

Rhys made a sweeping gesture that took in their surroundings. "I like what you've done to this room. 'Twas always far too dark; with the lighter hangings and the paint, it's much cheerier. And there's more furniture, isn't there?"

"Only that *cwpwrdd tridarn*." She pointed to her pride and joy—a Welsh court cupboard made of mahogany, with intricately carved doors. "I commissioned it from a joiner in Carmarthen."

"I suppose you paid for it out of Llynwydd's profits."

She shook her head. "I bought it before Llynwydd was doing well, so I used my allowance on it."

He looked at her oddly. "Your father approved that?"

"He didn't know."

"How much of your annual portion went to sustaining the estate?"

"Sometimes half. One year, two-thirds."

He frowned. "That was good of you, but it shall end now. You don't need to support Llynwydd anymore; I have ample money for that. And we should probably discuss pin money and the like, so you can buy gowns, jewelry—"

"I'd rather spend my money on Llynwydd." She rose. "There's still so much to be done."

"And I shall do it. If you want a piece of furniture, tell me, and I'll take care of it. Otherwise—"

"You'll do everything yourself? Why must you do it alone? I've proven I can take good care of this estate, so surely you can allow me to do my part now. I won't sit in the drawing room and embroider all day, when I could help you run Llynwydd."

His gaze darkened.

"I know you think to punish me by reducing me to a guest in my own home, but can't you see how foolish that would be? Together, we can do more good for our estate than you can do alone. And if we're to live as husband and wife—"

"Ah, but therein lies the problem," he said tersely. "You're my wife only when it suits you—in the study, in the kitchen. But not in the bedroom, eh?" His expression chilled. "You directed the footmen to move your belongings out of our bedchamber and into the Blue Room, after I'd expressly forbidden it."

She thrust her trembling hands behind her back. She'd done that while he was touring the stables, and she'd instructed the footmen not to mention it to him. "How did you know?"

He walked up to where she stood. "Remember, I told the servants to come to me when they had a question. They're not fools; they know who's master. So they are moving your belongings right back as we speak."

He pulled her so close, she could feel his breath. "If you want the privileges of running a household, you must also take on the duties of a wife." When he slid his arm about her waist and pressed a kiss to her hair, he made it clear what those duties entailed. "Will you share my bed? Willingly?"

She ached to say yes. His breath against her cheek was warm and inviting, and his hand at her waist skimmed up along her ribs, tempting her to make the small shift of her body that would put her in his arms.

But she couldn't. If she let him buy her like this she'd regret it, for he only wanted her body—to treat her as a faithless betrayer even while making love to her. He'd never see her worth. "I won't share your bed until it means more than a conquest to you."

With a growl, he whirled away from her. "Fine. Sleep wherever you like. But prepare yourself for long days of embroidering and thumb-twiddling. Because you won't be mistress in this house until you're mistress to me."

And with that, he left.

14

All the old loves I followed once
Are now unfaithful found;
But a sweet sickness holds me yet
Of love that has no bound!

—WILLIAM WILLIAMS PANTYCELYN,
"I GAZE ACROSS THE DISTANT HILLS"

Darcy strode up to Lettice's cottage, not knowing what to expect. She'd never sent him a note asking him to come before. She'd always waited until his obsession got the better of him and he came to her. It was her most maddening quality—that she never needed him as badly as he did her.

He could think of only a few reasons she might want to see him, none of them good. Either Vaughan had spoken to her or brought her a message from Pennant—or worst of all, Morgan Pennant was here in the flesh.

The place was ominously silent as he approached. Of course, Edgar would be in bed by now. With his heart hammering in his chest, he walked up to the door and opened it, not bothering to knock.

And there was Lettice wrapped in the arms of another man.

With a curse, he slammed the door behind him. Instantly, Lettice jerked away from the damned scoundrel, her eyes wide with guilt. Pennant, damn him. He'd come straight to Lettice, and she'd welcomed him with open arms.

"Get out of my house!" he growled at Pennant. "You have no right."

Pennant blocked Lettice from his sight. "I have more right than you. 'Tis my woman and my son you've kept here with your lies."

Darcy was stunned. Edgar was Pennant's son? No, it wasn't true.

Lettice thrust Pennant aside. "Hush, I'll handle this in my own way."

"As you handled it before?" Pennant snapped. "Believing his lies and letting him take advantage of you? No. This won't go on any longer. There will be truth between us all now."

He fixed Darcy with a fierce gaze. "Tell her the truth. She knows you had me impressed. Now tell her what you said about her six years ago. Tell her how you tried to destroy my love for her."

Darcy cast about in his mind for some plausible tale, something that would keep her from hating him.

"Careful now," Pennant hissed. "If you lie, I'll bring Vaughan into it. He was there. He heard everything you said, too."

"Lettice, you mustn't listen to him. He and Vaughan have been spreading this mad tale that I—"

"Please, Darcy." Tears shone in Lettice's eyes. "Don't lie to me."

"You'd believe him over me? He wants you, damn him! He's always wanted you, and he doesn't care what he says if it'll bring you back to him."

"Are you any different? You're lying to keep me, too."

He felt the room closing in on him. "Am I the only one who lied?" A painful pressure built in his chest. "You told me Edgar is mine. Pennant says the child is his. Which is the truth?"

She paled, and Pennant put his arm about her shoulder. But she shook him off to stand apart from both men.

"Is Edgar mine or not?" Darcy persisted. "I want the truth, and I swear it won't make a difference to me either way. I'll love the boy and care for him, no matter whose he is. But I want to know if he's mine." When pity showed in her face, he winced, feeling as if someone had cleaved him in two. "He's not, is he?"

She shook her head. "I know I shouldn't have deceived you, but—"

"But you thought I was some stupid, lovesick fool who'd believe whatever you said." Anger made him want to hurt her. "You pretended to love me, hoping all the while that one day your lover would return. Well, I pretended to help you, when it was me—yes, me—who sent your lover away."

He stepped closer, unable to contain his rage. "Do you think I didn't see you pining for him when you thought I wasn't watching? Every time you asked if any mail had come for you at the house, I ached inside. I happily sent back the one letter that arrived from him. God, I hated him for having your heart."

"And so you told me that she'd betrayed me," Pennant bit out. "You lied to me."

"With great pleasure, seeing the love die a little in your eyes."

When Lettice moaned, her face full of misery, he caught himself. He'd wanted to wound her, not destroy her. Even though she'd used him, he still loved her.

He turned a pleading gaze on her. "Please understand, I wanted you so badly, and I knew he'd do anything to return unless he believed you unfaithful." His voice grew choked. "I know *I'd* have done anything."

"And did," she said accusingly. "You told him horrible lies about me."

"Because I loved you! Because I wanted you for my own."

"And were those the only lies you told?" Pennant cut in. "You said terrible things about your sister to separate her from Vaughan, too—that she'd gotten cold feet and backed out of the marriage, then urged you to have him taken by the press."

Devil take him! Must Pennant tell Lettice about that?

"Did you truly speak such lies?" Lettice asked.

He dared not admit to that, for Pennant would go straight to Vaughan, and Vaughan wouldn't rest until he'd ruined the entire St. Albans family. "It was the truth."

Lettice's eyes widened. "Your sister would never have done such a thing."

"This isn't your concern, Lettice. Juliana summoned me

to the inn that night to rid herself of Vaughan, and I did so. That's what happened."

She turned to Pennant. "My mistress was so upset when she heard he'd been taken. Don't believe these lies— she would never do such an awful thing!"

Pennant stared tenderly at her. "If you say it, I believe you."

A painful knot tightened in Darcy's stomach. "Why? She lied to me about Edgar. She might be lying to you about this. It's not as if she's a complete innocent herself."

Lettice rounded on him. "And what do you mean by that?"

"I haven't been taking care of you and Edgar without any reward. Pennant has come here, thinking to start again where the two of you left off, but he can't." Darcy turned to Pennant. "She has shared my bed through six years of nights. Through six years of days, she has looked to me for help, and I've cared for her. You won't erase that by whispering sweet promises in her ears."

Pennant's eyes blazed. "And what of your wife during that time? You only shared crumbs with Lettice. I, on the other hand, want to marry her."

"You can't have her. She's mine."

"She may have given you a great deal," Pennant said, "but she never gave you her heart."

"You don't know that!"

Lettice placed her hand on Pennant's arm. "I can't bear this. You must leave and let me speak to Darcy alone. I need time to set things right."

Pennant frowned. "You said you'd be ready with your answer tonight."

"You've been here before?" Darcy roared, but the two of them ignored him.

"I'll be ready in the morning, I promise," she told Pennant. "Please, Morgan. Do as I ask."

The Welshman hesitated, then he stalked for the door, stopping in front of Darcy. "If you harm her, Northcliffe—"

"I wouldn't hurt her if my life depended on it."

"Ah, but you did once—by lying about her to me. But if you try to turn her against me again, I'll choke the breath from you. Do you hear?"

"Get out," Darcy hissed. "Get out of my house!"

Pennant glanced at Lettice. "I'll be back for you and the boy tomorrow."

"You can't have her!" Darcy cried as Pennant left, slamming the door behind him. He whirled on Lettice. "You're not taking up with him again, are you? Surely these years between us have meant *something*."

Her face was pale in the firelight. "You know they meant a great deal."

"I don't know what to believe. I thought Edgar was my son, and he isn't." He stared at her. "But I meant it when I said it doesn't matter. No matter how you've lied to me, I want you and Edgar. Don't let Pennant destroy what it took us years to build."

"You speak as if we're married, but Morgan's right. You have a wife."

"My wife detests me, as you well know." When she turned away, he caught her by the arm. "She hasn't once come to my bed unless I begged it of her for the sake of my heir." His throat tightened. "I will leave Edgar everything that isn't entailed, if you'll only stay with me."

He tried to draw her close, but she resisted. "Christ, I need you. You can't abandon me!" Desperation wasn't the way to keep her, but he couldn't bear the thought of losing Lettice. "I know I haven't been mistaken these past years. You felt real affection for me. I know you did."

"I did." Her eyes deepened with pity. "And I truly thought of you as Edgar's father, for you've always been kind to him. But it doesn't excuse your lies about me and my lady."

"Juliana has naught to do with it," he snapped.

"But the lies you told about her do." She pulled free of his hold. "I thought you were a generous and kind man. Instead I find you're a stranger, a deceiver—"

"You deceived me, too."

"To protect my child from starvation. You lied to gain something that didn't belong to you." She moved away from him, and he could feel her emotionally withdrawing.

"Let me make it up to you."

"It's no use. It could never be the same between us." She dragged in a heavy breath. "When Morgan comes tomorrow, Edgar and I are going with him."

"And if I marry you?"

She gaped at him. "What in heaven's name are you talking about? You're already married."

"I'll divorce her." He strode toward her, his purpose firming as he got closer. "I'll divorce Elizabeth and marry you."

"You're mad! An earl divorce his lady wife and marry a servant? Even if you could manage it, you'd lose every social advantage you've gained. You'd never risk that. You *shouldn't* risk it."

What she said was true, but he didn't know how else to keep her. "I'd risk anything to keep you with me."

"I couldn't accept such a sacrifice from you, Darcy." She straightened her shoulders. "Not when I love Morgan."

Those words exploded in his brain. He seized her in an unyielding hold, refusing to let go when she pushed against his chest. "You *don't* love him. I can prove it." He tried to kiss her, but she twisted her head away. "Let me make love to you, and I'll show you what still lies between us."

"Don't." She fought him in earnest now.

Her fear only enraged him. He grabbed her chin, forcing her head still so he could kiss her on the mouth. But when he tried to force his tongue between her teeth, she bit him.

He jerked back, then slapped her. Hard.

Then horror consumed him. "Oh God, Lettice . . . I'm sorry—"

She pushed him away and fled for the stairs. "Leave, Darcy." She held her hand to her cheek, which bore the imprint of his hand. "Please, just leave."

He took a step toward her.

"You promised not to hurt me. Did you lie about that, too?"

The words slid into his gut like a sharp blade. She feared him now, and rightfully so. He'd made her fear him.

He backed away, afraid of what he might do if he got

any closer. Right now she had cause to fear him. But if he came near her again, he might give her cause to hate him.

"Please go," she repeated.

He felt as if someone had wrenched his heart from his chest. "All right. But you'll come to your senses eventually and see that you love me as I love you. He'll never be good enough for you."

When he walked out and closed the door, he stood there listening to her sobs. Despite his brave words, he knew he'd lost her in a moment of blind stupidity.

How in God's name would he ever endure it?

15

No profit, though near dead,
I've had of this white maid,
Save to love all entire
And languish with desire,
To praise her through the hills
Yet, solitary still,
To wish her at nightfall
Betwixt me and the wall.

—DAFYDD AP GWILYM, "THE GREY FRIAR"

And will dinner be at the usual time?" Mrs. Roberts asked, three days after Juliana's return to Llyn-wydd.

"Yes." Juliana rolled her eyes. "Unless Squire Arrogance decrees otherwise."

Mrs. Roberts laughed. "He still thinks he makes the rules? Men are such fools."

Generally Juliana ignored Mrs. Roberts's thinly disguised attempts to find out what was going on between the master and the mistress, but today she was just angry enough to give the woman an earful. "Yes, but they all certainly stick together. I've won a skirmish in the kitchen, but lost one in the stables."

"The groom refused to saddle you a horse again, eh?" Mrs. Roberts clucked sympathetically. "Well, milady, I'm sorry for it. I know you miss your daily ride. But you'll be at it again once the master realizes how silly it is to keep you from it." She smoothed her apron. "I'd best get back to work."

As the woman bustled off, Juliana frowned. The household had fallen into two distinct camps divided entirely by sex. It infuriated her.

All the wretched footmen and grooms were under Rhys's thumb. Some of them were newly hired, so their loyalty was understandable. But she had hired the blasted groom who'd thwarted her this morning. He'd hemmed and hawed and begged her pardon, but in the end, he'd refused to saddle her horse.

Like his male companions, he'd thrown in his lot with Rhys. Her husband had only to spin a few tales about his battles at sea and his experiences in America, and they were ready to die for "the brave master."

At least the women were on her side, too practical to be swayed by stories of adventure. Behind Rhys's back, they came to her for instructions. Mrs. Roberts was the most blatant, nodding and saying, "Yes, sir," to Rhys's commands, then coming to Juliana to ask what she wanted done.

And Cook! Juliana chuckled. Cook had baldly told Squire Arrogance that she wasn't so foolish as to take her orders from a man who hadn't the faintest idea what went on in a kitchen. He'd pointed out that he could dismiss her for such insubordination, and she'd told him he knew better than to dismiss the only woman who could cook a *cawl* fit for a king. She'd been right, of course.

So Juliana had gone on planning meals, and Rhys had kept silent on that, just as he'd acquiesced when she'd had the maids move her clothing and jewel cases to the Blue Room.

But he and Moss discussed all improvements without her. She was forbidden the stables. And any outing she took in the carriage had to be approved by him, which invariably meant he went along.

It was insulting. And she dared not complain, for his answer was always "When you share my bed, I'll share the estate." Since he accompanied the pronouncement with a look that sent dangerously delightful shivers along her spine, she'd stopped complaining.

Instead she'd thrown herself into improving the squire hall. While he surveyed the tenant farms with an eye toward improvements, she clandestinely used her funds to order new drapes and linens. While he consulted with the estate blacksmith, carpenter, and gardener, she consulted with the housekeeper and oversaw the maids. It wasn't hard to keep busy, although many of her former duties had been taken from her. She used the time to catch up on tasks she'd put off before—cleaning out the attic, taking stock of her wardrobe, deciding which books needed new bindings.

She rarely saw Rhys, and when she did, he was unrelenting in his determination to shut her out of the workings of the estate. Only when they shared dinner were they cordial, as if there was an unspoken truce. He continued to recount tales about America, and she'd begun relating all that had happened to the estate after he'd left.

But once dinner was over, she always excused herself before he could turn the full force of his seductive talents on her. Fleeing to the Blue Room, she spent her nights remembering every blazing look he'd given her at dinner, every brush of his hand as he led her to her place, every kiss he pressed to her cheek.

As if guessing what his reticence did to her, he hadn't again tried to kiss her mouth or hold her. He had to know it was driving her insane.

"Milady?" asked the butler.

Oh bother, she'd been standing here like a half-wit. "Yes, what is it?"

"Master Evan is here. He said you're expecting him for a lesson."

She groaned. "I completely forgot." And she hadn't even gotten his paper ready yet. "Send him to the kitchen and tell Cook to give him some tea and apple tarts to take up to the schoolroom. I'll be there shortly."

As the butler left, she hurried into the study and drew ten sheets of paper from the drawer. Then she held the edges over the candle flame to singe them, waving them in the air to dispel the smoke.

"What in God's name are you doing?" came a voice from the doorway.

She whirled to face Rhys. "I swear, you have the most disturbing habit of sneaking up on a person."

"You have some peculiar habits yourself—like destroying perfectly good paper."

"I'm not destroying it. I'm merely . . . dirtying it up." She pulled out ten more sheets. "It's for Evan."

He leaned against the door frame. "Ah, yes. The boy who took the stained paper off your hands. I take it the 'staining' was no accident, either."

"Of course not. He won't take good paper from me, so I have to spoil it for him. He's here for his lesson, and I'd forgotten all about the paper."

"May I come along?"

Her gaze shot to him. "Why?"

"Since I've agreed to do what I can to provide an education for your charge, I ought to be allowed to meet him. Don't you agree?"

"I suppose it wouldn't hurt." Except that it would mean spending time with Rhys.

Gathering up the sheets, she walked toward the door. "I usually tutor him in the schoolroom."

Rhys shifted position, but didn't give her enough room to pass without touching him. She could feel his eyes hot upon her, and imagine she felt his breath on her neck.

As soon as she was past him she quickened her pace, but he fell easily into step beside her, settling his hand on her waist in that possessive gesture so common to men. Her breathing began an uneven rhythm she could hardly hide. Nor did it get any better as they climbed the stairs, with his hand riding on her waist as if to steady her when she knew he really did it to provoke her.

Unfortunately, it was working. She was overwhelmingly aware of his lean body beside her, moving with the lithe grace of a Thoroughbred—his thighs flexing beneath the glove-tight breeches, his arm brushing her back every time she took a step, his fingers resting in the small of her back just inches above her hips.

Oh bother, he was such a devil. So what if he had a fine body? He was an untrusting, stubborn wretch, and totally unworthy of her attention.

Still, by the time they'd reached the schoolroom, her blood was racing and her body aflame. With profound relief, she escaped him to cross the room.

Thankfully Evan took her mind off Rhys. He had apparently either refused the tea and tarts or had wolfed them down, for he now sat engrossed in a book she'd acquired yesterday—Daniel Defoe's *Robinson Crusoe*. Oblivious to her and Rhys, he hunched over the book, eating up the pages. It never ceased to astonish her that he could read at such a pace.

"Sorry I kept you waiting," Juliana said gently.

Evan gave a start, his cheeks flushing as he saw her and Rhys. Shutting the book, he jumped up and gave a bow. "Good day, my lady. I hope you don't mind. I saw the new book and—"

"Don't be silly." She smiled. "I'm glad you took the chance to look it over. How is it?"

He shrugged. "Interesting, I suppose."

"I thought it might amuse you." When Evan cast Rhys a curious glance, she said, "Allow me to introduce my husband, Squire Vaughan. He wants to observe the lesson today."

Evan's eyes widened. "'Tis a pleasure to meet you at last, sir."

"For me as well," Rhys said with a hint of amusement.

Juliana took her seat and barely gave time for Rhys and Evan to sit before she launched into the lesson, eager to get this over with so she could escape her husband.

If Evan was surprised that she spent no time chatting with him about his mother or the farm, he didn't show it. Nor did he seem uncomfortable having Rhys watch them. If anything, he showed off—conjugating French verbs with obvious pride, then reeling off a dozen new words he'd learned from the poem she'd assigned him to memorize.

"And what is Gruffydd's speaker lamenting here?" she prompted after he recited a particularly complicated line.

Evan thought a moment. "Is he saying he can't talk poetry while he's wandering?"

"'Recite' poetry," she corrected. "But that's not it exactly. He grieves for the old ways that are no longer valued. He says no one wants to hear Welsh verses recited anymore, so he must keep his 'poet's trade' hidden."

Rhys spoke for the first time since they'd begun the lesson. "In Gruffydd's day, there were few who would stand up to the English. The Welsh language was considered ignorant, and some Welshmen refused to use it. So Gruffydd felt like a stranger in his own land, 'betrayed to wander the world in search of aid.'"

She swung her gaze to Rhys, who was watching her as if trying to fathom her. Gruffydd's poem had been one of their mutual favorites. Did he remember? And had he guessed that she'd chosen it for Evan for that very reason?

His gaze was soft as he stared at her.

Evan spoke up, oblivious to the sudden current in the air. "Mr. Gruffydd is like you, Mr. Vaughan, isn't he?"

Rhys lifted an eyebrow. "How so?"

"Well, you had to wander the world, too, and give up your poet's trade."

When Rhys glanced at her, she said coolly, "Evan has always been interested in your . . . situation."

"Oh, more than that, sir," Evan blurted out. "I think you're a great hero, to fight so nobly for the Welsh cause, even when it meant being taken by the press gangs."

She could still feel Rhys's gaze, but she wouldn't look at him. "I told Evan how you were forced into the navy."

Evan warmed to his subject. "She told me how you said we should speak Welsh if we like. And she told me about your poetry. I've read all your poems."

"How did you manage that, when they were never published?"

"Lady Juliana let me read them in the book you gave her. Oh, sir, they were wonderful."

"Really?" His gaze now bore into her.

"Aye. She told me all about you." Evan leaned forward confidentially. "She said you were very special."

Oh, why must Evan be so talkative? "Let's get on with the lesson, shall we?"

"No, this is much more interesting," Rhys said. "So Evan, did she tell you what she meant by 'special'?"

"I don't know. Like a hero. You know, like the man all the girls in the books fall in love with."

"And did she say she'd fallen in love with me?"

Evan shot Juliana an uncertain glance. "Well, not exactly. But she talked about you like . . . like my sister Mary when she talks about that shopkeeper in town."

Rhys leaned back to cross his arms over his chest. "Ah, but if I were her 'true love,' why did she go off to marry that other fellow?"

Juliana fought down anger. Dear heaven, would he never understand?

"She said 'tweren't a husband she wanted, but children. And since you weren't here, and she thought you were never coming back—"

"Didn't she say *anything* about love?" A faint mockery was in his tone.

Juliana glared at him. Rhys had never bothered to ask *her* if she'd been in love with Stephen, yet here he was, badgering the poor boy for his answers.

"My, but we've gone far afield of our lesson." She tried for a light tone. "Let's get back to it, shall we?"

Rhys's gaze locked with hers. "Evan hasn't answered my question. Tell me, lad—did Lady Juliana say she was in love with Lord Devon?"

"Not to me." Evan shifted uneasily, having finally begun to sense tension in the air. "She wanted a husband who would give her children. That's all."

Rhys's mouth tightened. "But I was already her husband. Did she admit that?"

"No." When Rhys frowned, he added, "But you mustn't blame her for it. She thought you were dead. Everyone thought you were dead."

Rhys smiled ruefully. "You do have a point, Evan."

"She used to cry about it," Evan persisted, determined

to defend Juliana. "I'd hear her after we'd read one of your poems. She would cry in the garden."

Rhys's gaze burned into her, and she turned away.

"That's enough. Evan has lessons to do and—"

"I think Evan has done so well today that he deserves a rest from lessons," Rhys broke in. "Evan, why don't you go down to the kitchen and tell Mrs. Roberts I said to give you a pork pie?"

Evan looked to Juliana, and she sighed. There was no point in trying to continue the lessons with Rhys asking probing questions. In truth, she'd rather have Evan out of it. "Do as Rhys says."

"Should I come back tomorrow?"

She nodded, her throat too tight for speech.

Only after he left did she remember she still had his charred paper. She leapt up and said, "Oh dear, I forgot to give him—"

Rhys stayed her with one hand. "You can give it to him tomorrow."

They listened until the sound of Evan's footsteps faded. Then Rhys took the paper from her and laid it aside.

He was so close now that she could smell the musky scent of him, see the glitter in his eyes. There was no telling what he thought of Evan's revelations. He might even think she'd put Evan up to it.

His back was to the window, and the late afternoon sunlight glanced off his hair, giving him a halo. Yet he was no angel. He'd had heaven dangled in front of him and snatched away one too many times.

Even now he looked as if he waited for the push that

would send him plummeting to earth. "Tell me, wife. Were you . . . *are* you in love with the marquess?"

She met his gaze boldly. "Nay. I once thought I could grow to love him. But I know better now."

Something flickered in his gaze. Relief? Hope?

Then he drew her into his arms. "Why did you tell Evan about me and let him read my poems?" he asked in a rough rasp. "Why cry for me, after you tossed me aside so easily?"

"I told you: I loved you."

"But you kept our marriage secret, even from the boy. Why, if you were in love with me?"

She tensed. "Because I was scared and weak. No more."

He searched her face. "I no longer know what to believe. My mind tells me your claims make no sense. And yet—"

"You know the truth in your heart," she said, laying her hand on his cheek. "If only you'd heed it."

"I only know one thing for certain. That I still want you." He pressed a kiss to her hair. "God, how I want you."

Next he kissed her temple and she nuzzled his chin, seduced into forgetting that he didn't believe her . . . *wouldn't* believe her. His heart knew the truth, and his heart was guiding him at the moment.

His mouth skirted the edge of her cheekbone, gliding down the curved line of her jaw so he could tongue her throat. "'Tis like the men who disappear into the fairy circle." He tugged her mob cap loose to bring her hair down about her shoulders. "While they are in the enchantment, they know no rational thought. Only when they leave do they realize they've been seduced by a dream."

"Am I a dream, then?"

His lips hovered above hers as he stared down at her, eyes glittering. "One of you must be. Either the woman I fell in love with—or the woman I hold in my arms now."

"They're one and the same, and no dream, either. That, I can prove." Then she lifted her lips to meet his.

With a groan, he took her mouth, burying his fingers in her hair to hold her still. Desire jolted her. She'd lain awake too many nights remembering their last kiss, too many years remembering their lovemaking. It would turn a nun into a wanton, and she was no nun.

So when he sought to deepen the kiss, she let him. She opened her mouth so he could tangle his tongue with hers so wonderfully that her pulse quickened and her blood heated.

"By thunder," he murmured, "you taste sweeter with each kiss. What sort of sorcery is this?"

"The best kind."

Hunger leapt in his eyes and he plundered her mouth once more. With his hands clasping her head, he drove his tongue deep, delving for sweetness, offering heat in return. His body strained against hers in an ancient fight for domination that she was only too happy to yield. Winding her arms about his waist, she dovetailed into him, curving her body around his taut arousal.

"Ah, *cariad*." He lifted her onto the table and fitted himself between her legs. Before she could even respond to that blatant act, he captured her mouth once more in a sense-stealing kiss.

Through a haze of voluptuous enjoyment, she felt him shove up her skirts and petticoats. Then one hand stroked gossamer caresses up her bare thigh, while his other tugged loose her fichu, then inched her bodice down to free her breasts.

When his mouth left hers to trail kisses down her throat to the cleft between her breasts, she moaned. He caught her about the waist, stretching her back until she was arched over his arm, laid out for his pleasure. And he took it with obvious delight, sucking each breast in turn.

At the same time, he inched his other hand higher until his fingers were stroking the swirl of hair between her legs. When he rubbed her there, she nearly came off the table, arching into him for more.

So he plunged his finger inside her, in and out, making her insane. She clutched his shoulders, and his mouth teased one nipple with teeth and tongue until she thought she'd die from the intense pleasure. The assault on two different fronts so aroused her that she writhed against him, seeking more.

"Yes, my darling wife," he murmured against her breast. "Be the wanton for me again."

She only became that when he did these enticing things to her. Yet how could she resist when his mouth sent myriad sensations rocketing through her and his finger slid so seductively inside her?

He was watching her, his eyes like sapphires at the bottom of a clear stream. Unnerved, she turned her face away. "Please . . ." But what to beg for? Mercy? Forgiveness? He was incapable of either.

She pushed at his chest, but he held her unbalanced, hovering over the table, her breasts raised for his mouth and her legs held open by his thighs. And she didn't really want to escape him, did she?

"I won't hurt you," he murmured.

As if to prove it, he sought her mouth once more for a gentle, coaxing kiss; that of a lover, not a conqueror. She could almost believe it was the old Rhys kissing her, the old Rhys working magic between her legs.

"Oh . . . yes . . . yes . . ." she moaned as he increased the pace of his strokes, until she was climbing Icarus's path to the sun, willing to risk total destruction if only she could soar. She scarcely noticed the sheen of sweat forming on his brow, nor the mad way he plundered her throat and breasts while he fondled her harder, deeper, faster.

Her enjoyment blinded her to anything but his body half-covering hers as he sought to make her part of him at every point—kissing, sucking, urging her up toward oblivion.

Then a thousand sensations exploded in her, thrusting her into the sunlight she craved and feared. With a cry, she dug her fingers into his shoulders and writhed against him, crushing her breasts against the wool of his waistcoat.

For a moment, he held her suspended. Then as her need faded to warmth, he withdrew his hand from between her legs. He thrust against her so that she could feel the rigid flesh trapped inside his breeches.

The rasp of wool against her skin yanked her from her sensual haze, and she tore her mouth from his. What was she doing? They were in the middle of the schoolroom, for heaven's sake, with the door wide open!

He fumbled to open his breeches, and she struggled to right herself beneath him. "We can't do this here."

His eyes smoldered. "But we are, my darling. And it's too late for regrets."

"It's not that. I do want you to . . . to—"

"Make love to you?" Triumph flashed over his face.

"Yes." She wished she could deny her unholy craving to join her body to his, but she couldn't. "But anyone might walk in and see us here."

"All right, my lady wife." He gave a pained smile. "I suppose I can make it to our bedchamber without devouring you."

They restored their clothing and hurried down the stairs. They'd nearly reached the State Bedroom when a footman hurried toward them, waving a piece of paper. "I've an urgent message for you, sir!"

Rhys barely spared the man a glance as he opened the door to the master bedchamber. "Not now."

"But it's from Mr. Pennant," the servant persisted. "His man is waiting outside to accompany you."

That made Rhys pause. He took the note and read it, then swore under his breath. "Tell Pennant's man I'll be right there."

As the footman scurried off, Juliana asked, "What is it? What could possibly make you leave when we're about to—"

"I don't want to go, believe me." He ushered her into the bedchamber and shut the door. "But I must."

"At least tell me why."

"I can't." He sat down to change his shoes for heavy riding boots.

Her stomach sank. "You mean you won't. You're quite

happy to make love to me, but you still don't trust me with your business affairs."

He said nothing, drawing his boots on with jerky movements.

"You call me your 'darling wife,' but you mean only your 'darling bedmate.' And you only want me for that when it's convenient."

A muscle tightened in his jaw. "It's not my fault you waited so long to do your duty."

Her *duty*? She bit back a hot retort, knowing he just wanted to distract her from his plans. "So you won't tell me where you're going or why."

"That's right." He went to change his coat with the feigned nonchalance of a man who knows he's wrong and refuses to admit it.

She strode for the door.

"Where are you going?" he bit out.

"You're finished with me, so I'm returning to my other 'wifely duties.'"

He was across the room and turning her around to face him before she could even open the door. "Ah, but I'm not finished with you." His voice was dangerously soft. "This is merely an interruption. When I return late this evening, I expect to continue exactly where we left off."

"You expect to find me warm and willing, do you? And what will you give me in return?"

He blinked. "What do you mean?"

"You want me to sell you my soul—to be a docile wife outside the bedchamber and a wanton inside the bedchamber. You want me not to ask questions when you leave to go on God knows what fool's errand for Morgan. In return, you offer me only the ashes of your mistrust. Unfortunately, my price is higher than that."

"You can't ask a price for what is mine by right—what you gave me and then took back." When she lifted an eyebrow, he added sullenly, "But if I did decide to pay your price, what would it be? Complete run of the house? Me trailing obediently after you like that lapdog betrothed of yours?"

The thought of Rhys trailing obediently after anyone brought a bitter smile to her lips. "I only want your trust."

He stared her down. "Your price is too high."

Her hopes faltered. She'd thought he might be softening, that he might one day come to trust her. But the navy had sucked the trust out of him, leaving his heart to calcify.

She pulled free of him and went to open the door. "Then don't expect me to be waiting in this bedchamber for you when you return."

16

Find her, if you can, and bring
My sighs to her, my mourning.
You of the glorious Zodiac,
Tell her bounty of my lack.

—DAFYDD AP GWILYM, "THE WIND"

Fighting the urge to run after Juliana and pick up exactly where they'd left off, Rhys reread Morgan's note:

> John Myddelton, current holder of the seat for M.P. of the borough, is dead. Northcliffe is trying to force through his own candidate tonight at the council meeting, so the Sons of Wales are planning to storm Common Hall. They're already furious over what Northcliffe did to us, and now they're determined to rout him. I fear there will be bloodshed. But they'll listen to you. They're meeting in the basement of Gentlemen's Bookshop, as usual. Come help me stop them before it's too late.

Crushing the note, he stared out at the sinking sun. Carmarthen was two hours' hard ride from here. If he left now and drove his horse to the limit, he could probably get there in time.

But he'd lose any advantage he'd gained in his struggle to bed Juliana.

Damn it all to hell. Why must Myddelton have died *now?* The M.P. had been a moderate Whig respected by both sides, but if Northcliffe were to replace him with his own man . . .

Years ago, he'd have enjoyed being in the thick of it, urging on the fight, ready to cudgel freedom into the thick skulls of the Carmarthen burgesses. But war had made him more cautious. This wasn't the way to go about effecting change. His experiences in America had taught him that.

The colonists had advantages in their rebellion that the Welsh lacked—distance from their oppressors, trained militia and navy, and a great deal of wealth. If the Sons of Wales thought they could rid themselves of the English simply by trouncing a few burgesses, they were mad. Possibly fatally so.

Rhys sighed. He had to act.

I only want your trust.

Right. He strode out the door. If he told her what was going on, she might send a messenger to warn Northcliffe before Rhys could convince the men to choose another path. Then there would be bloodshed anyway.

She'd betrayed him and his friends once. She could easily betray them again.

She wouldn't do that, his conscience said as he mounted his horse.

Damn. He spurred his horse into a gallop, striving to wipe her from his mind, but he couldn't stop thinking about the Juliana who taught Welsh children in their own language.

Who claimed the loyalty of her Welsh servants with the flick of a finger.

Who'd cried over him and kept his poems.

Who steadfastly proclaimed her innocence.

His gut knotted up. What if he'd been wrong?

If he were, his refusals to trust her must be like a slap in the face. Many more of those, and her onetime love might turn to hate. And he couldn't bear having her hate him. Not now. Not after this afternoon.

He grew hard just thinking about her response to him, the arch of her back as she'd pressed into him, how she'd felt when he'd fondled her honeypot, all tight and wet and warm.

"Damn it all!"

He couldn't go on like this. He'd done the right thing by not telling her everything. Innocent or no, he couldn't have risked her thwarting his plans this night. The damned woman had been going behind his back to make the servants do as she pleased, treating him with defiance . . . refusing to share his bed.

With a snarl, he tightened his grip on the reins. *That* at least would stop after tonight. He'd nearly seduced her today; he could do it again.

It would be easy. Although she hadn't been sharing his bedchamber, she hadn't been locking her door against him, either. He knew that, because one night he'd slipped inside to watch her sleep, torn between his craving for her and his determination that she come to *him*.

He'd resisted the urge to seduce her when she was half-asleep. But now that he was sure she wanted him, he could be blatant about it. He would kiss and caress that exquisite body until she moaned and writhed, wanting his touch as she had this afternoon.

First, however, he must take care of this problem with the Sons of Wales.

They shouldn't be taunting a power like Northcliffe without considering the consequences. For God's sake, half of them were family men with children. He had to stop them.

But how? Though they might be hotheaded radicals, they were also right. If Northcliffe convinced the burgesses there wasn't enough time for a proper election, and got them to move up the election day to make it impossible for any other candidate to campaign, then whomever he chose would skate right in.

Somehow Rhys must stop Northcliffe without provoking a bloodbath.

Suddenly an idea came to him. By the time he reached the bookshop basement two hours later, he'd formulated a plan. And judging from the noise spilling out from the bookshop into the street, he'd come none too soon.

Relieved that the watch hadn't already arrested the lot of them, Rhys strode down the stairs into the basement. Morgan was on the platform, trying to make himself heard, but the crowd was too inflamed to listen. A fiery young laborer had garnered their attention and was inciting them to riot.

The familiar smells of book paste, dust, and sweat jolted Rhys back to when he'd been the young man on the platform. It had been the first—and last—time he'd shouted revolution. 'Twas the same crowd, the same discontented tradesmen's sons and farmers and dissidents who had come to hear him that night.

Except that these men carried hammers, picks, and staffs as they echoed the young radical's cries for justice. Rhys wanted justice, too, but he'd learned it was damned hard to get.

He pushed his way through the crowd to climb up on the platform beside Morgan. "How long have they been at this?" Rhys shouted.

"An hour. The council meeting will be starting soon, and they want to remove Northcliffe's candidate forcibly."

"The last time that happened, five men were arrested and sentenced to service in the navy." Rhys gestured toward the young radical. "Who's he?"

"His name's Tom Ebbrell. That's all I know."

"Listen to me!" Rhys shouted at the crowd, but couldn't make himself heard. He grabbed someone's cudgel and smashed the nearest chair with it.

That got everyone's attention.

"For those of you who don't remember me, I'm Rhys Vaughan," he said in Welsh. "I'm one of the men Northcliffe got impressed into the English Navy."

There was a murmur throughout the crowd.

Ebbrell came over to extend Rhys his hand. "I've heard much about you, sir. I read your pamphlets when I was but a stripling, and 'twas them that made me learn about the blindness of Wales. 'Twas them that awakened my heart to our plight."

Rhys shook the man's hand. "Those pamphlets gained me a long stint in the English Navy," he said, loud enough for the crowd to hear.

"'Twasn't the pamphlets that did it, but that devil Northcliffe. Ever since his father's death, he's been casting about for a man he can own, and he thinks he's found one in Sir Davies. We'll show him otherwise, won't we, boys?"

That brought a roar of assent from the crowd, but when Rhys held up his hand, they went silent.

He put all the force of his old revolutionary zeal into his voice. "'Tis a noble fight you're choosing!" It had been so long since he'd commanded men in Welsh that he feared his words creaked with misuse, but he tried to make up in fervor for what he lacked in eloquence. "You should thwart Northcliffe's attempt if you can."

He held the cudgel aloft. "But this isn't the way to do it—with truncheons and axes. 'Twill only make the burgesses dismiss you as rebels whose opinions can be ignored."

Angry mutters rippled through the crowd, and Tom Ebbrell's face reflected outrage. "Don't you want to see justice done, to see Northcliffe suffer? What happened to all your words about making Wales free?"

"Freedom comes at a price—and sometimes that price

means acting with forethought, instead of rumbling forth like a herd of bulls."

Rhys stared into the faces of furious, tired men and found himself thinking of their wives and children. How many other wives tonight had protested their husband's activities? Six years ago, he hadn't cared when Lettice had protested. But tonight, he couldn't help seeing Evan's face—and Juliana's—as the boy had described Juliana's tears when Rhys left.

"The colonies resorted to battle only when they couldn't have representation. Yet we've been given the right to representation—"

"Aye!" shouted a voice near him. "We have Northcliffe's puppet!"

A swell of disgruntled voices filled the room.

"If you pull down his man he will only find another," Rhys called out, "and you'll be branded as 'rough, un-schooled Welshmen' bent on violence. You'll find your-selves impressed as I was, made to serve the very men you detest—all for nothing but to vent your spleen."

Some fellow in the crowd cried out, "Why are we lis-tening to this coward? He returned to make Northcliffe's sister his wife! He has gone over to the enemy!"

The crowd took up the cry. "The enemy! He's the enemy!"

Rhys banked his fury with effort, pounding the floor with the cudgel until he got their attention once more. "I want Northcliffe's hide as much as you. Perhaps more so, for he kept me from my wife, who is sympathetic to our cause and a Welsh scholar besides."

No matter why Juliana had rejected their marriage, it hadn't been hatred of the Welsh. And Northcliffe had been the instrument of her distress, so it wouldn't hurt Rhys's case if they saw her as her brother's victim. Nobody loved a romantic tale of star-crossed lovers more than the Welsh.

"If I've learned one thing in America, 'tis that the only way to free Wales is to gain a voice in Parliament. Tonight you are planning to keep one pro-English voice out of Parliament, but all that does is delay the inevitable."

"Perhaps so," Ebbrell snapped. "But what else can we do? Trot off like sheep to the slaughter?"

Rhys addressed the crowd. "I have a better idea." He paused to sweep his gaze over the expectant faces of men who'd long been oppressed by English landholders. "I say put forth your *own* candidate. Tonight. Then you'll have your voice. And that's the first step to freedom."

The crowd fell into a stunned silence so complete, Rhys thought he could hear the collective beating of their hearts.

Then Tom Ebbrell cleared his throat. "'Tis impossible. Although I daresay many on the council dislike Northcliffe as much as we do, they're afraid of him. You are the only fellow to match him in wealth and influence, but you're not of this borough."

Rhys shot Morgan a quick glance, relieved when his friend nodded. "That's why I'm offering to put my resources behind someone who *is* of this borough, and who has considerable consequence both here and in London. Morgan Pennant."

After a stunned silence, the crowd broke into cheers. Morgan had always been a favorite with the Sons of Wales, and no one begrudged him the money he'd made in the colonies. Morgan was also better educated than them, yet as Welsh as the triple harp and the *eisteddfodau*. No one would question his suitability. Thank God.

"You don't object, my friend?" Rhys said under his breath to Morgan.

"Nay. I have a score to settle with Northcliffe. And I suspect a beating won't hurt him as much as this challenge will."

"Is it agreed?" Rhys cried to the crowd. "Will you lay down your arms and put forth Morgan Pennant as a candidate? If we produce a suitable one, the council will be forced to allow an election and give time for the campaign. So—will you go with me to the meeting to serve the writ for Morgan, then join me in a campaign that will shame Northcliffe forever?"

"Aye!" Tom Ebbrell clapped his hand on Morgan's shoulder.

"Aye!" the crowd echoed.

Tossing the cudgel aside, Rhys raised his fist. "To Morgan!"

The hall rang with the thunderous noise of weapons being dropped. "To Morgan!" they cried.

Rhys felt the old zeal swell in him again. "And to Wales!"

"To Wales!" they cried.

This time, he'd fight the battle with the Englishmen's weapons.

Three hours later, Rhys cast Morgan an amused glance as they rode away from Common Hall. "How does it feel to be a candidate for Member of Parliament?"

"Ask me tomorrow. I suspect I'll have a more sober view in the morning." Morgan gazed off into the distance. "Tonight was only a skirmish in the battle. 'Tis easy to serve a writ, especially when the council is sorely tired of dealing with pompous noblemen like Northcliffe. But to put a man like me into office is not so easy."

"'Tis still worth a try."

"Aye. But this plan could wring you dry. Disputed elections for Parliament nearly always devastate the loser financially. And sometimes the winner, as well. There are the banquets to pay for and palms to grease and—"

"I know." Rhys rubbed his weary neck. "Father considered running once and decided against it when he counted the potential cost. But you and I are not my father. We're far more responsible. Between us, I think we can pull it off."

"I hope so. Did you see Northcliffe's face after you agreed to donate enough money to refurbish Common Hall? I thought his eyes would pop out of his head. He's no fool; he knows 'tis easy to buy the votes of the burgesses. And when you're buying them for *me*"—he chuckled—"to have me steal the election from him after I've already stolen his mistress is the worst indignity of all."

"Does this mean Lettice has come to live with you?"

"Aye. We married yesterday by license." A thread of steel entered Morgan's voice. "She and Edgar are my family now."

"I see." Rhys couldn't quite hide his envy. He and Juliana could be a family, too. If he let it happen. If he could see his way through to trusting her.

Morgan cast him a look of pity. "From what you said earlier, I thought perhaps you'd changed your mind about the women's part in our impressment. I take it you and your wife are still at odds."

Rhys gritted his teeth. "I can't believe I'm so bedeviled by one small woman. 'Tis enough to make me doubt my own sanity. The night of the engagement party, she threatened to make my life hell if I continued to distrust her. I thought she meant she'd be a shrew or do some petty nonsense like throw tantrums and defy me. I could handle that." A groan escaped his lips. "But I've discovered there are other kinds of hell."

"That, I can well imagine," Morgan said with a laugh. "So you still distrust her?"

"I don't know what to think anymore."

"Lettice says Juliana was Northcliffe's victim. She's convinced the girl would never have done what Northcliffe claims. She told Northcliffe that to his face, too."

Five days ago, Rhys had argued vehemently with Morgan over the absurd idea that Juliana might be innocent. Now the idea seemed much less absurd. "And what did he say?"

Morgan sighed. "He kept insisting he hadn't lied. Unfortunately, there seems to be no way of knowing the truth if the innkeeper and the St. Albans brothers stick to their story. Even Lettice has no real proof of her innocence."

"So Lettice admits that it's possible Juliana betrayed us."

"Nay. I think Lady Juliana would have to confess it under oath before Lettice would believe ill of her."

Rhys suppressed a curse. No one believed ill of Juliana. The women at Llynwydd deferred to her wishes no matter what he said. They looked on him as a wolf preying on the poor lamb.

Hah! That poor lamb was rapidly twisting everyone in the household about her little finger. Before long, he'd find even his own valet taking her side.

"One thing you should know, however," Morgan went on. "Northcliffe did admit to keeping my letter from Lettice, which means it's likely he did the same with yours to Lady Juliana."

"Yes. And it's even likely that Northcliffe lied. But how do you explain the fact that someone told him where to find us? And why did Juliana hide her marriage from everyone from the very beginning?"

"What reason does she give?"

"Youth . . . fear . . . weakness—"

"All valid reasons."

"And all reasons for her backing out of the marriage. Can't you see? She must have kept it hidden because she didn't want it. And if she didn't want it, then she betrayed me."

"Perhaps it's not as simple as that."

"I don't know. I can't even think straight anymore. I want to trust her, even though I know she must be lying."

"Perhaps you're thinking straight when you want to trust her." Morgan remained silent several moments before venturing, "Has it occurred to you that you may be choosing not to trust her for reasons other than evidence?"

"What in God's name do you mean by that?"

Morgan shrugged. "If you accept that she didn't betray you, then you can't force her to stay with you. You'd have to let her choose between marriage to you or separation. You'd have to take the chance of losing her—as I took the chance of losing Lettice to Darcy. And you won't risk that, will you?"

Rhys fisted his hands on his reins. There was too much truth in Morgan's words.

If Juliana were innocent, he'd been unfair and callous. To think of how he'd treated her this afternoon, walking away and not trusting her with something she couldn't have altered anyway . . .

He resisted the thought. "She can't possibly be innocent."

"Only you can know, I suppose."

Rhys chafed at Morgan's veiled reproof. Thankfully, they were approaching the road to Llynwydd, where he could escape his companion.

As he turned that direction, Morgan halted his horse. "You're not staying at your town house tonight? 'Tis near midnight, and with the moon setting early, you may not have much light to ride by."

Rhys thought of Juliana lying awake in bed. She'd said she wouldn't be waiting for him, but he couldn't take the chance. This afternoon's encounter had sharpened the keen edge of his hunger for her, and he wouldn't be able to sleep until he'd satisfied it.

"I'm going home. I'll come to town in a few days so we can plan the campaign."

"Fine. Good luck with your wife."

Aye. He would need plenty of that tonight.

Juliana jerked up straight in her bed, cocking her head to listen. There it was again—someone was trying to open the latch on her door. She groaned. Only one person would be attempting to enter her bedchamber in the middle of the night. The male curse that followed confirmed it.

Hadn't he heard a word she said before he left? Had he really expected her to be waiting in his bed, warm and willing? Of course he had. He was a *man*, and a randy one at that.

The crack of a fist against the door sent her shrinking against the headboard. "Go away!" she called out.

"Open this door," he commanded. "I must talk to you."

"Is that the new term for seduction?" she asked sweetly.

"I want to tell you where I was tonight," he said at last. "Please, Juliana."

The "please" nearly shattered her resolve. She moved to the door, then paused, her hand on the latch. Was this simply another trick? After this afternoon, he was bound to know that all he had to do was kiss her and she turned into wax in his hands. "You can tell me from where you are."

There was a long silence, then a heavy sigh. "I was at a Sons of Wales meeting. The men were threatening to riot at the council meeting, and Morgan asked me to come stop them."

Her heart lurched in her chest. Not again. She couldn't bear to lose him a second time. "And you went? Without telling me why? Without stopping to think about how dangerous and stupid and—"

"Damn it, Juliana, open up so I can explain."

She slumped against the door. What he meant was, *Open up so I can take you in my arms and make you forget that I don't trust you with anything.*

"You can explain just as well from out there."

"I've told you what you wanted to know." Irritation crept into his voice. "Isn't that enough?"

"Why didn't you tell me before you left?"

Another long pause ensued. "Because . . . your brother was going to be there at the council meeting and . . . well . . ."

When he trailed off awkwardly, everything fell into place. Darcy had mentioned he would be putting forth his candidate at the upcoming council meeting. Apparently the Sons of Wales hadn't wanted that, and Rhys had been only too happy to help them thwart his enemy. Even when it meant leaving her side to rush off to Carmarthen.

"You thought I might warn him, didn't you?" she whispered.

"I didn't want you to worry—"

"Don't lie to me. You went off without a word because you didn't want me to warn Darcy." She snorted. "As if I could, when you won't even let me saddle a horse from my own stables or call for the carriage!"

"Damn it all, I'm sorry." When he spoke again, his voice

sounded strangled. "I was wrong to run out without any explanation. It was a gut reaction. I didn't stop to think . . . I just—"

"Didn't trust me."

"Let me make it up to you." His rumbling voice made it absolutely clear how he intended to "make it up" to her. "Open the door and let me show you I'm sorry."

She tensed. She desperately wanted to see what it would be like to have him make love to her again, fusing his naked body to hers, driving himself deep inside her. Her knees went weak.

But she knew what would happen afterward. He would distrust her again tomorrow. And the next day. And the next. He would keep shielding his heart, even while he made love to her.

And that would hurt far more than this absence of him.

"Go away, Rhys," she whispered through a raw throat. "Go back to your radical companions and leave me in peace."

The door shook as he pounded his fist into it. "I know you want me, wife. You can't deny it."

"I don't want you to hurt me. I'm afraid of you, Rhys."

"Nay." His voice sounded so close to her ear, she had to remind herself of the stout oak door between them. "You're not afraid of *me*. You're afraid of yourself. That's why you haven't locked your door until tonight—because this afternoon you almost gave in. And you're terrified that you might do it again if you unlatch the door."

"I'm not . . . I won't . . ."

He gave a bitter laugh. "Good night, *cariad*. I won't

make a liar of you tonight." He dropped his tone to a satiny caress. "But you can't stay in there forever."

As his footsteps echoed, she cursed. It was only a matter of time before he took complete advantage of her weakness for him. She could only hope that, by that time, his weakness for her would be just as great.

17

Sea on the shore no longer
Stays than this outlaw in care.
So I'm bound with pain, shackled
Straitly, and my breast is nailed.
Scarcely, beneath her goldhead,
Shall I have my wise young maid.

—DAFYDD AP GWILYM, "HIS AFFLICTION"

*I*t was already midmorning when Lettice entered the bedroom to find her husband still asleep, sprawled across the mattress like a conquering hero. Ah well, it was Sunday, and he'd had a late night in town.

She still could scarcely believe he was hers. All these years of aching for him in secret when Darcy came to her . . . and now they were bound by vows that even the mighty Lord Northcliffe couldn't break.

As she studied his familiar tanned face and the long scar that divided his bristly cheek in two, she sighed. Could they ever put those years behind them? Could he ever completely forget she'd spent that time in the bed of his enemy?

As if feeling her presence, Morgan opened his eyes and swiped back his unruly hair. "Good morning, sweetheart." He patted the bed.

She sat down beside him. "Good morning, Mr. Candidate for Parliament."

He laughed. "So you actually heard all that muddle I told you last night. Your 'hm' and 'um' sounded suspiciously like someone talking in her sleep."

Playfully, she punched his arm. "Oh, I heard all right. And while you've been sleeping the day away, you and Rhys have become the talk of the town."

He pulled her atop him, settling her against the length of his body. "What are they saying?"

"That you'll be a 'force to be reckoned with' and other such nonsense."

"And are they admitting what clever devils we are, to rout Northcliffe at his own game?" When her smile faltered, he added hastily, "I'm sorry, love. I didn't mean to bring him up."

She brushed her lips over his. "It's all right. It's not as if we can erase what happened by not talking about it."

"I suppose you're right. But I wish I could." His voice turned grim. "I wish I could blot the devil completely from your mind . . . and your memory."

"You've nothing to worry about. Those years were like wandering through the mist to me. These few days with you have been more real than all my years with Darcy."

His eyes searched hers. "Still, it must bother you to hear me speak of him with venom."

"Nay." She rested her head on his chest. "I understand

why you want him to pay for what he did. But you can't expect me to feel the same urge. I've already made him suffer by leaving him. Nothing I could do would punish him more."

Morgan stroked her hair. "If not for what he did to us, I could almost like the man. His father was a stupid noble who let his holdings fall into disrepair, but Northcliffe turned that around and made it profitable in a short time. He's got a good mind. 'Tis a shame he uses it only to gain power."

"He won't be doing that much longer. With Rhys's money and influence behind you we'll soon be putting M.P. after your name, and that will sound the end to Darcy's power, I suspect." She kissed his scruffy chin. "I'm only hoping you don't grow a big head once you're an M.P. I won't countenance that."

He thrust his hips suggestively up against her. "I'm already growing a big . . . something, my love. Do you think you can 'countenance' that?" He reached down to drag her skirts up her thighs.

"Stop that! Edgar might come in and see us!"

He clamped his hands on her backside and squeezed. "Then he'll learn a thing or two from his old Da, won't he?"

"Why, Morgan Pennant, you . . . you . . ." His fingers slid between her legs, and she said his name again, this time more of a sigh than a protest. "Let me at least close the door."

A sound from the doorway made her look around, and there stood Edgar, round-eyed and bewildered. In a thrice, she jerked down her skirts and scrambled from the bed, hearing Morgan groan behind her.

"What are you doing with Father?" Edgar asked, shoving his thumb into his mouth.

It had taken only a day for Edgar to accept that Morgan was his father. Apparently, he thought fathers appeared magically from the sea every day.

Lettice hurried over and wiped a smidgen of food from his cheek. "Mother and Father are . . . playing a game, dear. Why don't you finish eating, and then play with the toy ship Father bought you yesterday?"

She glanced back at Morgan, who regarded her with frank male appreciation. "Mother and Father will be . . . finished in just a bit, and then we'll do something fun. Does that sound good?"

With a nod, he walked off. She shut the door, but before she could even flip the latch, she heard a timid knock.

"What is it, son?" Morgan called.

"Can Mr. St. Albans have some flummery, too?"

"Oh Lord," Lettice muttered as she swung the door open. "Mr. St. Albans?"

"He's in the kitchen. He's come to see you and Father. He asked me to fetch you, but I can tell him you're playing a game."

"It's all right. I'll come talk to Overton." She quickly straightened her skirts and smoothed her hair.

Morgan was already out of bed, pulling on his drawers and hunting for a shirt.

When the three of them entered the kitchen, Overton was sitting at the table, staring into Edgar's bowl as if hoping to find a secret in the hot mixture of oatmeal flour and milk.

"Do you want some flummery?" Edgar chirped.

Overton's head shot up, then he looked warily at Morgan. "I'm not hungry," he said to Edgar. "Listen, my boy, I need to talk to your . . . parents. Could you go play in the garden for a bit?"

"I suppose. Will you let me feed your horse?"

"Certainly." Overton watched as Edgar skipped out to the garden. "He's fond of horses, isn't he?"

"My son is fond of many things," Morgan gritted out. "Of course, I'm only now learning what those things are."

When Overton colored, Lettice laid her hand on Morgan's arm. "It's all right. Overton has always been a friend to me and Edgar."

Overton rose. "Not always. Darcy didn't send Mr. Pennant and Mr. Vaughan to the press gangs by himself—I had a part in that. I should have told you the truth about it from the beginning, but Darcy . . ."

Lettice knew perfectly well that if Darcy asked his brother to go to sea in a leaky coracle, Overton would set sail.

"All that matters is that I know the truth now," she said. "Darcy has already admitted to what you and he did."

"Well . . . as long as you know. But that's not why I've come. I need your help." His voice tightened. "I'm worried about Juliana, out there alone with that bloody crazy Vaughan."

"He's not crazy," Morgan bit out.

"Isn't he? I heard what he did at the council meeting, showing up with those radicals to . . . to . . ."

"Put me forth as his candidate?" Morgan said.

"I don't give a damn about who's M.P., as long as it's not me." He jutted out his chin. "But I heard that Vaughan is going to put all his money into your campaign. He'll lose everything, trying to fight my brother."

"He's willing to risk that," Morgan said. "I'm not sure what concern it is of yours."

"My brother hates Ebbrell and all his lot. He couldn't wait to have them come to the council meeting with cudgels in hand, so he could have them arrested. And now that you've thwarted him—"

"Wait a minute. How did your brother know that the Sons of Wales had planned to riot?"

"Because . . . well . . ." Overton cast Lettice an uncertain glance.

She smiled. "Go on. He may be gruff, but he won't hurt you."

"Don't be so sure of that," Morgan muttered, but she pinched his arm and he added, "Just tell me the truth. I'm a reasonable man."

"Darcy has a spy among the Sons of Wales."

Morgan clenched his fists, and Lettice stepped between the two men. "Hear him out, Morgan, before you lose your temper."

"I want to know who the wretch is," Morgan ground out.

"I thought you might." Without hesitation, Overton offered a name Lettice recognized. "'Twas he who revealed that you and Vaughan printed those pamphlets years ago. That's how Darcy justified handing you over to the press gang."

Morgan stared at Overton. "So it had nothing to do with Lettice and Juliana?"

Overton shook his head. "He first learned of it when he overheard you and Lettice in the forest. Then he paid one of the radicals to get more information, so he could convince the press to take you without letting you ransom yourselves, as is sometimes done."

A muscle worked in Morgan's throat. "Good God."

"That also means my lady was faithful to Rhys," Lettice said. "She didn't betray him, did she?"

"Nay. She knew naught about it until after the men were at sea."

"Then how did you find her and Rhys at the inn?" Morgan asked.

"The innkeeper recognized her and sent for us at once."

Lettice's eyes narrowed. "*Which* innkeeper?"

"The owner of the White Oak."

She sank into a chair. "That *bastard*!"

"Who is he?" Morgan asked.

"A former suitor of mine who used to come to Northcliffe Hall. He knew Juliana from there, although I think she only saw him once. He was always angry that I spurned him. And apparently he found a way to get even."

Morgan loomed above Overton. "The innkeeper helped you that night, and he's been lying about it ever since."

"Aye. Darcy paid him well."

"We've got to tell Rhys," Morgan said. "He thinks she betrayed him."

"I know." Overton paled. "That's why I'm here. I want to ride out to Llynwydd and tell him everything, but I don't dare go alone. He might refuse to see me. But he'll see you, and perhaps me with you."

"Why didn't you tell the truth before?" Lettice asked. "Why has Darcy continued to insist that Lady Juliana wanted to escape from the marriage? She's his sister, for heaven's sake! And yours, too."

Overton wrung his hands. "'Tis a bloody mess. Darcy wanted a better husband for Juliana than a Welsh squire, and I just went along because I thought he might be right."

"Yes, but why did he keep lying even after the marquess spurned her?" Morgan demanded.

"Because he was afraid Vaughan would turn his wrath—and newfound influence—on him. Besides, Darcy thinks Vaughan is bewitched enough by Juliana that he won't hurt her."

"And what do *you* think?" Lettice asked.

"I'm afraid Vaughan will turn his wrath on all of us anyway. Last night, he proved that not knowing the truth won't keep him from destroying Darcy. I don't want him to destroy poor, innocent Juliana, too."

Lettice said, "I truly don't think Rhys would—"

"There's no telling what a man like Rhys might do when he's angry," Morgan said with a warning glance.

Then she realized what Morgan was up to. If Overton were reassured about his sister, he might not be so eager to tell the truth. And Rhys needed to know. He wouldn't trust Lady Juliana until he was sure of her.

"So." Overton leveled his gaze on Morgan. "Will you go with me to Llynwydd?"

"Of course we'll go," Lettice said.

Morgan shook his head at her. "You're not going, love. Rhys isn't kindly disposed toward you, either, for he still believes you had a part in the whole thing. 'Twill be better if I go alone."

"No," Overton said. "I have to see my sister. I must make certain that she's well." Pain slashed across his face. "And I must explain why we've wronged her. You're not going without me."

"As you wish. Give me a moment to dress, and we'll be off."

When Morgan disappeared into the other room, Lettice took Overton's hand. "Don't worry about Juliana. It will all come right in the end. I'm sure of it."

He ventured a smile. "I hope you're right."

"How's Darcy?"

"As well as can be expected, now that the light has gone out of his life."

"He's not taking it well, then?" she said, refusing to feel guilty about that.

"Nay."

"I'm so sorry."

"It's not your fault. He was the fool, to toy with your life and expect you not to hate him for it."

She sighed. "I don't hate him. I just pity him."

Overton stared at her. "When Darcy first became obsessed with you, I didn't understand it. He had a rich, beautiful lady betrothed to him and was heir to an earldom. I thought he was mad to dally with a lady's maid."

"He *was* mad," she said, attempting a laugh.

"Nay. Now that I've come to know you, I think he should have done more than make you his mistress. He should have married you."

"Don't be silly," she murmured, but his words warmed her. She'd always received the brunt of the town's disapproval. No one had chastised Darcy for keeping a mistress, but everyone had criticized her for being his kept woman.

Sometimes she'd even believed they were right. And telling herself that she'd had no choice didn't lessen the pain or self-doubt. After a while, she'd begun to believe she didn't deserve to be a wife. That in taking Morgan away, God had deemed her unworthy of it.

Morgan entered, and she smiled at him. Thank heaven time had proven her wrong. It had brought Morgan back to her.

And now Morgan must bring Rhys back to Juliana.

The house was as quiet as a tavern at dawn, but Juliana still couldn't concentrate. Every time she started reading the larder inventory, her mind wandered to Rhys, still asleep down the hall. She'd instructed his valet not to wake him, mostly to put off the inevitable.

The blasted man had known exactly what his words would do to her last night. All she could do was wonder when and where he would catch her alone, and try to seduce her. Then she started remembering his heated kisses and tempting caresses and—

"Oh bother!" She set the inventory aside. She should lock him in the State Bedroom. Then she wouldn't have to worry about it.

The thought made her smile. Of course, some wretched footman would let him out at once, but still it was lovely to think of him at her mercy, forced to follow her whims for a change.

"Milady?"

She turned to find Mrs. Roberts in the doorway. "Yes?"

"Your younger brother and a man named Pennant are here to see the master. I told them he was asleep, but they're insisting."

She scowled. "Send them up here." This time, she'd make her betraying wretch of a brother listen to her.

When Mrs. Roberts returned with the two men, Juliana dismissed her and closed the door to face Overton. "I can't believe you have the audacity to visit, after what you've done. Are you here to tell Rhys more lies about me?"

"I've come to tell him the truth."

"Isn't it a little late for that?"

The anger in her voice made him blink. "He hasn't hurt you, has he?" He looked her over as if for signs of physical injury.

She deliberately kept quiet. *Let him worry. He's done little enough of it until now.*

"I swear, if Vaughan has hurt you, I'll throttle him!"

She rolled her eyes at her brother. The last thing she

needed was Overton engaging Rhys in fisticuffs. "He hasn't harmed me. Not physically anyway."

Overton clearly didn't know what to make of that, although Morgan's eyes narrowed.

"I'm fine. As you can see, I have the run of the house and . . ." Her voice faltered at the half-truth, then she went on coldly, "Anyway, you needn't worry."

"But I do," Overton said.

"And when did this change of heart occur? Before or after you publicly proclaimed me a heartless witch and betrayer to my husband, who already had reason to resent me? Surely it occurred to you that your lies would turn a tormented man into an unreasonable tyrant."

"Oh God, I'm so bloody sorry, Juliana. That I let Darcy convince me to lie to you in the first place years ago. That I kept secret what he'd told your husband. And that I didn't speak the truth at your engagement party, even if Darcy—"

"'Darcy this' and 'Darcy that'—is this all his doing? What kind of hatred must he bear for me that he'd lie so?"

"You must understand—Darcy thought Vaughan had married you to regain Llynwydd. He thought he was saving you."

"Did he, now? And when Rhys returned and he *kept* lying?"

"Darcy thought Vaughan would want to be rid of you, once he was convinced you'd betrayed him."

Behind Overton, Morgan snorted. "Obviously your brother had no idea of how strongly Rhys cares for your sister."

Hmm. Rhys had a funny way of showing it.

Overton went on quickly. "Once he realized that Vaughan was serious about revenge, Darcy got scared—afraid that Vaughan would destroy him."

"And of course, it didn't matter at all that Rhys might destroy me, did it?" she snapped.

Overton paled. "What has he done to you? If he has abused you—"

"He hasn't." She stiffened. "But Darcy gave permission to Rhys to do with me as he wished, without a care for what that might be. I can never forgive Darcy for that."

"Where is Rhys now?" Morgan asked.

"Asleep." She faced him. "Surely that doesn't surprise you. He had a late night, since he went out at your behest to take on Darcy. I suppose you two are trying to get yourselves impressed all over again."

"I think Northcliffe knows better than to try that now."

A sudden fear gripped her. She knew only too well how desperate Darcy got when he was cornered. "Darcy isn't going to take all of this lying down. He'll strike out at Rhys somehow."

"Don't tell me you're worried about your 'unreasonable tyrant' of a husband," Morgan said dryly.

Though she was tempted to give him an earful of just how her husband had been behaving, she was more concerned with making him understand the treacherous path Rhys was on. "Of course I'm worried. I don't want to lose Rhys again."

Both men looked relieved, especially her brother. "So things are going well with you and your husband?" he asked.

"I'm sure things will go better after you tell him the truth about the night we were impressed," Morgan said. "Once you explain how you knew where to find her."

"Yes, how *did* you know?" Juliana asked. "That's the one thing I haven't figured out."

Overton shifted from foot to foot. "The innkeeper recognized you and sent word. Once we explain that Darcy paid the innkeeper to lie, surely Vaughan will realize you had nothing to do with it."

His statement brought her up short. She'd been too focused on chastising Overton to realize the full implications of his visit. He'd come to tell the truth. To vindicate her to her husband. At last.

Hope swelled in her. Finally, someone would tell Rhys what had really happened. Then he'd be suitably chastened and beg her forgiveness. All would be well, and they could put this terrible time behind them.

Until the next time.

Her hope faltered. This wasn't the first instance of Rhys believing the worst of her. Years ago he'd accused her of spying on the Sons of Wales, only to realize his mistake when her father had threatened to cane her.

Each time *she* told him she was innocent, he remained distrustful. Someone else had to say it for him to believe it.

Despite all she'd done for Llynwydd and her explanations of why she'd hidden the marriage, he persisted in taking Darcy's word over hers.

His *enemy's* word.

And now Overton wanted to prance in here and tell Rhys everything, to act as if none of her suffering had occurred. He thought to wipe away the years with a few words—and Rhys would probably believe him. Then he would act as if none of it had happened, as if she hadn't been publicly maligned and betrayed by them.

She clenched her fists. A pox on him! And on them, too! How dared they think they could simply trot in here and make it all right with a few words!

She wouldn't give them that—nor him, either. Not this time.

She'd told him she was innocent. It was time he considered her life and character to determine whether to believe her. It was time he listened to his heart. Otherwise, the distrust would never end.

"I don't want you to tell him the truth," she said. When Morgan and Overton gaped at her, she added, "Please go now, before he awakens."

"Why the bloody hell would you want that?" Overton asked.

"Because I want him to believe *me*—to trust *me*. And if you tell him the truth now, he won't learn that."

"But Juliana—" Overton began.

"She's right." Morgan cast her an enigmatic glance. "But do you realize what you're asking of him? In the navy they battered his pride, stole his dignity, reduced him to an animal. And he's lived for years believing that you helped put him there. Even before that, he'd had few in his life he could trust. You're asking him to ignore his entire past. Speaking as his friend, and one who thinks highly of him, I don't know if he can do that."

Tilting her chin up, she said quietly, "He'd better learn to do it. You seem to forget he's not the only one who suffered through this. I may not have suffered exile or floggings, but I had to live in a perpetual limbo, never knowing if I was widow or wife, never knowing what had happened to him. I even went through the agony of grieving for him, after that investigator falsely told me he was dead. Then, once Rhys returned, he treated me with a contempt I didn't deserve."

"Yes, but—" Overton began.

"If you tell him, he'll say he's sorry, and it will all be better—right? Men! You think a few apologies will wipe away the heartache you cause by your refusal to see a woman's true character." She stared hard at her brother. "Either Rhys learns to trust me, or he lives with the consequences of his distrust. I won't give him this easy solution. I can't, if I want our marriage to last."

She stared them down, trying to hide her trepidation. She was taking a big chance. But she had to.

"You love him, don't you?" Overton said. "You still love that bloody Welshman, or you wouldn't care if your marriage lasted."

The painful truth hit her. She *did* love him, despite everything. "Unfortunately, foolish though it may be, I do."

Overton got a sheepish look on his face. "Then I suppose that takes care of my other reason for coming."

Morgan's head shot around. "What other reason?"

Avoiding his gaze, Overton drew a folded sheet of paper out of his waistcoat pocket, along with a sealed envelope. "Well . . . you see . . . I didn't think I should tell you, Pennant, since I knew you wouldn't approve. But I promised to bring this to Juliana."

When Overton handed it to her and she unfolded the paper, she recognized the crest at the top. And the signature at the bottom.

Dropping into a chair, she read it, then opened the sealed envelope and read its contents, too.

"What the devil is it?" Morgan asked when she lifted her head to stare into space.

"Apparently," she said in a strained voice, "Lord Devon has decided he wants to resume our betrothal."

18

I'm her true lover always
While the quick life in me stays.
Without her, I go lovelorn—
If it's true she's not foresworn.

—DAFYDD AP GWILYM, "THE WIND"

Rhys woke from a dreamless sleep to find himself utterly alone in the massive state bed with its ivory-embroidered silk hangings.

He hadn't thought this far when he'd planned his vengeance, when he'd decided to make Juliana pay for her youthful betrayal. He hadn't considered what it would be like to live with a stranger he'd taught to despise him.

Or to be so heart-wrenchingly alone.

He craved her more each day, no matter how he blocked her from his activities. And it wasn't just the pleasures of her body, but the way she startled when he entered a room, the smile that broke over her face when he amused her with a funny tale, her endearing turns of phrase and her quick wit.

What would it be like to have her be his wife entirely? To have her share not only his bed, but his thoughts, his plans, his hopes for the future? To wake up beside her in the morning? To have her rub his back? To help her dress, letting his fingers linger as he fastened everything he'd unfastened the night before?

He'd never lived with her like that . . . never spent more than one night in the same room with her. But his imagination painted a picture too tempting to be borne.

This was insane. If he wanted Juliana to be his wife in every way, he could have her. She was willing. She only required his trust.

Yesterday, he'd said he couldn't pay her price. Today, he wondered why not. She'd betrayed him once, but that was long ago. Had she betrayed him since his return?

Nay. She'd defied him, but her household rebellions commanded his respect, not his distrust. She hadn't tried to rouse her brothers against him . . . she hadn't tried to run away. She'd endured his petty tyrannies with grace and forbearance.

Would it be so impossible to give her what she asked?

Glancing at the clock, he got a start. It was almost one. She must have ordered the servants to let him sleep.

He left the bed, smiling as he quickly dressed. No doubt she had a reason for that. Some plot to arm the footmen against him, or ordering the cook to feed him gruel so he'd have no strength to seduce her. With Juliana, there was no telling.

The urge to see her grew so great, he hurried out to find her. Hearing voices in the salon, he strode that direction. Just as he reached the door, a faintly familiar voice halted him.

"So what do you want me to tell him, Juliana?" the man said. "You've read the letter. Lord Devon insists that you meet with him, and he's appealing to me and Darcy to arrange it. I have to give him some answer."

It was St. Albans. Come to wrest his wife from him.

Fury ripping through him, he jerked the door open. Both St. Albans and Juliana whirled around. He didn't need to see her guilty flush or St. Albans's terror to know he'd stumbled onto a discussion he hadn't been meant to hear.

In two quick strides, he was across the room and drawing his brother-in-law up by the collar. "You tell that bastard Devon that my wife is no longer his to command!" He twisted the collar until it tightened about St. Albans's neck. "And if I ever find you bringing letters to Juliana from him again, I'll bind you hand and foot and sink you in the Towy!"

"Rhys!" Juliana yanked on his arm. "Let him go! Please!"

"What's he doing here?" Rhys shook St. Albans, who was starting to turn blue. "Why is he bringing letters to you from Devon?"

"Let him go, Rhys," said another voice.

Releasing St. Albans, he turned to find Morgan standing there. "What are *you* doing—" He glanced at St. Albans, who was pulling at his collar, gasping for breath. "Surely the two of you didn't come here together."

But obviously they had. "What the hell is going on?"

"St. Albans wanted to make sure Juliana was all right, and I accompanied him because he was afraid you wouldn't let him see her."

"Damned right I wouldn't have," Rhys bit out. "Especially if I'd known he was playing messenger for that damned marquess. How could you bring him here to coax my own wife away from me? What kind of friend are you?"

"I didn't know he had letters from Devon with him."

"Be quiet, the lot of you!" Juliana turned on Rhys, eyes flashing. "How dare you say who I can and can't receive letters from? Overton brought a letter addressed to me, and I had every right to read it."

He bore down on her. "How many letters like this has he delivered? How many times has he sneaked in here behind my back to help you carry on a clandestine correspondence with your former betrothed?"

"Don't be absurd! As if anyone could sneak in here with the footmen and butler and maids running about. This is the first time Overton has visited, and I assure you I didn't know he was bringing letters from Stephen."

More than one letter. And she'd used Devon's Christian name. That sent him over the edge. "Well, it's the last time your brother will be coming here. And there will be no more letters from your precious Stephen, if I have to lock you into your bedchamber to ensure it."

"Juliana!" cried St. Albans. "You must let me tell Vaughan what—"

"No!" She fixed her gaze on Rhys. "Go home, Overton. Thank you for coming and thank you for your offer, but I'll handle this my own way."

"Yes, go home, St. Albans," Rhys echoed. "And don't come back."

Juliana settled her hands on her hips. "Pay my husband

no mind. He becomes irrational whenever Lord Devon's name is mentioned."

"Irrational!" Rhys growled. "Because I take umbrage at having my wife—"

Juliana turned her gaze to Pennant. "Morgan, take him out of here and go. Both of you, please. I need to talk to my husband. Alone."

"Come on, lad," Morgan said.

"I can't leave her with this madman!" St. Albans protested. Only when Rhys fixed him with a murderous glare did he let Morgan drag him from the room.

Rhys closed the door behind them. "The letters." He snapped his fingers. "Give them to me, if you please."

"Oh, you blasted fool." She threw them at him. "Read my 'clandestine' correspondence if you wish."

Both were from Lord Devon. The first was addressed to Lord Northcliffe and St. Albans, asking them in cordial terms to arrange a meeting between him and Juliana.

But the other was addressed to "Lady Juliana, my one true love." Full of effusive apologies and compliments, it stated Lord Devon's desire to renew his courtship of her if she could arrange a divorce from her husband.

The letter would have enraged him, except for one fact. It was clearly the first, and it didn't appear to have been solicited by Juliana.

"So your titled former betrothed wants a meeting, does he?" Rhys tossed the letters into the fire. "Well, he's not having one."

"I know this is upsetting," she said calmly, "but I must explain that—"

"He's had his explanation!" The thought of her meeting with Lord Devon struck him with such fear, he couldn't govern his words. "I'm forbidding you to see him or write to him, and I will hold firm on this."

"Why are you being so pigheaded? I've already told you I don't love him. What would it hurt for me to write a letter explaining—"

"What?" Jealousy rode him hard. "That your cruel husband won't allow you a divorce? He knows that. Or will you offer him an alternative . . . an affair perhaps, to give him what you deny me?" When she stared at him in horror, he realized he'd gone too far. "Oh God, I'm sorry. I didn't mean—"

"Yes, you did." She backed away. "No matter what I do, you still think I'm a despicable creature who would betray you at every turn."

All he'd meant to do before he'd come in here was tell her that he cared, that he wanted to change things between them. "That's not—"

"You won't be happy until I've received my just deserts for what I supposedly did to you . . . and for what I *really* did by stupidly keeping our marriage secret."

Her voice grew choked. "It's not enough to make me a prisoner in my own home, or cut me off from my family, or refuse my help in caring for the estate. Nay, you must punish me more, mustn't you? So perhaps I should help you, so we can be done with this once and for all."

She flew past him to open the door and call for the housekeeper.

"What the devil—"

Mrs. Roberts appeared almost instantly. "Yes, milady?"

"I've decided on the marketing list. You won't find most items in Carmarthen, but I'm sure Simms can get them from a warship in the bay. I'll need hardtack, the oldest and most maggot-ridden you can find, some salt beef, and grog—let's not forget grog."

Mrs. Roberts was aghast. "Why would you and the master want—"

"Oh, not for the master." Her voice had gone cold. "This is to be my diet. The master will eat his usual fare, but for the next three years or so, I'll be having—"

"That's enough!" Pulling Juliana back into the room, Rhys turned to the startled housekeeper. "Your mistress has had some upsetting news. Ignore what she just said. She's overwrought." Then he shut the door.

As Juliana wrenched free of him, the deadness in her eyes chilled him. "I should have realized that wouldn't be harsh enough for you. It doesn't entirely live up to what you suffered, does it? Mere food deprivation wouldn't satisfy your desire for punishment."

"Don't be ridiculous. I don't want you punished." He fought to stay calm when all he felt was growing fear at the strange, lost look on her face.

She didn't seem to have heard him. "Perhaps a few floggings would satisfy you. But that wouldn't take care of those years you spent in America." Her voice was so distant that it clutched at his heart. "You were wounded and cut off from your home."

He caught her in his arms and held her close. "Hush, my darling." He'd never seen her like this. He'd driven her to it with his foolish accusations. "I don't want to hurt you."

"You must help me think of a suitable punishment," she said hoarsely. "Tell me what you require as penance, so I can be done with it."

"I don't want a penance. God knows I don't want you to suffer what I did."

"Oh, but you do. You want to strip me of everything, to make me your slave."

He tightened his arms around her. "I want you to be my wife. Nothing more. I want to put the past behind us and go on." When she stared at him as if uncomprehending, he said hastily, "You said we should find peace together—and I want that, too. Peace with you. Here at Llynwydd."

She shook her head. "You want nothing but my body, and certainly not peace. You told me you don't even know what it is. And now I believe you."

Her face was so desolate, fear clawed at him. This acquiescence worried him far more than all her anger.

He caught her head in his hands. "You said you'd teach me to find peace. I'm holding you to that promise."

She closed her eyes. "I can't. You'll only hurt me again."

"I swear I won't." He sought for something to pull her out of her hopelessness. "You can't give up on me. If you do, I'll . . . I'll turn into a beast. I'll terrorize my tenants and run roughshod over the servants."

"It doesn't matter."

He made his voice deliberately provoking. "You don't care? Then I'll throw your precious *cwpwrdd tridarn* out in the rain, and I'll . . ." God, she was limp in his arms, as if she truly *didn't* care what he did anymore. He forced steel into his voice. "I'll cut off Evan's lessons. I'll not even give him any paper."

Her eyes shot open. "You wouldn't dare! The poor boy never harmed anyone in his whole life. I won't let you—" As relief flooded his face, she broke off. "You wouldn't hurt him, would you?"

Encouraged that her expression had lost some of its bleakness, he murmured, "Who knows what I'd do without you? I can be a monster."

"I know." She gazed at him a long moment, her vision seeming to clear. When she spoke again, her tone was more pointed. "How well I know."

The numb creature of a moment ago seemed to have dissolved, leaving his Juliana, full of stubborn rebelliousness. Thank God. "Then tame the monster. You're the only one who can."

"I haven't had much success with that," she said. "I've obviously been going about it all wrong."

"Nay. You've been driving me mad with wanting you, and surely that's the first step."

She glanced uncertainly at him. "I think you're worse when you want me. You become so jealous and wholly irrational."

"And I say stupid, regrettable things. I shouldn't have said what I did about you and Devon. I went a little insane at the thought of him trying to get back into your life. But 'tis only because I want you so very much." He nuzzled her temple, feeling the pulse quicken beneath his lips. "'Tis only because I've spent endless hours remembering the feel of your hair, and the taste of your mouth."

She tried to push away. "You say these lovely things one minute, and then the next—"

"I'll turn over a new leaf." He lowered his head. "I promise to be a monster no more, if you'll only satisfy this craving that's eating me up." He brushed a kiss over her cheek. "Only you can assuage this hunger." He closed his mouth over hers, fearful she wouldn't respond, that he'd driven her out of his reach.

But although she stilled, her mouth softened. He lingered over her lips, drinking her hot little breaths until he could stand the beckoning heat no more. Then he plunged his tongue inside.

By thunder, she was wonderful. And she was his, all his, whether she admitted it yet or not.

Taking his time, he explored the hot satin of her mouth, the slide of her tongue around his. And when she slipped her arms about his waist and pressed against him, he took the invitation to grow bolder, rubbing his palm over her breast, groaning when she arched into his hand.

"That's it, darling," he whispered against her lips, then trailed kisses along her cheek. "That's the way to tame the monster."

"You're not acting tame," she grumbled. But when he ran his tongue along the rim of her ear, she curved her body against his like a cat.

"Neither are you." He found the hooks that held her bodice together.

"Rhys!" she protested when he worked them loose.

"For God's sake, 'tis daylight and we're in the middle of the salon."

"Aye, and after yesterday, that's where we'll stay. I'll not lose you on the way to the bedroom again."

He kissed her hard then. Peeling open her bodice and drawing down the neck of her shift, he filled his hands with her breasts, thrust high by her corset. Then he thumbed her nipples until they were hard as cherry stones. Hard and sweet and driving him utterly mad.

He wanted to tear the clothes off her, to devour those luscious breasts as he thrust into her delectable body over and over and . . .

Mustn't do that . . . mustn't scare her. Must make her want me. Like she used to.

He skimmed his hands over her gown, unlacing and unpinning what he could, desperate to have her naked so he could make her desire him. But it had been too damned long since he'd undressed her, and she was wearing far too many clothes. Despite what he'd told her, he'd been celibate since he'd left her. No one had been able to tempt him.

Except Juliana, and he was ready to explode with wanting her. He fumbled with her corset laces, cursing when he couldn't unknot them.

Juliana was touched by his ineptness. Perversely, it made her desire him more. "Let me," she whispered and worked loose the knots of her front-laced corset.

That she felt almost as much urgency as he terrified her. After his fury, she didn't want to need him so much.

"Take it off," he said hoarsely as she undid the last knot.

A shiver passed through her, for his words echoed those

of their first night together after his return. Yet as he lifted his hands to drag the shift and corset down her with aching slowness, she knew this wasn't at all like that night.

His eyes were still that intense blue, raking hotly over her bared breasts and belly, and his brow was still furrowed with concentration. But when he grazed his fingers over her skin, it was with a gentleness near to reverence. "How can you have grown only more lovely in six years?"

He'd never denied that he found her attractive. Still, his words gratified her female urge to be admired, and she smiled in feline satisfaction.

With a scorching look, he dragged his finger down to the waistband of her petticoat.

"Take the rest of it off," he said in a husky voice. "I want to see all of you."

She started to obey, then paused. "Only if you remove your waistcoat."

He quickly acquiesced, going one step further to remove his shirt.

"Well?" He tugged at the waistband. "I'm waiting, my darling."

Suddenly shy, she removed everything else, hiding her blushing face from him as her shift slid to the floor last, leaving her naked.

She heard his quick indrawn breath, felt the heat of his gaze on her. Then he caught her up in his arms and strode to the sofa. Laying her down, he knelt beside her. She swallowed when she saw the desire flaming in his eyes.

He ran his thumb over her lips. "You have nothing to fear from me. I want only to please you."

"And not yourself?"

"Aye, and that, too. Surely you won't deny me that. I've spent too many nights longing to touch your 'sweet body that from faith can guile.'"

She recognized the lines from Robin Ddu's poem. "Oh, unfair. You know I can't resist when you quote poetry to me."

His low chuckle echoed down deep inside her. "I know." He kissed her forehead. "'Your brow like a daisy bright.'" He swept her hair off her shoulder to fan out on the upholstery. "'Your hair like a tongue of gold.'"

Then he kissed her neck, before running his tongue down the slope of her breast to curl it about her nipple. "'Your throat's upright growth, / Your breasts, full spheres both.'"

He tugged at her nipple with his teeth, shooting such sparks through her that she whimpered and clutched his shoulders. His mouth inched lower as he trailed his tongue in a line down her belly to her navel, dipping it there before sliding lower.

"Your belly like a ripened peach," he said, then sucked the skin lightly into his mouth, making her squirm beneath him.

"Those aren't . . . Ddu's words," she choked out as his lips brushed the edges of her silky triangle of hair.

"Nay, those are mine." He skirted the aching place between her legs to press a kiss to her thigh. "Your thighs smooth as polished beech."

"That's enough," she said as his tongue spiraled higher and higher toward the spot no man had ever kissed.

"Poetry?" he rasped. "Or this?"

Then using his fingers to part the delicate folds of skin, he darted his tongue over the nub he found there, and she thought she'd die.

It was like being stroked by lightning, courted by sunshine, and caressed by moonlight all at once. The heat made her buck beneath him, trying to get more, yet afraid she'd never get enough to satiate the tension he was building with each flick of his tongue.

He shifted to crouch over the sofa, his tongue licking up at her like flame, laving her, teasing her. She thrust against his hot mouth, wanting something she couldn't fathom, feeling the tension lengthen and stretch and grow tauter by the second.

"Oh . . . Rhys . . . Rhys . . ."

His mouth suddenly left her and she moaned, undulating against the sofa in a fruitless attempt to ease her craving.

"I can't wait any longer," he ground out as he tore off his breeches and drawers.

Suddenly, she was looking at his erect shaft.

She stared at it in blatant fascination. On her first night with him, she'd been too shy to actually look at the part of him that had thrust up inside her. But age had made her curious.

Pushing up onto one elbow, she reached out to stroke the smooth skin. When he groaned and thrust against her hand, she encircled him with her fingers. With a curse, he clasped her wrist.

"If you touch me like that, I'll explode." Then he climbed on top of her. "And I want to explode inside you."

She grew warm again. That was what she wanted. Rhys inside her.

He nudged her legs apart. "I need you, Juliana. God, how I need you."

She caught her breath. The first time they'd made love, he'd said, *I love you.*

Then he eased into her, making her forget everything but the present. "Christ, you're tight as a virgin." Satisfaction flashed across his face. "Tight as that first time . . ."

"You've been the only one to touch me." She moaned, half in distress, half in pleasure when he began to move in slow, enticing strokes.

"And I will always be the only one to touch you," he vowed, his face darkening as he quickened his thrusts. "Oh God . . . Juliana . . . it's been so long."

The sense of invasion began to lessen as his movements drew the silken tension taut in her again. She strained against him, clutching his behind to anchor him between her thighs. She felt his muscles flex as he lunged against her, inside her, filling her so fully she cried out with the thrill of it.

"That's it, my darling." He plunged to the very heart of her. "If you only knew how incredible you feel."

She knew how incredible *he* felt, driving into her like thunder, bringing her closer to the dark explosion lying in wait for her. Each time their bodies slammed together, she went a little insane, twisting beneath him as she tried to seal herself more to him.

He bent to kiss her mouth, stabbing his tongue in perfect rhythm with the thrusts of his hips. She met every kiss with her own wild hunger. She wanted to devour him, to trap him in her heart so he could never doubt her again.

The words *I love you* burned the back of her throat, but pride kept her silent. Instead she yielded her body completely to him, sure that one day she'd be able to give him the words, too.

When the explosion finally hit, she wasn't prepared for the pure, white heat of it . . . the power that hurtled through her, shattering all her control. She gasped and surged up, feeling her body pulse against his as the force shuddered through her, in her, around her.

"*Cariad!*" He drove into her one last time. His body convulsed and he spilled his seed inside her. "By thunder, you're mine . . . all mine . . ."

Muttering Welsh endearments, he collapsed atop her to bury his face in her neck. She felt spent, drained of both will and strength. There was something deeply satisfying about being in his arms, knowing that she'd just pleasured him and found her own enjoyment. His weight upon her contented her.

After several moments of lying there with limbs entangled as their heartbeats slowed, Rhys kissed her jaw. "Now that, my darling, was the way to tame a monster."

"Mmm." She skimmed her fingers down his back. "I shall have to try it more often."

A mischievous smile crossed his lips. "A great deal more often. In fact . . ." He pushed up against her.

Good Lord, he was growing hard again. "Is it normal for a man to be lusty again so soon after lovemaking?"

His gaze burned into hers. "Six years is a long time.

And contrary to those ugly words I said to you our first night together after my return, you were the only woman I wanted in all that time. The only woman I craved."

Something unknotted inside her at his confession. It had driven her mad, thinking of all the women who must have pleasured him in America.

"So I have all that hunger for you stored up inside. And it'll take me at least six more years to reduce it to a manageable level." He slid off her and held out his hand. "But what I wish to do with you requires a more comfortable setting. Let's continue this in our bedchamber. We've got all day, and all night, and I intend to use every minute of it."

The thought of spending the day in bed with Rhys made her heart pound all over again. Taking his hand, she rose from the sofa.

They drew on a minimum of clothing between quick kisses. When they left the salon, no one was around, but as soon as they took a few steps, Mrs. Roberts rushed up the stairs. She'd obviously been waiting in the hall below.

"Milady, are you all right?" the housekeeper asked in alarm as she noted Juliana's dishabille.

"I'm fine." She couldn't repress the lilt in her voice as she gazed up at Rhys. "Go back to the kitchen. Everything is fine."

The housekeeper hesitated as Rhys and Juliana swept past. As they reached their bedchamber, Juliana paused. "Oh, and Mrs. Roberts, tell the servants I will personally dismiss anyone who ventures up here in the next few hours."

Rhys chuckled as he drew her into their room. "Aren't

you worried about what the servants will think, my lady wife?"

"They'll think I've decided to share a bed with my husband," she said, echoing his words of a few days past. "I should hope they'd realize that."

With a crow of triumph, he caught her up in his arms and carried her to the bed.

19

Three things are reckoned wealth:
A woman—sunshine—health—
And in the heaven's dower
(Save God) a maid's the flower.

—DAFYDD AP GWILYM, "THE GREY FRIAR"

Juliana stared up at the threatening clouds. Just what they didn't need for the harvest—a thunderstorm. She hoped that since it was near dusk, the men were close to being finished.

She ordered the footmen to hurry loading the carts with the feast that the farmers expected the squire to provide as reward for their work. But her mind wasn't on that.

In the two weeks since Rhys had carried her into their bedchamber, much had changed between them. True to his word, Rhys had treated her as his wife from that moment. He'd given her all the freedom and privileges a wife deserved and more, for he'd made her his equal partner in running the estate.

Their days were busy and full. She usually rose before Rhys and attended to breakfast. Then they went their separate ways, having found the tasks that suited them best and appropriated them accordingly. Sometimes they lunched together, sometimes not. And they took the occasional ride in the late afternoon.

It wasn't until evening that they truly had time for themselves. Dinner was leisurely. They played backgammon or chess. Sometimes they read. And afterward . . .

Her cheeks flushed as she helped a footman slide a large pan on top of another and secure it in place. Some nights Rhys peeled her gown slowly from her, lavishing kisses over every inch he bared, then lingering over her body for what seemed like hours as he brought her to the heights of pleasure. Other nights, they tore off each other's clothes and came together like animals, writhing and straining in their haste.

She'd grown to know every inch of him . . . every scar, blemish, and muscle. She loved how he clutched his pillow in sleep, how he stretched his legs and groaned when he awoke, then opened his eyes with a slow smile meant only for her. She loved everything about him.

She loved *him*, period.

A splinter pricked her finger, and with a frown she sucked off the drop of blood. She still didn't know how he felt about her. He often said that he needed her. That he desired her. But never that he loved her.

It wouldn't have bothered her so much, if not for one thing—they never spoke of what had happened years ago. The one time she'd brought it up, he'd refused to discuss it. He'd insisted upon putting the past behind him; he'd said it didn't matter what had happened.

But it did. She could feel it in the wary way he sometimes looked at her, in the sudden shuttering of his expression whenever his impressment was mentioned. He still couldn't bring himself to trust her. Or love her.

She helped a footman spread an oilcloth over the cart. She *had* made progress with her husband. When she'd accidentally mentioned Stephen yesterday, he hadn't exploded or baited her with questions about Lord Devon's courtship of her. And in time—

Two hands closed over her eyes. She dropped the oilcloth with a shriek.

"Good evening, my lady," murmured a husky voice in her ear.

"Rhys Vaughan!" She wriggled away from him. "I swear, if you don't stop creeping up and frightening the life out of me, I'll—"

He muffled her words with a long kiss meant to rouse her blood. His face was grimy and he smelled of hay and they were surrounded by curious footmen, but she still responded.

When he drew back, he laughed. "What were you saying, darling?"

She glanced around to find the footmen grinning as they went about their work. "You're the most infuriating man I've ever known."

He chuckled.

With a little sniff, she headed to the last cart, which the footmen were already covering with oilcloth. "What are you doing here anyway? I thought you were overseeing the haying. Surely they're not finished."

He fell into step beside her. "Almost. We worked fast to beat the rain."

"How did it go?"

"Very well. The farmers were pleased that I joined them, since they're used to having Moss oversee everything. I've come back to fetch the harvest feast. And to fetch you to join us."

She looked down at her dirt-stained gingham gown and touched a hand to her flushed face. "Like this?"

He laughed. "Believe me, you look a lot better than the rest of us."

"I'm sure. But they won't expect me to attend. There's so much to do, and"—she gestured to the sky that threatened rain—"I don't know if I want to be caught in that."

"It'll hold off awhile longer. Besides, I have reasons for wanting you there this evening. I need your help."

"For what?"

"I'll tell you on the way." He removed a burlap bag from his saddle, then tossed it into the cart before lifting her onto the perch and climbing up to sit beside her. With a click of his tongue, he started the horses into a walk as the footmen took their places on the carts and fell in line.

She looked over at him. "So, Squire Arrogance, why are you dragging me off to the fields?"

"Thomas Newcome helped us bring in the hay harvest today, and Evan was there, too."

"They usually are."

"You told me you wanted to see the boy in school."

"Yes, but if you're thinking of talking to Mr. Newcome about Evan, you must abandon that idea. Evan's terrified

of what his father might do if we try to force his hand."
She caught her breath. "Sometimes I worry that he beats
the boy."

"I imagine you're right about that." He stared grimly
ahead. "Which is why I don't intend to talk to him. I have a
better method of convincing him to let his son go to school."

"Oh?" She laid her hand on the seat, only to feel the
burlap bag. It squirmed, and she shrieked, yanking her
hand back. "What in heaven's name—"

"It's all right. It's just a garden snake, perfectly harmless."

"A snake!" She scooted as far away as she could manage.
"Why on earth are you carrying a snake about?"

He grinned at her. "Well, my darling, it's like this . . ."

By the time they'd arrived at the hay field, Juliana was
grinning as widely as Rhys. Only he could come up with so
devious a plan. She glanced up at the dark sky. Now if only
the rain would hold off long enough for them to attempt it.

The workers cheered at their approach, having just finished loading up the hay. As the burdened wagons lumbered off to the barns, Rhys stopped the carts full of food,
and the workers crowded round—burly men and stout
women, their faces and clothes caked in dust and sweat.

Among them, she spotted a very dirty Evan, his young
face aglow, and she was glad she'd come.

Rhys stood up in the cart and said in Welsh, "Good day,
friends!"

"Good day," the workers echoed, clearly pleased to hear
the squire greet them so amiably.

"You've done well by me and my wife today," Rhys continued. "Now it's our turn to do well by you." He gestured

to the carts behind him. "There's mutton with potatoes, pottage, pudding, cheese, spiced fruitcakes, and light ale, compliments of my wife and her excellent kitchen."

Cheers rose up all around. Sometimes the harvest feast was nothing more than barley bread and salt pork with watered-down buttermilk. So a dinner of costly mutton stew and cheese washed down with ale was considered generous indeed.

Juliana smiled. Rhys was canny in the ways a laborer's mind worked. Later they'd be saying what a "good fellow" the squire was, "not one of those stingy nabobs who spends all his time in London, but a man who knows how to fill a body's stomach."

Rhys made a wonderful squire. As she'd known he would.

Grinning, he handed her down from the cart, and soon they were too engrossed in serving the meal to even speak to each other. He cut slabs of rice pudding as she doled out stew into earthenware basins, then cut hunks of the cheese.

As she worked, she kept a wary eye on the burlap bag she'd tucked under her cloak. Rhys had assured her that the snake wasn't poisonous, but she wasn't taking any chances.

Once everyone was served and sitting in groups about the field, Rhys came over. The light was failing, and a contented quiet filled the air as some workers ate and others built a fire, surrounding it with stones bared by the reaping.

"Let's do it now, before the light is completely gone," Rhys murmured.

They walked to where Evan and his father sat alone. As she and Rhys approached, she flashed them a smile.

"Good evening," she said brightly, ignoring how Thomas Newcome scowled at her. "I hope the meal is good."

The father merely grunted, but Evan mumbled, "Very good, my lady," shooting his father an anxious glance.

"I'm so glad you're here, Evan. I have some plums I wanted to send back to your mother. If you'll accompany me to the wagon, I can give them to you."

Evan looked at his father, who shrugged. "Go on, then. Your ma would like a plum or two, I'll wager."

Obediently, Evan stood and began to walk with her. As soon as she heard Rhys saying, "I need to have a word with you about the barley harvest, Mr. Newcome," she pulled Evan close.

"Do you want to go to school?" she asked.

"You know I do, but Da—"

"Never mind him. Do exactly as I say, and I think your da will be willing to send you."

She murmured instructions, and as soon as they'd moved as close to the abandoned scythes and as far from the workers as they could while still heading for the cart, she reached under her cloak for the burlap bag.

Glancing around to make sure no one watched, she dumped the snake onto the ground, then let out a blood-curdling scream.

Every man and woman around jumped to their feet. Even though Evan had been told to expect the scream, he stood there frozen.

"A snake! A snake!" she cried, shooting Evan a stern glance. Shaking off his surprise, he ran toward a scythe.

The blasted snake started to crawl off so she had to

do some quick maneuvering to make it look as if it were headed for her.

On cue, Rhys started running from across the field. Then Evan returned with the scythe and chopped down, cutting the head off the snake just as Rhys reached them.

Feigning tears, she collapsed into Rhys's arms. "It was coming for me ... oh, Rhys, it was dreadful!"

"My God, 'tis an adder," Rhys said as he peered at the dead snake.

"An adder," murmured the men crowding in around her.

"You might have been killed, my darling." He stared at Evan. "You saved my wife's life, lad."

Evan beamed, thoroughly caught up in the deception.

"What happened?" Mr. Newcome asked as he approached. "What happened?"

"Your son has saved my wife's life," Rhys repeated.

Juliana continued to shake, her trembling real this time. The most important part was still to come.

"God have mercy. A snake! Did my boy kill it?"

"Yes, thank God," Rhys said. "The reaping probably flushed him out." Releasing her, he bent to point out some faint markings on the snake's head. "You can clearly tell it's an adder."

Mr. Newcome nodded sagely. Vipers were rare in Wales, so he'd probably never seen one. And in the fading light, he wouldn't be able to tell much anyway.

Another man bent to examine the snake. "One bite from this and milady would have been dead in an instant."

Juliana reminded herself that their trick was for a good cause.

Rhys straightened. "For this, Newcome, your son deserves a reward."

Mr. Newcome's face brightened. "He does?"

"I am forever in his debt for saving my beloved wife." Rhys clapped his arm about Evan's shoulder. "Juliana tells me you're an intelligent boy, that you could make your mark in any school. How would you like to go to Eton, if your father will allow it?"

The stunned expression on Mr. Newcome's face was matched by Juliana's. Eton? That was exceedingly generous, far better than she'd dreamed.

Evan stared up at Rhys in wonder. "You'd send me to school, sir? Do you mean it?"

"Aye. 'Tis the least I can do."

"But isn't Eton that grand school for the sons of rich men and lords? Are you sure I could manage there?"

"If my wife thinks you're ready, I'm sure you are. But if you're worried, she would no doubt be willing to tutor you for the rest of the summer, so you won't be lacking."

"Hold on here," Mr. Newcome burst out. "The rest of the summer? Send him away to this Eton place? The boy has to work the farm. He can't be going off to some bloody English school!"

The frosty gaze Rhys leveled on Mr. Newcome was so quintessentially aristocratic, it would have made any English nobleman proud. "Are you refusing to let me repay your son for what he has just done?"

Mr. Newcome paled. "N-No, sir, but what about my farm?"

"You have another son, don't you? Surely you can spare the younger."

It was clear from the other men's scornful looks that they thought Mr. Newcome a fool for not snapping up the squire's offer.

"Or perhaps the way I've chosen to show my gratitude is not to your liking," Rhys added coldly. "I didn't realize you wouldn't want your son to be educated. I'll just send someone back to the house for my purse."

"Oh, no, sir!" Mr. Newcome broke in as the men began to mutter about "stupid fools" and "those who looked a gift horse in the mouth." "Whatever you see fit to do is . . . is fine. I'm very grateful you would honor my son this way."

Evan and Juliana both let out a breath.

"Good," Rhys said. "Then Evan shall start spending half a day at the house until it's time for the Michaelmas term. I will, of course, pay for all his expenses." He softened his tone. "And you might consider, Mr. Newcome, that if your son succeeds at Eton, he'll one day bring the family a far greater income than he could ever bring as a farmhand."

Mr. Newcome cast a startled glance at Juliana. "Do you think he's really that bright, milady?"

She smiled. "Evan is the most brilliant child I've ever seen. He will do you proud."

"So it's settled." Rhys thrust his hand out to the older Welshman.

Juliana held her breath until Mr. Newcome took it. "Aye, sir. It's settled."

The poor man wore a look of dazed confusion. Tomorrow he'd be much more unhappy about all this. But if he was as proud as he'd always seemed, he wouldn't go back on the agreement he'd made before his neighbors.

As Rhys led the man off to discuss the details, she went to Evan's side. He was looking a bit dazed himself. Perhaps they should have given him more warning about what they intended to do.

She laid her hand on his shoulder. "You do *want* to go to Eton, don't you?"

He shook himself. "More than anything."

"You know it means you'll be living away from home most of the year."

"Aye. I don't know how Da will manage."

"Let the squire take care of your father. And don't forget what I told you. If you ever need me for anything—" She drew a sharp breath. "If your father should try to punish you for this, you tell me, all right?"

"I will, thank you."

"'Tis the least I owe to the boy who saved my life," she teased him.

But he looked solemn. "'Tis you and the squire who have saved me, my lady. I will always remember that."

"Evan!" shouted his father. "Come on, m'boy, we're going home."

"Go on," she murmured, chucking him under the chin.

As he walked off, a smile spreading over his face, she called out, "I'll give you a day's respite, but I expect you to be ready to go right to work day after tomorrow, you hear?"

"Aye, my lady!" he called back.

As the Newcomes left, Rhys picked up the snake with a stick and tossed it into the fire. "We don't want anyone examining that too closely."

"I suppose not." She laughed. "What you did just now was wonderful."

He slung his arm about her shoulders. "I told you I'd take care of it."

"Yes, but Eton?" She stared up at him as he led her back to the cart. "Aside from the expense, I'm surprised you chose an English school."

He was silent a long moment. Someone had brought out a fiddle and was playing a dance as couples rose, flushed with ale and ready to extend the celebration into the night.

When he spoke, he had to raise his voice over the music. "Much as I hate to admit it, there are no schools in Wales that can prepare someone as gifted as Evan." He looked back at the dancing couples, whose fire-lit shadows made them appear larger than life. "But perhaps one day . . ."

She stood with him, watching a man caper here, a woman twirl there, their bodies extensions of the leaping flames. "'Tis better for him to go to England anyway, where his father can't hurt him."

"There are worse things than physical pain," he murmured, and she knew he meant his years of exile. Then he shook off his brief melancholy. "Well, wife, now that you've been saved from certain death, shall we celebrate the harvest with our friends?"

She grinned. "I'd like that. Nothing builds a woman's hunger so much as playing the damsel in distress."

20

My breast is pained with passion,
Pining for love of a girl.
—SION PHYLIP, "THE SEAGULL"

The celebration at the field ended an hour later when the rain came down in a torrent. Amid laughter and shouting, Rhys grabbed Juliana and dashed to the cart. With rain half-blinding them, he drove home, and by the time he pulled up under the eaves of the stable they were soaked to the skin.

But he didn't feel the least bit cold, having drunk enough ale to fend off the chill. He jumped down and helped Juliana out, hands lingering on her waist as the groom emerged to pull the cart into the stables. They stood where it was warm and dry under the eaves, and Rhys kissed her hair, damp and rich with the scent of rain and lavender.

"Thank you again for what you did for Evan," she said. "You've saved him from a cruel father."

He hesitated, wondering if he should tell her that life at Eton would probably be harder for Evan than it had been at home. Canings and other harsh punishments were still routinely given, although it wasn't as bad as it had been in his day.

But it was still better for a brilliant child like Evan to be at Eton than serving a wasted life as farm help.

"Also," she continued, "thank you for taking me tonight. I enjoyed it very much."

"You're welcome." He dropped a kiss on her forehead.

She toyed with the buttons on his waistcoat. "I only hope I didn't make a complete fool of myself, dancing out there with the others like a ten-year-old girl."

He thought of how she'd looked whirling in the circle, her hair a nimbus of fire and her green eyes glowing like cut jade, and desire uncurled in him. "Nay, you were wonderful." He coaxed her lips open with a finger. "Only one thing could make this night more enjoyable."

"And what might that be?" She caught his finger in her teeth, swirling her tongue around it with a mischievous smile.

He pressed her against the stable wall to let her feel the hard ridge of flesh in his breeches. "I'll give you three guesses." He drew his finger from her mouth to run it down her collarbone into the hollow between her breasts.

"Hmm," she said. "A nice hot cup of tea by the fireplace?"

"No." He slid his finger beneath her sodden bodice until he found her nipple.

As he rubbed the hard tip, her breath quickened. "Perhaps a . . . quiet game of chess?"

"Definitely not." He pushed the wet gingham material of her bodice down to free her breast, then lowered his head to suck at the damp skin.

"Rhys!" she protested, pushing his head away. "What if someone should come along?"

His eyes gleamed. "Wouldn't they get a show?"

She drew up her bodice and shoved him away. "Not here, my lusty husband."

The rain still came down in sheets, but she ran out into it laughing. She raced toward the house and danced up the wide steps as he followed at a more leisurely pace, letting the rain beat the grime of a day's work from him. At the top she paused to blow him a kiss, then opened the door and slipped inside, giggling as she closed it.

"God save me from teasing wenches." Shoving the wet hair from his face, he hurried up the stairs. If it was a game she wanted, she'd best make it quick. That one taste of her hadn't been near enough.

But when he opened the door and walked in, she was standing stock-still in the hall, holding a sealed envelope, with Mrs. Roberts at her side.

Mrs. Roberts glanced over. "Oh, there you are, sir. Don't you look a sight, the two of you. I was telling milady that you'd best get out of those wet clothes before you—"

"Who's the letter from?" Rhys interrupted, alarmed by Juliana's pale cheeks.

"Oh," said Mrs. Roberts. "It came from Northcliffe Hall while you were at the harvest."

A sudden vise clamped down on his heart. The last time someone had brought a message from Northcliffe Hall—

"Darcy sent it," Juliana whispered.

The vise tightened. "How do you know?"

"'Tis his handwriting." She stared at it a moment longer, then ripped it open to draw out a letter. She read it quickly, then gazed off into space.

Rhys fought the urge to snatch the letter and toss it into the nearest fire. "What does it say?"

She stiffened and nodded at the housekeeper. "Thank you, Mrs. Roberts. That will be all this evening."

As the woman left, her eyes bright with curiosity, Juliana handed him the letter, then headed for the stairs.

He started reading. It was indeed from Northcliffe. Apparently her brother and Devon had been involved in some investment together, and now Devon was threatening to back out if Northcliffe or St. Albans didn't arrange a meeting between him and Juliana. "One final meeting," it said, "to satisfy Lord Devon that Vaughan is not holding you in the marriage against your will."

Against your will. Damn them all! How dared they!

Worse yet, Northcliffe had apparently responded to Devon's blackmail by setting up the meeting. The marquess was invited for dinner at Northcliffe Hall two days hence, and Northcliffe was *commanding* his sister to attend.

It didn't help that the bastard included Rhys in the invitation. Not one bit.

Rhys shoved the letter into his pocket. The audacity of the man!

Juliana was already halfway up the stairs, and he hurried up to fall into step at her side. "Where are you going? We must talk about this."

"Yes, but not here."

He gritted his teeth as he followed her to their bedchamber. She was right. This was definitely not something to be discussed in front of the servants. Because he suspected that she planned to go.

And there was no way in hell he'd allow it.

As soon as they were inside their bedchamber, he closed the door and tore off his drenched coat. "You want to attend, don't you?"

"No. But I have to." She undressed, letting her wet clothes fall into a puddle, then donned a shift and her silk wrapper. "I must settle this matter once and for all."

"It was settled when I told Devon you were married and he bowed out of the engagement. He has no damned right to come back asking for you."

She sat down on the bed. "Are you ordering me not to go?"

He clenched his fists, fighting down the fear twisting inside him. "I don't think it's a good idea." He held his breath, waiting for her to explode. He could deal with anger. He could fight her when she was shouting at him much better than he could battle this quiet acquiescence that increased his fear.

But she stared calmly at him, as if she knew his weakness. "Why? What are you afraid will happen?"

The rational question took him aback. He raked his fingers through his hair. "That should be obvious. I don't want you anywhere near that damned marquess."

"That's not what I asked. What do you think will happen if I go 'near that damned marquess'?"

You'll leave me. You'll realize what you're missing and you'll run away, as you did before.

He concentrated on peeling off his wet clothes to keep from saying things he'd regret.

As he jerked on his drawers and dressing gown, Juliana rose and came toward him. "Are you afraid Stephen will kidnap me and carry me off to his estate? I hardly think even my brothers would allow that. Do you fear he'll present proof of a legal claim to me? There is none. So what is turning you into a beast at the very idea of my meeting him over dinner? There will be other guests present—you, for one, since you were invited."

"I was present at your engagement party, too, yet that didn't keep you from choosing him over me. If I'd released you from your vows that night, you'd have gone with him. You wanted a divorce then. You said so."

"That's true. I was very angry." She tilted her chin up. "And I think I had a right to be. But a great deal has changed between us. Surely you realize I've been more than content to be your wife these past two weeks."

"Then why must you see Devon again?" he snapped.

She laid her hand on his chest. "Can't you understand how he must feel? To have his betrothed leave him at his own engagement party, and not know what has happened to her?"

"He can't feel any worse than I did to have my wife leave me on my wedding night."

Paling, she dropped her hand. "You still believe I betrayed you. You're afraid I'll run off with Lord Devon, and betray you again."

The terror churned in him more fiercely. "Nay," he protested.

Thunder cracked the air outside, as if to echo his fears.

She gazed steadily at him. "If you trusted me, you

wouldn't be afraid to let me go to this. You'd have faith in me to handle whatever Lord Devon requests."

She didn't understand the irrational clutch of fear in his heart at the very thought of her speaking with Devon. He'd nearly lost her to the bastard, and only by force had he gained her back. How could he ever endure losing her for good?

Or . . . would he lose her if he refused to trust her?

"It's not that simple." He turned away, unable to bear the look in her eyes.

"Oh, but it is." She came up behind him to encircle his waist and lay her head against his back. "It's as simple as deciding to trust me or not."

He could feel the damp from her hair soaking through his dressing gown, could see her hands linked over his belly. Two weeks ago she wouldn't have held him so easily, nor touched him with the casual intimacy of a wife.

He didn't want to lose that. "It's not you I don't trust," he said, striving for a calm tone. "It's those treacherous brothers of yours . . . and Devon."

She sighed. "What are they going to do? Have me impressed? If you're so worried about what will happen, come with me. The invitation included you."

He twisted around to face her. "Aye, doesn't that surprise you? Your brother is furious over what I did at the council meeting, so why invite me to his home? This could be a trap. Perhaps your brother is doing this on purpose, to lure you—and me—to Northcliffe Hall, so he can . . . can . . ."

"Can *what*? He can't have you impressed again, for your

powerful friends would protest and he'd find himself in trouble. He can't kill you. If he'd wanted to, he'd have done it before now. These are all just excuses, and you know it."

He did, but how else could he keep her away from her *former betrothed* and her devious brothers?

"Rhys, listen to me." She lifted her hand to stroke his cheek with a tenderness that made him ache. "I told you I didn't love Lord Devon." She dragged in a deep breath. "I love *you*. So why would I toss aside a marriage with the man I love for a man I don't?"

He froze. *I love you.* He'd waited so long for her to say those words again, even though he'd been unwilling to say them himself and allow her that hold on his heart. But what if she were saying them only because she wanted him to give in?

He caught her hand. "If you love me, you'll stay here and not give those bastards the chance to separate us again."

He knew he'd said the wrong thing when the blood drained from her face. "I bare my heart to you, and that's all you can do? Use my love as a lever to get what you want?"

He closed his hands on her shoulders. "You don't know what you're asking."

"I do know." Her face was drawn now. "I'm asking you to trust me. And it's clear that you can't."

The air in the room grew arctic, despite the closed window and the fire blazing in the hearth. Juliana's expression of pain drove icicles through his heart. Damn it, he was losing her—he could feel it. Despite everything, he was losing her.

And he simply couldn't. "I do trust you, *cariad*. I do."

Her silence spoke her disbelief.

He stumbled for words and could only come up with the ones he'd spoken years before. "And . . . and I love you."

Her gaze shot to his, wild and luminous in the firelight, but her expression was skeptical.

As it should be. He could scarcely believe he'd said the words himself. Yet he felt them. In the past two weeks, the beauty of what they'd had before had echoed in what they had now. He loved her now as much as he'd loved her then; perhaps more. It didn't matter if she'd betrayed him. Nothing mattered but her.

"Yes, I do love you," he said. This was even more important to him than the first time he'd declared his heart to her. "I've loved you from the day I first saw you. I never stopped."

When she said nothing, he sucked in a harsh breath. "That's why it nearly killed me to think you'd betrayed me. And then to see you with that damned English lord—"

"He doesn't mean anything to me, I swear." There was frustration in her voice. "'Tis *you* I love."

"Then show me." He hauled her into his arms. "Make love to me, darling."

"But Rhys—"

He kissed her hard, urging her to respond. At first she resisted, but when he swept her lips with his tongue, she moaned and her mouth opened like a flower. He drove into her mouth, wanting to strike deep into the heart of her, to find that place she held separate from him and make it his.

She pulled away. "This won't solve anything . . . we have to talk about—"

"I need you." The savage need to make her forget everything but him clawed at him. "I love you more than breath, more than life. I have to know you need me, that you love me. Show me that Devon means nothing to you."

He drew her hands to the sash of his dressing gown. "Please," he whispered through a throat taut with fear. "Make love to me." If she rejected him now . . .

Her eyes met his—then she undid the knot and peeled off his dressing gown.

He reached for her, but she shook her head. "I'm making love to *you*, remember?" Keeping her eyes fixed on him, she shed her wrapper. When she shimmied out of her shift he caught his breath, drinking in the sight of her finely sculpted form—all feminine lines and curves and smooth, tempting surfaces.

With a sensuous look, she drew his hands to her waist, then stretched up on tiptoe to fit her mouth to his. He reveled in the way her hard nipples pressed into his bare chest. Wrapping his arms about her, he opened his mouth over hers. His flesh strained against his too-snug drawers, wanting to be inside her.

And when she darted her tongue into his mouth, he thought he'd lose his mind. He'd had no idea how it would affect him, to have her initiating everything. She teased his tongue with sweet, coaxing thrusts that intoxicated him.

She smelled of spiced fruitcakes and ale, but before he could fully satisfy his craving to taste her, she was kissing down his throat and then his chest. When she stopped to tease his nipple, he uttered a groan that became a moan when she ran her tongue down the furrow of dark hair on his chest, scorching him. Her tongue delved into his navel, and the shock of pleasure that shot through him was so intense that he buried his fingers in her lush curls to hold her still.

But she wasn't finished with him. Her fingers worked loose the buttons of his drawers and then she tugged them down, freeing his aching shaft. She was kneeling now, and he suddenly realized through a haze of shock and excitement what she intended to do.

"No," he muttered thickly. Lightning illuminated the room with its quick flash, and when she touched her hot mouth to the tip of him, then swirled her tongue over the tight, aching skin, he thought the lightning had surely struck him. With a choked curse, he pulled away. "No, no, 'tis too much."

He dragged her up into his arms. "You're a seductress, you know that?" he rasped as he scattered rough kisses over her rounded cheek . . . her damp, tangled hair . . . her wide, flawless brow.

"I'm merely doing what you asked," she said in a throaty voice, rubbing up against him, against his arousal full to bursting.

"You're driving me to distraction." With a savage growl, he bent to suck her breast.

She pushed him from her, then slowly circled him until she stood at his back. He could feel her breath on his tense muscles as she glided her hands over his back. Without warning, she cupped his buttocks, then smoothed and squeezed them in her deft hands.

He flung his head back, his eyes sliding shut as she grabbed his shoulders and molded herself to him.

He could feel her triangle of hair against his arse, the dewy fleece crushed against him. That was titillation enough—but when she anchored him to her by clasping his thighs so that her fingers were inches away from the part of him that ached to be buried inside her, his eyes shot open.

"Is this to be my punishment for all my demands on you?" he asked hoarsely. "Are you deliberately tormenting me?"

She went still. "Surely you know by now that I could never hurt you," she said, her voice muffled against his back. "Do you so doubt my love?"

He saw their images reflected in the wide pier glass hanging next to the bed. Her arms were around his hips and her hands on his thighs. The top of her head showed above his shoulders.

Clasping her by the hand, he drew her to stand beside him, then nodded at the gilded mirror. "Look there." He touched their clasped hands first to her creamy shoulder, and then his own scarred one. "While you're as sweet and smooth and lovely as your skin, I'm grievously marred and angry and dark. Since my return, I've tormented you and deliberately sought to hurt you, even when you met my anger with kindness. If I doubt your love, 'tis only because I can't believe you'd love me when there's so little in me to love."

She faced him, eyes glowing. "You blind fool." As he watched in the glass, she ran her hands over his ravaged shoulders. "For surviving this, I love you." She fingered the scar at his temple. "For turning my brother's punishments into a triumph, I love you." She bracketed his face in her hands. "And most of all, for putting aside your vengeance so you could be my husband completely, I will always love you. Don't you see? As long as I have life or breath, there will never be anyone else."

With a choked endearment, he lifted her into his arms and strode to the bed, laying her down and covering her with his body. "I don't deserve you, but I don't care. I love you, and I want you so badly, I'm drowning in it."

"Then take me," she murmured, spreading her legs to fit him against her.

With a guttural moan, he sheathed himself in the warmth he needed so badly. She was glove-tight and wet, and when she began to move under him, undulating to create the friction he craved, he thought he'd go mad.

"Juliana . . . sweet Juliana . . ." he rasped against her neck as he joined her motion, sinking into her, wanting to lose his soul in her, to bury his fears in her welcoming body.

Her breasts were crushed against him, and she smelled of rain and smoke and lavender. He wanted to devour her or have her devour him . . . to be so much a part of her that she could never leave him.

Rain pounded the roof in time to the pounding of his heart as he thrust into her over and over. She was making enticing little cries and moans and her body moved against him, seeking fulfillment. He wanted her to find it . . . to find it in him, so he struggled to hold back his release until she could find hers as well. He fingered her until he felt her writhe beneath him urgently.

"That's it, *my love*," he said in her ear. "That's it . . ."

She strained suddenly against him as her release overtook her. "Oh, Rhys . . . my husband!"

It was the first time she'd called him that since his return, and it sent him over the edge. He erupted in her with a guttural moan, her sweet spasms wringing him dry.

Then he collapsed on her, feeling her shake beneath him with the aftershocks of her pleasure. Never had he known this with any woman. He was awestruck that making love to her was so entirely satisfying.

Outside, thunder and lightning still rampaged, but here in the cocoon of their bedchamber, with the fire blazing and the light of the candles reflecting off the creamy bed linens, he felt secure. Her body beneath him was warm and yielding, and he wished he could wrap it around him forever. This was what marriage was meant to be. The security of being locked away with one's love, not needing the rest of the world.

It wasn't distrust that made him want her to stay here with him. It was love, only love.

He rolled off her, pulling her against him until they lay spoon-fashion, and then nuzzled the drying ends of her hair aside so he could kiss her shoulder. "I love you."

"I love you, too," she whispered.

He lifted himself on one elbow to see her face better. Her eyes were closed, and her breathing seemed to have evened out. "Juliana?"

"Hmm?" she said dreamily.

"You like being here with me, don't you?"

"Mmm." She snuggled against him.

"And you understand why I can't bear to let you go to

this dinner, don't you? You'll stay here with me. You won't leave me."

When she was silent, her breathing slow and deep, he realized she was asleep.

No matter. He drew the counterpane up over them and sank onto the pillow. After tonight, she must understand how he felt. And surely in the morning, when they could discuss it more rationally, she'd agree with him. Let her sleep.

But Juliana wasn't sleeping as she lay with her body curved into his, fighting hard to keep her breathing even.

Just as she'd warned him, making love had changed nothing for him. But it had changed a great deal for her. She couldn't go on with him like this. The truth of what had happened six years ago had to be faced. His overwhelming jealousy and fear of letting her out of his sight showed that he still didn't accept that she hadn't betrayed him.

That hadn't prevented him from recognizing that he loved her. And doubtless he accepted that by telling himself she was different now—that her betrayal no longer mattered, that it was all in the past.

But nothing was ever completely in the past. Like a thorn that festered if it wasn't removed, his doubts about her would eat away at him, and his love for her, if he didn't face them.

So she must make him face them—and she could think of only one way to do that. Go to the dinner, with or without him. Leave tonight, before he could make it impossible for her to leave by going back to his old ways of having the grooms refuse to give her a mount. Then she'd have to pray that he followed . . . or that he didn't spurn her when she returned.

The storm finally subsided, and the rain dropped to a gentle drizzle. Shifting to her back, she peeked at him. He was asleep, his breath even. She stared at the lips half-parted in sleep, the jaw shadowed with his evening whiskers, and the dark slashes of his eyebrows. His peaceful expression clutched at her heart.

What if she took this bold step and it proved too much for the fragile trust he'd begun to feel for her? What if it shattered everything between them?

But if she didn't do this, how long before fear of betrayal devoured him until he couldn't let her out of his sight? How long before she struck out against his unreasonable demands and destroyed whatever remained between them?

No, she had to do this. He had to learn if he loved her enough to brave his fears. Or there was no chance for them.

Her decision made, she slipped out of bed and began gathering clothing for a trip to Carmarthen.

21

Sad outlaw, I've no ransom,
Shut out from her town and home.
She to her outlaw's bosom
Sent but longing, bitter doom.

—DAFYDD AP GWILYM, "HIS AFFLICTION"

Rhys awakened to find the room empty. His wife had certainly risen early. Where the devil was she?

He got up and dressed. He was about to ring for a servant when he saw a note propped against the pier glass addressed to him. In his wife's handwriting.

That couldn't be good.

With his heart thundering, he opened the note and read:

Dearest Rhys,

I've gone to Northcliffe Hall. If you search your heart, you'll understand that I must settle matters between me and Lord Devon. I also wish to be reconciled with my brothers, devious though they are.

I know you don't see matters as I do and will be

furious at me. I realize that my furtive departure may only increase your distrust of me, but you left me no choice. I only pray you can find some measure of forgiveness in your heart.

You told me you wanted me to share your life in every way, and I agreed to that. Now I'm asking you to share mine. Put aside your fears and come to me at Northcliffe Hall. Sit beside me when I face Lord Devon. Show me that you trust me to do the right thing.

I well know what a great thing I ask of you. If you can't do it, I will understand. In either case, know this: You always have my love.

Juliana

He could hear the words as clearly as if she stood right there entreating him, and every one was a dagger through his breast. He read the letter thrice, trying to fathom her thoughts, but each reading only tormented him more.

She'd promised him her love forever, but she hadn't said when she would return . . . *if* she would return. Worst of all, she hadn't said what she'd do if he didn't come—though he feared he knew. If he refused to be husband to her in this, wouldn't she have the right to refuse to be wife to him?

Put aside your fears and come to me at Northcliffe Hall.

With a curse, he balled up the note and threw it at the pier glass where their images had been linked last night, when she'd opened herself to him so passionately.

And then had slipped out of their bed, leaving just this foul note asking him to sell his soul for her. Devil take her! Was this her way of repaying him for all his misuse of her?

She said she knew what she was asking of him—but obviously she didn't, or she wouldn't ask it.

Go to the house of his enemy? Break bread with him? Watch her greet a man who'd once sworn to marry her, and pretend it didn't ravage him?

She had no right to ask this! Her brothers had sent him into hell, and Lord Devon had meant to enjoy the fruits of that betrayal. Damn the lot of them! How dared she expect him to go and pretend civility, when he detested them? If she loved him, she wouldn't ask this.

Damn her if she thought she could bend him to her will! She'd disobeyed his direct order, and she thought to force his hand.

Well, he was not so easily manipulated. Let her sup with her foppish suitor and her infernal family. He wouldn't come to heel like some sad hound trailing after the master. Nay, he would not!

And if she couldn't accept his terms, then that was her loss. He wouldn't force her to remain in a marriage she found too binding.

At that thought, such pain tore through him that he swore and swept her dressing table clean with one fist. He watched with bitter satisfaction as perfume bottles shattered and the jewelry she kept in several small chests went flying. He stalked toward the door, his boots crunching over the broken glass as the stench of mingled perfumes assailed him.

He nearly slipped as his shoe came down on something larger, and his weight snapped it in two. He kicked it aside—then froze as he saw what it was.

A love spoon. The one he'd carved and given Juliana on the night he'd proposed.

Oh God. He crouched to pick up the two halves, then spotted the jeweled case she'd kept it in. The cloth that he'd used to wrap it in was lying inside, worn and yellowed with age.

He stared at the case, crafted to fit the love spoon, and then at the two pieces. She'd kept his gift all these years. She hadn't thrown it away. She might have kept their marriage secret from the world, but here was proof that she'd remembered it in private.

He closed his fingers around the ancient emblem of Welsh marriages . . . the emblem he'd broken, as surely as his refusal to go to Northcliffe would break his marriage.

"Ah, my love," he whispered hoarsely. "What have I done to you?"

How foolish his plans had been when he'd stormed into Northcliffe Hall a few weeks ago. He'd thought to make her suffer, but it didn't matter how much he railed against her. It didn't matter that he'd lived without her once, and ought to be able to live without her again. He couldn't. If she left him, there would be nothing in his life of worth.

And the choice was wholly his. She was forcing him to choose whether to live with her or without her. And if he chose wrongly, he'd have no one to blame but himself.

It was the hour when breakfast was served at Northcliffe Hall, and Juliana sat at the table awaiting her family. No one yet knew she was here. Since she'd arrived in the middle of the night, she'd asked the housekeeper not to awaken anyone and had retired to her old bedchamber.

Unfortunately, she'd slept little. How could she, when all she could think of was Rhys's face when he'd touched their joined hands to his scars? He'd been so unsure of her, and now she'd given him new cause to doubt her loyalty and love.

But she couldn't have acted any other way. And by now, he'd read her note and realized what she intended.

Would he come?

Would he follow her here in a fury, ready to drag her back to Llynwydd? That would devastate her, for it would show that he still lacked regard for her needs and wants.

If he didn't attend the dinner, that would devastate her, too. How could she bear it if he refused to give her this proof of his trust?

"The housekeeper said you were here," Darcy said from the doorway. "Thank God you've come."

It had been three weeks since she'd seen him, but the changes in him made it seem like a lifetime. His face was as gaunt as a death mask; his eyes glittered like a man too aware of the pain being inflicted on him. His clothes hung on him, and he seemed uncharacteristically lethargic.

Despite all he'd done, she pitied him. "Good morning, brother," she said, more softly than she'd intended.

The gentle greeting seemed to startle him. "I feared you would ignore my summons. You had every right to do so, after what I did."

"Darcy, I—"

"Please, Juliana, let me speak first. There's nothing you

could say that would be crueler than the words I've said to myself."

He paced beside the table. "After Overton told me how Vaughan spoke to you, I thought I'd go mad. I wanted to rush there and bring you back, to force you from the bastard's hands, but Overton said you wouldn't wish it."

"Yes, that's what I told him."

Darcy fixed her with a panicked gaze. "But here you are. I can't believe Vaughan would allow it. Not after the council meeting, where he effectively ruined all my future in politics by nominating Morgan, who'll probably win. That's when I knew he's not through tormenting me."

"Rhys knows I'm here. He may join me tomorrow evening, although we were both surprised you invited him."

Darcy dropped into a chair. "Overton insisted. He said it was time we treated you as husband and wife. As family."

She should have known Overton would be the one to act with compassion. Darcy never would.

When had he changed from an overprotective brother into an obsessed politician? And was his present self-deprecating air an act?

"Did Lord Devon really threaten to pull out of your mining project, or did you invent that so I'd return and you could throw me at Stephen?"

Darcy looked stricken. "It's the truth, I swear. The man's besotted. And ever since Overton told him the kind of life your husband intended for you, he's been wracked by worry." He glanced away. "Especially once he learned my part in all that happened. Only by promising to arrange this meeting did I keep him from bowing out of our venture."

"Stephen is a man of character." Bitterness crept into her voice. "You should be grateful he didn't call you out. 'Tis what you deserved."

"I know that only too well." He leaned forward. "I can't excuse what I did back then. If I'd known how unhappy it would make you, I'd never have done it."

"That's not true."

"It is! I only did it to protect you from that . . . that scoundrel!"

"I was in love with that scoundrel." She leveled an accusing gaze on him. "You did it to get rid of a penniless Welsh radical who might ruin all your plans for political gain."

He didn't try to deny it. "If you still hate me for what I did, why are you here?"

"I have my own reasons."

When she said no more, a sigh escaped him. He knew he'd lost her trust. "Whatever they are, I'm grateful you've come. It will help me a great deal if you can put Devon's mind at ease."

She regarded him warily. "If that means reassuring him that I'm content with my marriage, then yes, I'm happy to do so."

"I suppose it was too much to hope that Vaughan would let you go, if you wished to leave."

Darcy would never change.

"I don't want to leave. I love him, and he loves me, despite what you did to part us." Though she had yet to see if he trusted her.

"He treats you well, then?"

"Very well."

"If that's true, then perhaps all has not been lost."

Not yet. Although Darcy had set the events in motion, it had long ago stopped having anything to do with him. Rhys's decisions were now governed by other things. She could only pray his love for her won out.

Darcy cleared his throat. "Do you think you could ever forgive me for what I did?" When she frowned, he added, "I now know what it is to suffer as you did. I've lost the woman I loved, for Lettice has left me for Pennant. And I've lost my position in the community, and my wife."

"Your wife?"

"Elizabeth is leaving me." He tried for a nonchalant shrug, but looked whipped instead. "Not legally; a divorce is impossible. But she intends to live apart from me. Since we have no children . . . she thinks it's best."

"Oh, Darcy, I am sorry," she said with genuine feeling.

"Don't be. We were never well suited." He came to sit beside her and take her hands. "But if I lost you, too, I'd have nothing. Even Overton can scarcely bear to speak to me. Please say you won't always hate me for what I did."

His expression triggered all her memories of when they were children and she'd begged him for his help. He'd always given it. This time it was him begging, and try as she might, she couldn't find it in her heart to refuse him.

"I don't hate you," she said. "I can't forget what you did, but I'll try to forgive you. In time, perhaps we can put it behind us."

He kissed her hand gratefully, but her mind was already on another man who said he wanted to put the past behind him.

Would he? And if he didn't, how would she ever endure it?

22

I'm but an ailing poet,
I cannot keep it secret:
My voice grows faint for her fair face.

—SALBRI POWEL, "THE LOVER'S HOPE"

Evan stood waiting in Llynwydd's entrance hall two days after the harvest as Lady Juliana had said, but something was wrong. There were no maids chattering, no footmen humming. Everyone walked about in a hush.

A murmur from a nearby room coaxed him to eavesdrop.

"I'd swear the poor man hasn't eaten a morsel since the mistress left yesterday." It was Mrs. Roberts.

"He said she went to visit her family." That was Mr. Moss.

"There's more to it, to be sure," Mrs. Roberts said. "They quarreled. You should have seen their bedchamber. Broken bottles and perfume stink everywhere. The master only said 'clean up this mess,' but he's been drinking himself sick in his study ever since. A crying shame, it is."

The squire and Lady Juliana at odds? But he'd seen them dancing in the fields only two days ago.

"Good morning, Evan."

Oh God, it was the squire himself, and he looked awful—scruffy and unshaven, with no coat or neckcloth and his waistcoat buttoned wrong. And Evan could smell the brandy on him.

"G-Good morning, sir," Evan stammered. "I-I came because Lady Juliana said I was to start my lessons today."

"Aye, I know." Mr. Vaughan's eyes had an unnatural glint in them. "We need to speak about that."

He led Evan into the drawing room, then gestured to a chair. Evan sat gingerly, schooling his face to show nothing. Years of living with his father had made him good at that. It had often saved him from his father's quick fist.

"Lady Juliana won't be able to tutor you today. She's in Carmarthen, visiting her brothers."

Evan's heart sank. "If I may ask, sir, how long will she be gone?"

"She may return tomorrow." A muscle worked in Mr. Vaughan's jaw. "I don't know. She has gone to speak with the man she'd planned to marry before I returned." He stopped, as if realizing he'd revealed too much.

The squire looked so bereft, Evan couldn't help reassuring him. "I'm sure she'll be back soon, sir. She doesn't care for that other fellow at all. Not like she cares for you."

Evan's words seemed to startle the man. "I wish I shared your certainty."

"Oh, but you should! Anyone can see she only wants you for a husband."

The squire stared into the fireplace. "She hasn't always felt that way. She wanted to spurn me upon my return." His voice fell to a hoarse whisper. "And 'twas said that she had a part in sending me into the navy."

Evan's mouth dropped open. "Whoever said that is a bloody liar, sir! My lady never spoke of you without saying how wise and good and clever you were. Surely she wouldn't have sent such a man to suffer."

At the man's continued silence, Evan stood and drew himself up stiffly. "I could never believe that of her, when she's been nothing but kind to me and everyone on this estate. I don't understand how you can believe it, either."

The squire looked at him with a wan smile. "You're very fond of my wife, aren't you?"

A tight knot formed in Evan's throat. "Aye. I think she is the finest woman in all of Wales."

"She is indeed." Mr. Vaughan raked his fingers through his unkempt hair. "No doubt you're right and she'll be coming home soon. Why don't you return tomorrow, eh? I'm afraid there won't be any tutoring for you today."

With a nod, Evan left.

Rhys watched the boy go, a painful tightness in his chest. What a strangely perceptive child Evan was. And what had possessed him to confide in the boy?

His overwhelming desire to have someone counter his bitter doubts and fears. Evan was so sure of Juliana, so very stout in his defense of her character. It made a mockery of his own attitude toward his wife.

Coming on the heels of his ghastly night spent alone in their bed, it forced him to admit the truth, which she had known better than he. It came down to a refusal to trust her.

But it was worse than that, for his deepest fear was that the dinner was another setup for betrayal. That he would go to Carmarthen only to find her willingly allied with Devon as her brothers protected her.

It was easier not to face it—to wait here like a coward and see if she'd spoken truly of how she felt for him.

Shudders racked him. Evan was right. How *could* he think such terrible things of her? This past two weeks, she'd been everything he could dream of in a wife. To believe that she would betray him again would be to ignore the many demonstrations of her affection that she'd given him from the day of his return.

And to believe that she'd *ever* betrayed him was to ignore her true character.

What *had* happened on that night years ago? If it had been as she'd said, her brothers had somehow found out about the marriage on their own and taken steps to prevent it.

Was that so impossible to believe?

Nay. Her brothers were deceitful enough to do such a thing. Whereas everything he'd seen of her since his return had shown him a responsible woman, who wouldn't ignore a vow as holy as matrimony. Especially for the reasons Northcliffe had provided.

And what were those reasons, which had seemed so convincing at the time?

Reason one: dislike of his Welsh blood. It was unlikely that the woman who'd danced with Welsh laborers, who'd endured holding a snake under her skirts so she could help a Welsh boy receive schooling, would be ashamed of her husband's Welshness.

Reason two: a desire for riches. If living with Juliana had taught him anything, it was that she wholly lacked that desire. Though he'd made all his wealth available to her, she hadn't ordered expensive gowns or pressured him to buy frivolous items for her.

Reason three: his lack of a title. That one, he couldn't be entirely sure of. Yet her concern for her betrothed had revolved around the man's feelings, not his status. She didn't seem to care that she'd lost her chance to be a marchioness.

Now he came to the last, most convincing one.

Reason four: her fear that Rhys was marrying her for her property.

It was true that if Juliana had believed that, she would have rejected him. She'd put much store in having a husband who wanted her for herself.

But he hadn't known Llynwydd was deeded to her, and he felt certain she'd realized that. Besides, she'd asked him once if he was marrying her to strengthen his claim on Llynwydd, and when he'd denied it, she'd seemed to believe him.

Now that he considered it all together, none of Northcliffe's reasons were that convincing. Faced with everything he knew of her, Rhys couldn't believe she'd have thrown him aside so ruthlessly.

But what about the damned innkeeper? What about the fact that no one could have known where to find them without her help? What about Northcliffe claiming to have learned about the Sons of Wales from her? And why had her brothers continued to insist that she'd betrayed him, even after he'd returned?

She'd given him no reason for that.

Yet there must be one. And like her reasons for hiding the marriage, which, though they rankled, were sound, there must be a good explanation for everything. Perhaps if he hadn't been so busy convincing himself that she'd betrayed him, he might have examined it more thoroughly. If he asked the right questions, he could probably find answers.

But he didn't need to anymore. He simply couldn't believe she'd betrayed him, no matter what the innkeeper or her brothers said. Her brothers had lied, the innkeeper had lied . . . damn it all, the whole world had lied.

She was innocent. He would swear it. And he'd known it for some time.

So what was preventing him from putting all his faith in his lovely wife, who, in Evan's words, was "the finest woman in all of Wales"?

Morgan's words from weeks ago hit him full force. *If you accept that she didn't betray you, then you can't force her to stay with you. You'd have to let her choose between marriage to you or separation. You'd have to take the chance of losing her . . . And you won't risk that, will you?*

With a curse, Rhys jumped to his feet. Morgan was right. At the root of his distrust was a horrible fear—that given the choice, she would not choose him.

And how could she? He'd refused to have faith in her when she'd waited for him until all hope was gone. After his return he'd publicly maligned her, carried her off like a pirate with his booty, and nearly raped her.

And she was a sweet, generous woman whom he shouldn't even be allowed to touch! Why had he mistreated her so?

He thought back to when he'd first discovered her identity. He'd been angry that he couldn't have the English earl's daughter, so he'd struck out, trying to bring her down to his level by accusing her of being a spy.

The fear that she would find herself too good for him had made him mistreat her. It was like what the navy had done to him. Each time they'd lashed him to that spar, each time they'd brought the cat down to tear the skin from his back, they'd told him he was miserable and worthless, a puny Welshman not good for anything but fish bait.

But what they'd really meant was, *You damned squire's son, with your education and your proper manners—you're too smart and too strong willed for the navy, and we hate you for it.* So they'd sought to chain him by making him like them—scared and stupefied by grog.

And he'd tried to chain her, too. He'd bullied her, and when that hadn't worked, seduced her to stay, all the while trying to tell her that she wasn't worthy of him, when he knew in his heart that he was the unworthy one. Worst of all, he'd never given her the choice of staying.

How could he have? She wouldn't have chosen the despicable creature who'd been nothing but a torment to her.

Yet the image of them standing together before the mirror flickered into his mind. *I will always love you. Don't you see? As long as I have life or breath, there will never be anyone else.*

He shoved his hand in his pocket to grip the pieces of the love spoon that he'd carried around with him ever since yesterday.

It made no sense that she would love him, that she'd choose him over a wealthy English nobleman. His mind told him it couldn't be true. But for once, he had to believe what his heart said. And his heart said that she loved him, and would never betray him. His heart said to trust her.

So trust her, he must. For there was no other way he would find peace and keep her love.

23

I have my choice, beauty bright as a wave,
Wise in your riches, your graceful Welsh.
I have chosen you.

—HYWEL AB OWAIN GWYNEDD,

"HYWEL'S CHOICE"

Rhys wasn't coming, or he'd surely have been here by now. Juliana had half-expected him to appear yesterday to bear her away from the lion's den, but he hadn't . . . nor sent word, either.

A footman entered the drawing room and handed her a package. "A messenger brought this for you, my lady."

There was no card. She opened the expensively wrapped box to find a lace purse. She looked inside and found a slip of paper bearing only one sentence—*Everything I own is yours.*

Rhys! She leapt up. "Where's the man who brought this?"

"'Twasn't a man, my lady, but a boy. And he's gone."

She sank into the chair. She knew it was from Rhys; it was his handwriting. He'd sent a gift, but hadn't come himself. There was no cause yet for joy.

Two hours passed, and a second gift arrived—a heart-shaped gold locket in a Celtic design. This time the slip of paper inside the box read, *My heart is yours.*

It was sweet, but she wanted him, not his gifts, dear as they might be.

By the time the third gift, a volume of ballads by Dafydd Jones titled *Bloedeugerdd Cymru*, arrived, she sighed as she opened it to find inscribed on the frontispiece the words, *My soul is yours.*

Oh, my darling, my soul is yours, too. But if you give me your soul, you must give me your trust. So where are you?

She fretted while she dressed for dinner, donning her best gown of emerald satin. It made her eyes sparkle and her skin glow like cream, but if Rhys didn't come it didn't matter. Nothing mattered anymore if he refused to be here with her.

She spread his gifts out on a writing table. What was he trying to say? If he was asking her forgiveness, he'd certainly chosen a dramatic way to do it. But Rhys had always known how to hold an audience.

And she wanted more than gifts and sweet words. If he couldn't be here to show her his love and trust, then he was not the man she wanted. And no amount of gifts would change her mind.

She glanced at the clock. It was nearly time for dinner.

A footman appeared at the door. "My lady? Another gift has arrived, and the bearer wishes to speak to you."

She nodded, her heart sinking. This meant one thing—Rhys had refused to come to dinner, and had sent someone to make his excuses. Numbly, she followed the footman to the entrance hall.

And there, staring at her with a solemn gaze, stood her husband.

Hope leapt in her chest. He was splendidly bedecked in a cobalt coat and breeches of shot silk that made his eyes burn brightly in the candlelight. His embroidered waistcoat was his best, his neckcloth was immaculately tied, and his shirt sparkled white against the dark blue of his coat.

He looked like any gentleman arriving for dinner with an earl and a marquess. But his rigid stance told her this wasn't easy for him. He was a proud man being forced to bend his will to another, and he clearly disliked it.

Which made his coming all the more wonderful.

"Leave us," he commanded the footman.

She bit back a smile. His arrogance wasn't gone. But he'd come to join her, which was all that mattered.

She walked toward him, her breath quickening as he followed her with a hungry, ardent gaze. Then he held something out to her—the love spoon split in two.

Her breath caught. Surely he wasn't saying . . .

"In my thoughtless anger, I broke it." He closed her hand around the pieces. "And I need you to help me mend it, my love. For I can't live in peace until it's whole again. I only hope I haven't left the repair until too late."

Her heart swelled with love that he could take his pride in his hands and come to her like this. He wasn't easy to live with. His years at sea had made him more impatient and quick to find fault. But he was fair and truthful, even in his arrogance. And he did love her. She could see it in his eyes.

"It's not too late," she told him joyously. "It's never too late."

At her words, the fear drained from his face. He dragged her into his arms and caught her mouth in a long kiss so gentle and loving, she knew she'd remember it for the rest of her life.

He drew back to cup her face in his hands. "Never leave me again. Ask me for anything else. But never leave me."

She pressed a soft kiss to his lips. "I have no intention of leaving you. Not now, not ever."

He buried his face in her neck. "Good. These past two days have been torture. If you'd wanted to punish me, you couldn't have found a better way."

"I didn't want to punish you, but to make you see what we could have if you would trust me."

He looked up to meet her eyes. "And I do. I've learned that if I don't have faith in you, I can't have faith in anything in this world. For you're the only one I trust—even more than myself."

"Oh, Rhys," she said, melting. "I have waited so long to hear you say that." She scattered kisses over his lips, his cheeks, the tip of his nose. "But why did you send me all those gifts? I was afraid it was in lieu of your coming."

He nuzzled her hair. "I was afraid to just show up on your doorstep with my heart in my hands. I thought you might be so angry at me for waiting to come here, that you wouldn't even speak to me."

"I am much happier to have your heart and soul, as you have mine. And your trust. At long last."

He rested his forehead against hers. "I've been such a fool, my love. In so many ways that I scarcely know where to begin apologizing, but—"

A knock at the door made them both start. It took them a moment to come back to earth, to realize they stood in Northcliffe Hall.

She flashed him a rueful smile. "I hate to interrupt your lovely confession, dear husband. But that is probably Lord Devon."

To Rhys's credit, he managed to keep an even expression.

"I must let him in, you know," she added.

"Yes. I know you must."

"And it would probably be best if I greeted him alone first."

"As you wish. I came here because I understand what you feel you must do."

She handed him the pieces of the love spoon, then pointed to the dining room. "Go there and wait for me. I promise I'll only be a few moments."

He nodded, but as she slid past him, headed for the door, he caught her and bent her over his arm to give her a hot, possessive kiss.

When he let her up, her head was spinning. "What was that for?"

"To give you something to remember while you're speaking to your former betrothed." Then he strolled off, looking markedly more sure of himself.

With a laugh, she opened the door.

It was indeed Stephen, who looked startled to see her answer it. "Good evening, Juliana."

"Good evening, Stephen. Won't you come in?"

He entered the house, watching her with a sober look as a servant hurried in to take his greatcoat and hat.

"The others haven't come downstairs yet. Shall we wait for them in the drawing room?"

"Whatever you wish."

As soon as they'd gone inside, she closed the door. Now that she was face-to-face with him, it was hard to know exactly what to say. His air of aloof dignity made him look so terribly noble, she wasn't certain how to approach him. Had she once thought to live with him, to share a bed with him and bear his children? No doubt they would have had a tolerable marriage, but compared to what she had with Rhys, it would have been a pale substitute.

As if sensing her discomfort, he spoke first. "Seeing you here at least answers one of my questions. Vaughan is obviously not keeping you a prisoner."

"No." She managed a smile. "I'm at Llynwydd because I choose to be. I'm happy there."

He looked skeptical. "With him? I'd hate to think he is treating you with the same contempt he showed you the night of our engagement party."

It was hard for her to even remember that Rhys; he'd changed so much since then. "That was a difficult time, I'll admit. But things have gotten better. We've found we suit each other very well."

"But is that enough?" Stephen stalked forward to

clasp her arm. "Tell me the truth. Does he make you happy?"

He looked so forlorn that she wished she could comfort him. But she could find no way to soften the blow. "Aye. We've found again what we once had."

"I see," he said stiffly.

"I can't tell you how sorry I am for deceiving you. If I'd known he was still alive, I would never have accepted your offer. But I truly believed him dead. And Darcy insisted that I keep my brief marriage secret to protect the family name."

He nodded. "Overton has told me something of what happened then, and how you dealt with it. I gather your brothers were largely to blame for separating you from your husband. And for keeping the marriage secret from me."

"Aye." Perhaps learning that had prompted him to threaten to pull out of the mining project with Darcy. "You mustn't blame them. They thought they were acting in my best interests."

He snorted. "Perhaps Overton did, but Darcy had only his own interests at heart."

"True." Still, she didn't want Stephen to strike at her brother on her account. Darcy had suffered quite a bit for his mislaid ambition. "But his machinations wouldn't have caused nearly as much havoc if Rhys hadn't believed his lies."

She averted her gaze. "And I played my own part by keeping my previous marriage secret from you. I should never have let you court me when my heart belonged to

Rhys. So any quarrel you have with my family must be with me first."

He said nothing.

"I know you won't believe this, but it was probably best that Rhys returned when he did. I don't think I ever could have been yours entirely. And you are too wonderful to have a wife who doesn't love you."

He winced. "I would have been happy to have you in any case."

"Believe me, marriage is much more satisfying when you love your spouse."

He fixed her with a keen gaze. "And do you love yours?"

"Aye. And he loves me."

"Well, then, I suppose it's pointless for me to stay for dinner. You've made your position clear, and there's nothing left but to accept it."

Relief swept her. At least she wouldn't have to bear an entire meal with Rhys and Stephen glaring at each other. "I hope someday you can forgive me."

He smiled sadly. "It would be fruitless to do otherwise, wouldn't it? Bad blood between us would serve no purpose."

How different he was from Rhys. Stephen would never let his emotions push him to do anything impractical, while Rhys had to fight to keep his emotions from consuming him. Perhaps one day, Stephen would meet someone who could rouse him to show some feeling. But she hadn't been the one for that.

"I hesitate to mention this," she said, "but I promised Darcy I'd speak to you about your project."

"It's all right," he said tersely. "I told your brother I wouldn't pull out if he arranged this meeting, and he kept his part of the bargain." He lowered his voice. "But surely you won't blame me if I sever the relationship in every other way."

"Nay. I doubt even Darcy would blame you for that."

Silence fell between them, awkward and uncomfortable.

"Come, I'll see you out," she said, opening the door.

"Yes, that would be wise."

As soon as they reached the entrance hall, she rang for the footman. Rhys emerged as well, his expression hooded as he halted beside her.

"His lordship is leaving," she told the servant. "Fetch his coat and hat."

As the footman scurried off, Lord Devon stared Rhys down.

"You're not staying for dinner, Devon?" Rhys asked, tension in his voice.

"Nay. It seems I've been mistaken in some of my assumptions."

She could almost feel Rhys's tension ebb. "At least you're good enough to admit it."

"Goodness has nothing to do with it," Stephen clipped out. He took his coat and hat from the footman. "And you should know one thing, Vaughan. If I ever suspect you are treating Juliana as harshly as you did the night you took her from me, I'll do my best to steal her back from you."

Juliana gaped at him. Perhaps there was some depth of feeling in him after all.

Rhys slid his arm about her waist. "I shall never give

you a reason to try. Rest assured that I know the worth of what I have."

Stephen smiled for the first time since his arrival. "Then I wish you both luck. So few of us learn the worth of what we have until it is beyond our reach."

As soon as the door closed behind him, Rhys said, "I hope you know I've suffered a thousand deaths in the last ten minutes."

She couldn't help but tease him. "And you must suffer awhile longer, I'm afraid." She went to pull the bell summoning the family to dinner. "There's still my brothers to endure."

He groaned.

She stretched up on tiptoe to kiss his forehead. "But if you're very, very good, I promise that I'll give you a reward to remember."

He slid his hand over her behind, his eyes gleaming brightly. "I'll hold you to that."

With Juliana's hand in his, Rhys watched Northcliffe descend the stairs, accompanied by his mother and brother. Rhys briefly wondered where Northcliffe's wife was, but that thought left him when Northcliffe's eyes met his.

They hadn't seen each other since the night of the council meeting, and the change in the man was shocking. His cocksure arrogance had disappeared, and his skin bore an unhealthy pallor.

Still, he managed to look aloof. "Good to see you, Vaughan."

Rhys bit back a retort to that blatant lie. For Juliana's sake, he must be civil. "Good evening, Northcliffe."

Northcliffe turned to his sister. "Where is Devon?"

"He left." When Northcliffe went white, Juliana hastened to add, "He promised not to withdraw from your project."

Overton came down the last two steps to approach Rhys with an outthrust hand. "I'm glad you've come, Vaughan." His gaze flicked to Juliana, and Rhys wondered how much she'd confided about her marriage. "We're *very* glad to have you here."

"You look well, sir," said the dowager countess as she gazed down her nose at him. "My daughter told me that Llynwydd thrives under your care."

Rhys cast Juliana a quizzical glance. "Did she indeed?" What else had she told her mother about him, about their marriage?

"Mama was concerned you might not be able to support me in a style befitting an earl's daughter, but I put her fears to rest."

In that sentence, Juliana had completely summed up her relationship with her mother. So, she couldn't have told her mother much; the dowager countess was obviously not the kind of woman Juliana could confide in.

A quick stab of pity went through him. It was a miracle that his lovely wife hadn't turned into a spoiled noblewoman, having such selfish creatures for parents.

"Let's go in to dinner," her mother said. "By now, the servants are probably buzzing with gossip about us, and we'd best squelch it."

Northcliffe patted his mother's hand. "Why don't you take Juliana and Overton in? I'd like a word with Vaughan in private."

Juliana tightened her fingers on Rhys's arm. "Not without me present."

"And me, too," Overton added.

Northcliffe stiffened. "Very well. Let us all go into the study, then."

Their mother rolled her eyes. "Since the three of you are determined to foment speculation, it's left to me to squelch the rumors. I shall be in the dining room when you are ready." With a regal sniff, she walked off.

Northcliffe led the way. As soon as they entered the room and Northcliffe closed the doors, Rhys said, "Before you speak, I have something to say myself."

Three pairs of eyes fixed on him. The St. Albans siblings bore a remarkable resemblance. Juliana might be superior in character, but no one could mistake that they were her family. Unfortunately.

He dragged in a deep breath. "I believe that you lied to me about my wife's part in the impressment. I believe you lied to me twice—on the night you took me from her, and on the night I took her back. And now I want to know why."

Northcliffe's gaze shot to Overton.

"I didn't tell him," Overton protested. "Although I would have, if Juliana had let me."

Rhys gazed at his wife in blank astonishment.

She wouldn't look at him. "That's the main reason Overton came to Llynwydd two weeks ago. To tell you everything. To explain that the innkeeper, who'd once courted Lettice, had recognized me and that's how they knew to come after you. Overton also came over to tell you about the spy in the Sons of Wales. That's why Morgan agreed to go with him—to help Overton tell you the truth."

"But she wouldn't let us say anything," Overton interjected.

Rhys covered her hand with his. "Why? If they had told me—"

"You would have believed them. I know. I didn't want you to believe them. I wanted you to believe *me*. And I was willing to wait until you could say you trusted me despite all the damning evidence."

As he remembered that day in the study, the wave of self-hatred that swept over him was so intense, he nearly reeled. After she'd made such a sacrifice for their marriage, he'd responded by accusing her of infidelity. No wonder she'd been so angry. He'd deserved that and more from her.

Instead, she'd given him her body. And her heart, though he hadn't realized it at the time. "I've been more of a monster than I realized. How can you ever forgive me?"

"How can I not?" She squeezed his arm. "No matter what the truth, you thought I had betrayed you and sentenced you to a living hell. That day in the study, you forgave everything to make me your wife. I could hardly do otherwise."

His gaze locked with hers, and something more profound than anything he'd ever known passed between them. Suddenly he knew he would barter his soul to keep the glow on her face and the smile in her eyes, to keep her looking at him like that. For without her beside him, life was nothing but one empty step after another, all of them leading into a void.

Northcliffe broke the silence. "I can see my confession would be somewhat anticlimactic."

Anger flared in Rhys. "Not entirely. Juliana explained how you could succeed in convincing me of her betrayal, but I still don't understand why. I can guess why you wanted me away from Juliana in the first place: You had bigger plans for her. But why lie to me that night? And why keep lying later?"

With a tortured sigh, Northcliffe turned to face the fire. "I lied the first time in a futile attempt to keep you from wanting to return."

"And after I came back?"

"I thought if you believed her to be a betrayer, you would grant the annulment."

"But I made it clear that I wouldn't, and you still kept lying. Why?"

Northcliffe stiffened. "The reason is so contemptible, I'm not sure I can speak it."

Juliana snorted. "After you told him how much influence and wealth you'd gained, Rhys, he was afraid of what you might do to him if you knew the truth. So he let me stand between you and him to take the brunt of your anger."

Shocked, Rhys gaped at Northcliffe. What kind of brother hid behind his sister's skirts and made her face an angry man alone? Northcliffe ought to be flogged, and then shot.

Of course, Northcliffe wouldn't have succeeded if Rhys

hadn't believed the lies. Rhys remembered how firm he'd been about what he'd do to Northcliffe if the man thwarted him, not knowing he was sealing Juliana's doom.

No, the events of that night hadn't been entirely Northcliffe's fault. If Rhys had been less angry and more determined to ferret out the truth that night, he could have saved them both some heartache. Instead he'd let Northcliffe use her as a shield, because he'd been too jealous to hear the truth, too furious over finding her betrothed to another.

"I am so sorry, my love," he whispered. "Sorry for all that you've been through. We've made your life hell for quite some time, haven't we?"

She touched her hand to his cheek. "I must take the blame for some of it, too. If I hadn't let Darcy talk me into keeping the marriage a secret, none of it might have happened."

Northcliffe faced them. "'Tis still mostly my doing. I toyed with people's lives and coerced Overton into doing the same. For that, I can only offer my deepest apologies."

Juliana glared at him. "You think your apologies will wipe out all that my husband suffered? That it will bring back the years of marriage we lost, the times I wept for Rhys while he withstood flogging after flogging? How dare you offer something as meager as apologies!"

When Northcliffe looked stricken, Rhys lifted Juliana's hand to his lips. "It's all right, love. I appreciate and share your fury. But I have a more productive response to your brother's offer."

He leveled a solemn gaze on Northcliffe. "Though you

and St. Albans can do nothing to repay Juliana and me for those years, you can do something to show your remorse. At Llynwydd there's a Welsh boy whose genius is being wasted, thanks to the shortsightedness of his father and the refusal of your countrymen to provide for his education. I'm sending him to Eton, because there is nowhere here in Wales for him to find such an education.

"But there are others who yearn for schooling and have no chance of it. So take some of that money and influence you've gained by walking over people, and turn it toward opening a school as respected and prestigious as Eton, where Welsh children can go to learn about their own country's glories."

He glanced at Juliana, who nodded. "That would satisfy us far more than any apology. And you may find that it will satisfy you more, as well."

"It will be done," Overton vowed.

Northcliffe hesitated, then nodded. "I will make sure that it is done."

Rhys smiled. At present he felt charitable toward the whole world, even Juliana's family. His wife was at his side, full of love and hope for the future. They had Llynwydd and each other. And one day soon, perhaps, they would have children.

Indeed, life was good.

Overton stepped forward. "And now, my friends, let us seal the agreement with dinner. I fear if we linger here much longer, Mother will wash her hands of us."

Northcliffe turned to the door and Juliana started to follow.

Rhys caught her arm. "We'll be there in a moment. I'd like a word with my wife in private."

As soon as they left, Rhys slipped his arms about her waist and kissed her long and deep, reveling in the ardency of her response.

Then she drew back, laughing. "I thought you wanted a word? It appears to me, my impatient husband, that you wanted to do something else with your mouth. But now is not the time or place."

He thought of the long two hours ahead before they could even think of excusing themselves. With a grin, he walked to the door. After everything her family had made him suffer, they could wait awhile longer to watch him play the dutiful in-law.

Shutting the door, he turned the key in the lock.

"Rhys!" Juliana scolded.

Yet her eyes smoldered as he stalked back to haul her into his arms, sliding his hands down to cup her bottom and pull her up against him.

"My life on't, you're a wicked man, Rhys Vaughan!"

He nuzzled the top of her breast. "Aye, *cariad*. But no more wicked than my wife, I suspect. Shall we find out?"

Her breath was already quickening, and she slipped her hands around his waist. "Well . . . I suppose we can always join the family for breakfast . . ."

Then she smothered his laugh with her kiss.

EPILOGUE

And though in the desert night
I've wandered many a year
And often had to drink
Of the bitter cup, despair;
The yoke I suffered was my gain
And not for nothing came that pain.

—WILLIAM WILLIAMS PANTYCELYN,
"FAIR WEATHER"

Mother, I want to go home!" Five-year-old Owen threw himself across the bed in Northcliffe Hall's nursery. Enveloped from head to toe in a flannel nightshirt, he tossed his auburn curls and crossed his arms, looking for all the world like his father.

"Shh! You'll wake the baby, and I had a wretched time getting her to sleep."

Thankfully, Margaret merely turned over and chewed on the corner of her blanket before settling down once more.

Owen lowered his voice to a stage whisper. "I'm not sleepy. Can't I stay up?" A wily look crossed his face. "Mrs.

Pennant is letting Edgar come over tonight, and Uncle Overton is going to let Edgar look at his French pictures. I want to see them, too!"

Juliana sighed. Much as she loved her brother, he was such a bachelor. French pictures indeed! Lettice would be appalled to know her son was being corrupted by Overton while Morgan was away. It made Lettice uneasy to have her son at Northcliffe Hall, even though Darcy spent little time here now and was in London at present.

"No, you may not stay up. Tomorrow your father will be back and there will be plenty of things to do, not to mention the ride to Llynwydd. So be a good boy and go to sleep." She blew out the candles in the sconce by the bed.

"But I'm not sleepy." He yawned wide enough to swallow a small cat and settled against the pillow. "I'm . . . not . . ."

She watched him a moment. Although he'd gotten his auburn hair and green eyes from her, he was like his father in every other way—cocky and confident and arrogant.

And utterly lovable. With a sigh, she tucked the covers around him. "Sleep well, *cariad*."

Picking up the brace of candles, she headed for her own bedchamber. Only one more day until Rhys returned. Although she was glad that he'd won a seat in Parliament as M.P. for the shire, joining Morgan as M.P. for the borough, she hated the long absences when Parliament was in session.

Coming to Northcliffe for part of the session had been a good idea, since it provided a change for the children and allowed her to visit with her family. And it was always nice to see Lettice. Between Lettice's son and daughter and Juliana's own two, there was plenty to talk about. But like Owen, Juliana was eager to return home. Even after years with Rhys, she couldn't get enough of his lovemaking.

With a sigh, she entered her bedchamber and began to disrobe. It was still early, but she didn't feel like dealing with her family tonight. She wanted to lie in bed and read. And dream about tomorrow.

A noise at the window startled her. It sounded like . . . like . . .

She whirled toward the window, her heart jumping into her throat as she saw Rhys perched on the branch outside, tossing pebbles at the glass with a rakish grin.

She flew to open the windows. "Rhys! You're here!" Then she looked down. "Are you mad? You could fall and break your neck, you blasted—"

"I'm coming in." He gave her only a second to back away before he swung onto the sill and into the room. He kissed her soundly, then murmured, "God, how I missed you."

She covered his face with kisses. "I missed you, too. But if you'd broken your neck coming in that window—"

He laughed. "I'll leave the tree-climbing to Owen from now on, but I couldn't resist tonight. I saw the light in your window, and I knew if I entered downstairs, I'd have to endure an hour of Overton's questions and your mother trying to force food on me, before I could finally get you alone." His voice dropped to a husky murmur. "And I very much wanted to get you alone, *cariad*."

He began to loosen the ties of her night rail.

"Why are you back so soon?" she whispered. "We weren't expecting you until tomorrow."

He quickly shed his clothing. "The session ended early. I am yours for the next year." His eyes gleamed as he jerked down his drawers. "*All* yours." Then he carried her to the bed.

Much, much later, she lay beside him, sated and content, their bodies curved together spoon-fashion. His legs were draped over hers as he kissed her shoulder.

He splayed his hand across her belly. "Do you realize it's been almost exactly six years since I returned to Wales? Yet we've been married twelve." He nuzzled her neck. "Have you ever wondered what might have happened if the coach hadn't been late? If we'd been able to leave together as planned?"

She covered his hand with hers. "We'd have had six more years together. Sometimes I hate Darcy for taking them away from us."

"Me, too." He laced his fingers with hers. "But other times, I wonder if our years apart made our marriage stronger. Perhaps we wouldn't have known the depths of our love without our separation."

She turned to face him. "An interesting thought, my love. You are either the wisest man I know . . . or utterly mad. I'd have rather had the years with you and saved us some pain."

He chuckled. "I figured I should find some silver lining in the cloud Darcy created, since he's established not just one but several schools in our names." He sobered. "But really, don't you think our marriage might have faltered if we'd been left to our own devices? We were so young and foolish."

She stared up at the man she loved more than life itself. Was it possible their marriage might not have been so full and rich if they'd thrown themselves recklessly into it from the beginning? If they hadn't been forced to overcome so many obstacles to be together?

"I think, my dearest husband, that time and place have had little bearing on our love. If we'd spent one hour apart or an eternity, I know I would have always loved you. We were meant to be together. Compared to that, six years apart means nothing, don't you think?"

He smiled as he pulled her into his embrace. "Aye, my love," he murmured. "Nothing at all."

Want even more sizzling romance from
New York Times bestselling author
Sabrina Jeffries?

Don't miss

The Danger of Desire

the next installment in her
sizzling and sexy Sinful Suitors series.

Coming in Fall 2016 from Pocket Books!

London
August 1830

When Warren Corry, Marquess of Knightford, arrived at a Venetian breakfast thrown by the Duke and Duchess of Lyons, he regretted having stayed out until the wee hours of the morning. Last night he'd just been so glad to be back among the distractions of town that he'd drunk enough brandy to pickle a barrel of herrings.

Bad idea, since the duke and duchess had decided to hold the blasted party in the blazing sun on the lawn of their lavish London mansion. His mouth was dry, his stomach churned, and his head felt like a stampeding herd of elephants.

His best friend, Edwin, had better be grateful that Warren kept his promises.

"Warren!" cried a female voice painfully close. "What are you doing here?"

It was Clarissa, his cousin, who also just happened to be Edwin's wife—and the reason Warren had managed to drag himself from his bed at the ungodly hour of noon.

He shaded his eyes to peer at her. As usual, she had the look of a delicate fairy creature. But he knew better than to fall for that cat-in-the-cream smile. "Must you shout like that?"

"I am not shouting." She cocked her head. "And you look ill. So you must have had a grand time at St. George's Club last night. Either that, or in the stews early this morning."

"I always have a grand time." Or at least he kept the night at bay, which was the purpose of staying out until all hours.

"I know, which is why it's really unlike you to be here. Especially when Edwin isn't." She narrowed her eyes at him. "Wait a minute—Edwin sent you here, didn't he? Because he couldn't be in town for it."

"What? No." He bent to kiss her cheek. "Can't a fellow just come to a breakfast to see his favorite cousin?"

"He can. But he generally doesn't."

Warren snagged a glass of champagne off a passing tray. "Well, he did today. Wait, who are we talking about again?"

"Very amusing." Taking the glass from him, she frowned. "You do not need this. You're clearly cropsick."

He snatched it back and downed it. "Which is precisely why I require some hair of the dog."

"You're avoiding the subject. Did Edwin send you here to spy on me or not?"

"Don't be absurd. He merely wanted me to look in on you, make sure everything was all right. You know your husband—he hates having to be at the estate with Niall while you're in town." He glanced at her thickening waist. "Especially when you're . . . well . . . like that."

"Oh, Lord, not you, too. Bad enough to have him and my brother hovering over me all the time, worried about my getting hurt somehow, but if he's sent you to start doing that—"

"No, I swear. He only asked that I come by if I were attending this. I had to be in town anyway, so I figured why not pop in to Lyons's affair?" He waved his empty glass. "The duke always orders excellent champagne. But now that I've had some, I'll just be on my way."

She took him by the arm. "No, indeed. I so rarely get to see you anymore. Stay awhile. They're about to start the dancing."

"Just what I need—to dance with a lot of simpering misses who think a coronet the ideal prize."

"Then dance with me. I *can* still dance, you know."

No doubt. Clarissa had always been a lively sort, who wouldn't be slowed by something as inconsequential as bearing the heir to the reserved and rather eccentric Earl of Blakeborough.

Clarissa and Edwin were so different that sometimes Warren wondered what the two of them saw in each other. But whenever he witnessed their obvious affection for each other, he realized there must be something deeper cementing their marriage. It made him envious.

He scowled. That was absurd. He didn't intend to marry for a very long while. At least not until he found a lusty widow who could endure his . . . idiosyncrasies.

Clarissa stared off into the crowd. "As long as you're here, I . . . um . . . do need a favor."

Uh-oh. "What kind of favor?"

"Edwin would do it if he didn't have to be in Hertfordshire helping my brother settle the family estate, you know," she babbled. "And Niall—"

"*What's the favor?*" he persisted.

"Do you know Miss Trevor?"

Miss Trevor? This had better not be another of Clarissa's schemes to get him married off. "Fortunately, I do not. I assume she's one of those debutantes you've taken under your wing."

"Not exactly. Although she was just brought out this past season, she's actually my age . . . and a friend. Her brother, Reynold Trevor, died last year in some horrible shooting accident, and she and her sister-in-law, Mrs. Trevor, have been left without anything but a debt-ridden estate to support. So Miss Trevor's aunt, Lady Pensworth, brought the two of them to London for the season."

"To find them husbands, no doubt."

"Exactly, although I think Lady Pensworth is more concerned about Miss Trevor, since the late Mr. Trevor's wife has already borne him a child who will inherit the estate, such as it is. To make Miss Trevor more eligible, Lady Pensworth has bestowed a thouand-pound dowry on her, which ought to tempt a number of eligible gentlemen."

"Not me."

She looked startled. "I wasn't thinking of *you*, for heaven's sake. I was thinking of someone less wealthy, with fewer connections. And decidedly younger. She's only twenty-four, after all."

Decidedly younger? "Here now, I'm not that old. I'm the same age as your husband."

"True." Her eyes twinkled at him. "And given your nightly habits, you apparently possess the stamina of a much younger man. Why, no one seeing you in dim light would ever guess you're thirty-three."

He eyed her askance. "I seem to recall your asking me for a favor, dear girl. You're not going about getting it very wisely."

"The thing is, I'm worried about my friend. Miss Trevor keeps receiving these notes at parties, which she slips furtively off to read; she falls asleep in the middle of balls; and she seems rather distracted. Worst of all, she refused my invitation to our house party next week, which I had partly planned in hopes of introducing her to eligible young gentlemen."

"Perhaps she had another engagement."

Clarissa lifted an eyebrow at him.

"Right. She needs a husband, and you're nicely trying to provide her with a selection of potential ones." He smirked at her. "How ungrateful of her not to fall in with your plans."

"Do be serious. When was the last time you saw any unmarried woman with limited prospects refuse a chance to attend a house party at the home of an earl and a countess with our connections?"

He hated to admit it, but she had a point. "So what do you want *me* to do about it?"

"Ask around at St. George's. See if anyone has heard any gossip about her. Find out if anyone knows some scoundrel who's been . . . well . . . sniffing around her for her dowry."

The light dawned. During her debut years ago, Clarissa had been the object of such a scoundrel's attentions, and it had nearly destroyed the lives of her and her brother. So she tended to be overly sensitive about women who might fall prey to fortune hunters.

"You do know that if I start asking about an eligible young lady at the club," he said, "the members will assume I'm interested in courting her."

"Nonsense. Everyone knows you prefer soiled doves to society loves."

That wasn't entirely true. He did occasionally bed bored widows or ladies with inattentive husbands. There were a great many of those hanging about—one reason he wasn't keen to marry. He had a ready supply of bedmates without having to leg-shackle himself.

"Besides," she went on, "that *is* the purpose of St. George's, is it not? To provide a place where gentlemen can determine the suitability of various suitors to women?"

"To their female relations," he said tersely. "Not to the friends of their female relations."

Clarissa stared up at him. "She has no man to protect her. And I very much fear all of the signs lead to her having found someone unsuitable, which is why she's behaving oddly. I don't want to see her end up trapped in a disastrous marriage. Or worse."

They both knew what the "worse" was, since Clarissa

had gone through it herself. Damn. He might not have been her guardian for years now, but she still knew how to tug at his conscience.

"It would be a very great favor to me," Clarissa went on. "I tell you what—let me just introduce you. You can spend a few moments talking to her and see if I'm right to be alarmed. If you think I'm overly concerned, you may leave here with my blessing and never bother with it again. But if you think I might be right . . ."

"Fine. But you owe me for this. And I promise I will call in my debt down the road." He grinned at her. "At the very least, you must introduce me to some buxom widow with loose morals and an eye for fun."

"Hmm," she said, rolling her eyes. "I'll have to speak to my brother-in-law about that. He has more connections among that sort than I do."

"No doubt." Her brother-in-law used to use "that sort" of women as models in his paintings. "But I don't need you to talk to Keane. So I suppose I'll settle for your promise not to be offended if I also refuse your invitation to your house party."

"There was a possibility of your accepting? Shocking. But since I've never seen you attend a house party in your life—unless it was to some bachelor's hunting box—I didn't bother to invite you."

"Good," he said, though he was mildly annoyed. Marriage had obviously changed her. A year ago, she wouldn't have stopped plaguing him until she'd convinced him to attend. Surely she had not given up on him already.

Unless this was her sly way of once again trying to get

him married off. He'd best tread carefully. "So where *is* this woman you wish me to meet?"

"She was right over there by the—" Clarissa scowled. "Oh, dear, that's her by the fountain, but what the devil are those fellows doing with her?"

She stalked off across the lawn and he followed, surveying the group she headed for: a woman surrounded by three young gentlemen who appeared to be—fishing?—in the fountain.

He recognized the men. One was a drunk, one a well-known rakehell, and the third a notorious gambler by the name of Pitford. All three were fortune hunters.

No wonder Clarissa worried about her friend.

He turned his attention to the chit, who had her back to him and was dressed in a blue-and-green plaid gown with a pink-and-yellow striped shawl.

Good God. Any woman who dressed that way was bound to be a heedless young twit, and he disliked that sort of woman. Unless she was sitting on his lap in a brothel, in which case intelligence hardly mattered.

As they approached the group, Clarissa said, "What on earth is going on here?"

The jovial chap with cheeks already reddened from too much champagne said, "The clasp broke on Miss Trevor's bracelet and it dropped into the fountain, so we're trying to get it out to keep her from ruining her sleeves."

"I would prefer to ruin my entire gown than see you further damage my bracelet with your poking about," the chit said, her voice surprisingly low and throaty. "If you gentlemen would just let me pass, I'd fish it out myself."

"Nonsense, we can do it," the other two said as they fought over the stick wielded by the drunk. In the process, they managed to poke Miss Trevor in the arm.

"Ow!" she cried and attempted to snatch the stick. "For pity's sake, gentlemen . . ."

Warren had seen enough. "Stand aside, lads." He pushed through the arses. Shoving his sleeve up as far as it would go, he thrust his hand into the fountain and fished out the bracelet. Then he turned to offer it to the young lady. "I assume this is yours, miss."

When her startled gaze shot to him, he froze. She had the loveliest blue eyes he'd ever seen.

Though her gown was even more outrageous from the front than from the back, the rest of her was unremarkable. Tall and slender, with no breasts to speak of, she had decent skin, a sharp nose, and a rather impudent-looking mouth. She was pretty enough, but by no means a beauty. And not his sort. At all.

Yet those eyes . . .

Fringed with long black lashes, they glittered like stars against an early-evening sky, making desire tighten low in his belly. Utterly absurd.

Until her lips curled up into a sparkling smile that matched the incandescence of her eyes. "Thank you, sir. The bracelet was a gift from my late brother. Though I fear you may have ruined your coat retrieving it."

"Nonsense." He extended the bracelet to her. "My valet is very good at his job and will easily put it right."

As she took the bracelet from him, an odd expression crossed her face. "You're left-handed."

He arched one brow. "How clever of you to notice."

"How clever of you to be so. I'm left-handed, too. So I generally notice another left-hander because there aren't that many of us around."

"Or none that will lay claim to the affliction, anyway." And he'd never before met a lady who was.

"True." She slipped the bracelet into her reticule with a twinkle in her eye. "I've always been told it's quite gauche to be left-handed."

"Or at the very least, a sign of subservience to the devil."

"Ah yes. Though the last time I paid a visit to Lucifer, he pretended not to know me. What about you?"

"I know him only to speak to at parties. He's quite busy these days. He has trouble fitting me into his schedule."

"I can well imagine." Pointedly ignoring the three men watching them in bewilderment, she added, "He has all those innocents to tempt and gamblers to ruin and drinkers to intoxicate. However would he find time to waste on a fellow like you, who comes to the aid of a lady so readily? You're clearly not wicked enough to merit his interest."

"You'd be surprised," he said dryly. "Besides, Lucifer gains more pleasure in corrupting decent gentlemen than wicked ones." And this had to be the strangest conversation he'd ever had with a debutante.

"Excellent point. Well, then, next time you see him, give him my regards." She cast a side glance at their companions. "He seems to have been overzealous in his activities of late."

When the gentlemen looked offended, Clarissa said hastily, "Don't be silly. The devil is only as busy as people allow him to be, and we shall not allow him to loiter around here, shall we, Warren?" She slid her hand into the crook of his elbow.

"No, indeed. That would be a sin."

"And so are my poor manners," Clarissa went on. She smiled at her friend. "I've forgotten to introduce the two of you. Miss Trevor, may I present my cousin, the Marquess of Knightford and rescuer of bracelets. Warren, this is my good friend, Miss Delia Trevor, the cleverest woman I know despite her gauche left hand."

Cynically, he waited for Miss Trevor's smile to brighten as she realized what a prime catch he was. So he was surprised when her smile faded to politeness instead. "It's a pleasure to meet you, sir. Clarissa has told me much about you."

He narrowed his gaze on her. "I'm sure she has. My cousin loves gossip."

"No more than you love to provide fodder for it, from what I've heard."

"I do enjoy giving the gossips something to talk about."

"No doubt they appreciate it. Otherwise they'd be limited to poking fun at spinsters, and then I would never get any rest."

He snorted. "I'd hardly consider you a spinster, madam. My cousin tells me this is your first season."

"And hopefully my last." As the other fellows protested that, she said, "Now, now, gentlemen. You know I'm not the society sort." She fixed Warren with a cool look. "I do better with less lofty companions. You, my lord, are far too worldly and sophisticated for me."

"I somehow doubt that," he said.

"I hear the dancing starting up," Clarissa cut in as she released his arm. "Perhaps you two can puzzle it out if you stand up together for this set."

He had to stifle his laugh. Clarissa wasn't usually so clumsy in her social machinations. She must really like this chit. He was beginning to understand why. Miss Trevor was rather entertaining.

"Excellent idea." He held out his hand to the young lady. "Shall we?"

"Now see here," Pitford interrupted. "Miss Trevor has already promised this dance to me."

"It's true," she told Warren. "I'm promised for all the dances this afternoon."

Hmm. Warren turned to Pitford. "Lord Fulkham was looking for you earlier, old chap. He's in the card room, I believe. I'll just head there and tell him he can find you dancing with Miss Trevor."

Pitford blanched. "I . . . er . . . cannot . . . that is . . ." He bowed to Miss Trevor. "Forgive me, madam, but I shall have to relinquish this dance to his lordship. I forgot a prior engagement."

The fellow scurried off for the gates as fast as his tight pantaloons would carry him. Probably because the wretch owed Fulkham a substantial sum of money.

Pitford's withdrawal was all it took for the other two gentlemen to excuse themselves, leaving Warren alone with his cousin and Miss Trevor.

With a smile, he again offered his arm to Clarissa's friend. "It appears that you are now free to dance. Shall we?"

To his shock, the impudent female hesitated. But she obviously knew better than to refuse a marquess and quickly recovered, taking the arm he offered.

As they headed toward the lawn where the dancing was taking place, Miss Trevor said, "Do you always get your way in everything, Lord Knightford?"

"I certainly try. What good is being a marquess if I can't make use of the privilege from time to time?"

"Even if it means bullying some poor fellow into fleeing a perfectly good party?"

He shot her a long glance. "Pitford is deeply in debt and looking for a rich wife. I should think you would thank me."

She shrugged. "I know what Pitford is. I know what they all are. It matters naught to me. I have no interest in any of them."

Pulling her into the swirl of dancers, he said, "Because you prefer some fellow you left behind at home? Or because you have your sights set elsewhere in town?"

Her expression grew guarded. "For a man of such lofty consequence, you are surprisingly interested in my affairs. Why is that?"

"I am merely dancing with the friend of my cousin," he said smoothly. "And for a woman who has 'no interest' in the three fortune hunters you were just with, you certainly found a good way to get them vying for your attention."

She blinked. "I have no idea what you mean."

"The clasp on that bracelet wasn't broken, Miss Trevor." When she colored and glanced away, he knew he'd hit his mark. "So I can only think that you had some other purpose for dropping it into the fountain."

As they came together in the dance, he lowered his voice. "And if it wasn't to engage those men's interest in you personally, I have to wonder what other reason you might have to risk losing such a sentimental heirloom. Care to enlighten me?"

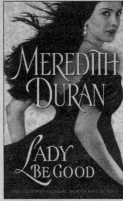

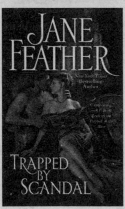